William Henry Thomes

The Bushrangers

A Yankee's adventures during his second visit to Australia

William Henry Thomes

The Bushrangers
A Yankee's adventures during his second visit to Australia

ISBN/EAN: 9783337180041

Printed in Europe, USA, Canada, Australia, Japan

Cover: Foto ©Andreas Hilbeck / pixelio.de

More available books at **www.hansebooks.com**

THE

BUSHRANGERS.

A Yankee's Adventures

DURING HIS SECOND VISIT TO AUSTRALIA

BY

WILLIAM H. THOMES,

"A RETURNED AUSTRALIAN." AUTHOR OF "THE GOLD HUNTER'S ADVENTURES, OR LIFE IN AUSTRALIA," ETC., ETC.

CHICAGO:
DONNELLEY, LOYD & CO., PUBLISHERS,
1883.

CONTENTS.

CHAPTER I.

PAGE

The Yankee and his Quartz Crusher.— A Start for Australia. . . . 9

CHAPTER II.

We arrive at Melbourne, and meet old Friends. 18

CHAPTER III.

The stolen Diamonds.—The lovely Bar-maid and her Father. 27

CHAPTER IV.

The Prize-fighter and his Daughter.—The Row.—The Signal. 36

CHAPTER V.

Mrs. Trotter's Castle. 45

CHAPTER VI.

The Exploration.—The Quarrel and the Murder. 52

CHAPTER VII.

The lost Diamonds recovered.—The Escape.—The sudden Alarm.—The unpleasant Position.—Hez plays the "Injun."—The Pet and his strong Arm. 60

CHAPTER VIII.

An Escape from the Pet.—The Pursuit.—The Jolly Sailors.—The Arrest and Discharge. 67

CHAPTER IX.

Hez and his Feelings.—The fat Porter and the Page.—The Governor's Wife. 78

CHAPTER X.

The Governor and his Wife.— A strong Pull for a Commission. 83

CHAPTER XI.

The Red Lion. — Miss Jenny and her Temper. — Her Warnings. — Arrival of the Pet. 94

CHAPTER XII.

The Red Lion. — A desperate Struggle. 98

CHAPTER XIII.

The [illegible]. — The Accusation of Miss Jenny. — The Despatch. 103

CHAPTER XIV.

The first Hunt for Bushrangers. — Webber and his Family. — The sleeping Tramp. 109

CHAPTER XV.

A suspicious Sleeper. — The Meeting in the Bush. 114

CHAPTER XVI.

Webber and his Guest. — The Pursuit. — The Escape. — The stolen Horses. 119

CHAPTER XVII.

Lost in the Woods. — My Horse's Death. — Night and Mosquitos. — An unwelcome Bedfellow. 125

CHAPTER XVIII.

A Night on the Mountain. — A strange Meeting. — The Cave. 131

CHAPTER XIX.

The unexpected Arrival. — The Concealment. — In a tight Place. 138

CHAPTER XX.

Face to Face. — The Struggle. — The Compact. — The Surprise. — "Death to the Spy." 143

CHAPTER XXI.

Mother Brown and her Friendship. — The Disguise. — An Attempt to escape. 151

CHAPTER XXII.

An old Acquaintance. — The Pursuit. — Bushrangers and their Consciences. 157

CHAPTER XXIII.

A poor Shot — A freed Fugitive. — An old Friend. — The Kiss of Welcome. 162

CHAPTER XXIV.

An Australian Farmer's Experience. — His Wife and Family. — Bushrangers in Pursuit. — Barricaded. 164

CHAPTER XXV.

A Skirmish with the Bushrangers. — Our Defence. — Attempt to burn the House. 173

CHAPTER XXVI.

Arrival of Murden and his Men. — Great Joy of Hopeful. — The Fire subdued. — Change of Mind. 179

CHAPTER XXVII.

Dead Bushrangers. — Hopeful and Amelia. — A Warning. — Old Love forgotten. 186

CHAPTER XXVIII.

A Coquette at Work. — A jealous Lover. — An attempted Murder. — An Alarm. 191

CHAPTER XXIX.

Moloch in a Fit. — His Disappearance. — A close Shot. — Preparations for a Tramp. 199

CHAPTER XXX.

An Expedition. — Crossing the Valley by Night. — A Confession. — Point Lookout. — The Sentinels. 205

CHAPTER XXXI.

An Attempt to extort a Confession. — The Perils of Travelling in Australia. — A Surprise. 211

CHAPTER XXXII.

The Robber's Death. — Bushrangers surprised. — The Attack and Flight. — Murden's Alarm.. 218

CHAPTER XXXIII.

Rescue of an English Baronet. — His Adventures. — A strange Sight. . 221

CHAPTER XXXIV.

Mother Brown's Mystery. — A Search for Gold. — A terrible Surprise. . 226

CHAPTER XXXV.

A Visit from Keeler. — He is urgent for our Company. — Doings at Point Lookout. 232

CHAPTER XXXVI.

An unexpected Visitor, but a pleasant One. — The Treasure. — A great Surprise. 240

CHAPTER XXXVII.

Miss Jenny and her Position. — As handsome and vulgar as ever. . 246

CHAPTER XXXVIII.

A Coquette's Contempt. — The Disappearance. — Amelia and Moloch. . 252

CHAPTER XXXIX.

The Abduction. — A Native on the Trail. — The Pursuit. 259

CHAPTER XL.

The Pursuit. — Bridge of Salt. — Mysterious Sounds. — Alligators and their Attacks. — An Escape. 266

CHAPTER XLI.

Perilous Position. — Escape from Alligators. — On Foot. — A Western Man in Australia. — He joins us. 272

CHAPTER XLII.

A tedious Tramp. — An unexpected Enemy. — A strange Sight. — Serpents in Pursuit. — A Fight. 277

CHAPTER XLIII.

Moloch and his Victim. — He explains Matters. — Negotiations. — Failure. — We raise the Siege. 287

CHAPTER XLIV.

Gloomy Prospect. — A bright Light. — Friends or Foes? 294

CHAPTER XLV.

On the Trail. — A young Girl's Distress. — A Ruffian's Threats. — Forward to the Rescue. 301

CHAPTER XLVI.

On the Mountain. — Amelia's Grief. — She demands Vengeance. — Preparations for Hanging. 307

CHAPTER XLVII.

The Hanging. — An Interruption. — The Tables turned. — Escape of Amelia. — A Tableau. 314

CHAPTER XLVIII.

An unexpected Tumble. — The Rescue. — A private Conversation. . . 320

CHAPTER XLIX.

A tiresome Ride. — Arrival at the Station. — Departure for Melbourne. . 326

CHAPTER L.

A Row at the Red Lion. — A Baronet in Danger. — To the Rescue. — The Pet knocked out of Time. 333

CHAPTER LI.

Ten Minutes in Jail. — A belligerent Cabman. — A Fight and Knock-down. 338

CHAPTER LII.

Mother Brown's Pardon. — Her Confession. — My Astonishment. . 343

CHAPTER LIII.

The Baronet's Confession. — A Comparing of Notes. — The lost Child. — A Tableau. 348

CHAPTER LIV.

Explanations. — Mother Brown and Tom. — An Interview with the Baronet. 355

CHAPTER LV.

Mother Brown's Confession. — The stolen Child. — The Locks of Hair. . 362

CHAPTER LVI.

Preparations for an Arrest. — The Pet on the Watch. — Bad News. . . . 368

CHAPTER LVII.

A sudden Disappearance. — The Pursuit. 372

CHAPTER LVIII.

The Hunt for the Baronet's Daughter. — A Midnight Adventure. 375

CHAPTER LIX.

Meeting an old Friend. — A disagreeable Surprise. — A Council of War. . 380

CHAPTER LX.

In Pursuit. — A Surprise. — A Blow on the Head. — The Conference. — A Prisoner. — A few Remarks by Miss Jenny. — Her Visit and Assistance. 385

CHAPTER LXI.

A momentous Question. — A terrible Struggle. 396

CHAPTER LXII.

The Haunted Station. — No One at Home. — Perseverance of a Blue Man. — In Sight. 403

CHAPTER LXIII.

An important Capture. — The Pet's Regrets. — Jenny and Mad Dick. . . . 408

CHAPTER LXIV.

Mad Dick makes Proposals. — A scornful Rejection. — Violence. — To the Rescue. 417

CHAPTER LXV.

An agreeable Surprise. — Father and Daughter. — The Pet's Regrets . 424

CHAPTER LXVI.

A little Love. — A few Explanations, and a Tableau. 433

CHAPTER LXVII.

A Life for a Life. 441

CHAPTER LXVIII.

A private Conference. — A plain Talk. — A stern Refusal. 448

CHAPTER LXIX.

On the Tramp. — A wonderful Lake. — A warm Reception. 458

CHAPTER LXX.

A wonderful Lake. — The Quartz Crushers. — A Separation. 464

CHAPTER LXXI.

General Events. — Hasty Weddings. — Conclusion 478

THE BUSHRANGERS.

CHAPTER I.

THE YANKEE AND HIS QUARTZ CRUSHER.—A START FOR AUSTRALIA.

HEAVEN only knows what sent me to Australia the second time. I was very comfortable in Boston, for I had money, and it was safely invested. I had friends, or rather those who professed to be such. I had pleasant rooms, and a pair of fast horses; and men said that I was a lucky dog, and deserved my good fortune, and I have no doubt they were sincere in their expressions. But still I was not happy or contented. I missed the dear companion who had travelled with me in California, and starved and suffered, prospered and grown rich, in Australia.

In my first series of Australian sketches,* I spoke of the sudden death of my friend Frederick; and after his decease I don't think that I felt as though I could settle down and remain a quiet citizen, although I strove to do so, and made desperate attempts to convince myself that I was happy. But all in vain. I found that my thoughts would revert to Australia, its gold mines, its immense prairies, extensive sheep pastures and flocks of sheep, its sharp business men, desperate convicts, savage bushrangers, and roving police, and with the latter I numbered some friends; for had we not witnessed many a battle, and defeated some of the most desperate bands that roved the plains, and lived on mutton when it could be obtained, and starved when it was scarce?

---

* THE GOLD HUNTER'S ADVENTURES; OR, LIFE IN AUSTRALIA. 1 Vol. 12 mo. 4 Illustrations. Published by LEE & SHEPARD. 1865.

All these things came to my mind, and I longed for a renewal of my adventurous life; and yet I struggled in secret against the fate which would consign me to danger, privations, and innumerable hardships. I thought of the clouds of blinding dust which drive the inhabitants of Australia frantic as it fills their eyes, noses, ears, and mouths, and burns the skin of the face like caustic I recollected the wet winters, when rain falls as though rivers in the clouds had broken loose, and were determined to sweep away all vestige of land; the piercing cold which is encountered on the mountains; the mud; the snakes; the millions of insects, which drive sleep from the eyes of the tender-skinned; and, remembering all this, I still felt as though I must once more visit Australia.

When I mentioned the subject to my friends, they laughed at the idea. One of them advised me to marry a nice girl and settle down; another said that he knew a lady who would suit me. After an introduction, I found that the prediction was false; so I gave up all thoughts of matrimony, for I was convinced that my affinity and I had never met, and that I must search for her if I desired a wife.

But still I had not fully made up my mind that I would return to Australia, until, one day, I was seated in the office of my lawyer, when who should enter but a thin, wiry, sharp-eyed man, with a freckled face and sandy hair, clothes clean but stout and coarse, and hands which looked as though accustomed to toil!

"I want to see," he said, in tones peculiar to certain districts in Vermont and New Hampshire, "the feller what writ them ere Australian stories."

He had been told, it seems, that I might possibly be found there. He continued,—

"I've a notion of takin' a trip to that island, whar the gold is so plenty that a feller can make a fortin in no time; so I want to see the feller what wrote them stories, and get his 'pinion on a machine what I've built, which I s'pect will chaw up more quartz and spit out more gold than anything that ever was built in these ere United States of Amereky."

The lawyer pointed to me, and the visitor turned round with a stare of astonishment.

"You don't mean to tell me that you are the feller what dug all that gold out there, and had sich high old times with the bushrangers; do you?" he cried.

"I am the person," I replied.

"Wal, I'll be darned if you ain't the man I want to see, and no mistake. I'm glad to shake hands with sich a feller as you; now that's a fact."

He gave my hand a squeeze that proved most conclusively he possessed enormous strength, but at the same time the man's freckled face lighted up with such genuine satisfaction that I began to feel glad at having met the fellow.

"Now," continued the countryman, "will you jist take a look at my machine, and see if it's good for anything? I reckon it is; and so does some fellers that has seen it; but, then, they don't know, p'aps. Will you come with me for a little while, and jist tell me what you think my crusher will do?"

"Is it far from here?"

"No, sir; it's jist down here, in a room what I've hired. I've practised with it for a month or two, an' it goes like thunder."

"By steam?"

"Sartin — by steam," was the answer.

"I will go with you," I replied, although I did not anticipate much of a treat; for I had seen hundreds of quartz-crushing machines, and yet never met with but half a dozen that would do good work or pay for the material used in their construction.

We passed down the street to a machine-shop, and in a room that was double locked I saw a quartz crusher that met my ideas of what was required for the work it had to perform. I cannot describe the machine without illustrations, and there is no necessity that I should bother the reader with an account of its wheels and cogs, hoppers and springs. It is enough if I state that it reduced paving-stones to powder, filtered the latter through a sieve, and left a few grains of gold, which I had mixed with the stones, as they passed under a crusher, in a receiver, glistening as though just from the bowels of the earth. I had put in twenty scales of gold dust. I took out the same number.

"Wal," asked my Yankee friend, "what do you think of it?"

"It is a good machine, and will do just the right kind of work. In Australia a fortune can be made with it."

"I rather think so," drawled the Yankee, as though he was fearful of being too enthusiastic on the subject; and his calm, calculating gray eyes looked thoughtful as he surveyed the machine and its ponderous jaws.

"Is this of your own invention?" I asked.

"Wal, I reckon it is. You see, I've bin a sort of inventor all my life; and arter I'd sold the patent of my sassenger machine, I jist thought I'd turn my 'tention to a quartz crusher. I heard a Californy chap describe one, and I thought I could improve on it. I worked a year on this thing, and here it is."

"And now what do you propose to do with it?"

The sandy-haired genius scratched his head as he answered, —

"I've put all my money in the thing, and now I'm pumped as dry as a yearlin' heifer."

I looked over the machine once more, calculated its enormous strength, and its capacity for work, and then I said, —

"I will purchase one half the patent right of the quartz crusher, and furnish the money for building a second one, and after it is constructed we will start for Australia, and work them in partnership."

The Yankee seized my hand, and shook it in an enthusiastic manner.

"You're the man I has been lookin' for!" he cried. "We'll make our tarnal fortunes in less than no time, arter we has once got near a ledge of rocks what contains the right kind of stuff. But you is in arnest?"

"I am, and to prove it, commence work on the second

machine as soon as possible; and now we will go and look over your patent and make out the papers."

The Yankee's eyes lighted up at the thought of making his fortune.

"I'm your man," he said. "If we don't make things howl in Australia, then it ain't no matter; and arter we get our machine in workin' order, we'll eat the island up but we'll find gold;" from which remark I thought that he entertained but a slight idea of the extent of Australia.

"Now one question more," I said, as we left the building. "Tell me your name, and where you are from."

"Hezekiah Hopeful, of Hillsborough County, New Hampshire," was the prompt answer.

"Are you married?"

"Get eout!" was the bashful reply. "No, I ain't got no wife, but I has a gal, and when I'm rich we'll be one, but not before, if I knows it."

I was satisfied. Once in Australia, he would not be continually moping about a wife. The more I saw of the man, the better I liked him. He was a rustic genius, with courage and fidelity, and I thought that we should have no trouble in performing the work before us.

As we returned to the office, I talked with Hopeful about Australia, and found him a good listener; and after I had concluded, I drew from him, little at a time,—for he was cautious and shy,—an account of his life, how he had invented, and lost money by the operation, until he was compelled to recruit his exhausted finances by working at journey work in a machine-shop. His father had left him a few thousand dollars at the time of his death; this was gone, and some hundreds with it, and yet Hopeful assured me that he had invented some useful articles, such as the "Patent Flying Clothes Horse," "The Enlightened Mouse Trap," "The Enchanted Wash Tub," "The Baby's Delight," a sort of swing, on the perpetual-motion order, so that mothers could leave their pets for some hours without trouble.

All of these inventions Hopeful said were patented, but he did not hold the rights, on account of his being compelled to sell as soon as completed, for the want of money, although my new-found friend acknowledged that some parties had made fortunes through his aid.

"But they don't come it any more, I'll be goll darned if they do," cried Hopeful, with an angry gesture. "If my quartz crusher works like all thunder, and gobbles up the gold and spits it out like fun, I shall make somethin' out of it; shan't I?"

"A fortune, I hope," I answered.

"Is we goin' into the thing on equal shares?" asked Hezekiah, after a moment's thought.

"Yes, if you are disposed to accept of me as a partner. I'll buy one half of your patent, and you shall name the price. I'll furnish the money for the new machine, and the funds for a passage to Australia, and run my own risk about payment. How does that suit you?"

Mr. Hopeful uttered a crow of satisfaction as he exclaimed, —

"I'll have to write to Martha about this; and she'll yell, I know; but she'll be glad too, 'cos the critter always is when I'm in luck."

"Who is Martha?"

Hopeful looked at me from the corners of his gray eyes, as though doubtful if it was proper to trust me with so important a secret; but at length he said, —

"She's a gal."

"I supposed so."

"And a plaguy handsome gal she is, too. There ain't a handsomer one in all Hillsborough County, now I tell you."

"And this girl you would marry if you had the money to support her?"

"I reckon;" and then Hopeful burst from his reserve, as he exclaimed, "Goll darn it! the gal is too good for me, I know, 'cos she has got a dad what is worth ten thousand dollars. I tell you, he's got the putty, and jist 'cos he has, he don't want me to hitch on to Martha. She's bin willin' for a year, but her folks ain't, 'cos they say I'm only a genius, and won't be worth a darn cent. Yes, sir, it was on account of Martha I invented my quartz crusher. A Californy chap helped me with the idea, and I thought if I could sell 'em the gal would be mine."

We soon finished the business that took us to the lawyer's, and before night Hopeful was hard at work in a machine-shop, superintending the casting of wheels, pulleys, and massive pieces of iron beds; and, while he was doing his part of the work, I was getting ready for the voyage to Australia. I engaged a passage in the clipper ship Morning Light, Captain Keelhaul, who swore by his maintopmast that he would make the passage from Boston to Melbourne in ninety days, or carry all the spars out of the ship, and ruin one or two insurance companies. I collected and boxed up such articles as experience told me would be useful. I laid in a good stock of tobacco, a keg of pure brandy, a tent, a good supply of ammunition, and the saddles which I had brought home with me, confident that I could find none in Melbourne or Sydney that would compare with them for comfort or convenience.

At last Hezekiah announced that his second machine was ready and boxed up, and the day after the quartz crushers were stowed away in the hold of the Morning Light, and Hopeful was on his way to Hillsborough to have a parting interview with Martha, to tell her that he would be faithful, and beg of her to remain the same, — to shed some tears, to dry them, and to inform the young lady's parents that he should return with lots of money, and to receive an answer on their part that they would like to see it, merely out of curiosity, if nothing more. But, from what Hez let out, I think he was quite satisfied with all that transpired at Hillsborough. Perhaps Martha was more tender than he expected. At any rate, I noticed that he had a daguerreotype in his hands quite often, and once or twice I saw him kiss it with frantic devotion and very moist eyes.

But time passed rapidly, and at length we were ready to sail. All of my friends were taken leave of, and all of them promised to write quite often — pledges which it is useless to say were not kept, except by one or two men who had a personal regard for me, and without the slightest expectations of being remembered in my will.

"All aboard, gentlemen," roared Captain Keelhaul, one bright morning in the month of October, as we stood on Lewis's Wharf, and saw that his topsails were sheeted home, and that all were ready to cast off the lines as soon as the pilot gave the word.

"Come, Hopeful," I said, as I laid a hand on the shoulder of the genius, and pointed to the ship.

"I'm ready," he answered; "but it's an all-fired do..e, to leave home; now ain't it?"

"Not when you are used to it," I answered.

"Yes, I know you don't care, 'cos you ain't got no gal or wife; but I tell you it is tough on me, what leaves a heart and bright eyes. If you don't believe it, jist you try it."

"I will, some time, but not now."

Hopeful took a long look up the wharf, and a glance overhead, as though he hoped to see a familiar face before he separated himself from the world, and then gulping down a deep sigh, he stepped on board the vessel, and the next moment the lines were cast off, and the Morning Light was heading down the harbor, under the influence of a five-knot breeze from the westward.

"Come, gentlemen," cried Captain Keelhaul, who had nothing to do as long as the pilot was on board, "I've got one of the best bowls of punch mixed that man ever tasted. We must get acquainted over it. Walk into the cabin, and let us drink to a successful voyage and a quick one."

On the whole, I rather liked the appearance of the passengers, and when I was called upon for a sentiment I said so, and for half an hour we talked and drank punch; at the end of which time the breeze had freshened, and I felt the motion of the ship, and so did the young fellows who were near me; for I noticed that they no longer smoked with an apparent relish, that their cigars went out for the want of suction, and that some pale cheeks began to appear around the board.

"Gentlemen," cried Captain Keelhaul, on whom the punch

had no more effect than if it had been emptied into the harness cask, "one glass more, and then we will go on deck."

Only by the most determined spirit were some of them enabled to comply with the request; and as soon as the liquor was worried down, there was a rush for the deck, a decided tendency to look over the ship's side, as though something of an attractive nature could be seen in the water; and, after some internal commotion had been subdued, my fellow-passengers retired to their state-rooms, and were no more seen on deck for a week's time. As soon as I left the cabin I searched for Hopeful, and found him paying tribute to Neptune.

"How long," he asked, "must I suffer with this gol darned sickness? I feel as though I should throw up my boots."

"It will depend upon yourself."

"Then I'll be well to-morrow, sure."

But he was not well, or so that he could eat his rations, for a week; and then we were across the Gulf Stream, and steering for the coast of Africa.

I do not mean to tell the reader of the fun that we had on board, of the calms that we endured, of the gales that we encountered, of the petty quarrels that occurred among the passengers, of the good nature of Hopeful, who was a favorite fore and aft, and thought seriously, before we had been out six weeks, of constructing a steam engine and propeller, so that we could make headway during a calm. He gave up the undertaking when he found that the cook could not spare one of his coppers to be used as a boiler, and that Captain Keelhaul would not allow the spare iron to be hammered up for the purpose. All of these things I need not tell, for I know that the reader is impatient to land at Melbourne; and one morning in the month of January we dropped anchor in Hobson Bay, opposite the village of Williamstown, and our voyage was ended, for the land of gold was near us; and so were some of the ill-dressed vagabonds of the landing, for they swarmed off to us and came on board, clamorous for money, whiskey, or tobacco, while the work which they proposed to do in return for such favors was of a very slight nature, and not such as called for an outlay of much strength.

"Is that what you call Australia?" asked Hopeful, as he looked at the boatmen with a species of awe.

"Yes, Hez; here we are, safe, in just ninety days from Boston. What do you think of it?"

"I was thinking," replied the genius, in a thoughtful tone, "whar in all creation they got their old clothes from." And this was Hezekiah's comment on his first introduction to the cheerful, refined, and intensely honest people of Australia.

CHAPTER II.

WE ARRIVE AT MELBOURNE, AND MEET OLD FRIENDS.

From the time I left Melbourne until my return was just three years; consequently many changes had taken place, and many new faces had crowded out the old ones which I had been accustomed to see. Among the boatmen, I did not notice a man whom I had known in former years, and I must confess that I felt a little homesick to find that such was the fact, although I did not allow the feeling to manifest itself; for I knew that Hez was just about as miserable as a man could be, and not shed tears like a child. While I was packing my trunks, and thinking how I could get my tobacco on shore without paying duties, the custom-house officers came on board and took charge, and following them was a steamer to take the passengers and luggage up the river to Melbourne.

"Now, then, gents," shouted a fat and wheezy Englishman, who seemed to be a custom-house inspector, "just rouse your luggage on deck, and let us have a look at it. No tobacco, gents, and no cigars. You Americans are fond of the weed, but you mustn't smuggle."

"You hear him," cried Hopeful, with staring eyes. "You can't get that 'backer on shore. Don't you attempt it."

I laughed at his fears. I knew Australian officials much better than he did. My trunks were passed on deck, and I thought were going on board the steamer without an examination; but I was mistaken.

"Open 'em sir," cried the official.

"Nonsense!" I replied, and tipped the wink; but to my surprise the fellow did not respond, for he whispered, "I can't do it, sir, 'cos there's a d—d purlice lieutenant on board the steamboat, and he's watching me."

I looked up and saw a fine, soldierly-appearing man, with the uniform of a lieutenant of police on his back, standing near the guards of the steamer and composedly smoking his pipe, while his eyes were turned towards me. I thought that the man's face appeared familiar, and I glanced at it two or three times, and endeavored to recall it to mind, but could not; and I commenced to unlock my trunks, when I heard a peculiar sound, such as I had not heard for three years, or since I had given up hunting bushrangers and gold digging.

In an instant I looked up, as suddenly as though I had been warned by the tail of a rattlesnake. In fact, under the excitement of the moment, I sprang to my feet, and laid my hand on my revolver, while I glanced around in a hurried manner; for the signal which I had heard meant that there was danger near, and that I must be prepared for it. It was a peculiar hiss which the police force had adopted to communicate with each other while in search of convicts who had escaped to the bush.

As I said before, I looked aloft, and then around the deck, but saw nothing to attract attention; and I began to think that I must be mistaken, and was just on the point of handing my keys to the custom-house officer, who manifested some impatience, when the second signal was heard, sharper than before.

"There is no deception this time," I muttered, and instantly replied to it; for I knew the answer as well as the cavalry soldier knows the blast of the trumpet.

As I did so my glance fell upon the lieutenant of police I saw a smile pass over his face, and the next instant he had left his high position on the paddle-box, and was standing on the deck of the Morning Light, by my side, with his strong, sunburnt right hand extended, as though desirous of giving me a warm welcome.

"Your honor recollects me?" the officer asked.

"I have seen your face before, but I can't call your name," I replied.

"And to think that you should forget me, after all the fights we have mixed in," the officer cried, in a reproachful tone. "I am sure that your friend would not."

"You mean Fred?"

"Yes, sir."

"Ah! he is dead."

"A brave man has gone to his final account," cried the officer, reverentially; and he removed his official cap, and exposed his head, and as he did so his name flashed across my memory like lightning.

"Maurice!" I cried, and seized his extended hand.

"Yes, sir, that is my name, and very thankful I am that you have not forgotten it. I thought that I knew you, but I was not sure; so I tried the signal, for I was positive that you would not forget that. Ah, how many times we have used that, and successfully, too!"

"I recollected your face—I was positive that I had seen it; but it is so many years since we have met, that you must pardon me for not calling your name as soon as you spoke."

"Don't say one word," cried the officer; "a man who has proved himself as good a friend as you have, need not apologize."

I smiled and bowed, for I did not know to what he alluded, and I thought that it was best to remain quiet until he gave the cue.

"Yes, sir," continued Maurice, who had served in the Australian police force for many years, and was a sergeant at the time of my former visit, "to you I am indebted for my present position. You recommended me for the office, and I got it in less than three months after you left us. You shall find that I am not ungrateful."

"Don't mention so slight a service. I am sure that you deserve all that you got, and more too; for I have seen you under fire, and you stood it like a hero."

"Ah, those were times for men like us. Now nothing is doing. The bushrangers can kill and rob, and nothing is done towards rooting them out. They don't care for us 'traps,' and laugh if we talk of hunting them. Four weeks ago, ten convicts, transported for life, escaped from the hulks, and are now on the road, eating mutton, killing miners, stopping the mail, and raising the devil generally. I offered to take a squad of men and hunt them out of the bush, but I can't get the chance."

"But where is Captain Murden? He used to be fond of such adventures. He has not grown old and stiff, I hope."

"Ah, sir, it is because he is no longer a captain that such things are permitted. I suppose that you know he is discharged from the force?"

"No; this is the first intimation that I had of it."

"Come here one moment, sir," the officer said, as he motioned for me to move towards the cabin, where Hopeful stood with eyes greatly distended at the fact of my meeting an old acquaintance.

"Well, give me the keys of your luggage, so that I can search your boxes," cried the custom-house officer, as we moved towards the quarter-deck, where the crowd was not so great.

"What do you say?" demanded the lieutenant, turning upon the pursy custom-house officer with an expression of surprise.

"Why, I want to search the gentleman's luggage, you know."

"Search the devil! What do you mean? Put it on board the steamer, and don't disturb a single article."

"But our orders —"

"I'll take the responsibility," cried Maurice. "His luggage contains nothing but such as I can vouch for. If you knew the gentleman you would say so."

"One moment," I whispered to Maurice. "I have some twenty pounds of costly smoking-tobacco in one of those boxes."

"I am glad of it, and I wish that you had twice as much; for I hope that you will remain with us for some years, and that we shall have many quiet smokes together. Ah, if we could have a few more expeditions, what fun we should have!"

"Don't tempt me," I said. "I have come here to crush quartz, not bushrangers. If Fred were alive I might do something for you, and with you; but now I don't feel enthusiastic."

"What, not even to restore Mr. Murden to his rank of commissioner?" asked Maurice, with an eager look. I was silent, for I liked my former friend too well to refuse or make a rash promise.

"Let me tell you how Commissioner Murden lost his position, and then you can think what can be done to restore him to his former rank. You see he was appointed, after you left us, for good conduct in breaking up Black Darvil's and Darnley's bands, and ridding the country of such pests. You know what trouble we had in clearing them out?" I nodded, for I recollected the circumstances quite well.

"Well, Mr. Murden earned his promotion," continued Maurice, after a pause, "and there was not a man in the force but was rejoiced when he was appointed commissioner, because we knew that he would do what was right with the force under his charge. He had a roving order, went where he pleased, remained away as long as he pleased, and returned when he pleased. Of course I was with him and the force he commanded, and a good time we had of it. We were all growing rich, for we divided on the square—" At this point of the narrative I smiled, and I could not help it, for I recollected several dividends in which I had had a large share.

"O, you may laugh," cried Maurice, "but it was a dividend that cost Commissioner Murden his head. You see, we had driven the bushrangers all out of Victoria, and sent them flying in terror towards Sydney; but one fellow gave us some trouble, for he was mounted on the best horse that was ever raised in the colony, and we might chase him all day, and still not overtake him. But at last we come the woman game over him. You know what that is, I suppose?"

I nodded. It meant that some good-looking girl, a convict, and perhaps sent to Australia for life, had received the promise of a ticket of leave, or a pardon, if smart, if she would manage to inveigle the bushranger and deliver him up to his enemies.

"We found a smart wench, and put her on a sheep farm, and told her to keep her eyes open. She did. The bushranger, one day, while sweeping down for a fat lamb, caught sight of the girl, and that settled him. In three days we had him ironed, hands and feet; and then we began to tease him, just to find out where his gold dust was stored, for we knew that he had an awful lot of it somewhere, for he had been in the bush for nearly two years."

"You mean by teasing," I said, "that—"

"Just so," replied Maurice, with a cool smile. "We were not permitted to torture prisoners to find out their secrets, and as this fellow refused to tell where his money was stored, we just laid him down near an ant-hill, and let him rest while we cooked dinner."

"That was horrible," I muttered.

"I know; but what could we do? He wouldn't utter a word nor make a sign: so we put him near the ant-hill, and, would you believe it, the cuss did not whimper for half an hour. At the end of that time he began to groan, and turn, and twist, and in three quarters of an hour he shouted for mercy, and promised to tell all that we wanted to know. Ah, there's nothing like an ant-hill to bring a man to his senses."

"And you found the place where the dust was stowed?"

"Yes, and made a good thing out of it. We divided five hundred pounds each, and returned to the government two thousand pounds, or nearly ten thousand dollars, which, you will admit, was liberal."

"Of course."

"And not only that, we brought in the prisoner; but the cove was ungrateful, for he told the court that we had robbed him, and the court ordered an investigation, instead of laughing at the charge. Well, one of our fellows, who was never fit for a policeman, while in his cups split on us, and made a confession; and that is the way Commissioner Murden lost his head."

"Is he stopping at Melbourne?"

"O, yes, and has petitioned for reinstatement; but he has not had a hearing, and I don't think he will, unless he can bring strong influence to bear."

"In the mean time the bushrangers are on the rampage between Melbourne and Ballarat?"

"Yes, sir. As soon as they heard that Murden was off duty, they came back to their old quarters, and remained there in force; for when a platoon or company is sent against them, they scatter in all directions, and we return home."

"But how does it happen that I find you on the water, instead of doing duty on the land?"

"Simply because the officer who has charge of this kind of business is sick, and I was detailed to take his place. I am glad I came, for I have the pleasure of meeting you."

I bowed, and as the baggage was all on board the steamer, there was nothing to detain us on the Morning Light. I shook hands with Captain Keelhaul, promised to see him at Melbourne, and then Hez, Maurice, and I went on board the steam tug, the lines were cast off, we steamed past Williamstown, entered the river, and in a short time were moored at the docks, if such they can be called, of Melbourne.

"Will you go to a hotel, or drive direct to Mr. Murden's house?" asked the lieutenant.

"Thank you," I said. "I know something of Melbourne hotels. I have even stopped at them when I was in Australia on my first visit."

"Pardon my forgetfulness," cried the police officer. "I did not think of that. You know all about high charges, poor fare, bad accommodations, and the bugs."

"I should think that I did."

"Then you must go to a private house, or else stop with Mr Murden. He can accommodate you. He is not married, has a good establishment, and a well-stocked cellar. I know that he would like to have you visit him." But I thought that it was rather rude to force myself on a man without an invitation; so I concluded to take lodgings, as the cheapest and most convenient way of living while we remained in Melbourne.

"I know just the place that will suit you," cried Maurice; and he held up his hand for one of the numerous carts near the steamer to approach. The dray was loaded, and started, and we followed on, through some of the principal streets, until we stopped at a respectable-looking house.

"Here is the place for you," said Maurice. "Off with the load."

We found the woman who had charge of the house willing to receive us at a reasonable compensation, and in a short time we were installed in our apartments; and then Maurice took his leave, promising to call and see us in the course of the evening. As soon as he was gone, Hopeful lighted his pipe, and sat down opposite to me.

"Wal," he asked, "what is the next move?"

"We can't move until the cargo is out of the ship. We must remain here until our quartz crushers are landed, and then we will see what we can do with them."

"And you still think our prospect is good?"

"Of course."

"Wal," said Hez, with a sigh, "I don't know as I feel as hopeful as I did when I was in Boston; but if you think it's all right, then I s'pose it is. But it don't seem to me that they is making much fuss about the gold here."

"What did you expect?"

"Wal, I s'posed that every man I seed would have a bag full on his arm, and that the shop winders would be full of it. But I ain't see no gold as yet, and I am fearful it has all been dug out and carried off."

"Patience, Hez," I replied. "You will see gold in the course of a few weeks, and I hope that in that time we shall own some."

"I hope so, too," Hez replied; but he was not in a hopeful mood, and I saw that his thoughts wandered back to the cherry-cheeked damsel of Hillsborough County, and that he was a little homesick, and would like to have had a good cry, but his manliness had come to his aid, and prevented the tears from falling. I saw what was wanted, for I had felt the same sensations many times; so I opened our trunks, gave Hez a good dose of whiskey, put a pipe in his mouth, and commenced relating some of my former exploits in the land of bankruptcy and gold. I soon saw smiles on my friend's face, and was warmed up in good style, when I heard steps on the stairs, and the next instant a knock on the door.

"Come in," I shouted; for I thought that it was some one belonging in the house.

The door opened with a crash, and in rushed my old friend Murden, the very man I wanted to see of all others. He seized my hand, and for a moment neither of us could speak, so overpowered were we by emotion; but, while we were waiting for words to come, we scanned each other's faces with much interest. I saw that Murden had changed but little during the three years that we had been separated; that his eyes still retained their fire; that his face still looked determined and resolute; that his form was wiry as ever, and just as capable of receiving and giving hard knocks as when we roamed together on the banks of the Lodden.

"Well, of all the men in the world that I desire to see most, you are the one," Murden remarked. "Why, it was only this morning that I commenced writing a letter to you, and begging that you would once more visit Australia. Half an hour since, Maurice walked into the house, and informed me that you were here, and I hastened to meet you as soon as I had made a few preparations for your supper. Come, pack up. A dray is at the door to take your things. My house is your home, and at no other place shall you remain quiet."

"But, my dear sir —"

"No excuses. Call the woman up, and pay her for the rooms for a week's time, and then we will be off."

I saw that remonstrance was useless; so, after introducing Hez to Murden, I paid for our lodging, and then followed Murden to his comfortable house, and was instated in neat apartments; and while I was dressing for supper, or dinner, — for it was just six o'clock, — Murden came to my room and talked with me.

"Maurice has told you the particulars of my discharge from the service," he said, "and now I want your help to get restored. You are still remembered at headquarters, and your good word will do much for me. But there is another plan which will accomplish the object, if fair words fail, and I will let you into the mystery of the matter." Just at that moment, dinner was reported ready, and we proceeded to the table.

CHAPTER III.

THE STOLEN DIAMONDS. — THE LOVELY BAR-MAID AND HER FATHER.

It was very evident that Murden did not neglect his table, even if he was out of employment; for I saw all the fruit of the season on his sideboard, and several bottles of wine cooling in ice, while the ware upon the table was the richest china, with several pieces of silver scattered around; but as none of the silver matched, I was at no loss to account for the manner in which it was obtained; and in fact Murden made no secret of the fact that he had taken the plate from bushrangers during some of his excursions.

"And they obtained it from—"

"How should I know?" was the answer. "They stole it, of course; but I did not hunt for the owners after I had recovered it. I needed a few pieces of ware to decorate my table. I did not feel like buying, and I had no occasion to. But come, the soup is growing cold."

We sat down to dinner, Hez wondering at the good fortune which had befallen us, and willing to do justice to the cheer spread before him; but after the dessert was set on the table, and the wine had circulated two or three times, Murden spoke on the subject nearest his heart, although he first sent the servant out of the room with the following advice: "Tom, leave the room; and remember that I intend to talk confidentially to these gentlemen. If I catch you listening at the door, I'll cut off your ears, and send you back to the chain-gang. You know me."

"Yes, sir," was the only reply; and the man left the room apparently impressed with the conviction that Murden would keep his word.

"Now, my dear fellow," said Murden, as he filled the glasses and lighted a cigar, "let me tell you that I am anxious to be restored to my position as commissioner; because, in the first place, I had no idea that I should lose it, and after it was lost I felt as though I should regain it In the second place, the position is profitable, and gives one a rank that cannot be obtained in any other branch of the government, unless one goes in for some of the high offices; and I'm not fit for that, you know."

"How do you propose to get back?" I asked; "and how can I be of service to you?"

"Listen, and I'll tell you. Your deeds, and those of your brave companion, poor Fred, are not forgotten by the government. They are treasured up and talked over, and compared with the dashes of the police of the present day; and I need not say that every fresh bushranger outrage is the signal for tongues to commence wagging, and then your name is mentioned. Now, such being the case, it stands to reason that you must have influence with the government, and that a word from you would set me all right."

"You shall have half a dozen words if you want them," I answered, with a laugh. "Why, you know that I would do all in my power for your restoration."

"Thank you. I not only want a word or two, but I desire a little of your assistance in another direction; and if your friend here can do something to aid me, so much the better."

"Darn me if I don't do all I can," cried Hez, on whom the wine was operating, and who forgot his homesickness for the moment.

"Thank you. I supposed that you would. Try one of those oranges; after a long voyage they taste delicious."

Hez complied, and then Murden continued, sinking his voice to a whisper, "Let me tell you how I expect to get reappointed. A week ago some ticket-of-leave man or person whose time is out entered the government house, and stole all the diamonds belonging to the wife of the lieutenant-governor. They are worth some five thousand pounds, and of course no woman likes to lose such jewels; so for days and nights the police have been on the watch in hopes that they will turn up; but thus far no one has been lucky enough to lay hands on the thief, or thieves, or the precious stones."

"Probably the scamp has run to Sydney with them," I remarked.

"No, I think not; for the roads and boats have been watched, and not a suspicious character has left the city without being thoroughly searched."

"They may have gone to the mines — to Ballarat or Bathurst," I suggested.

Murden shook his head as he replied, "The police in that section of the country have been on the watch, and they would not fail to find the jewels if they had been taken to the mines."

"Then of course you think that the diamonds are in the

city; that the robber or the party who took them has not left town."

"Such is my opinion," responded Murden; "and I will tell you why I think so. In the first place, the rogue — and I have no doubt that he is a cunning one — would naturally suppose that every person leaving the city would be watched. Such being the case, a crafty rascal would argue that it is better to remain quiet for a few weeks, or until the affair has blown over, than run any risk by leaving in a hurry. In the second place, diamonds of much value cannot be sold in Australia without exciting suspicion and an investigation. They must go to England to get rid of them at a fair price, for the Jews of Melbourne would not think of paying one tenth part what they are worth. You follow me in my argument?"

"Yes; I think that you are sufficiently lucid."

"Well, then, pass the bottle to your friend, and we will wet our lips; for talking is dry work, at the best. At the same time light one of these fresh cigars — they are genuine Havanas, and were given me by a Spaniard to whom I did a little service a year or two ago. You will like them, for the tobacco is rich and agreeable."

We performed our allotted parts in a short time, and as the white clouds of smoke encircled our heads, Murden continued: "Now, if I could find those diamonds, my restoration to rank would be certain and speedy, for I should refuse the reward which the governor has offered, and which has set all the *traps* of Melbourne on the alert. I should decline the reward," said Murden, after a moment's thought, and with an honest expression of countenance, "because I know that I could make much more in my old position with one month's successful foraging."

"You are candid," I remarked.

"I am with friends, and with one who has shared with me in many a spoliation. Why should I not express myself in plain terms?"

"'Specially if there's money to be made," cried Hopeful, pricking up his ears.

"Just so," replied Murden. "Restore me to rank, and I'll warrant that we find something worth picking up."

"We will do what we can for you; but you must remember that we came here for hard work, and not for bushranger hunting. We are going into the quartz-crushing business, and have machines for that purpose."

"And I know where the richest quartz veins in the country are to be found."

"Whar?" asked Hez, with his usual bluntness.

Murden smiled, and did not reply directly. "The information will come in due time. But we will not talk of the matter now. Let us settle the diamond question first."

"Go on. State your proposition, and I will agree to it," I said.

"I know the party who stole the diamonds is in the city, waiting for a chance to get to England. Now, we must arrest him, and recover the property; and to do so I shall need your assistance."

"I have already promised it."

"I know it, but you have not promised to commence operations this very night."

"It is sudden."

"And therefore the more liable to be successful. Will you go with me?"

"Yes."

"Good! Then we will commence our rounds at nine o'clock, and as we will have to visit the lowest dens in the city, we must change our clothes, and put on garments that will not attract attention for their novelty. Each of us will want a revolver, a lot of impudence, and a determination to make love to half a dozen good-looking bar-maids."

"O, but I can't do that," cried Hez, with a very blank face. "I'll help all I can, but I can't be false to Martha."

Murden raised his eyebrows, — all the surprise that he allowed himself to express, — and remarked, "Well, we'll excuse you in that particular, although you are the first man that I ever saw that could remain faithful such a distance from home. You are a species of the genus homo that is rarely found in this section of the country; and if I should proclaim that so faithful a fellow was in the city, I should not be believed. Jack and I will do the love-making, but you must help us drink. You must keep quiet, and not utter a word, for I'm afraid that Yankee twang of your tongue would set some of the old heads to gossiping; and that we must avoid."

At nine o'clock we changed our clothing, assuming the garb of common sailors, such as blue shirts and trousers, thick Scotch caps, and leather belts around our waists to keep up our pants. In an inner pocket of our shirts we placed our revolvers, for we did not know but that we should need them in case of trouble or any sudden outbreak. We were all of us salt enough to pass for sailors without much suspicion; and with a dozen or twenty shillings in our pockets, just enough to pay our way, and yet not invite an attack for the purpose of robbery, we sallied forth, and sauntered slowly through the streets, meeting policemen at every turn, and encountering their keen glances without the slightest apparent notice; for Murden wore a false gray beard and wig, while Hopeful and myself were not well enough known to care for such disguises. After walking a short distance we heard the sound of violins, guitars, and pianos, the latter most shockingly out of tune.

"Now, then, we must have our wits about us, for we are in the den of the enemy," whispered Murden. And he spoke truly, for we saw bloated monsters of both sexes flitting in and out of the dance halls and drinking saloons, some of them drunk, and others in a fair way to reach an inebriated condition. Sailors and pimps were lounging on the narrow sidewalks, and women were at the windows of all the houses, exchanging chaff with those in the street, and soliciting visits from those who passed near them.

At length we came to a saloon called the "Red Lion," which looked a little more pretentious than the rest, and seemed cleaner. Murden glanced in at the door for a moment, and then entered, with a careless, indifferent swagger that was quite taking. Hez and I followed him.

and took seats at a table, and then, for the first time, I glanced around to see who were our neighbors. There were about a dozen people in the room, which was a long one, with a door at the end farthest from the street. On the left hand side, on entering the saloon, was a bar, and behind that bar, — a rather substantial one, of solid oak, — was a red-faced, broad-shouldered man, with a bull-dog sort of expression about his jaws, that was not intended to inspire confidence in those disposed to create a disturbance, or to take liberties with him. His hands were large and bony, and his arms were of immense length, and wonderful in their muscular strength; for the man had his shirt-sleeves rolled up, and showed all the flesh to the elbow. But I was not so much attracted by the man whom I have described as I was by the young girl at his side. At the first glance I thought that I was mistaken, and I rubbed my eyes and took a second look. No, I was not dreaming. Behind the bar, standing by the side of that muscular giant, drawing ale, half-and-half (half ale and half porter), was the handsomest girl that I had ever seen. She was all English, with large blue eyes, of a dark hue, and the sweetest red and white skin, so pure and transparent that I could hardly believe she was not painted. Her hands and arms were splendidly proportioned, for the latter were bare, although they were encircled by bracelets of a costly pattern; but the gold did not look as well as the pink and white flesh. On her long and tapering fingers I saw several rings, and as they were set with diamonds, brilliant flashes of light followed all her movements. She was dressed with most exquisite taste, a light dress revealing a pair of plump, white shoulders, upon which not a speck or blotch was to be seen. Never before had I been so taken with the face and form of a woman; and Murden had to speak to me three times before I was recalled from dream-land, where I had wandered when I was feasting my eyes on the face of the young and tender-looking bar-maid.

"What is the matter with you?" Murden asked. "I

have spoken to you three times, and inquired if you would have plain ale, half-and-half, or a shilling's worth of gin We must call for something, you know."

"Who is she?" I asked in a whisper, regardless of his question. "Tell me something about her, for she is the handsomest woman that I ever saw in my life."

"Whew!" whistled Murden. "Sits the wind in that quarter?" and then, with a grave face, he continued: "Don't lose your heart there, Jack, for she is colder than ice, and all the gold in Australia would not tempt her virtue. She has broken more hearts than any woman in Victoria, and the little jade is proud of her triumphs."

"And no one has yet touched her feelings?"

"No one, so it is said. See, here she lives in the worst section of the city: she is surrounded night and day with escaped convicts, pardoned convicts, and convicts whose time has expired. She waits upon murderers, thieves, gamblers, men of the most licentious character, all the scum of the world, which drifts to the surface and bubbles in Melbourne, and yet she stands behind that bar as virtuous and chaste as Diana."

"Jist like my Martha," murmured Hez, with a suppressed sob and a long-drawn sigh.

Just at that moment the young girl flitted towards us, and after a hasty glance at our faces to see if she had ever met them before in the saloon, she turned to me for orders, and with the sweetest smile and the most fascinating courtesy that I had ever seen, asked, —

"What will you please to order, gentlemen?"

"Some of your best ale; and I know that it must be good if you draw it," I said, hastily, fearful that Murden would get the start of me. In an instant her calm blue eye scanned my features, and then fell upon my hands. I thrust them out of sight, for I recollected that they were not rough enough for the character I had assumed, and that I had forgotten to stain them. She seemed to have read me in an instant, for the light vanished from her red, sweet lips, and she drew herself up and looked as cold as an iceberg.

"A pint or a quart of ale for each?" the bar-maid asked.

"A pint, and half a dozen of your best cigars. Remember, not German."

"I understand, sir;" and she glided from me towards the bar, where the muscular individual with the red face was reading, with the most intense interest, an English sporting-paper. There were but two persons in the room, with the exception of our party, and the bar-maid, and the individual who was reading. In the farthest corner of the saloon, near the door, two men were seated at a table, with a pot of ale between them. They were talking in low tones, so low that we could not hear the first whisper they utterred; but we noticed that they were earnest, and rather apprehensive, for they often glanced towards the door, and seemed to shrink if any one passed it. I did not pay much attention to them, although I suspected that they were burglars; but Murden scanned them closely, while I was ordering the ale.

"Tell me more of that girl," I said, as soon as she turned towards the bar.

"Confound your curiosity! She is the daughter of the 'Manchester Pet.'"

"And who is the 'Manchester Pet'?"

"There he stands behind the bar. He was once a prize-fighter in England, and even to this day he delights to break people's heads, unless they are civil to him and his daughter. But here comes the ale and cigars. I'll tell you more of the matter in a minute."

CHAPTER IV.

THE PRIZE-FIGHTER AND HIS DAUGHTER. — THE ROW. — THE SIGNAL.

"FIFTEEN years ago," said Murden, raising the ale to his lips, and taking a long and refreshing draught, and then smiling at the bar-maid in token that he appreciated the quality of the drink, "the Manchester Pet was one of England's wonders. His correct name is Sam Sykes, and for ten years he worked at bricklaying; but as he had had two or three fights, and showed great pluck and powers of endurance, the London fancy took him in tow, trained him, bet their money on him, and matched him for a fight, which he won; and he continued to win battles, until, in one contest, he fortunately, or unfortunately, just as you please, crushed his opponent's skull, and killed him. Well, the traps or peelers of England didn't look at the matter in the light of a joke; so they searched for the Pet, discovered him, tried him for manslaughter, found him guilty, and the judge sent him to this country for five years. His wife, this child, and another woman, followed him, opened a bar, and supported themselves until the Pet's time had expired. Miss Jenny was three years old when they landed at Melbourne; consequently she is eighteen at the present time. Don't look at her in that way," continued Murden, "or she will know that we are talking about her."

"How can I help it?" I replied, with a sigh; "for she is very beautiful."

"Jist like my Martha," muttered Hez, sucking away at his cigar, with his cap on the back of his head, and his frank, open face once more clouded at the thought of the New Hampshire beauty.

"Don't be spoony," cried Murden. "She is not the sort of woman you want for a wife; and as for a mistress, your life would not be safe to mention such a thing. She is a jewel, but the setting is not such as you would like for permanent wear. Will you hear the rest of my yarn?"

"With pleasure, or rather, I should say, with pain; for it does pain me to think that so beautiful a creature should be here, surrounded by crime and wretchedness."

"Don't be spoony, I tell you," continued Murden. "It is a bad sign for your success in Australia."

I laughed, and withdrew my eyes from the calm, self-possessed face of the young girl, and prepared to listen to Murden; but even while I was listening, I could not help thinking that with such a companion for life, my career in Australia would be very short. Had she been owned by respectable parents, and brought up in seclusion, I might, I thought, have seriously contemplated a short courtship; but a prize-fighter's daughter, and a bar-maid—this was too much.

"What, in the devil's name, are you thinking of?" asked Murden, who had talked for some time, but whose words I did not understand, because my mind was filled with other matters.

"I have heard all that you said," I replied.

"Nonsense! I know better. You were thinking of that girl's blue eyes."

"Jist like Martha's," muttered Hez, looking at the bottom of his pewter beer pot.

"Go on with your yarn. I will hear it, unless you are too tedious," I said.

"Well, I will be as brief as possible, although you don't deserve such mercy. As I said before, the party arrived at Melbourne with a little money. They went into the public-house business, and the Manchester Pet went up the country and into the road-mending line. He used his strength to some advantage, was civil and obliging, helped the overseers to subdue several rebellious convicts, and, in the course of two years, was enabled to rejoin his wife and child as a ticket-of-leave man. The family had managed to exist, and save a little money. The Pet knew how to dispose of it to advantage. He rented this place, the Red Lion, and cus-comers crowded around him. He made money, and now is reported worth something handsome."

"And the daughter — has she remained with him ever since?"

"Yes; but, at the same time, she was not allowed to grow up in entire ignorance. She has received a little education; knows how to read and write after a fashion; but that is about all."

"Jist like my Martha," cried Hez; and then recollecting that he had made a mistake, he added, "except that Martha knows most everything."

"Anything more?" I asked.

"No, with the exception that the Manchester Pet saw that his daughter's beauty attracted custom; so he has kept her behind the bar ever since her mother's death."

"Then her mother is dead?"

"Yes; died some years since." At this moment the Manchester Pet seemed to have finished his reading, for he folded up the paper in a dignified manner; and, as he laid it under the counter, remarked to his daughter, in rather an animated tone, —

"The Birmingham Chicken and the Dublin Porcupine have made a match, and will fight for the belt in October."

"What's the stakes?" asked the young lady, looking up with an unusual degree of interest.

"Two hundred pounds."

"Which's the best man?" continued the young lady with the dark blue eyes.

"O, the Chicken. He's got more science than the Porcupine. I'll bet on him, and give the odds — not much, you know, but a little."

Murden touched me with his foot, and laughed beneath his false beard. "What do you think now?" he asked.

I was a little disconcerted by the conversation of the blue-eyed beauty, but still I was not disgusted. Man will stand much nonsense when it is backed by a handsome woman's face. Perhaps, if I had been her husband, I should not have liked it. As it was, I thought that such unwomanly conversation could be cured or abolished in the course of time, provided the girl had a teacher whom she loved. But while I was ruminating,—regretfully, perhaps,—the Pet left the bar, yawned, stretched his enormous limbs, glanced around the saloon, looked at the two men who were in the corner near the door, hesitated for a moment as though he had half a mind to speak to them, and then his sharp eyes fell upon us, and he seemed to look us over in an instant. Then he came towards our party.

"Well, my men, how's the beer?" he asked.

"So good," I answered, "that we want more of it."

"Jenny, more beer here," cried the Pet, turning to his daughter.

"Are you in search of a ship?" asked the Pet, as the blue-eyed girl took our pots.

"We wouldn't mind if we had a good offer," Murden replied.

"Come to me if you want to cut and run for it," said the Pet, under the impression that we thought of running away, and would need a chance to ship. "I can find you a good vessel and good wages."

"I will talk with you on the subject some other time," I said. "We shan't go on board for twenty-four hours. We've got liberty for that length of time."

During this conversation, the bar-maid had suspended her labors, and listened to our words with much attention. Her eyes wandered from face to face, and at last rested on mine, with a long, steady stare, as though she was determined to remember it in case we again met. I had removed the common cap that covered my head, and I must confess that vanity prompted me to the act, and I will also acknowledge that I was not a bad-looking fellow when I was dressed as a human being, and not as a monkey, which, I feared, the Scotch cap made me resemble. The Pet winked, yawned, and then walked towards the door, as though he was about to look up some customers; but, not finding any on the sidewalk, the publican walked off for a short distance, and no sooner did he disappear than the two men in the farther corner of the saloon — the same fellows who had whispered together so earnestly all the time that we were present — arose and walked towards the door, which was near them. They attempted to open it, but found it locked; and, with an air of surprise, they turned to the bar-maid.

"Miss Jenny," they asked, "what is the door locked for?"

"To keep out those whom we do not wish to enter," was the pert reply.

"Damn it, what do you mean by that?" one of them asked.

"Just what I said. Father don't want you to enter the private room until you pay what you owe."

"Do you think that we intend to bilk you out of your pay? We have —" Before the fellow could finish his sentence his companion put his hand over his mouth and stopped him.

Murden and I exchanged glances. My friend leaned over and whispered to me, "I know them both, now that I have seen their faces. Both of them have been confined in the hulks, and both of them enjoyed the reputation, in England, of being daring burglars. One of them I suspect is —" Murden did not conclude his account, for the suspected men, who seemed furious at the idea of being debarred from entering the private parlor, raised their feet and kicked at the panels of the door, as though they meant to break them in. Miss Jenny did not manifest the least sign of alarm. She did not exhibit the least tremor, nor did her sweet face flush with an indignant blush, as she walked towards the two men who were committing the assault on the door.

"Pat Doland and Bill Thrasher," said the young girl, "you'll get your heads knocked off unless you stop that noise, and go about your business. Father is only a few steps from here. If you don't stop I'll call him."

"Will you open the door?" demanded the fellow whom she called Pat Doland.

"No; I'll call father first," was the firm answer; and I looked at the dark blue-eyed girl with increased admiration

"Your father be d—d," was the reply of the men. "We can pay him what we owe him, and a hundred times more, but not to-night. Let us into the private parlor, where we can settle a little matter."

"You can't go in," she answered.

With an angry oath the men dashed at the door; but as they kicked at it, Jenny threw herself in front of them, so that they could not touch the door unless they injured her person. I arose from my seat, but Murden laid his hand on my arm.

"Don't interfere," he said. "The quarrel is none of yours."

Perhaps I should have taken his advice, had not the fellow who was known as Thrasher suddenly raised his hand, and struck the sweet-faced Jenny upon her shoulder, so fair and white.

"Coward!" she cried; but she did not leave her place near the door.

I could not stand that. So I left my seat, in spite of Murden's remonstrances, and ran to that part of the room where the ruffians were still swearing and threatening vengeance on Jenny for the stand she had taken. In my movements I was none too soon. Thrasher, finding that oaths could not frighten Jenny from her position, had raised his arm for the second time, and I saw that it was directed towards her face.

"Take that, you ——," cried the ruffian; and his heavy fist was about to fall, when I struck him in the region of his right ear, and over he went; but in an instant Doland turned on me, to revenge the fall of his companion.

"Blast your eyes for that," the ruffian said; and he left the door and Jenny, turning square round, and aimed a blow at me with a slung shot, which he took from his pocket. Luckily I saw the missile coming, and had a chance to dodge. The slung shot passed within a few inches of my head, and the blow was so well intended that the assailant had to turn half round to recover his balance; and he had hardly done so before he fell at full length upon the floor; and looking up I saw that Hez was beside me, and had done a manly part with his strong arm and hard fist.

"Gol darn a man what don't fight fair," my friend said. "If I can't lick a man with my mawlies, I won't take no slung shots or knives, I won't."

I did not have time to compliment Hez on the activity which he displayed, for the fallen ruffians were moving, and making demonstrations. I saw Doland put his hand in his coat pocket; but before he could draw his pistol I was kneel ing beside him, with one hand on his throat, while with the other I wrenched the pistol from his jacket, and as I did so, saw that Hez was following my example.

In the mean time Miss Jenny had maintained her position near the door, looking upon our proceedings without mani festing the slightest alarm. Perhaps she had seen too many rows to care for them; or perhaps she wanted to see which would come out best. If such was the case, she must have been more than satisfied; for she said, as soon as we had disarmed the ruffians, "Now let 'em up, and if they don't pay and go off peaceable, kick 'em into the street."

"You'll regret this," cried Doland. "We might have spent all our money in the Red Lion; but now we'll see you hanged first."

"Don't be impudent to the lady," cried Hez. "I'll be gol darned if I'll stand that, you know."

"I don't see any lady here," answered Thrasher. "I see a bar-maid, or a pot-girl, I don't know which. Ladies don't live in this part of the town."

Jenny's cheeks flushed, and her eyes flashed; but I saw that she managed to retain her calm exterior in spite of the insult.

"Shall I kick them into the street?" I asked the young girl.

"No," was her prompt answer; "they are not worthy of your rage. Let them go. My father will wax 'em when he hears of their doings."

As she spoke the Manchester Pet entered the saloon; and his heavy face lighted up at the least appearance of a disturbance. He strode towards us, and asked, "What's the matter, girl?"

"Doland and Thrasher wanted the private room. I told 'em that they couldn't have it. They insisted that they would go in, raised a row, and struck me, and if it hadn't been for these two coves I should have got a black eye."

The face of the Pet was fearful to behold while she was relating her grievances. He set his heavy jaws firmly together, and looked as though he was about to enter the prize-ring and fight a desperate battle with an adversary whom he hated most terribly. He struck his huge fists together, and then rushed on Doland.

"Keep off," shouted that individual, and he made a show of placing himself in a boxing attitude; but the rush of the Pet was like that of an enraged bull. He bore down all opposition, caught Doland around the waist, struck him once or twice on his face, and then carried the man to the door and threw him into the street. He fell with a crash, and was covered with blood when he arose and staggered off.

The Pet returned for Thrasher; but that cautious individual dodged, and shouted, "Let me alone; will you?"

The Pet made a rush, but Thrasher avoided him, and left the saloon in a hurry, and the Pet came back, after a vain pursuit.

"I'll break their blasted necks, some day," muttered the Pet, as he went behind his bar and refreshed himself with a pot of porter. "I'll kill the man who dares to insult my darter."

Jenny whispered a word to her ferocious father, and he looked at us for a moment with some attention, then came towards us.

"Give us your hand, my fine feller," he said. "You is worthy of shaking hands with me, and I tell you that is an honor I don't grant all sailor-men. You floored them 'ere coves, and the gal tells me that you did it in style. Now you shall take a drink with me. Come, girl, bring some ale, and draw it mild, from the best taps.

The giant shook hands with me in a boisterous manner,

and then served Hez and Murden the same way. Jenny brought the ale, and I was pleased to notice that the mug which contained my ale was brighter than the rest, and that the beer was more lively than that which Hez or Murden put to their mouths. Did I argue from this that the bar-maid appreciated the devotion which I had shown, and was willing to give me positive proof, in her own delicate way, that I was not disagreeable to her? I don't know that I thought much about it that night, for I could think of but one thing, and that was, that the bar-maid was the handsomest woman I had ever seen, and that I wished that she was in a different sphere of life, so that I could feel as though she was worthy of my love."

"You coves has acted in ship-shape fashion," said the Pet, bringing his hand down upon the table with such force that the pots jumped several inches.

"Keep your hands quiet," said the girl, for she still remained near us.

"All right, lass," the Pet answered. "I'll mind my eye. You go behind the bar, and I'll talk with the sailor-men." But the girl did not obey, for she sat down near the table, and looked at me attentively, as though she had seen me before, and wanted to recall the time and place.

The Pet did not notice it. He commenced talking with us, praised us for what we had done, and intimated that his house was open to us in case we were disposed to run away from our ships.

"Don't talk nonsense, father," said the girl. "Don't you see that this man is no sailor?" She pointed to me, and the Pet cast his eyes over us as though to judge of the truth of her assertion.

"How is it, youngster? bean't you a sailor-man?" he asked.

"Look at his hands," said the girl. Her sharp eyes had noticed that they were too soft and clean to pass for a sailor's.

Before I could answer, some one entered the door of the saloon, and remained there a few seconds; and during that time I saw him make a signal with his hands, and then return to the street, as though the person he was in search of could not be found in the Red Lion. The Pet arose, stretched his huge arms, and said he was going out for a walk.

"Look to the bar, lass," he said; "and don't charge these coves for their drink. I'll come back afore long."

He left the saloon, and just as he cleared the threshold, Murden said, "We must move, lads, or we shan't see much sport in Melbourne to-night. You pay, Jack, for I want a little fresh air;" and off Murden walked.

As I threw down a couple of shillings on the counter, and turned to leave the saloon, Jenny laid her hand on my arm, and looked up at me with a pair of eyes that a princess might have been proud of. What man could hesitate when uch orbs asked for a moment's conversation?

CHAPTER V.

MRS. TROTTER'S CASTLE.

As the handsome bar-maid laid her white hand, covered with diamond rings, upon my shoulder, I saw Murden standing on the sidewalk, and signalizing me to make haste and join him; but how could I leave such a pair of eyes in a hurry?

"Let me speak with you," she said. "Will you listen to me?"

"Yes, for an hour, if you will not tire of my company."

She did not blush or smile at the compliment; but she fixed her calm blue eyes on my face, and said, "Tell me your occupation."

"Does not my dress proclaim it?" I answered.

"No, it does not. What is your business? Are you like most of the company that come here? Do not deceive me."

"What do you suspect?"

"That you and your companions are cracksmen," was the prompt answer; and those blue eyes did not relax the firmness of their gaze when the words were spoken.

"Well, what more?" I asked, in as calm a tone as I could assume.

"Then turn your attention to other business, or come here no more," was the low answer.

I looked at her in surprise. "Do you forbid me to see you again?" I asked.

"Yes, unless you can come here as an honest man Look you, covey; you have done me a service to-night. I am grateful, womanly grateful, and for that reason I would save you. You are surprised; but you would not be if I told you all. If you have committed a robbery, come not here with the proceeds, for you will lose your liberty and all your unlawful gains. Do I speak plain enough?"

"Yes, but I have no fear."

"I tell you that you will be sold, and yet I cannot inform you who will do it."

"I can suspect."

"And yet keep a secret?"

"Yes, if it belongs to you." I bowed, and would have taken the lady's hand, but she drew back and stood on her dignity.

"Hands off," she said, with a slight flush on each cheek. "I want no love-making. I cannot stoop to a cracksman or a bushranger; and an honest man would not bend to me."

"Will you come?" shouted Murden from the door.

"In one moment," I answered. "To-morrow I will call and see you. Are you willing?" I said in a low tone.

"The saloon is open for customers," was the answer. "If you come, appear with clean hands, and talk but little with my father. You understand me?" and as she asked the question, she raised her dark-blue eyes, and gave me a look that I could not mistake. It told me as plain as words that her father was in the habit of selling to the police those adventurous gentlemen who risked their lives and liberty for the sake of silver ware, gold, or colony bank notes.

"I thank you," I said, "I have no fear."

"So others have said, and met with misfortunes. Let me warn you in time."

"From your words it is evident that you do not think I am a sailor," I remarked; for I relished her company so much that I prolonged the conversation in spite of Murden's impatience.

"You are no more of a sailor than I am. You are from Sydney, and have just arrived in Melbourne."

"Go on. You are good at guessing."

"You were compelled to leave Sydney for fear of the traps."

"That is enough for one night. I will hear the rest when I call to-morrow," and I left her and joined Murden.

"I thought that you meant to talk all night," that amiable gentleman said. "I am afraid that I have missed my game by delay."

"Well, it is not often that a man has a chance to talk with a pretty woman in this part of the world. They are not over plentiful, as you must be aware."

"I thought that you cared nothing about women?"

"I don't, for homely ones."

"Bah! that bar-maid has turned your head, and it will take six months in the bush to cure you. But come along. I have work that will interest you."

He led the way along the rough sidewalk, and at last we turned down a narrow lane, dark, dirty, and prolific of bad smells, and then halted near a cellar lighted by a spluttering candle.

"In the name of thunder, what did you bring us here for?" I asked.

"Hush! not a word," answered Murden in a whisper. "Step back a little, so that no one can see us." We retired to the shelter of an overhanging roof attached to a low wooden building, which was directly opposite the cellar.

"Feel to the right and left," whispered Murden. "We

want no listeners here." We felt our way to each end of the building, and returned without making any discoveries.

"Now, then, what is the project?" I asked.

"Before I answer the question, let your friend, Mr. Hopeful, enter the cellar opposite, and buy a candle, or make some excuse, and while there let him take a rapid survey, and note if the two men whom we saw at the Red Lion are in the place. If they are, say nothing to them; but return as soon as possible. If no one is there but an old woman, ask her if she has lodging rooms to let. Tell her that you want to hire, for the night, a room for yourself and friends. When she comes out of the cellar to show you the rooms, we will join you, and pretend to be drunk. Do you understand, Mr. Hopeful?"

"I rather think that I do," answered Hez, confidently, and away he went.

"Now, Murden," I asked, "what does this mean? It has some significance, I know."

"To be sure it does," answered the ex-police commissioner. "You noticed the two men at the Red Lion?"

"Of course. I knocked one of them down. You saw the operation; and I ask you, as an Englishman and a friend of the prize-ring, if the blow which I struck was not a scientific one."

"Nonsense! Listen to me," said Murden. "While those two fellows were talking, I caught a few of their words, and came to the conclusion that the rascals lodged here."

"Well, what of it?"

"Only this: those two men, I think, have got her ladyship's diamonds."

"The devil they have! What ground have you for such suspicion?"

"I haven't time to tell you all; but I am determined to see if my surmises are correct. If they are, my road to preferment is sure, and then you and your friend can command me at all times."

"Thank you. Here comes Hez."

Hopeful could be dimly seen emerging from the cellar,

and following him was an old woman hideous with wrinkles, tobacco, and snuff. We crossed the street, and stood before them, swaying back and forth, as though we were under the influence of liquor.

"I has a room that'll suit ye, divil fear ye but it will," cried the woman, unlocking the outside door, and bidding us enter.

"Ye are sailor-men, ain't ye?" she asked.

"Yes, mother, we've smelt of salt water," answered Murden.

"And ye has run from yer ships? Don't deny it, ye divils;" and the old woman chuckled.

Murden pretended to hesitate, as though he feared to make a confession.

"Don't mind me," lads, the hag said; "I'll keep ye safe. Divil a bit shall the purlice find ye; and when yer ship is gone, I'll get ye another. Now, tell me the truth, ye divils has ye any money?"

"Hain't we got some," replied Murden; and he produced a few shillings, and shook them in the old woman's face.

"Give me one for the lodgin'," she cried; "it's chape for a shillin'. The beds is illegant. Divil a better can be found in all 'Stralia, and ye'll say so in the mornin'." Murden put a shilling in her withered palm. She slipped the silver into her bosom, and then led the way up a flight of rickety stairs.

"Have you many lodgers, mother?" asked Murden, as we reached the first landing.

"Only two, as nice gintlemen as ever lived; but it's little they sleep in the night time. Day is night for them. But they pay well, and what more can I ask?"

"Do they sleep on the next floor, or on this?" asked Murden.

"Sure, it's on this floor, and in the illegant room that overlooks the big yard. Ye can have the front room if ye want it, but I must have another shillin'."

"Well, it's dear, but take it," said Murden, who for the past five minutes had been supporting me, as though I was under the influence of liquor, and needed a bed.

The old hag dropped the money into her bosom, and then unlocked the door, and ushered us into an apartment that contained a number of dirty blankets in one corner, a pine table covered with grease, and about a thousand flies and fleas to the square inch.

"Ah! this is comfortable," cried Murden, as though he had been accustomed to such lodgings all of his life. "Here we have everything that one can desire, except pipes, tobacco, and beer."

"Sure, I have all of 'em in the cellar, and for money ye can have 'em."

"And a candle?"

"Yes, the best in Melbourne."

Murden put a third shilling into her hand, and it went the way of the others.

"I'll bring 'em, I'll bring 'em up," the hag said; and leaving the light on the table, she felt her way down stairs in the dark, and closed the outer door after her. As soon as she had done this, Murden took the candle and examined the wall which separated the front and back rooms. The partition was composed of rough boards, unjointed and unpainted, with knot-holes in many of them, and rat-holes in all of those near the floor.

As soon as Murden had finished his survey, he went to the door of the back room, found that it was locked, and by the aid of some soft wax, took an impression of the key-hole, then returned to the room and examined it by the light.

"I can pick it in two minutes," he said.

"What in the devil's name do you mean to do?" I asked.

"I mean to enter that back room before morning," was the answer.

Before I had time to ask another question, the old woman's feet were heard on the stairs. She reached the room, and placed the pipes, tobacco, and beer on the table.

"Better stuff can't be found in all Melbourne," she said, "although it's I that say it."

She stood surveying us for a moment and then, finding

that we did not want any more of her stock, stuck the candle in the neck of a bottle, and left us. An hour passed away, and no one entered the house. We had smoked half a dozen pipefuls of tobacco, when Murden laid his pipe down, took from his pocket a piece of strong, crooked wire, cut the candle in halves, took off his shoes, and crept noiselessly towards the door.

"Do you want my help?" I asked.

"You may come if you please, and let Mr. Hopeful stand at the head of the stairs and give warning the instant he hears a key put in the outside lock. Remember, no noise."

We extinguished the light in the front room, and then went to the landing. All was quiet in the house, with the exception of the rats. Murden felt for the key-hole of the back door, and inserted the wire in it, and worked it back and forth, until the bolt slipped; and then he turned the handle of the door, and we entered the room. The apartment was precisely like the front one, and furnished in the same style. But we did not stop to notice matters particularly, for we had other motives in visiting the room, and to satisfy ourselves we overhauled the blankets, examined every corner of the apartment, and yet nothing but a few dirty pieces of clothing met our view. For the first time Murden's face wore an expression of dejection, as though he had been disappointed, and hardly knew which way to turn to retrieve his fortune.

"We must give it up," he whispered, after we had examined the floor to see if there were not some boards which had been recently disturbed, and found that there was no appearance of such a thing. "I am inclined to think that the diamonds are not here. The rogues have buried them or left them at some pal's house."

"Let us examine the walls," I said. "I don't feel like giving it up in this way."

"It is useless," said Murden. "I am satisfied that the jewels are not here. Her ladyship will have to weep for her loss a few weeks longer."

"And we must remain here all night?" I asked, as I

kicked at a rat that was advancing towards me with hostile intentions.

"Yes; I suppose so."

"Then let us arrange the partition so that we can hear some conversation if the occupants of this room should return before we leave the house."

"By Jove! but there is something in that," exclaimed my friend. "A word may lead us to the scent."

He drew his bowie knife and commenced cutting at the boards of the partition, and I imitated his example; but both of us worked so cautiously that we did not leave traces of our handiwork so that suspicion would be excited. We had just finished our peek-holes, when Hopeful opened the door, and whispered, "Some one is coming."

In an instant we put out the light and stole from the room, Murden locking the door with the skeleton key, and while he was thus employed, the street door was thrown open; but luckily the current of air extinguished Mrs. Trotter's candle, and left the lady in darkness.

CHAPTER VI.

THE EXPLORATION. — THE QUARREL AND THE MURDER.

Mrs. Trotter was not a delicate-minded female. In fact, she often gave vent to expressions which masculine ears should never hear in the presence of woman, whom we regard as pure and heavenly, and worthy of the best place at the breakfast table, the best seat in the concert hall, and the most comfortable box at the opera; and in return for all this we only ask that she will love us, that she will dress to please us, and that she will take care of our children when she has nothing else to do; therefore, when the candle was extinguished, and that amiable lady, who carried the candlestick, exclaimed, in a harsh voice, "Curse everything an inch high!" I, for one, felt shocked; and Hez, no doubt, was very much grieved.

"What did you let the light out for?" asked one of Mrs Trotter's companions. "You old fool, didn't you know better?"

"That is one of our Red Lion friends," whispered Murden

"Ye is smart beauties, ye is, to call a woman old enough to be yer wife a fool. It's the party up stairs that wouldn't do it, or I'm no judge."

"A party up stairs?" cried both men, eagerly. "What do you mean? Who are they, and when did they come here?"

"And do you s'pose I'll answer all yer questions? Don't I keep a lodgin' house, and didn't the three sailor-men pay me for pipes and the beer, and a shillin' for the beds?"

"The beds!" cried the two men, with shrill laughs. "Your beds consist of a blanket and a million fleas."

The old woman uttered a malediction, and hobbled off for a light, leaving the fellows in the entry; and although they lowered their voices almost to a whisper, we could hear what they said.

"The d—d traps are not on our trail, are they?" one of them asked.

"Nonsense! What should make you think that? We ain't known in Melbourne, and I've not seen a Sydney trap since I've been here. I tell you we are safe enough if we only work our cards right, and when we once dispose of our —"

"But these fellows up stairs — what of them?"

"They are drunken or runaway sailors, and the last men in the world to suspect us. No doubt they are snoring off the effect of the liquor which they have drunk; so don't be alarmed at phantoms of your own conjuring up." At this instant the old woman returned with the lighted candle, which they took from her hand. We withdrew into our own room, and closed the door so softly that a rat would not have been disturbed by the noise.

"Now, Hopeful," cried Murden, in a whisper, "can you imitate snoring?"

"Gol darn it, I can do it so nicely that you'll be tempted to throw a boot at me afore I've been underway two minutes," replied my original friend.

"Then start it at once, but don't overdo the matter." Accordingly Hez took a seat on the floor, leaned his back against the partition, and started his nasal music, which sounded like distant thunder.

We waited until Doland and Thrasher made their way up the crazy staircase and unlocked their door, and then we applied our eyes to the peep-holes. I saw that Doland was under the influence of liquor, but not so much as to make him reckless and noisy; while Thrasher, who looked like a cool hand at roguery, seemed quite sober. The men took a hasty survey of their apartment; put the light on the table, and pulled up two empty boxes and sat down on them. As soon as they were seated they took out their pipes, filled them, and commenced smoking; but they had taken only a few whiffs when Doland raised his head and listened.

"What, in the devil's name, is that noise?" he asked.

"It's the drunken sailors in the next room," answered Thrasher. "A crash of thunder would not start them. Let them snore, although I'm sorry the old woman took them in. If we get rid of the shiners, we leave for the mines for a few months, and then say that we have made a lucky hit; and who is to deny it?"

"We might have settled matters with the Pet, if we had only hinted what we wanted the private room for," Doland snarled.

"Yes, and had the brute claim one half for commissions. I know the cove by reputation. Didn't Sandy-Haired Bob tell me all about him?"

"But his girl is a good looker," muttered Doland. "I never saw a handsomer piece of calico in my life."

"But she ain't for the like of us; so it's no use getting spoony over her," Thrasher replied. in a hasty tone, as though he felt a little sore on the subject.

"I don't know about that," Doland said, in a dogmatical

manner. "If I should go to her all covered over with diamonds, and with gold in my pockets, I think she'd look at me in a friendly manner."

"Yes, and before she had time to give you a second look, the traps would have you; for I tell you, man, that a person can't walk the streets with a diamond ring on his finger, but he's asked to explain how he got it, and where. Give up all thought of the girl, for you can't get her after what passed to-night."

"If I sell my share of the sparklers, I'll try," muttered Doland, in a surly tone.

"I have a good mind to divide the sparklers, and let you run with your share. I would if I didn't fear that you would get caught and peach."

Doland dashed down his pipe and sprang to his feet. "Your words imply that I'm a traitor!" he cried, in a loud tone of voice. "I'll no longer keep company with a man who talks in that style. Let us make a division — you take your share, and I'll take mine, and we'll go in different directions."

"I would if I didn't think —"

"No think about it," cried Doland. "Down with the jewels, and let us share them."

I could hear Murden tremble, he was so agitated. He feared that the rogues would patch up a peace, and that the jewels would not be produced. All that we wanted to know was, where they were secreted; and if we could discover that point we were willing to run some risk in laying our hands on them. In fact, so interested was Murden that he whispered to Hopeful, "Don't snore so confounded loud. I don't want to lose a word that they utter." Consequently Hez held up a little, and we listened; but for some time not a word passed between them, for Thrasher sat motionless, staring at his companion as though he was debating what should be done with him and his demand.

The two burglars sat so that we could see their faces. Murden whispered, "That Doland is in more danger than he ever was before, for Thrasher is meditating whether he shall strangle him or strike him dead with a blow of his knife."

If Doland noticed the expression of his companion's eyes, he did not seem to regard it, for he met his gaze with a dogged resolution, like that of a man made obstinate with liquor; and as he dashed his hand on the table, he said, "I'll take my share of the sparklers, and do as I please with 'em. I did as much as you to get 'em, and you can't deny it."

"I don't want to; but I do want you to keep quiet. Wait until the traps give up the search, and then we can turn the jewels into gold, and spend our money like lords."

"I'll have my share now. Put the box before me, and let us make a division."

"Doland," said Thrasher, in a calm tone, "you are drunk. Sleep on the matter, and to-morrow morning we will see what can be done. If you are of the same opinion then, we will take our shares and separate. Does that satisfy you?"

"No, it does not," roared Doland, more drunk and obstinate the longer he was talked to. "Give me my share, and we part company. We have been pals long enough."

I saw Thrasher look around the room in a hurried manner, as though he was a little terrified at his own thoughts; his face lighted up with a fiendish expression, and his compressed lips and scowling brow revealed the workings of a temper that would not be controlled. He started to his feet, and I saw his hand steal into the bosom of his coat; but when Doland looked up, the hand was quickly withdrawn, and Thrasher asked, in a voice that was ominous, it was so calm, "Won't you wait till morning?"

"No, damn you for a sneak thief. Bring the box or I will—."

We watched every motion that Thrasher made, for we feared that he would strike a blow before the hiding-place of the jewels was revealed to us. He stood for a moment near Doland's back, and I thought that the latter's life was not worth insuring; but the fellow turned, walked towards the wall, and stooping down in one corner, removed a board, thrust in his hand, and drew out a parcel covered with a newspaper.

Doland watched his operations with dogged sullenness. He seemed determined not to trust Thrasher after the parcel was in his hand. The latter approached the greasy table, and laid the bundle on it. Doland seized it with eager hands, and tore off the wrapper. We saw that it had covered a rich casket, inlaid with gold, and I heard Murden sigh as his eyes fell upon the glittering box; and that sigh satisfied me that we had caught sight of the casket which belonged to the amiable lady of the lieutenant governor.

"Give me the key," said Doland, in a fierce tone, when he found that the casket was locked.

Thrasher handed him a golden key, without speaking a word. Doland unlocked the box, thrust in his hand, and held up to the light a necklace which contained a large number of diamonds. He then removed from the box a bracelet, and several other articles, all of them studded with precious stones; for, dull as the light was, I could see them glisten and sparkle at every touch of the rough hands that handled them.

"I'll make choice of the necklace for my share of the plunder," said Doland, after he had examined the jewels with drunken gravity.

"No, you don't," replied Thrasher; "you know that that is worth all the rest, and a thousand pounds added. Knock out some of the stones, and make the thing equal."

"Not a stone shall be touched. I've made my choice. You take the rest. I run more risk than you, and the best part belongs to me. You can't deny it. Didn't I enter the government house by climbing up the spout? Didn't I hang around there for two weeks?"

"And didn't I do the planning?" asked the other, with a malignant sneer.

"Yes, and left the work for me to perform. But I don't want to talk with you. I've got my share of the plunder, and you may take yours."

The fellow raised his voice so that we could have heard him even if we had not been listening; and this part seemed to strike Thrasher, for he laid a hand on Doland's shoulder, and said, "Not so loud; the sailor-men in the other room will hear you. Speak softly."

"I shall speak as I please, unless you are willing I should take this necklace for my share," returned Doland, in a dogged tone. I saw that Thrasher hesitated for a moment, as though uncertain what course to pursue; but as his eyes fell upon the jewels he looked dangerous.

"You consent?" asked Doland, and then, without waiting for an answer, he thrust the necklace into his pocket, and took up a pipe.

In an instant Thrasher's hand was on his neck, and with no gentle grasp. "You mean scoundrel," he cried, "give up that jewel, or I will strangle you!"

Doland made an attempt to start from his seat, but Thrasher held him as though he was in a vice; and a noiseless struggle commenced, for each party was fearful of attracting attention. We watched them with eager interest, and Hez left off snoring, and claimed a fair share of the peep-hole, so that he could see what was going on. I was not surprised to see Doland's right hand, which had been tugging at his opponent's arms to tear them from their hold, suddenly thrust into his bosom.

"Ah! you would stick me, would you?" cried Thrasher, on whom the motion was not lost. "You would kill your old pal, would you?" These questions were asked in hoarse whispers; and they were not replied to for the very good reason that the gentleman to whom they were addressed was not in a condition to answer pointed interrogations, his breath being hard to catch, and he had none to spare.

But the right hand which Doland had raised was still searching in his breast pocket, and at last a long and vicious-looking knife was drawn. Thrasher saw the danger, and prepared for it. With a vigorous shove he sent Doland backwards to the floor, whipped out a knife, and made a step forward; and as he did so he encountered Doland, who was vowing vengeance on his former friend.

"I'll kill you!" Doland cried, and I think he meant it: but before he had time to carry out his excellent intention, Thrasher had struck home, and the knife performed its allotted work. It entered the person of Doland just under the right arm, and was withdrawn in a second; and although the injured man made an attempt to stand and deal a blow in return, the effort was not successful.

"Curse you for a false pal," he gasped; "you have killed me."

"And saved my own life," was the cool rejoinder, as the fellow wiped the blade of his knife.

I could hardly remain quiet while all this was going on.

"Keep quiet," whispered the cool ex-police commissioner. "We want the jewels more than we want the man. Wait and see what he does with them." We did wait, although the murder so affected the nerves of Hez that he could no longer snore, or even make the attempt.

"He died d—d quick, it seems to me," I could hear Thrasher mutter, as though he was wondering why such was the case.

He laid his hand on Doland's breast, and felt of his flesh, and then appeared to be satisfied that the man was really dead. As he arose to his feet, his eyes fell upon the jewels, which still remained in the casket on the table. A smile of triumph passed over the man's face as he took up the bracelet and examined it.

"The fool lost not only his share of the jewels, but his life, by his obstinacy;" and as Thrasher spoke, a huge rat, gray and venerable, left its hole and walked to the middle of the room, stopped for a moment to utter a most doleful squeak, and then waddled off to a hole in another part of the room. Thrasher turned as quick as if some one had called him by name. The perspiration stood in large drops upon his brow, and he shuddered like one afflicted with the ague. But he soon saw what had occasioned the alarm, and he uttered a sigh of relief as he wiped the sweat from his brow. "D—n the rats," he muttered; "I thought some one was calling me by name. I must have some liquor or I shall be like an old woman before morning."

He turned and looked at the body, and then appeared to recollect that the diamond necklace was still in the dead man's pocket. He stooped down, removed the jewel, and put it with the others, and then closed the casket. He then meditated for a moment, and at last raised the casket and attempted to put it in his breast; but the box was too large, and after several attempts he walked towards the spot where the casket had been concealed, raised the board, dropped it out of sight, and then covered the place with the blankets — an act that met the approval of Murden, for he gave my arm an expressive pinch, and ventured on a low chuckle of delight. Thrasher, as though anxious to leave the place, hurried to the table, blew out the light, and then groped his way to the door, locked it after him, and stole down stairs. We waited until we heard the outside door close, and then lighted our candle in the entry, so that the reflection should not show through the front windows, while Murden once more picked the lock of the back room door; and then entering in a noiseless but hurried manner, we reached the body of Doland before we saw that he was sitting up and looking at us with some astonishment depicted upon his face, which was white and bloody.

CHAPTER VII.

THE LOST DIAMONDS RECOVERED. — THE ESCAPE. — THE SUDDEN ALARM. — THE UNPLEASANT POSITION. — HEZ PLAYS THE "INJUN." — THE PET AND HIS STRONG ARM.

As I have said before, Mrs. Trotter's castle did not enjoy a favorable reputation in the most criminal district of Melbourne, for more than one murder had been committed in her house — and it was supposed that those who had quietly yielded up the ghost, after repeated blows from bludgeons, hatchets, and knives, were disposed to assume a ghostly shape, and walk through the house in the night time; so when we saw Doland, whom we supposed dead, sitting up and staring at us as though he took us for supernatural visitors, we could not help starting back and retreating to the door; but before we gained the entry, reason returned, and I had just time to catch Hez by the arm, and prevent him from diving down stairs, head first.

"Let me alone," he said. "That dead man has come to life, and I don't want to see him."

"Hush!" cried Murden, in a stern tone. "We must make no noise, or we are lost. Come into the room. The man is not dead, and will not harm you." Thus assured, Hez became pacified. We found Doland still sitting up, and watching our motions with much interest.

"What do you want here?" he asked, as soon as he was assured that we were earthly visitors.

"We came here to save your life," Murden answered.

"Thank you, but I ain't in any danger," replied the man.

"And yet you are wounded, and pretended to be dead," Murden said.

"And if I hadn't pretended, I should have been dead in reality," was the curt answer.

"Explain yourself, and be quick about it, for we don't want to lose time," I said.

"Don't let me keep you up," the fellow said, with a grin. "I can take care of myself without your assistance."

We saw his motives, and exchanged smiles. The fellow wanted to get rid of us, so that he could seize on the casket and escape before his pal returned.

"Answer me this question," Murden said, speaking to the burglar, who still sat on the floor; "why did you pretend to die so easily?"

"Unless I had pretended I should now be in another sphere," returned the fellow, with a short laugh. "My pal struck at me before I was anticipating an attack. I saw that he had the advantage; so I let him shove his knife into me, and draw blood. And now that I have answered all your questions, you will please to leave my room." The coolness of the man was something amusing, and we could not but admire it under the circumstances.

"We came here," said Murden, in a decided tone, and in a quiet manner, "for the purpose of recovering some diamonds which were stolen a few weeks since from the government house. Do you know anything about them?"

Doland looked at us for a moment, as though he was judging how much knowledge we possessed; and then he said, "No, I don't. This is no place for diamonds."

"You are a liar, Mr. Pat Doland, alias Charles Brisley," cried Murden. "You see that I know you, and I know your history."

The fellow looked surprised and somewhat alarmed as he asked, "Who are you, and what do you know of my history?"

"No matter who I am, but in a few words I'll tell your history. You received a good education at the hands of an indulgent father; but you liked dissipation and bad company, and from petty crimes you took to burglary, was caught, sentenced, and since that sentence expired you have done some odd jobs, the biggest of which consisted in stealing a lady's diamonds. Now what do you say for yourself?"

"Nothing," answered the man, in a sullen tone.

"You see that I know you better than you know me," Murden continued.

The fellow looked up as my friend said this, and answered, "I know you now. This is Mr. Murden."

"You have guessed right. That is my name."

"And I thought that you had cut the police business, or I should not be here at the present time," Doland said.

"But you see that I have not. Now let us understand each other. You can give me some information respecting the jewels, and perhaps I can speak a good word for you before the beaks. What do you say?"

Doland shook his head as he answered, "Thrasher carried off the box containing the diamonds, and I never expect to see him or them again."

"Lying won't serve your purpose, Doland. I thought that you knew me better than to suppose that a lie would go down with me."

"So help me God, Mr. Murden, I speak the truth." My friend did not answer the fellow. but turned and spoke to me.

"Keep your eye on the man, and shoot him if he moves an inch," he said, and then walked to the corner where the casket was concealed.

Doland did not stir, but he watched Murden's movements like a cat in search of a rat. Murden kicked aside the blankets, raised the board, and drew out the casket. This was too much for Doland. He uttered a groan, and fell back full length upon the floor, as though all hope had deserted him.

"You see," cried Murden, "that I have secured your prize. Have you anything to say?"

"No, curses on your luck!" retorted the baffled burglar. "We were told in Sydney to look out for you, but supposed that we were safe."

"And so you are, in my custody. Come; I want you to go with me, and if you utter a shout, or seek to attract attention, I'll make short work of you. Do not hope for a rescue as we pass through Mud Lane. We are armed with revolvers, and you will be the first man shot."

Doland arose from the floor in a sulky manner, and held out his hands. "I suppose you want to put the bracelets on me, captain."

"I don't dare trust you without them." The handcuffs closed on the man's wrists. The prisoner did not utter a word of remonstrance against the treatment he received. He appeared to be thinking of other matters, and I supposed he was weighing all the chances of a trial, and wondering how many years' imprisonment he would receive; but I found that I was mistaken, for just as we were about to move towards the door, and make our escape from the house, Doland suddenly turned, uttered a shrill cry, ran across the room, and plunged headlong through one of the windows, taking glass and sash with him. We heard the fellow strike the ground in the yard, back of the house; but not a groan or a cry led us to imagine that he was injured, and though we rushed to the window and looked out, yet the night was so dark that we could see nothing, although Hez thought that he could hear footsteps retreating in a hasty manner.

We listened for a moment or two at the open window, for the purpose of obtaining a trace of Doland, for we did not like to think that he had outwitted us in spite of our precautions; but as all was quiet, we began to think that we were losing time, and we were reminded of this quite strongly when we heard Mother Trotter at the front door, blaspheming in a masculine sort of way at the destruction of a window. We did not care to encounter that Amazon; so we extinguished the light, and threw up the second window, and looked out. The distance to the ground was not more than six feet, less than we had calculated, and with a whispered injunction to follow, Murden dropped from the window.

"You next," I said to Hez; and he disappeared like a shadow.

I stepped to the window, and dropped to the ground; and the next instant I found myself in the strong grasp of two men, one of whom put a hand upon my throat, and the other pressed a pistol against my forehead. I was surprised, but not dismayed, for I had been in worse positions than the one in which I found myself; and if I remained quiet while the ruffian compressed my windpipe, it was simply for the purpose of improving the best opportunity that I could find of making my escape. Finding that I did not struggle, the men who held me eased up on their grasp; and one whispered, "Give me the box, and we'll let you go."

"What box?" I asked.

"Whist! and be —— to ye," was the answer. "Don't you make strange of it. Hand over the jewels, and we'll let you run. Be quick, now, for the boys is comin', and then we can't save ye. Do ye hear?"

"Yes; but I have them not. My friends have got them, and have run for it."

"Ah! now is that true?" demanded one of the ruffians: and he shook me in a fierce manner, as though to stir up the truth if I did not utter it.

"It is," I answered; and just at that moment a light was thrust from the window over our heads, and half a dozen wild faces, fierce and brutal, looked out upon us.

"We have one of 'em," cried my captors, in triumphant tones; and they shook me without opposition on my part for I did not think it best to show signs of strength. The ruffians at the window uttered a yell of triumph.

"The others is in the house," cried my captors. "This is the only one what has attempted to cut since we was here."

"Hold him till we comes out with the crowd," roared one dark-eyed fellow, with a face so thin and sharp that the light could not strike on it. "We'll break their bones and mince their flesh."

"Ah! we'll teach 'em to rob honest fellers like us," another one said, and then rushed to other parts of the house in search of Murden and Hez; old Mother Trotter urging them on in fierce tones, and vowing vengeance against us for deceiving her as to our character.

As soon as the light and crowd disappeared, the men who held me whispered, "Give us the jewels, or tell us where they is, and we'll let you cut, and divil a word shall the others know of it."

"I have them not, I tell you. Now relieve my neck, and let me get a breath of air."

"Divil a bit," was the answer. "You should be kicked to death by all the honest men in Mud Lane. Ye has cheated us, and ye know it; don't ye?"

I was about to reply; but casting my eyes on the ground, I saw something move towards me, in a slow and cautious manner, and without the least noise. My amiable friends, who had me by the neck, did not see the object that attracted my attention; for they were facing me, and jamming me against the wall just as though I had no feeling in the vicinity of my throat, and did not need breath to support my existence. At first I thought it was one of those huge black snakes which I had met with in the vicinity of Ballarat and the Lodden; but I was not long under such an impression, for just as the ruffians who held me were disposed to kick my shins and punch me in the ribs, the creeping object suddenly arose, and with a blow that would have done honor to the Manchester Pet, struck one of the rough gentlemen on the side of his head, and over he tumbled; and at the same moment, a form glided towards me on the left, and served the remaining inhabitant of Mud Lane in the same manner.

"Gol darn their pictures!" cried Hez, who had crawled on his stomach until he had struck a blow for my relief; "didn't I Injun 'em that time?"

"You'll make a bush-hunter in time," said Murden, in a tone that savored of admiration. "I never saw a thing done handsomer."

"Why did you leave me?" I asked.

"We heard a crowd of the Mud-Laners at the front of the house; so we started to see what they were after. Doland and Thrasher have joined forces, and raised the neighborhood. When we returned we found that the cusses had posted two men under the window. But come; we have no time for more explanations. The whole of the crowd will be after us in a few minutes."

As he spoke, we could hear the Mud-Laners in Mother Trotter's palace utter howls of rage because we had escaped from the place; and while we were talking, one of the windows over our heads was dashed out without ceremony, scattering the glass in all directions; and then Thrasher's head was thrust out, and he shouted, "Hold on to that man till we come down. We'll learn him to rob an honest man of his earnings." The head, and light that revealed it to our gaze, disappeared from view.

"We must leave, and in a hurry," said Murden. "We have no time to lose if we would avoid the beauties of Mud Lane"

Hitting the prostrate men a kick as we passed them, to see if they were conscious. and finding that they were not, we ran for a narrow alley that would take us to the head of Mud Lane; but we had not advanced four rods, before we saw a dozen of the neighboring roughs rushing towards us; but as they had not seen us, it was easy to avoid them. We retreated hastily, ran across an open space in the rear of some hovels which sheltered the worst people in Melbourne, and, late as it was, lights were still seen in the windows, as though the people sat up all night. These lights guided us on our way, Murden leading. He climbed over a fence, and we followed close at his heels. We stumbled through a ditch, were chased by dogs, and at last entered a narrow passage-way, rushed through it, and at the end found ourselves in the strong arms of the Manchester Pet, who saluted us with, —

"Now, you coves, I've got you. If you moves, I'll crack your bones like sticks;" and the strength of his arms showed that he was in earnest.

CHAPTER VIII.

AN ESCAPE FROM THE PET. — THE PURSUIT. — THE JOLLY SAILORS. — THE ARREST AND DISCHARGE.

Of course we struggled after we found the Pet had thrown his arms around us; but the muscular man held on to us, and seemed determined to crush us in his embrace. He had stationed himself at the entrance of the alley up which we had rushed, and caught us in a trap; and now that he had us, as he thought, secure, he did not call for help, or appear desirous of letting the rest of the Mud-Laners know that he had secured a prize. It was so dark that he could not see our faces; so he did not recognize us as the persons who had drank beer on his premises in the early part of the evening; but we easily detected him every time he jammed us against the wooden building, by his being without a jacket, and on account of his size.

"Give me the jewels, and you coves can run home as fast as you please. Don't say that you haven't got 'em, 'cos I knows better. Fork 'em over, and we'll quit company."

"We don't know anything about your jewels," Murden replied. "Let us alone, or it will be the worse for you."

"What! Rats that you are, do you threaten me?" roared the giant; and once more he commenced the business of cracking our ribs; but Hez, who had a strong prejudice against such treatment, slipped from the anaconda embrace like an eel; and although we had to receive a double dose of pressure on account of Hez's movement, yet we were not selfish enough to repine, and accuse him of a want of good faith.

"Ah, warmints!" cried the Pet, with a squeeze that nearly took away our breath, "will you give me the jewels, and say nothin' about 'em? Must I call the Mud-Laners here, and let 'em jump at you? Don't you provoke me too much, 'cos I can't stand it. If you want me for a friend, hand over the shiners?"

At this moment the giant's attention was attracted by something at his feet. He released us to look down, and that movement was fortunate for us; for we broke from his grasp, made a rush for the entrance of the alley, being stimulated by the shouts of the enthusiastic Mud-Laners, who, having started out for the purpose of shooting some one, or committing an outrage of some kind, were just now debating the propriety of hanging a peaceable man because he would not supply the crowd with gin, without price and without questions. We should have succeeded in effecting our escape if we had not fallen over Hez, whom we did not notice in our eagerness. As soon as we touched the ground, the giant rushed for us, uttering several oaths at our attempts to evade his embraces; but he had taken only one or two steps when he fell with a crash that shook the building in the vicinity, and the instant he touched the ground, Hez bounded over the prostrate form, and shouted,—

"Come on; the Pet can't come to time, if I know it."

We scrambled to our feet, and followed on, the Pet

uttering such oaths and yells that he attracted the notice of the Mud-Laners, and they came rushing down the dark street, howling and swearing, to see what the matter was.

We ran as fast as we could, Hez leading the way, although he had not the slightest idea where he was going. The Mud-Laners caught sight of us as we passed the door of a dance hall through which the light was streaming out, and they uttered shouts of warning for the purpose of rousing the denizens of the place, and getting them to head us off, and turn us back upon the main body. In fact their object would have been successful, had not a curious incident saved us.

The inhabitants of the district through which we passed were mustering to their doors and windows, attracted by the noise and the hope of plundering some one; and the Mud-Laners were close upon our heels, when we suddenly turned a corner, and entered a street which was very well lighted, and apparently filled with dance halls and drinking saloons Just at this instant, we saw standing on the sidewalk a dozen or twenty sailors, most of them with liquor enough on board to render them willing to espouse any cause. They were discussing the propriety of taking a drink when we hove in sight; but all such talk was abolished the instant that the tars saw that three men, dressed as sailors, were scudding before a lot of landsmen.

"Here's a row," cried one of the tars; "let's take a hand in it."

The sailors uttered a cheer, and rushed into the middle of the street, and thus we found ourselves between two fires; for we could not retreat, and to advance was dangerous.

"Leave all to me," I whispered to Murden and Hez, as we slackened our pace, and approached the sailors; for I had marked out the course which it was most desirable we should pursue.

"All right; go ahead," was the response.

"Ship ahoy!" I hailed, when within a few fathoms of the tars, who were expecting a charge, and had prepared for it.

"Ay, ay; what cheer?" was the answer.

"Brother sailors, with a signal of distress," I cried.

"Run under our lee, and we'll look into it;" and the men advanced to meet us.

We got in the rear of the sailors, and then they asked only a few questions; for the Mud-Laners were too near to permit much talk.

"What cheer, my hearties?" they said, as they crowded around us, and took a keen survey of our appearance; and although we were covered with mud and dirt, enough of our clothing was visible to show that we were sailors, or wore the garb of seafaring men.

"The sharks in our rear," I gasped; for I was tired after the hard run that the Mud-Laners had given us. "Want to sell us, and be —— to 'em."

"Are you runaways?" asked an old salt.

"Yes; we cut for it 'cos we had hard usage, and nothin' to eat but rice and wormy bread."

"Clubs and stones, lads," shouted an old salt, who seemed to be the leader of the men.

The sailors answered with a cheer, picked up all the stones, bottles, and tumblers that they could lay hands on, and then awaited the onset. The Mud-Laners noted the preparations, and paused some eight or ten fathoms from us.

"We want those cussed thieving coves," cried Thrasher. "They has stolen something from us, and run for it. Give them up, and we'll stand the liquor; refuse, and we'll come to blows."

"And does you think that we cares for your blows?" cried an old salt. "You just come to us, and we'll make you sing wuss than a feller what has to take four dozen afore breakfast. Now go home, and stay there, 'cos these men is shipmates, and we stands by 'em."

"But they has stolen something from us," cried Doland.

"Never you mind that," the old salt said, with a grave shake of his head. "If they has stole, you must prove it, and if you don't prove it, why, what is the consequence?"

"Ay, ay; what is they?" repeated the sailors, in an admiring tone. "Tom can beat the big wigs at hargument."

"It's cos I steers a straight course, and avoids the shoals and quicksands of nousense," was old Tom's contented remark; and although such sound sense and chunks of wisdom contented the jolly tars, it did not prove satisfactory to the Mud-Laners, and one of them, more impatient and impudent than the others, hurled a stone, near a pound weight, at the venerable head of the man who had propounded such logical questions for the admiration of his shipmates. The stone touched the old salt's tarpaulin, knocked it half off his head, and then glanced and went through the window of a porter-house.

"Steady," cried the sailor, who was an old man-of-war's-man, and had learned to take things coolly. "We has drawed their fire, and now we'll pipe all hands to quarters and return it. Hingland expects every man to do his duty. Nail our colors to the mast, and go in and lick the d—d landsmen clean out of their breeches."

This inspiring speech was received with cheers by the sailors. The Mud-Laners heard the cries, and knew that they had much work before them. It was not the first time that the Mud-Laners and a party of sailors had met in hostile array; but the cause of the fight was not, as a general thing, of a serious nature; a look, a word, a glass of liquor, was enough to set them at work. But this time the character of sailors had been assailed by imputation, and that was sufficient to cause the tars to fight most valiantly for their good name, while some of the Mud-Laners, who were ever ready to plunder, and cared but little for glory, backed out when they saw that hard knocks were to be exchanged, and nothing gained by it, except the opportunity of picking some person's pocket, while lying in the street insensible under the influence of a broken head. Even the Pet, who had vowed vengeance, suddenly recollected that his amiable daughter was all alone in his porter-house, and needed a father's protection. He slipped away to the rear, out across some dark alley, and got out of the affair with honor, as he thought.

All these things the sailors saw, and their spirits rose in

proportion. As they noticed the thinned ranks of their foes they cheered most lustily, and with the cheer poured in such a compact fire of stones, mud, and sticks, that the Mud-Laners wavered, fell back, and then, when they saw the sailors advance with triumphant yells, broke and run for the dark alleys. The tars uttered such howls of triumph that even the police were attracted by the sound, and came down the street in force; and as soon as the sailors caught sight of their enemies, the "traps," they delivered a parting volley at the Mud-Laners, cursed them for cowardly dogs, and then turned and fled to the nearest saloons.

It must not be supposed that we were quiet all this time. Far from it. We would not desert our brave allies, and when they charged we went with them, and when they hurled stones we did the same, and when they scattered to the right and left, we quietly walked off, but had gone but a few paces when the police, thinking that the time had arrived for them to distinguish themselves, and seeing that we were disposed to be peaceable, suddenly made a rush, and we found ourselves surrounded, to the great terror of Hez, who looked upon a police officer as a being of superhuman power and importance.

"We caught you at it," cried the sergeant, who had charge of the party. "Don't you go for to deny it. We seed you throw stones at those highly respectable citizens what run when we hove in sight."

"And who, in the devil's name, wouldn't run after catching a sight of your face?" returned Murden.

The sergeant of the force, who had never been outside of the city's limits in search of such game as bushrangers, eyed Murden with a glance that did not argue much for the ex-commissioner's happiness the coming six hours. In fact, he made such desperate attempts to pierce and freeze the very soul of my friend, that I could no longer contain myself, and I roared with laughter; and in this Hez and Murden joined.

"Ho, ho," croaked the sergeant; "we'll see who'll laugh after a night at the station-house. We'll see what you've got to say afore the beak in the morning. Damn your impudence, what do you mean by grinning at a hofficer of the law in that way?" The indignant fellow raised his club, and made a motion to strike us; but Murden drew back, and for the first time assumed a dignity that well became him.

"Hold your hand," he cried. "You have but a poor idea of an officer's duty if you think that he can club a man for laughing."

"Well, you is cussed impudent, at any rate," muttered the sergeant. "I won't strike you, but I'll take you to the station-house. Bring 'em along."

"Why not whisper to them who you are?" I asked Murden, as the officers closed around us.

"Hush! don't mention such a thing," was the reply. "We are not yet clear of the Mud-Laners. Keep mum; all will be well."

We marched along, Hez laboring under an impression that he was to be transported to the hulks, or sent up the country and set to work on the roads; and while whining we reached the vicinity of gas lights. Then, for the first time, did Murden begin to breathe as though he was safe, and as though the valuable jewels which he carried in his breast were to be the means of purchasing his restoration to rank and honor, riches and importance. In fact, so easy did he feel in regard to the future, that more than once he made an attempt to whistle a lively march, and only broke down when the gooseberry-looking sergeant ordered less noise.

At the station-house we were ushered into the presence of the officer who had command of the watch at that hour of the night. The official sat at a desk, writing. His back was towards us; so we waited for him to turn round and see if we knew him. At last he threw down his pen and faced us. To our surprise and pleasure it was Lieutenant Maurice, our old friend and companion. We pulled our caps over our eyes so that he would not immediately recognize us, and then waited for his judgment. It was given in a few words. Casting his eyes over us with a quick glance, he said,—

"Where did you pick up these miserable-looking devils?"

"Fighting, sir, in Wretched Cove Court," was the reply of the sergeant. "Caught 'em at it. This cuss was throwing stones. I seed him." He pointed to Murden. The police officer was a most proficient liar, and I looked at him with admiration, as a most excellent representation of a certain class of Australians.

"Put them in No. 5," said Maurice, "and bring me their names."

"Ha! ha! what did I tell you?" chuckled the sergeant, as he pushed us towards a cell.

"I'm not going in there," replied Murden. "I'm going home."

"O, you will, will you?" asked the sergeant in an ironical tone. "Perhaps you will let me accompany you."

"I have no objections, I'm sure;" and as Murden spoke he removed the false beard, and rubbed off some of the mud which had clung to his nose and eyebrows, and at the same moment he took off his cap and stood before the astonished officers, all of whom knew him as well as they knew each other.

I glanced at the sergeant. He was so surprised that he forgot to blush, or speak a word; but as soon as he recovered his presence of mind, he said, —

"I 'opes, Mr. Murden, that you don't think I would do this on a-purpose, do you?"

"I think this, Birney," was the reply: "You don't understand your business as well as you should. You have made a false charge against us, and if that was known at headquarters it would cost you your place."

"I 'opes, Mr. Murden, that you won't go for to speak a hard word agin a poor feller," whined the sergeant.

"Go to your beats, men," the lieutenant ordered, "and keep the Mud-Laners steady. Sergeant, you will report yourself under arrest."

As soon as the men left the station for their respective beats, Maurice called us into his private room, and asked in a whisper, as though he feared that the walls had ears,

"What is it all about? Something is going on, or you two would not be together at this hour of the night. Can I know the secret?"

"You should know it without our telling you," I replied.

Maurice thought for a moment, and then said, "It's the diamonds, I'll wager a nugget. Have you a trace of them?"

"Perhaps we have," Murden answered, "but it won't do for us to say much about them just at present. You know there is a thousand pounds reward."

"Yes; but if there were two thousand offered, and I thought that you could lay a hand on the sparklers, and through their means be restored to your former rank, I'd keep my mawlers off of them, although I'm a poor man, and the reward is a temptation."

"I believe you, Maurice," cried Murden, with a grasp of his hand. "I know that you have always stood by me during adversity, and if I am restored you shall not suffer for your friendship."

"Yes," said Maurice, with a bright smile and in a meaning tone; "let us once more beat for bushrangers, and I think that I can make more money than the diamonds would bring me. With you to command, and I to second you, I think that we should rake 'em."

I thought that I should laugh, but I managed to keep a sober face, as I shook hands with the lieutenant and bade him good night. Then we left the station-house, walked through the sultry, hot, deserted streets, and arrived home just as daylight began to show itself. A bath, a cup of good coffee, fresh from the plantations of the Philippine Islands, a mild cigar, a few words of congratulation, and a hasty examination of the jewels, to see if all were in the casket, and then they were locked up in a burglar-proof safe, and we retired to bed

CHAPTER IX.

HEZ AND HIS FEELINGS. — THE FAT PORTER AND THE PAGE. — THE GOVERNOR'S WIFE.

"Is it your intention to sleep all day?" asked Murden, when he saw that I had rubbed open my eyes and was glaring at him in rather a savage manner, for man's temper is never of a sweet nature if he is awakened from a deep sleep.

"Did you wake me up for the express purpose of asking such a question?" I replied, looking at Hez with a feeling of envy, for that universal genius was snoring the snores of the just.

"It's no use," cried Murden. "You can't go off again. I have business for you, and it must be attended to."

In half an hour we were sipping our coffee, eating cold kangaroo and dry toast, about as contented a body of men as could be found in Melbourne. As soon as breakfast was over, Murden announced the important information which he had but briefly alluded to.

"We must visit Lady Clemenstena, the wife of the governor," he said. "She will feel anxious to hear something of her jewels, and therefore will give us a cordial welcome. Besides, she is a pretty woman, and you like to look at handsome faces."

I thought of the dark, blue-eyed bar-maid, and sighed.

"Let us," continued Murden, "dress as becomes gentlemen. We have need of good clothes and much impudence if we seek to carry our point. To-day's work will decide my fate. If I am fortunate, in one week's time I shall be restored to my position, and if I am not, I leave Australia, never to return."

While on the way I stole a look at Hez's costume. It was better than I anticipated, although his vest was a little short, and his pants rather too tight for the warm weather. Murden was dressed in a thin suit, white linen pants and vest.

with a dark coat; and my costume was similar, for I knew what was expected at the government house, which I had visited many times during my first sojourn in Australia.

"You have the jewels?" I asked, as we drove through some of the streets.

Murden touched his breast pocket.

"And you intend to yield them up without conditions and without reward?"

"Only such as you can make for me," was the cool answer.

I looked at him in surprise. I did not understand him Murden smiled.

"You don't think me such a ninny as to ask for a favor just after I have conferred one, do you?"

"Why not?"

"Simply because it would not have the effect that I desire. Her ladyship is a romantic woman, and if I restore the jewels to her, and say that I ask for no reward, she would feel that I desired one. Don't you notice my strategy?"

I did begin to have a slight view of it.

"Then you stand on your dignity, and I act the friendly, disinterested part, which is to benefit you?"

"Precisely; so we need say no more on the subject."

We reached the government house just at twelve o'clock, and without waiting for an invitation — which it is extremely doubtful if we should have received, even if we had remained for a week in our carriage — we entered the palace, and found ourselves confronted by as bloated a looking porter as ever left the shores of old England to be bitten by fleas and other insects in Australia.

For a few minutes the porter looked at us without speaking, and then a frown gathered on his brow, and he said, "I shouldn't have expected it of you, Mr. Murden; no, I shouldn't."

"Why, what do you mean, Tony?" asked Murden.

"To think that you should come 'ere at this time o' day, jist when his lordship and her ladyship is a goin' to take lunch, is more than I can believe without seein' with my own hyes."

"But we have business with her ladyship, Tony, and she will feel offended unless she sees us; so, like a good fellow that you are, just pass the word, and let us slide by."

The addle-headed old fool shook his pate and sighed.

"I can't do it, Mr. Murden, indeed I can't, unless you can show me the keerd of invitation. It's as much as my place is worth, and you knows it."

"I know that I have some real English ale in my house. It came here in the British ship Noble Son, and is as fresh as the day that it was put on board; but not a drop goes down Tony's throat, if it was as parched as the Desert of Sahara, unless I speak with her ladyship within an hour."

The expression of the man's face was something wonderful to behold while Murden was speaking. His great, bloated tongue was thrust out, and licked his lips as though he could in imagination taste the beverage which Murden had spoken of. He pressed his fat hands upon his paunch, and, in a hoarse whisper, asked, "Is it the real stunnin' Hinglish hale?"

"As sparkling and lively as a young girl of seventeen in search of a husband," was the answer.

"And you have a cask of it?"

"Yes."

"And you won't give me a drop of it?"

"Not a drop, unless you send word to her ladyship that we wish to speak to her."

The fellow's face showed how much the struggle cost him; but at last a gleam of light seemed to flash over it, as though he could see his way out of all difficulties, and he whispered, —

"Mr. Murden, you have a woice that charms me; but you know I'd lose my place, unless I could give an excuse for sending you up. You see there's so many of the common trash what comes here, — men and vimen vot don't know nothin' about high life, — that I has to be on my guard all the time. Now, you see, if you could only say that you vanted to ax her ladyship about her lost diamonds, vy, it vould help you and me too, 'cos I could drink the hale vile you vas drinkin' her ladyship's vords. Ha, ha!" and the porter laughed at his jest until his fat sides shook like a jelly.

"You have hit the nail this time, Tony, as I knew you could if you tried," cried Murden. "Send word that we wish to speak with her regarding the diamonds."

"And arter you has made a few inquiries about the jewels," continued the porter, "vy, I don't care if you does speak to her about some conwict, or some ticket-of-leave man, vhom you vants pardoned. I knows nothin' about that, you know."

Murden looked sly, and that pleased the fat porter so much that he was seized with such a violent fit of internal laughter that I feared he would burst; but he recovered sufficiently to touch a bell, and look grave and profound, but terribly red in the face, as a page appeared.

"You lump of lampblack, these 'ere gentlemen vant to speak with her ladyship."

"Can't do it," said the page, standing on one foot. "She's eatin', and when she's eatin' she won't see any one; you know dat, Tony. We is jist takin' our lunch, and de wittles is good. I seed what it was, and I means to hav' some."

The little imp once more made the circuit of the porter, seemed inclined to stand on his head by way of diversion, thought better of it, and then butted Tony as a compromise.

"Look a-here, you imp of Satan," roared the fat Englishman; "go tell her ladyship that three gentlemen want to see her in the green room about her diamonds, and that one of 'em is Mr. Murden."

"If she shies a dish at dis head of mine, I shall pizen yer beer, Tony;" and, with these words, the imp left us, disappearing up the broad staircase.

"He's a warmint," said the fat porter, taking a seat, and crossing his legs in a reflective mood. "He vas took by his ludship from a Hamerican valeship. The Hamericans is all blacks, you know, every one of 'em, 'cept the Hinglish what lives there to instruct 'em and make 'em civil, like us

Britons vot knows everything, and more too, and larned it all ourselves."

The fat porter paused, thought for a moment, and then continued: "This black warmint belonged to the cap'n of the valeship, and very proud of him he vas. He used to lick him every day to make him civil; but I don't think he vas much improved by that operation, 'cos you can see vot the imp is now. But vot can you hexpect from Hamericans, vot is black, and don't know no better nor nothin'?"

Murden winked to me not to say a word in reply; so I remained silent, for the fellow was not worth the expense of an argument. And indeed I had no time to set him right, had I been so disposed; for the little page appeared at the head of the stairs, slid down by the banisters, uttered a subdued yell, danced around the porter once more, stopped suddenly, and jerked out a few words, which we understood to mean that her ladyship would see us. The fat porter aimed a blow at the page, but the grinning imp easily avoided it, and once more straddled the banisters, and attempted to slide up stairs; but failing in this, although somewhat puzzled to account for it, he commenced to go up the stairs on his knees, and he would have gone on his head if he could have done so.

We followed the little wretch, and were shown into the reception-room, furnished very plainly, with Canton matting on the floor, and green curtains, to repel the hot sun, at the windows. The chairs were willow, the lounge was bamboo — a Chinese institution, most exquisitely carved and figured, bearing the handiwork of that patient people, in every form and grotesque shape, that ornamented the front and back. Leading from the room, which was large and square, were folding doors, and through these we expected the lady to appear; nor were we disappointed, for the black imp, with a grin and a chuckle, said, —

"Now, you gemmen, jist stay here; sot down or stand up, jist as you please; but mind and keep yer hats off; and when her ladyship come in de room, do yer get up, lay yer hand on yer stomach, and bow jist as you see me now."

He bent over to illustrate, but Hez could no longer endure the little ape's airs. He was not so tolerant to the black race as the bold Briton who was with us; so when the lad's body had formed a curve, Hopeful's foot was raised, and landed on the centre of the grinning imp. He plunged forward, struck on his hands and knees, but was up in a moment.

"What for you do dat?" he asked. "What I do to you?"

"You little imp of darkness," said Hopeful, with a stern look, "do you mean to larn us free-born 'Mericans how to behave in the presence of company?"

"But how's I gwine to know 'bout dat?" said the imp, rubbing his person. "Don't I hab to tell most of de fat Englishmen how to act; and I s'pose you all de same."

And then his feeling of wrong was forgotten, as he thought of the fact that Hez was an American, and once more the grin returned to his face, as he asked, "What part you come from? Me come from old Maryland. Me slave at one time. Run away and go to sea. No like whaleship. Much work and no chance to sleep. Make me run arter tings all de time. Me 'Merican, and me is proud to see you."

It was impossible to withstand the advances of such a genius; so we smiled on him, and gave him a silver dollar, and the imp was just about to stand on his head, when the folding doors were thrown open with a noiseless slide, and we had just time to arise and form a group, when in glided a lady dressed very plain, but with an aristocratic-looking face that was quite taking.

We saw all that, and then a liveried servant announced, "Her ladyship, the wife of the governor-general." He uttered these words, and then disappeared.

CHAPTER X.

THE GOVERNOR AND HIS WIFE. — A STRONG PULL FOR A COMMISSION.

HER ladyship, the wife of the governor-general, was about thirty-five years of age, of commanding figure, graceful in her movements, with a full, round, English form, a splendid complexion, clear white and red, little pink ears, a most lovely hand, it was so small and transparent, and a little foot which peeped from beneath her thin white dress, and showed that it was clothed in a most unexceptionable slipper. In her hair was braided several roses, or plants indigenous to Australian gardens; but about her person there was no jewelry, with the exception of a plain gold ring, which all English women are proud to wear when married. It is the last ornament that is parted with in case of pecuniary distress, and violent is the grief which she manifests even when compelled to pledge the slim rim of gold for the sake of obtaining a little food. It is her badge of honesty, and with it on her finger, she can show her face to the world without a blush or thought of shame. And such is its sacred nature, that even those who should wear one for the sake of character and reputation, seldom impose upon the public by a false certificate of goodness.

But while I have been rambling the governor's wife is standing in the centre of the room, her eyes taking in our dimensions at a glance; for she was a woman of the world, and could read character like the open pages of a book. She knew Murden by sight and name, for he had met her once or twice when commissioner; but her station was so far above his own, that a slight smile and a mere nod of the head were sufficient to remind him that he was not forgotten.

During all this time we were on our feet, bowing quite low, with the exception of Hez, who whispered in my ear,

"She's jist like my Martha, only twice as proud, and not so purty."

"Hush!" I said. "She may hear you."

"I don't care if she does," was the answer. "It's true, by jingo; and I know it, if you don't."

Her ladyship saw the action, but did not catch the words, of course; so she paused a moment, put her gold eye-glasses to her eyes, and then said, in rather a low tone, to be sure, but still quite distinct, and with a rich voice, "This is Mr. Murden, I think."

Mr. Murden ducked his head, took a step forward, and then one backward, wiggled a little, and replied, "Yes. mum."

"And the other gentlemen," said her ladyship, "do I know them?"

"No, mum," was the reply; and Murden took another step forward, a second step backward and ducked his head as usual.

Her ladyship did not ask the question: but her looks said quite plainly, "Who are they?"

"This gentleman, mum," said Murden, pointing his thumb at me, "is no stranger in Australia. He spent some years here at one time, and now comes back 'cos he likes the country so much. He was very celebrated the time he was here. You may have heard of him, mum;" and Murden gave my whole name.

Her ladyship smiled in the most genial manner, as though she was familiar with some of my antecedents.

"Is it possible that I see one of those brave Americans who rendered so much service to the country a few years since, or before my husband took office?"

"Yes, mum, this is the man," cried Murden. "His companion is dead—died of what disease?" and Murden turned to me for information.

I did not answer Murden, for her ladyship, with ready tact, saw my position, and hastened to relieve me.

"I regret to hear that your brave and gallant comrade is dead. The world can ill afford to spare such heroes. I wish we had more of the same kind. If we had," — and here she looked hard at Murden, — "I don't think that so many robbers would go unpunished in the colony. I am sure it is very dreadful that they should be about, but it is much more dreadful that they should steal one's valuables and go unpunished."

"Yes, mum," Murden hastened to answer, "I wish we had a few more like the dead and gone Mr. Frederick. We would not allow bushrangers much peace. But why do I utter such a wish?" Murden said, as though he had just remembered a certain fact. "It is nothing to me. I am not in the department, and therefore should not repine because matters are not conducted to suit me."

The pensive tone in which this was uttered was most admirable. Murden was a skilful detective, and knew the workings of a human heart as well as most men; consequently, he was not surprised when her ladyship asked with a sort of fashionable listlessness, and with a slight flourish of her glass, —

"Why did you leave the department, Mr. Murden?"

"Because, mum," was the answer, "there were certain charges brought against me by a bushranger, a fellow whom I had captured, and whose word was not worth an Australian sheep. But I am content. I have escaped the vexations of office, and can live like a private citizen, happy and contented under the wise rule of your honored husband, whom all men praise and love."

"Except the opposition," cried the lady, in a quick tone, but with a sweet smile at the flattery respecting her husband. "You know they say that he is incompetent for the office."

She smiled as though she knew that such remarks were unjust, and before the sunbeam had died away, Murden had disclaimed the horrible insinuation.

"A more noble, honorable gentleman than the lord, your husband, never occupied the government house; and as for those opposition men, they would disgrace any country."

I saw that the conversation was assuming a political turn — a dangerous course unless a man is skilful with his weapons; so I winked to Murden to hold up; but just at that moment the folding doors were thrown open with a crash, and in strode a gentleman dressed in the most neglectful manner, and with the most common-looking clothes. I should have taken him, had I met him in the streets of Melbourne, for the head of some wholesale grocery store, or a grain merchant. He was rather short and fat, with a red face, leg-of-mutton whiskers and mustache, both about as red as they could be and go unpainted; and this man was lord and the governor-general of the province. I knew this by the workings of Murden's back, for it went up and down like that of a cat when in the presence of a strange dog, and he hopped and skipped about like a ballet dancer.

"O, my lord," cried the wife, "I am so glad that you have come! We have here one of the most devoted supporters of your government. He has a most appreciating regard for you and the measures which you have introduced."

"Egad! I'm glad of that, for I meet but few men who are of the same opinion," cried his lordship, with a jolly laugh that made his fat stomach shake like a jelly.

"The fact of it is," continued his lordship, wiping his eye-glasses, and then taking a cool survey of our party, "the opposition persist in calling me a blockhead, and a man that does not know the interests of the country. Now I can eat a good dinner and listen to long, boring addresses; and if those things are not of use to the colony, then I draw my salary in vain."

"By the way, my dear," said his lordship, after he had laughed enough to satisfy a reasonable man, "I hope that I do not interrupt you in your audience. I don't know the business which calls the gentlemen here, and I do not recognize but one of them. This is Mr. Murden, I think." Mr. Murden ducked his head and skipped around like a monkey on hot pavements.

"Yes, your lordship," he said, and smiled in the most affable manner.

"At one time police commissioner?" and his lordship once more raised his glass and looked at us.

"Yes, your lordship."

"And you want to go back to the force?"

"Yes, your lordship."

"And you expect that her ladyship will use her influence in your behalf?"

"Perhaps she may be induced to," was the evasive reply; for Murden began to lose his character of worshipper of rank, and assume that which was more natural to him, — an independent detective, afraid of neither man nor devil.

"What do you mean by perhaps?" asked his lordship, abruptly.

"I mean that if I should serve her ladyship most faithfully, that I have nothing to ask her for, although if I was restored to the police, I should feel grateful to the one who accomplished so desirable a result."

"O, but I can do nothing for you," cried her ladyship. "I supposed that you desired an audience for some other purpose."

"The fact of it is," said his lordship, with a good-natured, lazy yawn, "the office which you held is kept open to reward the man who is smart enough to recover her ladyship's diamonds. You know of the loss, I suppose?"

"O, if I could only find them!" and her ladyship wrung her hands and looked her distress.

"Well, you never will," was the consoling reply of the husband. "Your diamonds are out of the country long before this. Egad! I have a notion to ask Parliament to give me a donation to compensate me for the loss. Thunder it makes me feel like a poor man every time I think of the matter."

Then Murden looked sublime as he straightened up, smiled, put his hand in his breast, pulled out the casket, and exposed it to the eyes of the lady. She saw it, and flushed scarlet, so great was her surprise and fear, and then rushed towards my friend in a most unaristocratic manner, exclaiming, "O, Mr. Murden, don't deceive me, but tell me, have you found my jewels?"

"Egad! but it's the case at all events," cried his lordship

With a polite bow Murden placed the casket in her hand. "Your ladyship will find the jewels all safe. I have compared them with the list as advertised, and there are none missing. I give you joy at recovering them."

He turned and left the room, Hez following him. Murden had winked to me to remain, and I did so, the governor and his wife being too much absorbed in examining the lost treasure to pay the least attention to us. I heard their exclamations of pleasure, surprise, and admiration; and after they had got over the first burst of astonishment the aristocratic couple turned towards me.

"Why, Mr. Murden has left the room," cried her ladyship. "I am sorry that he has gone. I want to thank him for what he has done."

"Egad! I should think a man would want more than thanks for returning a box of jewels like that. There's a thousand pounds reward offered, and it must come out of your pocket-money; I can't afford to pay it."

"I hope that you will not offend Mr. Murden," I said, "by offering to reward him for what he has done. To be sure, he encountered great peril in his endeavors to recover the jewels; but I assure you that no mercenary motives actuated him to undertake the task. It was simply a desire to show the police force what one man, of a comprehensive mind, could accomplish after others had failed."

"Egad! it ain't every man who would refuse a thousand pounds. I should have hard work to do it myself."

"I have no doubt that you can inform us respecting the manner in which my jewels were recovered," her ladyship said, with a sweet smile, her white fingers still at work fingering the diamonds and emeralds.

I related in a brief manner some of the particulars of the case, showing up Murden in the most prominent manner.

"You give yourself and countryman no praise in recovering the jewels," she said. "Are all Americans as modest?"

"I speak sincerely when I say that unless Mr. Murden had joined in the search, your jewels would never have been recovered," I replied, evading the question.

"And your reward," said her ladyship, with a sweet smile, "for the part you have performed is —"

"Your ladyship's gratitude."

"You have that, most assuredly."

"Egad! I should think so; it's a cheap way of settling a debt," cried his lordship, with a jolly laugh, and a shake of his fat stomach that looked dangerous for his buttons.

"I am sure that you have some favor to ask of me?" the lady said, with an encouraging smile. "If not for yourself, can't you think of some friend who needs the government house patronage?"

"If he don't belong to the opposition I might do something for him," muttered the governor.

"I have a friend, as your ladyship surmises," I replied, "and that friend is quite dear to me. We have together encountered many dangers, and would seek more under certain circumstances."

"You speak of Mr. Murden," she said, with a smile.

"I do."

"But you know, egad!" remarked his lordship, "that he is accused of taking money from prisoners. That's a serious offence."

"But never proved," I replied.

"But one of the men supported the assertion," continued his lordship. "Egad! the evidence was said to be complete."

"The officer had been reprimanded for cowardice in the presence of an enemy. For that he vowed revenge. He accomplished his designs, and remains in the department, while an able man was compelled to leave it."

"You see, my lord, that the gentleman has an answer for every objection that you can urge."

"Just like the d—d opposition," muttered the governor.

"I need not remind you that a few minutes since you declared that the office would be bestowed upon the man who was so fortunate as to find her ladyship's diamonds." At this the lady laughed.

"You know you made such a statement, my lord, and I think that you should adhere to your word."

"But I shall have trouble, and you know I don't like trouble."

At these words I bowed and turned towards the door Both the governor and his wife looked surprised.

"You are not intending to leave us?" his lordship asked.

"I do intend to, for it is too much trouble for me to remain. I think that after a person has performed so important a service as Mr. Murden, that he should be entitled to a little consideration. But, as you do not seem to think so, I will take my leave."

"But look here. Egad! a man hasn't a chance to speak to you, you fly off so. Just like the opposition."

Her ladyship gave me a glance of approval, as though I had taken the right course.

"Egad! well, I'll think of the whole matter, and let you know in a day or two."

"It will then be too late. I shall not be in the city, perhaps."

"Give me a day to consult with my cabinet."

I shook my head and moved towards the door. The governor looked distressed.

"What will satisfy you?" he asked.

"Let me leave the house with the appointment in my pocket."

"Egad! that's sudden. What shall I do?" and he looked towards his wife.

"The gentleman's demands are reasonable. I should comply with them," the lady said.

Only for a moment did he hesitate; and then he cried, "Wait here one moment. My dear, you will entertain him."

CHAPTER XI.

THE RED LION. — MISS JENNY AND HER TEMPER. — HER WARNINGS. — ARRIVAL OF THE PET.

As soon as his lordship had left the apartment, a radiant smile was displayed on the face of his wife, as though she was much pleased at what had occurred.

"I am glad you assumed the position that you did," she said, "for I am deeply indebted to you and Mr. Murden."

I bowed, for it is not often that the blood of the Howards makes a confidant of a plebeian, and her conversing in such an unrestrained manner showed that she could confide in me.

"On Thursday evening," continued the lady, "the regular government-house levee takes place, and I should be pleased to see you here. You will meet some pleasant people, and some who may be of assistance to you during your residence in the country. If your wife is with you —"

I interrupted her by a smile.

"O, I see. You have not yet committed yourself by taking a wife."

But before her ladyship could ask more questions, the governor came in.

"Egad!" cried his lordship, with a rueful smile, "I haven't been so driven since the confounded opposition made me change my cabinet. Here is Mr. Murden's appointment; and tell him that I expect a good account of his doings. Don't forget to come to the levee. My wife will send you a card. Murden had better come also. It will look well."

"I have an American friend with me," I suggested.

"We will send him a card, never fear; and now good by."

I saw the carriage which brought us to the place waiting near the gate, with Murden's head and Hez's head out of the windows, watching my coming.

"Have you succeeded?" asked Murden.

I held the paper aloft, and shook it as an answer.

"Good God! I believe you have accomplished your object," Murden cried.

"I have," was my answer; "and here is the commission, signed and sealed."

My friend seized it, opened it, and read its contents. Then I saw a tear steal to his eye, and he extended his hand, and pressed mine with the grasp of a giant.

"I am indebted to you for all this," he said, "and if I live I will repay the obligation."

"Your own merit has contributed to the result," I remarked, in a quiet tone. "Without that, all pleadings would have been in vain."

"Well, I am thankful that I am restored. It is an unexpected result."

While he was laying out his plans for the future, we arrived home; and the instant we entered the house, Tom, the convict servant, was summoned. The fellow had been transported for attempting to burn up his grandmother, who had made a will in his favor, and then persistently refused to die. Tom entered the room, as though he expected to be commended for some of his good deeds. He had acquired a passion for burning people. Once he had seated the cook on a red-hot stove, because the latter did not please him; and once he had attempted to set fire to the chambermaid's clothes.

"Well, Tom," cried Murden, when he saw his servant waiting for commands, "have you burned any one to-day?"

"No, sir."

"Do you feel an inclination that way?"

"I did this morning, sir," answered the candidate, with great frankness.

"Ah! how was that?"

"The cook, sir, burned the curry, and I wanted to burn him."

"Restrain your passion, my friend," cried the commissioner, with the utmost coolness. "It won't do to indulge your appetite too often. I can afford one victim a year, but more than that makes the luxury too expensive. But I have news for you. I have been restored to my old position I am once more commissioner, and wish to celebrate the return to office. Furnish me, at six o'clock, with such a dinner as I shall feel proud of; and if you fail, I'll see what *I* can do in the burning line."

Tom left the room to prepare the dinner; and then Murden announced his intention of visiting a few friends, and inviting them to the feast.

"In the mean time, my boy," said my friend, "you can amuse yourself the best way that you can. I shall be home in the course of two hours."

He left the house, and Hez retired to take a nap. I had nothing to do; so it is not to be wondered at that I commenced thinking of Jenny, the bar-maid. At last I formed a resolution. I would go to her. I would look at her sweet face once more, and then forget it. I again assumed the garb of a sailor, put a revolver in my pocket, and left the house. I had no trouble in finding the street; yet when I entered it and neared the saloon, my heart began to fail me, and I was almost inclined to turn back, and let Jenny and her sweet face go; but beauty conquered, and at last I entered the porter-house and took a seat. Then, for the first time, I glanced towards the bar, and saw the girl I so much desired to see, with her large blue eyes scanning my face, as though she was trying to recollect where she had seen it. I felt the blood rush to my face, and for a moment I lowered my eyes; when I raised them, she was no longer regarding me, and appeared to be entirely unaware of my presence. I would have given much to have read her thoughts, and known that she had some slight regard for me. But I would not acknowledge that I was in love.

As the girl did not appear to pay the least attention to me, her eyes being fastened on a book, I knocked on the table, and when she looked towards me I said, "A pint of beer and a cigar, if you please."

As she placed the articles on the table, she said "You are here again. Did I not warn you last night?"

"You certainly did; but I would risk much to catch a sight of so fresh and fair an English face as you possess."

A proud curl of her lip was the response to the compliment; but her words were coarse as she replied, "None of your chaff, for I don't want it. You did me a service last night, and I attempted to repay it. I tell you to leave the city, for it is no place for you. If you do not, you will see trouble. Even now a policeman is spotting you from the other side of the street. Will you go?"

"No, I will stay."

"What fools you men are!" was her next complimentary remark. "You never will take advice, you never will see folly in the course which you pursue, and like a crazy bull you plunge headlong upon destruction, and then blame us women as the cause of it. I have no patience with you."

"And yet patience is a virtue, and I am told that you possess both patience and virtue."

"What's that to you?" she asked, with a flash of her blue eye that looked threatening.

I did not answer. I sipped my beer in silence, and admired the play of her handsome, regular features.

"You come here," Jenny continued, in an indignant tone, "after I have warned you to avoid this place. You take no notice of my advice, as though there were not half a dozen men within the sound of my voice who would sell you to the traps for a few shillin's. Take your plunder and bad company, and leave the city, or it will be the worse for you."

"As soon as I can obtain a ship," I commenced; but she interrupted me with an indignant gesture.

"Don't talk such blasted nonsense to me," she said. "You a sailor! Look at your hands; they are as white as mine."

"Let me see," I said, as though desirous of confirmation, and I laid one hand upon her own; but she threw it off in a scornful manner, and looked as though I meant to insult her.

"Hands off!" she cried. "This piece of goods is not in the market. I have struck many a man for a less insult."

"And why don't you strike me for what I have done?"

"Because your impudence protects you. What were you sent here for?"

"To make love to you, I suppose."

She frowned and pouted her red lips.

"Keep your love to yourself; I want none of it. Answer me at once. What were you transported for?"

I laughed and drank my beer.

"Are you a ticket-of-leave man? Have you served your time? or are you an escaped convict?"

"An admirable classification," I cried. "Can't you add one more, and think me a honest man?"

"No," was the prompt answer.

"Why not?"

"Because honest men, who wear diamonds on their fingers and trim their nails with care, don't visit the Red Lion."

"Not if they are in love?"

"Men like you don't love girls like me for any honest purpose."

I lighted a fresh cigar, and surrounded my face with a cloud of smoke. I did it to prevent the young woman from scanning my features as closely as she had done. I was successful in my object, for she dropped her eyes and asked, "Can't you tell me what lay you are on, and what you intend to do in Melbourne?"

"Most of my time will be spent in visiting the Red Lion and looking at you."

"Are you in earnest?"

"Yes."

"Then you are a fool, and will find every bone in your body broken after your money is gone. Do you understand?"

"No."

I was determined not to, for I read in her clear blue eyes an interest in my fate which the proud girl would fain have concealed.

"You make no attempt to understand me," she cried, in a passionate manner. "You are dull, or pretend to be. I have told you that I would do you a service in return for the one which you did me last night. You are young and brave Such being the case, why don't you seek some honorable employment, and lead an honest life?"

I appeared to think most seriously of her words.

"How much money have you?" she asked, in a blunt manner.

"Ten pounds or so," I answered.

"Then save it; for it will not last a week if my father sees it."

"Let me understand you," I said, in a determined tone. "Your amiable and gentle-hearted parent is in the habit of encouraging the visits of young men; he allows them to become infatuated with your beauty, but they can only gaze at the shadow, and not hope for the substance. When they hint at that, if their money is nearly gone, they are kicked into the street, or their bones are broken by a blow of the Pet's huge fist. Am I right?"

She nodded her head in a slight manner, and said, "You are no fool."

"Thank you. The Pet shall find that I am not. Now, I have taken care of myself for many years. Don't think that your father can deceive me, or that I am blind to your beauty or your defects. I know them, and, knowing them, I enter the field as an admirer."

"With what kind of intentions?"

"O, honorable," I answered, with a smile.

"You lie!" she cried, in a passionate tone; and she left me for her place behind the bar; and just at that moment the Pet entered the saloon from the door at the back part of the room.

CHAPTER XII.

THE RED LION.—DESPERATE STRUGGLE.

I RATHER think that even my impudence was dashed by the Pet's appearance; for I buried my face in the pot of ale, and hoped that he would pass on to the street; but he did not, for he saw that a customer was present, and that encouraged him to look and see who it was; and the instant his gray eyes fell on me, he uttered a grunt, and exclaimed,—

"Well, I'm d—d if you ain't here."

"This is as good a place as another," I replied, assuming all the coolness that I could command. "Give me another pot of ale, and let it be better than the last."

The Pet looked at me in the same manner that he would have looked at an opponent in the prize-ring. I returned the look as well as I was able.

"Look a-here, you young cove," the Pet cried, in a sullen tone; "what in the devil do you mean by comin' round here arter the way you treated me last night?"

"This is a public saloon, and I have a right to sit here as long as I pay my bills," I answered, in a slow, deliberate tone.

The Pet pricked up his ears at the word "pay."

"Of course, lad, you has the right to eat, drink, and be merry here as long as you has the spondulics; but, for all that, you served me a mean trick last night. It's your skull I should crush for it."

"Bah! Talk such nonsense to the marines. My head is safe enough. I have a pair of arms that can look after it."

Now I was uttering words which were intended for effect. This I knew; but the giant was not so well informed. He thought that I must possess an immense amount of science to talk so strongly; and thinking as he did, he cooled down, and assumed a friendly tone.

"Give the lad a pot of the best, Jenny, my lass; and if he wants to stand a treat, I'll drink with him."

I saw Jenny's eyes raised for a moment, as though she would warn me against such a course; but the devil prompted me to be obstinate just at that moment; so I answered,—

"Come on, old fellow. You shall drink with me until we are full, and unable to come to time. A full quart of ale for the Pet."

"And bring it in the spare parlor, lass," cried Sykes. "I want to speak with you in private."

I slapped the Pet on his broad back, and followed him to his private room.

We took our seats facing each other, and then Miss Jenny brought in the beer, and without a word or a look for me, left the room.

"Come," cried the giant, after he had fastened the door which led into the saloon, "let's be jolly and sociable. I'm a man what likes my hours of freedom from all care, when I can mix with my customers, and call myself one of 'em. Your good 'ealth, sir. Here's to our better acquaintance and mutual advantage. If you wants advice, come to the Pet; for, although I say it, Sam Sykes is not the man to steer wild in behalf of a friend. When you is in trouble, come to me, and I'll treat yer jist like a father. If yer can't come, jist send us word, and I'll come to yer, and go bail for yer." And then, as though he had said too much, he added, "Of course, I mean that I'll get bail for yer, if yer has anything to put down as security. You wouldn't ax a man to do it without; now, would yer?"

I nodded a negative, and the Pet continued: "I know a great many secrets, and I'm not the man to betray 'em. Not one has I peached; and the traps might tear me into ten thousand inch pieces, and I wouldn't blab. That's me. I'm a safe adviser for young men, I've seen so much of the world You is from Sydney?"

He asked the question suddenly, as though to surprise me into a confession; but I was not to be taken that way by such a thick-headed clown; so I answered, "Do I look like a Sydney man?"

"Then you is from Ballarat, by——;" and the giant struck his fist upon the table, and looked a little fierce.

"You think so?" I asked, and smiled.

"Where in h—l did you come from, then?"

The Pet glared at me in an angry manner, and didn't seem to like me as well as he did a few minutes before the conversation occurred.

"There is one subject I can talk about with you," I said, at last.

"Well, let's hear it," growled the Pet, who still thought me a burglar in the disguise of a sailor.

"Your daughter."

The Pet glanced at me in a hasty manner, as though doubtful whether to be angry or pleased; but, after a moment's thought, he concluded that it would be much better to look satisfied.

"Well, what of the lass?" he asked.

"She is very beautiful."

"So many men have said before you."

"Was the mother as handsome as Miss Jenny?"

To my surprise, the Pet turned towards me in a fierce manner, and raised his ponderous fist in a threatening attitude.

"D—n you, what do you mean?" he cried, in a fierce tone. "What right has you to talk about the mother of the lass?"

"Keep cool, my strong-armed friend," I said, in a quiet tone. "No offence was intended. I but asked out of curiosity."

"Well, don't you show too much of it round here, 'cos it won't pay; now I warn you."

"Very well," I said, rising, "I will visit some other saloon, and spend my money where I can be treated in a more civil manner."

The Pet suddenly changed his course, and became quite humble.

"Don't you go, lad," he said. "You'll find this the best house in town, and I'm one of the most good-natured fellers in Melbourne. Come, take a seat, and we'll have more beer."

I pretended to be appeased by this argument, and once more sat down; and as I did so, the Pet laid his huge hand on my shoulder, and said, "Then you likes the looks of my little lass, do you?"

"She is a clipper," I replied, in nautical language, "and the handsomest one that I ever saw."

"And you has taken a fancy to her, has you, lad?"

"She is very beautiful," I replied, in an evasive tone.

The Pet looked reflective for a few moments. "You know, lad,"—and he spoke in a slow, deliberate tone,—"that the cove what raises his eyes to the lass must possess the dosh to take care of her. Come to me with five thousand pounds, and then we'll talk the matter over. "Five thousand pounds is a big sum, lad, but ye can make it if ye is lucky and smart. There is the gold mines, and if ye don't like them, there's other mines what pays. Diamond mines pays well sometimes;" and as the old chap uttered the words, he stared full into my face, and winked with both of his gray eyes, in a manner calculated to lead one to suspect that he knew something of importance.

"Ah!" I replied, "do you know where there is a diamond mine. It must be valuable."

"Get out with you," he cried, and poked his finger in my ribs. "You is the lad for the diamonds. Who knows but you and the lass might jine if the swag was disposed of in a quiet way? Eh, lad, what do you think of that?"

"I don't know what you are talking about," I replied. "You must speak plainer."

"Why, d—n your eyes, does you pretend to say that you don't know what has become of the diamonds Doland and Thrasher prigged from the government house? Come, own up, 'cos you has nothin' to fear from me.

I pretended to be surprised, and the Pet grew enraged at what he considered my obstinacy.

"I knows all about it, and I knows all about you," the Pet continued, dashing his fist upon the table. I glanced towards the door.

"You don't leave this room till I is ready to let you go," the Pet cried. "Do you think I'll stand any of your nonsense? I is goin' to know what you done with them 'ere diamonds. I gives you fair warnin'. Don't you go for to get me mad. Now, then, tell me what you and your cronies done with the jewels?"

"Why do you think I know of the jewels?"

"O, thunder and lightnin'! don't bother me with such talk. Answer me at once, or I'll crack your bones as though they were egg-shells."

Perhaps I looked a little incredulous, for the man once more rapped the table, and uttered a volley of oaths.

"No Sydney thief can deceive me," he cried. "I'm up to your tricks, and knows all about 'em. Tell me what you did with the diamonds."

"Do you think it is any of your business where they are?" I asked, in a quiet tone of impudence, which I repented a moment afterwards.

With an oath and a roar the Pet threw himself upon me. So sudden and quick was the movement, that I did not have time to avoid the onset. I went down before it like a straw before the blast of a hurricane. Of course I struggled, for it was but natural that I should, but I could do nothing effectual. The Pet held me down with a grasp that could not be broken; and even while he did so, the wretch growled out words of denunciation and reproach.

"You chaff me, will you?" and here the rascal gave me a shake that made my teeth chatter. "You don't know me yet, I guess. D—n your impudence, what do you mean?"

"You scoundrel," I managed to gasp, "let me up, or the worse for you."

But instead of complying with my demands, the Pet gave me another shake, and hissed out, "Tell me of the diamonds or I'll strangle you. Where are they, and who has them?"

I don't know whether the giant suspected my intention of

letting a hole through his body or not, but this I do know; he held my arms so tight that I could not accomplish any object; so there was only one course to pursue, and that was to remain quiet, and submit to the pressure, or else utter a few startling yells, and see if I could not attract attention and a rescue.

While I was thinking of these things the Pet released my throat for the purpose of asking a question. It was the one that he was most interested in.

"Where's them diamonds?" he demanded.

Instead of replying, I uttered a shrill yell for help, and I had just time to do so, when the Pet's hands were at work in a fierce manner about my throat.

"You would, would you, d—n you!" cried the Pet; and he raised my head and dashed it to the floor, causing me to see more stars than agreeable at that time of the day; but such treatment only made me more determined, and with a sudden wrench I freed one of my hands, and struck the huge bully full in the face; and so well directed was the blow that a few drops of blood tricked down his cheek from the direction of the right eye.

For a moment the Pet was surprised at the suddenness of the attack. Still he held me with a giant's strength, and hissed out, "You can use yer mawlers, can yer, little bantam? Well, so can I; and let's see how you likes 'em."

He drew back his huge fist, like a twelve-pound shot, and aimed a blow at my face; but I dodged just in time, and the bunch of bones landed on the hard-wood floor with a crash that threatened damage to the boards or the man's hand, whichever were the strongest.

"O," roared the brute; and up went his fist to his mouth, and he licked the blood from the barked skin, like the beast that he was.

"O, cuss yer! that's yer game, is it? Yer think that yer has done somethin' smart, don't yer?"

"Now or never," I thought, and with a mighty effort I attempted to turn the man, and at the same time I uttered a second shrill yell for help.

"Blast 'yer for a screeching cove!" cried the Pet, in a fierce tone; and once more his hand clutched my windpipe

But there was a gentle rap at the door, and the Pet relaxed his hold a little to listen.

"O, dad," cried Jenny, "do stop your fighting, and let the poor young man out. If you don't I'll give an alarm."

"Away with you, girl," returned the father, fiercely. "Leave me to settle the matter."

"I won't," returned the independent girl. "Let him alone, or the traps will be here and jerk you off. Be warned in time."

"If I come out there to yer," said the Pet in a threatening tone, "ye'll remember me for a while."

"The diamonds, lad. Tell me of the diamonds, and I'll let you up," he hissed.

I did not reply, but made a desperate struggle, and was unsuccessful. I felt that my tongue was protruding from my mouth, that my eyes were starting from their sockets, that my breath was nearly gone, and that in a few seconds I should be unconscious; but just as I was losing all sense and feeling I heard a terrible crash, the door flew open, and in rushed half a dozen men. I heard a savage blow struck, and was instantly relieved of the pressure of the giant's body; and then I lost all consciousness.

CHAPTER XIII.

THE RESCUE. — THE ACCUSATION OF MISS JENNY. — THE DESPATCH.

I KNEW that I was relieved of the weight of the giant in a sudden manner; but that was all that I did know until I regained my senses, and the instant that I opened my eyes I heard a familiar voice exclaim, —

"He's all right now, gol darn it. I was afeard that the big cuss had killed him. If he had, I'd taken the law in my hands, and cut the brute into inch pieces."

"Is that you, Hez?" I asked, for I found that I was lying in some one's arms.

"Wal, I shouldn't wonder if it was. How do you feel now? Are you all right? Does your wind work well? Here, take a drop of this 'ere. It will do you a powerful sight of good." And he held a glass containing some brandy to my lips.

"We warn't none too soon for you," said Hez, when he saw that I was capable of standing and moving without assistance. "That big cuss was jist squeezing the life out of you. What did you come here for, at any rate?"

I did not answer, and there was no occasion for me to; for at this moment Murden entered the room in all the pride of blue coat and brass buttons and insignia of rank. His first look was towards the humbled Pet, and the instant the giant man noticed his glance, he said,—

"I'm glad to see you, Mr. Commissioner. I've news for you, sir—important news. You'll thank me when you hear it."

I was about to speak, but Murden made me a rapid sign to remain quiet and listen.

"Speak your mind. What have you got to say?"

"You remember, Mr. Commissioner, that some diamonds were nabbed at the government house, a few weeks ago?"

"Yes; what of them?"

"I know who has 'em."

"You do?"

"Yes, sir. I was trying to nab the man when you comes in. I will appear agin him if you will let me up."

"Do you mean to say that this man"—and he pointed to me—"is the one who stole the diamonds?"

"Yes, sir. I've been on his track for a week. He's a Sydney thief. I know him well. He's told me all his plans. There's more of 'em here."

"So you thought that you would make a capture for the benefit of the police."

"Yes, sir. I allers played in their hands, and I allers will."

Murden made a sign, and some officers raised the Pet and led him off to jail, to the intense consternation of the Mud-

Laners, who didn't understand it, and wondered who had got hold of the police bellows.

I passed into the saloon, and saw Jenny behind the bar, attempting to preserve her coolness and calmness; but the effort was not successful, and when she saw me her tears would flow in spite of her efforts to prevent them.

"You would not take notice of my warning," she said, in a bitter tone, "and now you see the result. You nearly lost your life; you are in the hands of the police, and my father is a prisoner for an assault on you. What more would you have?"

"And yet I made all this venture for your sake," I remarked.

"Don't talk such nonsense. I'm not to be gassed in that way. Go to your prison and leave me. Let me never see you again."

While we were speaking Murden came towards us. "Arrest that woman as an accomplice," he said, and pointed to Jenny.

The young girl dried her tears in an instant, and held out her hands.

"Put the irons on me if you will," she said; "I am not afeard of a prison; I am innocent, and can suffer."

"And suffer you shall. You knew of the attempt on this man's life;" and Murden pointed to me.

"I did, and tried to prevent it."

"It's false!" roared Murden, who cared no more for the girl's beauty than he did for her feelings.

"It's true," I said, in a calm tone. "The young lady did warn me of the danger that I incurred in remaining here; but I was heedless of her advice, and the consequences be upon my own head."

"Well, she must be made an example of, at any rate," replied Murden, who wanted to signalize his reappointment to power, and was loath to yield an inch.

The men looked to the commissioner for instructions; and that gentleman bit his lips, and was about to utter a harsh command, when I signalized for a moment's conversation.

"What is it?" he asked, impatiently. "It's something about that woman, I know. Now, let me dispose of her. I want to get her out of the way. You're in love with her. don't deny it. I discovered it last night. She'll ruin you, unless the whole thing is nipped in the bud. Be guided by me, will you?"

"No, I won't, not in this respect," I replied, very bluntly "I'm not in love with the girl." (Here Murden smiled in an incredulous manner.) "Of course, if you insist upon dragging the girl to the station house, I cannot interfere; but, remember, it is against my wish, and you know that —"

"O, d—n! don't talk in that style," cried Murden, in an impatient tone. "You know that what I am doing, and what I have done, is for the best. She is a dangerous girl. She has wrecked many a man through that face of hers."

"You think that my judgment is good on some points, don't you?" I asked.

"Yes; better than mine."

"Then believe me when I state that the girl is not as bad as you think."

"And you want her released?"

"Yes, most assuredly."

Murden turned towards his men, and held up his hand.

"Release that girl; she is no longer a prisoner."

The officers fell back, and left Jenny behind the bar. She raised her eyes for a moment to my face, and gave me one look; but it was such a contemptuous glance, that I did not desire a repetition of it. I did not understand it. What could she mean? Was she not grateful for what I had done? There was a mistake somewhere. I moved towards Jenny for the purpose of exchanging a word with her. She knew that I was standing by her side, and yet she would not turn her well-shaped, haughty head, so that the light of her dark-blue eyes should fall upon me.

"I thank you," I said, in a low tone, "for the interest that you have taken in me. How shall I reward you for what you have done?"

"By never speaking with me again," she said, in a crusty

tone. "I know you now, and hate myself for *yarning* with you."

"Yarning," I asked; "what is that?"

"Talking with you;" and the young lady made a gesture of impatience.

"O!"

"O! indeed;" and the girl turned upon me like a tiger. "It is well enough for you to 'O,' and look grave and pretty; but I tell you that I despise you, hate you, loathe the sight of your face. Now do you understand me?"

"I do not," I answered, quite calm and unconcerned; but admiring the girl more and more as she gave me evidence of her fierce, proud disposition.

"When you wish to play a part you are not so stupid;' and the girl looked at me with such a cold expression of contempt, that if I had not admired her very much I should have wilted under it.

"I cannot comprehend your meaning. Tell me in plain words what I have been guilty of."

For a moment she looked me full in the face without speaking. Then she said, in a cold, contemptuous tone, "A spy of the police department need not expect a civil answer from me. Look at me."

There was no need for such advice. I had been looking at her quite intently. She continued: "You see me here behind a bar serving out liquors to all sorts of customers, in one of the most detested quarters of Melbourne. It is a miserable employment for a young girl; but, low as my position is, and much as I despise it, I would not exchange it for yours."

I smiled at her vehemence, and that smile exasperated her.

"Laugh at me if you will; but a spy is something not to be laughed at—he is to be despised, spit upon, detested!"

"If I pledge you my word that I am not a spy, will you believe me?"

"No."

"If Mr. Murden pledges his word will you believe him?"

"No."

I would have made another attempt to reason with her if she had been like other women; but, as she was like steel in firmness, I turned away, and joined Murden.

"You make no heading with that woman," he said.

"No."

"I knew you would not. Other men have tried, and failed. But we must go to the station, and prefer charges against the Pet. It shall go hard with him for his murderous assault."

Jenny, as we were leaving the house, called to the commissioner, and Murden stopped to hear what she had to say. It took but a moment.

"Now," said Murden, as we entered the street, "tell me what mad freak sent you to the Red Lion at this hour of the day?"

"Curiosity," I answered.

"Which nearly cost you your life," was the dry rejoinder.

"But how did it happen that you arrived at such an opportune moment?"

"It was owing to the sagacity of your good genius, Hez. He saw you put on your disguise, and thought that you intended to look at Jenny's face once more; so, instead of taking the nap that he contemplated, he followed you to the Red Lion, saw you enter and call for beer, and then he left, for he felt that you was soft on the girl. While he was wandering around he met me, and told me what had happened."

"But one question more. Did Jenny give you any information regarding my condition?"

"Yes; she said, 'A young man is in the room; he has quarrelled with my father, and I wish you would separate them.'"

"Was she quite cool about it?"

"Like a cake of ice in July."

"Manifested no concern?"

"Not the slightest."

I sighed, and did not ask another question.

"Humph," growled Murden, "that woman's eyes have burned a hole in your heart, and that is misfortune number one, since you landed."

"And what do you call misfortune number two?"

"To marry her," was the blunt rejoinder; and without another word we entered the station house where the Pet was confined.

We found Maurice in charge. He received us with marked pleasure, for he had already heard of Murden's re-appointment, and was glad of it. We entered our complaint against the Pet, and then paid him a visit, for he was confined in a cell, and very repentant he appeared as we looked at him through the grates of his den.

"I hopes, gents, that you didn't think I was in earnest when I put my fingers to that young feller's throat. It was only a little fun. I wanted to know a certain somethin', and took that 'ere means of gettin' it. I'll make it all right with the young feller, and won't mind a pound or two if he'll settle."

"You're a precious rogue, Sykes," said Murden. "I've known that fact for a long time, and longed for a chance to lay hands on you. Escape is not so easy at the present."

The Pet uttered a howl of protestations respecting his innocence, but no notice was taken of them. We returned home, and, when we arrived there, found an official-looking document from the Home Department, in which was stated the fact that a gang of bushrangers was on the road from Melbourne to Bendego, and Commissioner Murden was ordered to take such force as he thought proper, and capture or disperse the rascals.

"This is marked for immediate service," Murden said, turning to me.

"Yes, I suppose so."

"I shall start at daylight to-morrow morning. Will you remain here or go with me?"

"I go with you. We shall not be absent more than a week. In the mean time we have nothing else to do."

"Good! I will make you and Hez aids, and order horses. Hez, will you go?"

"Count me in," returned the genius; and off went Murden to detail a certain number of men and horses and give orders for the expedition, and when he returned his guests began to arrive.

CHAPTER XIV.

THE FIRST HUNT FOR BUSHRANGERS. — WEBBER AND HIS FAMILY. — THE SLEEPING TRAMP.

No allusion was made during the dinner to the proposed expedition. The meal passed off in good shape. The wines were excellent, the food cooked to perfection, through the instrumentality of Tom, who had threatened to roast the head of the kitchen unless care was bestowed on the meat, and speeches and toasts as complimentary to the host as could be expected; and at two o'clock the company left the house, and those who remained in peace and quietness retired to bed for the purpose of obtaining a little sleep.

At daylight we were aroused by Tom. We dressed for a long and tiresome journey. Our costume was peculiarly fitted for the bush and horseback riding. We wore leggings of buckskin, which reached to the knee. They were light, yet strong enough to resist the thorns and brambles, and were also useful guards against the sudden attack of snakes, which must always be guarded against when travelling in the bush. We wore loose-fitting blouses of stout cloth, of a subdued color. Each blouse contained numerous pockets, which I had found extremely useful during my first visit. We had broad felt hats, and around our waists were stout leather belts, and attached to these were revolvers and bowie-knives, while we intended to strap to our backs two light but powerful repeating-rifles.

All ready for our journey, and with our rifles in our hands, we entered the dining-room only to find Murden radiant with gilt buttons and spurs.

"Do you wear your uniform?" I asked, astonished at his want of prudence.

"Certainly. Why should I not?"

"I supposed that common sense would tell you that if a mark is to be fired at, a lot of gilt buttons enables a man to obtain a good aim."

"Just as you say," returned the commissioner. "Tom, lay out my rough-and-tumble suit. I think that I shall feel better in it."

After breakfast, Murden retired for a moment, and came back shorn of his finery.

"Tom goes with us," said Murden, as we rose from the table; and that fire-loving young man grinned at the thought of displaying his talent in such a wide field as that which we were about to enter upon.

We found four perfect bay horses at the door, as good as the police force could muster, for they had been selected by Murden with special reference to speed and endurance. We each selected one, and mounting, galloped through the street.

"Strike for Webber's," cried Murden, when he saw that I was about to turn in the direction of the station house.

Webber's was a sort of stopping house, ten miles from the city.

"Where are the men?" I asked, as we turned a corner and dashed towards the country.

"At Webber's. I didn't intend that it should be known all over town that a troop of mounted men had gone in pursuit of bushrangers. If you are unsuccessful in your search, men swear at you; if you are successful, the fact will soon be known, and you gain all the credit that you deserve."

"So you sent them out last night?"

"Yes, they left the city one by one, so as to attract no attention. We shall find twelve good men at Webber's."

By this time we had reached the suburbs of the city, where a few half-naked natives were hovering over a smoky fire, — for the morning was cool, — endeavoring to warm a little offal or some refuse matter for breakfast, while near them and on each side of the road were rather pretty villas occupied by the merchants of Melbourne.

Past all this we galloped, and struck the dusty road which led to Webber's. Luckily for us, a heavy dew had fallen during the night, and the sun had not yet risen to drink it up; consequently we were enabled to escape the clouds of pulverized stones, blinding all who used the roads on a windy day.

But at last we left all traces of the town behind, and only at rare intervals came to a house. We passed through bushes which lined the road on each side, behind which a gang of resolute bushrangers could have wiped our party out of existence, and we should never have known what did it — through forests, on the branches of which chattering parrots and paroquets with gorgeous plumage mocked us, or else grumbled at the want of breakfast and the difficulty they would encounter in finding just such food as suited them — on to the cross roads, one of which led to Ballarat and the other to Bendego; and then we saw Webber's house, and in front of it were several heavy, lumbering wagons, some of them drawn by mules, and others by horses and oxen, while in the road, where the dust was knee-deep, were half a dozen little Webbers, clothed with scant garments, rolling up balls of dust by the aid of an ox horn filled with water. The little imps were having a jovial time, and were about the color of the dust in which they were playing, regardless of the mules, horses, or oxen stamping around them in every direction, while close to the children rolled several kangaroo dogs, long-legged fellows, with lean bodies like a greyhound, and the only species capable of keeping in sight of that bounding, singular animal, the kangaroo, peculiar to Australia, and no other country.

Opposite the house, which was one story and a half high, were half a dozen natives, who were nearly naked, basking in the sun, which had just begun to impart a little warmth to the atmosphere. The natives raised their little sharp black eyes as we passed them, scanned us for a moment, and then dozed like well-fed dogs, too lazy to stir.

We made our way through the crowd, carefully avoiding the tow-headed children, who rewarded us for our forbearance by hurling handfuls of dust and mud-balls at our heads, and at last drew up to the front door, where some dozen men, teamsters and miners, were seated, drinking gin and water, ale and beer, and smoking clay pipes.

Just at this moment, a fat, light-haired man, whom I recognized as Webber, looking no older than when I last saw him, came out of the bar-room. He waddled towards us, pipe in mouth, and in a calm, Teutonic manner, welcomed us to the house.

"I's glad to see yer, Mishter Murden, but I don't knows what brings yer here at dis time. I's glad to know dat you is got back to yer old place, 'cos de bushrangers eats my scheeps like ter tyfil, and I no help myself. I's much glad to see you, and I will have some breakfast for you right off immediately."

"We don't need it, Webber. Besides, we don't relish your cookery. You serve too many ashes with your mutton."

"By tam, but dat is true," and Webber scratched his head, as he continued, "But de beer is good, Mishter Murden, and you vill hab some of dat, or perhaps you vill take coffee. We always has good coffee."

We were willing to take his word for it, and followed him into the best room, on the walls of which were hung scenes in lager beer saloons in Germany, done in cheap style, yet faithful enough in their representations to cause many a Teutonic heart to sigh for faderland, and wish for home and lager, with an unlimited supply of cheese and sausage.

On the floor was a rough-looking fellow, with long, black hair, which fell in tangled masses about his shoulders and neck. His slouched hat was pulled over his eyes, and his great muscular arms were crossed over his breast; but they did not conceal the hilt of a knife, — a long and ugly-looking weapon, — and a pistol.

"Whom have you there, Webber?" asked Murden, and the commissioner pointed to the sleeper

"Ah, dat is a veller what is goin' to de mines. He stop here dis mornin', and he eat and drinks gin like de tyfil; and arter he eats 'im, he comes in and sleeps, I s'pose. He pays for all he gets, and dat's all I know of 'im."

"I must see his face," returned Murden. "He looks like a tough case."

"Don't you touch 'im," cried Webber; "he is von savage, and care for no one. Let 'im sleep, and den ven he vakes up he clears out, and says nothin' to any von. He pays me, I s'pose, for his bed."

But Murden was not put off by that excuse. He stooped down, and attempted to remove the hat from the man's face; but the fellow turned, uttered a deep growl, and struck at the commissioner, at the same time, saying, —

"Let me sleep, you Dutch hog, or I won't pay you for the bed;" and then the man pulled his hat over his eyes more firmly, and turned over and went to sleep, or seemed to, for he snored like a man who needed rest.

"Don't disturb him," pleaded the German. "He no pays me if you does. He calls it a bed, and I make him pay all de same as though it vas. Ah! here comes de coffee, and it smells bery nice. I makes good coffee here."

"Now, Webber," said Murden, as we tasted the coffee, after seeing that no flies were in it, "tell me some reliable news of the bushrangers."

I looked at the commissioner, and pointed to the man on the floor; but Murden laughed, and said, —

"O, he's too drunk and sleepy to know what's going on. No fear of him."

I was not satisfied, but still I had no more to say.

"Vell, Mishter Murden, to tell you de truth, I don't know much about 'em; but sometimes dey takes a scheep or two, and den dey leaves me for some von else, and I is glad of it. I vish dat dey would pay me for it, 'cos I's a poor man, and can't afford to lose 'em."

"Then you don't know of a gang near here?"

"Not shust at dis time. I heard dat dere vas some at

Sanderson's farm, or de udder side of de river; but dat vas a veek or two ago."

"And what do natives say? Do they bring any word?"

"Not lately, I dink. My stockmen no say dat dey see 'em."

Just at that moment I happened to look at the sleeping man, and was somewhat astonished to see a pair of wild, ferocious eyes glancing at me from beneath the slouched hat.

CHAPTER XV.

A SUSPICIOUS SLEEPER. — THE MEETING IN THE BUSH.

If I could have had a second glance at the man's face, I could have judged whether he was insane, or rational and wicked; but the fellow pulled his hat over his eyes, and appeared to sleep as deeply as when we first entered the room. At first I thought of calling Murden's attention to the man and his suspicious movements; but I recollected that the commissioner would probably laugh at me for my trouble; so I drank my coffee in silence, and listened to the conversation between Murden and Webber.

"Yes, Mr. Murden," said Webber, in continuation of some remark that he had made, "I should have heard of it, never fear, if der had been many bushrangers around here. So many people stop at my house dat I gets all de news. Dey tells me ebery ding dat is goin' on, and if I knew of a set of d—d rascals loafing round here, I should tell you about it like smoke."

"But you must have heard of some bushranger depredations near here," persisted Murden.

"To be sure I does. Some weeks I lose a scheep every day by a rascal who had to eat mutton or starve. But dey no come near de house — dey fear de traps too much for dat."

"And you have not heard of Keeler and his gang of bush-rangers?" asked Murden.

"Yes, I heard of dem last week. A miner he say dat Keeler away up near Bendego, and dat he rob ebrey one dat he meet. Dat all dat I hear of him."

Murden thought for a moment, and Webber seemed anxious for the result of his deliberation.

"Why not go and hunt 'em?" the German asked. "Dat Keeler bad man—all his gang bad men. Dink no more of robbin' a Dutchman dan dey would a Englishman. Great haul if you take Keeler. But he is smart, and say dat de tyfil can't catch him, and I begin to dink so."

"It is singular," at last Murden said, in a tone of soliloquy. "I heard from good authority that Keeler had been seen near this spot, and that he had a camp on the Lodden. The information must have been false."

"Let us get into the open air," I said; "these flies will kill me with their bites and stings."

We all moved from the room; but I left it last, and as I crossed the threshold I turned and glanced at the sleeping man. Once more I caught sight of those baneful eyes; but they were closed in an instant, and I left the room. Webber closed the door and locked it after we had passed out, putting the key into his pocket, and in reply to my look of interrogation, said,—

"I do dat 'cos de man might go off and no pay me. We has to look arter all de coppers, or we be ruined, the miners cheat so like de tyfil."

While we were lighting our pipes, the German asked, in a careless way,—

"Shall you go back to de city, Mishter Murden, or vill you push on for Bendego? It is early yet, and de heat no come on. If your horses fresh, you make ten miles afore ten."

"I think we shall push on," the commissioner answered; "but I am not certain what I shall do. I am half inclined to return to the city—and would if it was not so hot."

I thought I saw the faintest twinkle of satisfaction in the

dull, gray eyes of the German when this announcement was made; but Murden saw nothing. He chatted with the German, asked after his wife, his children, his cattle, and at last left the host, and strolled towards the place where the police force was encamped.

"Have you full confidence in that German?" I asked.

Murden stopped and looked at me, as though surprised at the question.

"Confidence in Webber?" he asked.

"Yes; have you confidence in his honesty and integrity? If I remember rightly, there were some few suspicions attached to his name when I first knew him; and it was even said that he had an understanding with ticket-of-leave men."

"And you still think that Webber is on the neutral order?" asked Murden, in a musing tone.

"It looks so to me. He may be a true man, but he does not appear so to me."

"Nor to me either," replied the commissioner in a low tone, as if fearful the bushes would hear his remark and repeat it. "I know the man most thoroughly, I believe; and while I think he would do most anything for money, yet I don't imagine he would dare to play us false unless laboring under the influence of bushrangers."

"And you will find that he is in that condition to-day," I said. "The fellow, while talking with us, was evidently desirous of keeping peace with a third party; hence his non-committal answers."

"But what third party did he fear while with us?"

"Did you notice the fellow who was lying on the floor?"

"Yes; sleeping soundly."

"Appearing to; for he was no more asleep than you were. He heard every word that was uttered."

"O, no! that can't be," replied Murden. "I should have noticed him if he had been playing the eavesdropper. I have a quick eye, and can see as far as most folks."

"I have no doubt of it; but just send one of your men to the house to keep an eye on the fellow. Let him slip on a miner's suit, and play the spy for a few hours. Do this to oblige me."

"O, anything for a quiet life!" answered Murden, with a shrug of his shoulders. "It's all nonsense; but I will do it to satisfy you that I am right, and that you are wrong."

By this time we had reached the camp, which was located in a grove so thickly studded with balsam trees that the sun's rays could not enter through the branches. The police officers were old stagers. Some of them had shared with me my former campaigns, and they knew all the woods and the habits of the bushrangers; so feeling perfectly satisfied, when ordered from the city, that a hunt in the bush was contemplated, they had packed up their mosquito nets, and now had them in use; for some of the men were sleeping, covered with the nets, and thus rendered impervious to the attacks of the blustering, bloodthirsty mosquitoes, and the inquisitive gnat with its painful bite. Such of the men as were not asleep were under their "protectors," reading or smoking; and among them I was pleased to see my old friend, Lieutenant Maurice, who did me the honor of throwing off his net, and arising and shaking my hand in a hearty manner.

"This," he said, "looks like business. Here we are once more on the war path, and may luck favor us;" after which remark he dove under his "protector," and appeared to be quite contented with himself and the world.

"I want you for a moment," said the commissioner, speaking to Maurice; and that gentleman at once arose without a sigh, and followed us to Murden's headquarters, which was a huge net, in the form of a bell-topped tent, capable of accommodating four or five persons, and breaking the legs of the most adventurous mosquitoes that ever walked over fine muslin, and butted their heads against its meshes. In the centre of the tent was a small table, made for being taken all to pieces in a moment's time; and on that table were several bottles, some crackers and cheese, and a box of sardines. All these things were the result of Tom's thoughtfulness, or Murden's discipline, it matters little which. By a vigorous effort we drove the insects from the front of the tent, and then entered, and found peace and comfort beneath the heavy folds of muslin.

"Come, let us take a drink," said the commissioner. "This is a dry country, and dryness is not conducive to health. Here we go!" We emptied the glasses, and lighted our cigars.

"What is the programme?" asked Maurice. "Do we remain here, or make a dash for Keeler and his gang?"

"Ah! Tell me where Keeler is, and I'll answer the question," Murden replied.

"In the first place, before you discuss his whereabouts," I said, "just send a man to Webber's, and let him watch both Webber and the fellow in the front room."

"You still cling to your idea," Murden said in a bantering tone. "I thought that you had forgotten it."

"No; I never forget. I claim your promise."

"And I will keep it. Maurice, put Sam in plain clothes, and send him up to Webber's. Tell him to spot a tall, dark, wild-looking fellow whom he will find sleeping in the front room. Find out his business, where he came from, and where he is going; and, at the same time, let him keep an eye on that Dutchman. I want to know if he has a double face."

"Yes, sir;" and off went Maurice to give Sam his instructions.

The heat now became oppressive, and as moving at that time of the day was out of the question, we just spread blankets on the ground, stripped off some of our clothes, and lay down, panting and gasping for breath.

"Rough weather this, for hunting bushrangers," said Murden. "We can only move early in the morning or late in the afternoon. The horses would melt under this sun."

Then he puffed hard at his cigar, and in a few minutes it fell from his mouth, for the man was asleep. Hez followed his example. I, too, fell asleep, and dreamed that a young lady had quarrelled with me, and then drenched me with scalding water; and this was so severe a joke that I awoke, and found that I was bathed in perspiration, and actually steaming.

Somehow, without thought or premeditation, I walked into the woods, and soon found myself in the rear of Webber's house. The trees were quite thick here, and the brush was dense; so I was about to return to the headquarters, when I heard some one tramping towards me, crushing the dry branches under foot, and apparently in an impatient mood. I dodged under a bush at the foot of a balsam-tree. It was best to be cautious, for I was some distance from the command, and no force was out on patrol duty. Not that I really thought that a bushranger would venture so near us; but there was no telling what might happen.

"De tyfil! we is far enough now," cried a voice, which I recognized as Webber's. "No von can hear us here; so dere is no use to go furder. Now stop and talk as much as you vant to, and be mighty quick vith it, 'cos I must go back to the house. Got for damn, man, you vill ruin me."

"Stop your noise, you blasted Dutchman, and tell me what you think the traps will do, or I'll roast you over a slow fire."

I pulled one of the bushes aside and looked out. I saw that the speaker was the black ruffian who had occupied the floor in the front room.

CHAPTER XVI.

WEBBER AND HIS GUEST.—THE PURSUIT.—THE ESCAPE.—THE STOLEN HORSES.

"So help me Got," cried the German, in answer to the demands of the dark-looking man, "I does not know one ding vot the purlice does. You hears me tell 'em to go home, or go to Bendego, 'cos no bushrangers here. I say all dat for you, and yet by damn you still kill my scheeps and lambs, and I lose much money by it."

"And you'll lose a d—d sight more if you attempt to play any of your Dutch games on me."

"So help me Got," commenced Webber; but the dark-looking man stopped him.

"Avast with your blarney," he said; "I don't want to hear it. All that I want to know is, will you stick to your bargain?"

"Ah, but vill you stick to yours?" demanded the Dutchman, with a chuckle, as though he had caught the man in a trap.

"None of your d—n nonsense," was the quick reply. "I'm in no mood for jesting. There's too much at stake with a gang of traps within a stone's throw of me. What in the devil's name prompted them to give that cussed Murden a command? I thought that he was shelved forever."

"Vell, dat is more dan I can tell, Mishter Kee—"

"Silence, you Dutch hog! How dare you pronounce my name?"

"Vy, dare is no one here, Mishter—"

Before Webber could finish the sentence the hands of the dark-eyed man were on his throat, and I saw the poor fellow strangle as though the pressure was more than was agreeable.

"Didn't I warn you?" the fierce man cried. "Fool! sourkrout-eater! swiller of beer! didn't I tell you that my name was not to be mentioned?"

"Yaw, I didn't dink," was the reply; and then, as Webber rubbed his throat, he continued, "I vish dat de tyfil had you. I shall find de tyfil to pay wid me by and by, and den vot shall I do?"

"Do as we do—run for it," answered the dark-looking man. "But I tell you that matters are pressing at the present time. Who is that young fellow with the sharp-looking eyes?"

"I don't know; I sees him somewhere afore."

"Does he belong to the police department?"

"How shall I tell? He no say dat he do."

"Well, d—n him, he acts as though he did, for the cuss kept his eye on me all the time he was in the room. Did he speak of me?"

"No, I dink not."

"Well, I'll warrant you that he whispered his thoughts to that bloody commissioner. Blast them both! what in the devil's name did they send a force here for? Just as I wanted to recruit my band and make expenses, these police officers come down on me; and if they press me hard, what am I to do?"

"Cut and run for it," replied the matter-of-fact German.

"If I do have to, I'll make havoc among your muttons before I go," the dark-eyed man said, in a savage tone. "I more than half suspect that you brought this cloud of pests down on me; and if I was certain of it, I'd make you suffer."

"So help me Got, I no do it," was the answer; and then the parties moved towards the woods on the right of the house.

When I reached the camp, Murden was just stirring, and near him stood the officer who had been sent to the farm for the purpose of acting as a detective. The officer made his report.

"I have looked after the man you told me to spot," the policeman said, "and I find that he is a dissipated miner, with money and a taste for liquor. He drinks a good deal, and tells of his luck at Ballarat and the South Mountain diggings. I think that he's an ugly customer when in his cups, but see nothing about him that don't look square."

Murden turned to me with a triumphant look.

"You see," he said, "your suspicions were unfounded."

"I see nothing of the kind. If you can't muster better detectives, you should import a few from Yankee land. Why, I have been gone from the encampment but a half hour, and yet I have learned more than your whole squad have done since they reached this spot."

"Gammon!"

"Is it? Well, then, let me tell you that I've seen Keeler, heard him talk, and know that he is near us at the present moment."

"Honest, or joking?" and Murden brightened up in an instant.

"I never joke on such serious matters with the head of the Melbourne police department."

"Excuse me, Jack; I know you don't. I thought that you were running a saw on me. Come, like a good-natured fellow that you are, tell me all that you know."

"Willingly; but you must listen to me with patience."

"Certainly. Go on."

"Well, then, in the first place, your innocent miner who slept so sweetly on the floor, was no other than the redoubtable Keeler."

Murden sprang to his feet and shouted, "To horse, men, to horse! and lose not a moment!"

The men within the sound of his voice sprang to their feet, and were about to rush to their animals, when I said, in a calm tone, "Countermand that order immediately."

"What for?"

"No matter at the present time. I'll give you reasons, if you want them, by and by."

"Saddle, and wait for further orders," the commissioner said, and then turned to me for further revelations.

"How do you know it was Keeler that you saw? Where did you see him, and why didn't you give the alarm?"

"Don't ask too many questions at once. Patience for a moment;" and then I informed my friend what I had seen and heard.

"That d—d Dutchman is in with them, after all. I have half a mind to arrest him."

"But now we must turn our attention to Keeler. I'll mount my men, and dash down to the house. We can take him by surprise."

"I doubt it, if that is the way you intend to capture him. The fellow is in the bush, awaiting information of your movements. Send the men out on foot, so that they can close in around the house."

"By Jove, your plan is the best. I'll adopt it;" and thrusting a revolver into his belt, he left the tent, and called his men around him, and told them what he expected them to do, and how to do it.

"If you see a dark-looking man," the commissioner continued, "just tell him to stop. If he refuses shoot him if you can."

The officers vanished like ghosts. Some disappeared behind bushes, and others dodged behind trees, and in a few seconds, only Hez, Murden, and myself, were to be seen. We walked slowly towards the house in hopes of meeting Keeler there, and arresting him before the police came up; but when we reached the building we saw Webber sitting in front of his door, smoking his long clay pipe. He got upon his feet when he saw us, and then I noticed that he had been patronizing his own bar.

"Webber," asked the commissioner, "where is the fellow whom we saw lying on the front-room floor?"

"Gone to the tyfil, I hopes," was the answer.

"In what direction did he go?" asked Murden.

"Yaw! what you ax dat for?" the German cried, his dull gray eyes assuming, for a moment, a cunning look.

"Tell me where that man has gone. I have business with him."

"Den you ain't a lucky man, and de business von't do vell. De man is a d—d rascal, and he eat my scheeps, and say dat he von't. I don't know vich vay he goes; I leave 'im in de bush."

Webber waved his hand in the direction of the bush back of his house, and then closed his eyes and nodded his wooden head; and as we found that no further information could be obtained of the man, we let him sleep until our forces closed in upon the house, which was speedily. They came from all directions, and met at the rallying point without having a word of information to impart. No one had seen Keeler or heard of him, although they had noted footprints in the bush, but had lost them, owing to the dry nature of the soil.

"Search all the buildings," cried Murden. "Don't leave a barrel unexamined."

"But leave all de liquor in dem," muttered Webber, who made an attempt to open his eyes, and found that the effort was a failure.

The officers departed to perform their duty. They were

gone for half an hour, and returned unsuccessful. As soon as the men had made their reports, Murden and I consulted together as to the next move.

"Take my advice," I said. "Put one of the natives on his trail. Let the man be followed for miles, if necessary, and report to us at the South Ford on the Lodden. We can be there to-morrow morning, and meet the fellow."

"I'll do it," Murden answered, and was just starting off to find a native tracker, a man that could keep on the trail of a cat, if such a thing were necessary, when one of our men rushed towards the house with consternation pictured on his English face.

"What in the devil is the matter with you?" asked the commissioner.

"Our horses," gasped the officer. "Four of 'em gone, sir."

"Gone! Where?"

"Don't know, sir. While we were in the bush they left; saddles and bridles gone with 'em."

I laid a hand on Murden's shoulder, and whispered, "Not a word of this to any one. Keep cool, and signalize to the men not to speak of the matter."

He saw that the advice was good, and followed it. By a peculiar movement of his hands the signal for silence was given, and then we strode towards the place where the horses were tethered. As I apprehended, the rascal had taken the best animals that he could find, and among them were the horses which Murden, Hez, Tom, and I rode, the flower of the flock, the very animals that I had felt so proud of when we left the city that morning. There was no longer a question about the heat. We thought of it, but determined to ignore it. We threw the saddles on the horses, got a lean native to examine the trail and follow it on the run, and then we dashed through the bush, determined to avenge the wrong which we had received. On we went, over a prairie where the soil was hot and dry, and through a dark wood, where it was necessary to sway from side to side to avoid the branches; and it was while we were in the wood that my saddle-girth broke, and I was compelled to haul up for repairs.

"Shall we wait for you?" asked Murden.

"No; I'll join you in five minutes;" and with this assurance my companions dashed on.

The girth required more repairing than I anticipated. Before I was ready to trust to it, half an hour had elapsed, and then I noticed that the sun was low, and that not a sound, except that made by insects, was to be heard in the woods. I was alone.

CHAPTER XVII.

LOST IN THE WOODS. — MY HORSE'S DEATH. — NIGHT AND MOSQUITOS. — AN UNWELCOME BEDFELLOW.

I PATTED the animal, and then mounting, rode quickly in the direction which my companions had taken, determined to overtake them as soon as possible. After I had ridden for five miles, the bush growing more and more dense, I was compelled to stop and look around me, having almost arrived at the conclusion that I had missed the trail, and that I was in the midst of an Australian forest, with the sun only an hour high, and the prospect of passing the night in the company of my horse and eight or ten billions of mosquitos, without counting other insects, of lesser note, but blood-thirsty propensities. I had eaten nothing since morning. My horse was tired, for his head drooped and his eyes were closed, and the sweat poured from his sides in streams. I dismounted, and as I did so I looked down and saw at once what was the matter with the poor beast. One of its hind legs was swollen in a terrible manner, so much so that the limb was almost powerless for locomotion. I removed the saddle, took off the bridle, and the animal made an effort to nibble a bush, but gave it up, and turned its sorrowful, dark, expressive eyes upon me, as though asking an explanation for its loss of appetite and all energy. I knew that it would not add to my peace or security to have the horse die near my camping-ground, for the dead body would attract myriads of insects, and perhaps dozens of wild dogs and other animals. I spoke a kind word to the poor brute, and then walked off some distance, the horse following me with slow and painful steps. The leg, which had felt a serpent's teeth, was swollen so much that the joints did not work, and the foot did not touch the ground. It had increased so much in size that I expected the skin would burst with every movement. I walked until the animal staggered at every step, and looked so piteous for help that I stopped, and was just about to pat the brute's neck, when it fell over; then with one convulsive struggle, the horses' life was gone; and hardly had the breath left the body before a cloud of insects settled upon it, eager and fierce for a feast.

I stood and watched them for a short time, but the darkness warned me that I had better retrace my steps to the spot where I had left the saddle, and with a terrible fear that a spotted snake would seize upon me as the next victim. To prevent such a fate, a careful avoidance of dry limbs and rotten logs was made on my way back to the place where the saddle was deposited.

But I did not meet with any mishap. I saw nothing more formidable than insects; and they punched away at me until I was forced to cover my face and hands with stuff which I had brought with me from Melbourne. In a few minutes it was so dark that I could not see my hand before my eyes. The wild dogs had already found the body of the horse, and were barking themselves hoarse in their struggles for a supper. I lay down at last, put my head on the saddle, and placed my revolver and bowie-knife so that I could use them at a second's notice.

I tried to sleep, but the barking of the wild dogs prevented me; so I just lighted my pipe, and puffed away most vigorously, much to the disgust of the mosquitos, which made frantic efforts to reach me through my protectors. But while I was smoking, napping, and swearing just a little, I suddenly, during a momentary lull, heard something rustle near the bushes, as though a creeping body was passing over dry branches, and moving in my direction. Suddenly it ceased its motions, and seemed to listen, as though waiting for definite information respecting my whereabouts. For ten minutes there was a profound silence, with the exception of the quarrel of the wild dogs, which were making a feast over the remains of the dead horse.

I began to doze, but was awakened in an instant by a rustling sound. This time it was nearer than before; so I hurled a dry stick in the direction of the noise, and the reptile remained quiet for a moment, and then recommenced its movements. I lighted a match and set fire to a dry branch which I had provided before dark to act as a torch. With a revolver in one hand and the torch in the other, I started off to search for the reptile that dared to disturb my meditations. I looked under the bushes and in the bushes, but not the least sign of a snake could I see; and after a search which lasted a quarter of an hour, I put out my torch, and went back to my hard bed, settled my head comfortably, and was just about to doze off, when the rustle of my old enemy once more startled me, and I found myself sitting upright, listening with all my might for further indications of an assault. Once more I lighted my torch and surveyed the premises. Ten minutes did I spend in trying to find the animal, and was unsuccessful.

"Blast the snake," I muttered; "I don't believe there's one within a mile of me. I won't search again."

I stamped the fire out of the torch, and lay down; but hardly had my head touched the pillow, when rustle, rustle, went the leaves close to my head. I remained quiet and listened.

Once more my torch was brought into requisition, and another hunt ensued, but with the same want of success. All was quiet. There was no more rustling of leaves and crackling of dry branches. The snake had left me for other quarters, as I supposed; so sleep sealed my eyelids, and I dreamed of grotesque and horrible things, and at last awakened with a start, and to the fact that I was quite chilly, and that on my heart, apparently curled up for warmth, and nestled as near the flesh as possible, was a living thing — the snake that had troubled me before I fell asleep. I did not dare to stir, for if I did I feared that I should receive a deadly wound; and if the customer on my breast was a spotted snake, a speedy death was certain, even if the skin was but grazed. It might be some other kind of snake; but it was not likely it was a harmless one, for but few reptiles that inhabit the dense woods of Australia are innocent of poison.

I listened carefully and attentively. The reptile was sleeping, or else curled up on the watch, prepared to strike at the first demonstration of hostilities. I made a first venture as a test, and to see what the result would be. I moved one arm in the direction of the torch which I had used in the early portion of the night. No corresponding movement on the part of the snake took place. This emboldened me to proceed and make another attempt. I thrust my right hand into a pocket where I kept my matches, and succeeded in obtaining several without disturbing the reptile. I thought that this was wonderful good fortune, and I grew bolder in consequence; but I was suddenly checked in my congratulations, for the reptile appeared to have been disturbed. It seemed to have raised its head, listened for a moment, and then curled down in its old place, and once more gone to sleep.

After this demonstration I did not move for a long time, although while I lay upon my back, and stared at the pitchy darkness, it seemed to me that I could see Jenny's face encouraging me to proceed, and save myself from the poisonous fangs of the monster. I waited until I thought that my visitor was quiet, and then I carefully lighted a match, and set fire to the resinous wood. Still there was no movement on the part of the snake. The flame burned quite feebly at first, and did not give me light enough to see the color of my strange bedfellow; but it gathered headway at last, and burned into a bright flame, that threw its rays for many rods into the dark forest. But there was no motion on the part of the snake. It remained curled up, as quiet as before the fire was kindled, and this gave me hope. I drew my bowie-knife, and prepared to give a mighty chop, in case the reptile made a spring; and then, with a faint prayer for success, I slowly raised my head, and took a survey of the monster. My movement seemed to disturb the sleeping animal; for as I raised my head and moved my body, a similar movement on the part of the reptile took place; and when I was able to rest on my left elbow, and look at the place where the snake was nestled, I encountered a glittering pair of eyes and an open mouth.

"Now or never!" I shouted, and let my knife descend upon the head of the reptile. It severed it at a blow, and the body, with a convulsive wiggle, tumbled from my breast to the ground.

As soon as I had severed the head from the body of the reptile that had made a bed of my breast, and nearly caused my dark hair to turn white from the effect of fear, I sprang to my feet, and for a moment contemplated the bloody work; and then all thoughts of danger gave place to merriment, and I laughed loud and long at the thought of what had happened, and could hardly realize that I had been suffering from the most intense fear for nearly an hour, as well as I could calculate the time. I think if any one had been within hearing of my voice, I should have been pronounced mad, and for a moment I feared that such might be the case; but when I raised my torch, and saw the wiggling, squirming body of a poor harmless forest lizard, minus its head, instead of a repulsive spotted snake, I knew I was sane, and that my eyes did not deceive me.

The forest lizard of Australia is a harmless, playful animal, about ten inches long, and weighs nearly a pound when full grown. It often seeks the company of human beings; and, if unmolested and petted, will lie on a man's breast, and protect him, in a measure, from the bites of flies and other insects, and will often give warning of the presence of a snake and even fight one, if all means fail to awaken the human being whom it seems to love

While I was regretting the death of the lizard, other thoughts entered my mind. I was hungry, and at my feet was meat more delicate and juicy than venison, more gamey than duck, and more palatable than chicken. Egad! I would have a feast, and without delay. Fire and dry wood were at hand, and it was but the work of a moment to dress my prize. A few minutes' time was sufficient to strip off the skin of my prize, and then I thrust a stick through its body, and roasted it to perfection; and even while I was thus employed, I was continually glancing around to see if I could not find a second victim worthy to be despatched for the purpose of appeasing a hungry man's appetite; but no other lizard ventured near me. I looked at my watch, and found that it was nearly two o'clock.

Throwing my rifle over my shoulder, I started on the trail, or the one by which I had entered the forest. I followed it for an hour or more, and then it grew indistinct, and at last I lost it entirely, and found myself wandering around, with no more idea how to find the way out than a child. I descended valleys, climbed hills, all covered with brush and trees; and at last, just about an hour before sundown, tired, thirsty, and hungry, I left the woods, and entered a rich valley, through which a small stream ran; but there was no sign of life near the water, not even a sheep greeting me with its honest "bah." I paused, and looked around for some sign of human habitation. I could see nothing. Not even a stockman's hut met my gaze. On each side of me were mountains, studded with white patches, which I knew were of a quartz nature; and I wondered if I had not stumbled upon a mine, such as would test the value of quartz-crushing machines, and make Hez's heart dance with joy.

CHAPTER XVIII.

A NIGHT ON THE MOUNTAIN. — A STRANGE MEETING. — THE CAVE.

As I entered the valley, I was too much pleased to complain of the solitude which reigned supreme in that district. I was too thirsty to find fault with the inhabitants of Victoria for not improving the advantages which such a spot offered; for after I had quenched my thirst, I looked around, and surveyed the valley in which I found myself. It was lying between two high hills, or mountains, as they would be called in this country, with rugged sides, with here and there a stunted tree, looking as though struck by lightning, and hit quite hard; and along the head-lands, the points most exposed to the storms, could be seen heavy masses of white rock, which the rains had left bare, and which the lightnings of heaven could not destroy, fair as was the mark. Where I was, I had not the remotest idea. I might be miles and miles from human habitation, and yet a stockman might reside within the sound of my voice. "At any rate," I thought, "it is better to be here than in the forest. I can see the sun, can obtain a drink of fresh water, and if no other course is left for me, I can easily follow the stream, for it must flow into the Lodden."

As I finished these reflections, I looked around, and thought I should have time to ascend the mountain on the opposite side of the stream; and from the summit I hoped to be enabled to survey the country, and shape my course for the next day. But as I was searching for a fording-place, I saw several dark forms glide under the shadow of the banks. I had a hook and line in my haversack, but no bait. I tried the virtues of a white rag, but the fish, which seemed to be a species of trout, and far from shy, did not bite at it. I drew out my line, removed the rag, and then commenced tearing up the sod near the water, and was rewarded by finding half a dozen angle-worms. I put one on the hook, threw in my line, and almost as soon as it had touched the water, a splendid speckled brown and gold looking fellow, made a jump for it. A swift turn of the line, a splash, a struggle, and the fish, weighing all of two pounds, was landed at my feet. It was all I needed for my supper, and after a short search I found a ford, crossed, and concluded to cook my prize before I made any further exertions for that night.

As soon as I had concluded supper and lighted my pipe, I extinguished the fire, for I did not want a party of natives or bushrangers hovering near me during the night. I smoked to keep up my spirits, but at last I could smoke no longer; so I picked out the softest place I could find, and lay down, pulled the saddle blanket over my shoulders, and went to sleep.

I was awakened by a footstep, or at least I thought I heard some one, with heavy boots, crushing down the dry leaves and branches, stumbling over rocks, and sliding down steep hills. I sat up and listened for a long time; but the sounds died away at last, and I began to think that all I had heard was a dream; and yet I could have sworn that a man — and a large one at that — had passed within a dozen feet of me, plunging along as though with a purpose, and acquainted with the ground over which he strode. As soon as I was on my feet, I commenced a search for the traces of the footsteps which I had heard during the night. But my search was in vain. The ground was too hard and dry to leave an impression, and only the experienced eye of a native could have found the trail.

I made a breakfast off of a fresh fish, and then commenced ascending the mountain in the hope of being able to see some sign of habitation. It took me nearly an hour to climb up, and after I had reached the top I could see nothing but chains of hills with deep rich valleys between them. Melbourne, I knew, was in a southerly direction, distant some thirty or forty miles; but what puzzled me most was the fact that I could see no traces of the Lodden, and yet I was positive that I was not many miles from it. At last I concluded that it was best for me to follow the stream at the foot of the mountain, in hope that it would lead me to some stockman's hut. Down the mountain I scrambled, and commenced my journey. I skirted the sides of the hill, avoiding the rank grasses for fear of encountering snakes, and walked on until nearly nine o'clock; and then I was too much fatigued to go farther at that time. During the morning I had seen nothing that evinced the least token that the valley had ever been inhabited. I threw my blanket down upon the ground, and was just about to lay my rifle on it, when I saw something that made me alter my mind. Within ten feet of me were beef bones, fish bones, and ashes, as though considerable cooking had been done in the vicinity. I examined to see how long a time had elapsed since fire was made where the ashes lay. They were fresh, and had not been undisturbed more than two days. I regarded it as a joyful sight, and was just about to congratulate myself on the prospect of meeting with company, when a thick clump of bushes suddenly opened, and before me appeared a woman, tall, masculine, dark, with a ragged dress, dirty and ill-fitting, and hair that looked innocent of comb and brush. Her astonishment at seeing me was as great as my own. She pushed her tangled hair back from her forehead, and stared at me for a minute without uttering a word. At last she spoke, and her voice was hoarse and masculine.

"Who in the devil is you?" she asked.

"A man," I answered.

"Can't I tell that, you fool, without word from you? Where did you come from, and what do you here?"

"I decline to answer the question until I know something of yourself."

"You fool," she sneered, "the less you know of me the better. I'm the devil when I'm crossed."

"Then I won't cross you, for I don't want to see a woman turn devil."

She looked at me for a moment in silence, as though

wondering what I was made of, and what kind of deeds I was capable of.

"Are you on the tramp?" the strong-minded female asked, making a comb of her fingers, and combing her tangled locks.

"Well, I've tramped a number of miles."

"D—n you, why don't you answer me in a civil manner?" cried the indignant female. "You'll catch thunder if you ain't all right."

"What do you mean by 'all right'?"

"Wait and you'll see;" and the dirty female tossed her dirty head and pulled her lank hair as though plucking it out by the roots.

"I'll wait," I said, in a quiet tone.

The eccentric and dirty female paused for a moment from her usual occupation, and asked, "Is you on the bushranger lay, or the private tramp?"

It was evident that the woman thought me a robber, and the question was, should I allow her to continue thinking so, or should I tell her at once what my real business was. I resolved to adopt the latter method.

"I'm neither a bushranger nor a tramp," I said. "I am a gold-hunter, have lost my way, and would feel obliged to you if you would show the road to Webber's."

The dirty-looking female eyed me in a suspicious manner

"You is sure that you isn't a spy? that you didn't come here to see what you could see, and then go off and blart like a bloody sheep?"

"I am sure that I'm no spy," I replied.

"And you ain't a ticket-of-leave man?"

"No."

"And you didn't escape from the hulks?"

"No; so far I have led an honest life."

The woman laughed in a scornful manner, and then approached me.

"Let me see an honest man afore I dies. You is the fust one that I has seen for many years. Come, take off yer cap, so that I can see yer face."

I did so, and the wild, dirty-looking woman put her head, repulsive as it was, close to mine, and scrutinized it closely.

"You look like my Bob afore he went to the bad. He had jist sich a face as ye has got. For his sake I'll do ye a favor."

"Then direct me to Webber's, and point out the shortest cut."

"You can't go there now," said the woman. "It's thirty miles from here, and the boys is all along the road. They'd pick yer up afore you'd cross the Lodden, and it's rough treatment they'd give you. You must wait till dark, and then start."

"Whom have I to fear?" I asked.

"Men who don't like honest faces."

"Do you mean bushrangers?" I demanded in an eager tone.

"The traps calls 'em that," the woman said, in a significant manner.

"And what do you call them?" I asked.

"Me? I don't call 'em. I cooks for 'em, and they comes when they is ready."

"How long have you lived in this part of the country?" I asked, seeing that the woman was inclined to be unconscious of my presence.

She looked up with a start, as though suddenly recollecting that I was near her.

"How long?" she repeated, with a bitter laugh. "How should I know, when all days and months is alike to me?"

"And have you no desire to leave such a dreary place for some town, where you can see and feel that you are in the midst of civilization?"

"Why should I?" she asked, and raised her head. "Who would notice an old woman like me — one what cares only for her bottle and gin? No; I'm better off where I is, with a party of savages, than with peoples what ain't so rough."

"And when do you think those savages will return?" I demanded, with an eye to my own safety.

"Not afore night, if they do then," she replied.

"And you would not advise me to start until night?"

"Not if life is sweet to you. Did you come from Melbourne?"

"Yes; I left there day before yesterday.'

"Did you know Sam Sykes, or the man what they call the Manchester Pet?"

"Do you know Sykes?" I demanded, in an eager tone.

"Ho! don't I know the mean coward, and all about him and his tricks. He'd sell his soul or his mother for gold. Ho! I know him well enough."

"And his daughter; do you know her?"

"*His daughter!* Ho! ho! yes, I know her; Jenny is her name."

"And she is very handsome, with large blue eyes and fair skin."

The old woman looked at me with a keen eye.

"Somethin' like me, hey?"

"Rather more youthful," I replied, with a laugh; and the woman grinned a dirty smile in response.

"Is yer in love with the fair-skinned and dainty Jenny?" asked the woman, combing her hair with her fingers.

"I've seen her, and admire her," I replied.

"And what said the lass to you?"

"Nothing."

"Humph! she's a proud wench, and might do worse, although it's little she knows —"

"Have you a cave here?" I asked.

"Of course we have, or how could the men hide when they were close pushed by the traps? One of the men was home last night, but he went away arly this mornin'."

As she spoke she pushed aside the bushes. I followed close at her heels, and saw before me the entrance to a cave, but so blocked up with bushes that a person would not have noticed it, unless special attention had been called to the matter. The sides of the cave were composed of soft quartz, and as I bent my head to follow the old woman, I saw, by the aid of the sunshine, bright specks interspersed throughout the mass, which my experience told me was gold, and that the mountain or ridge on which we stood was rich with ore. I stopped for a moment to examine the quartz and the woman turned back and joined me, finding that I had not followed her into the cave.

"You're lookin' at them specks," she said. "Ho! I know where they is bigger and thicker nor that."

"And will you tell me where to find them?"

"Not now," she said. "There's too much danger in this quarter for gold-hunters."

I followed her, with a determination to clean out the bush-rangers, who infested the neighborhood, at the first opportunity, and then set Hez's quartz-crushing machines at work in the valley, where wood and water were abundant, and where I had no doubt we could crush out enough gold to make our fortunes in a year's time, or less.

The old woman led the way through a short arch, and then we emerged into a dome-shaped cell, large enough to accommodate some twenty men. It was lighted at the top through the roots of a tree, the grass and earth being removed from them for that especial purpose. The light that came from the roof and that which came from the entrance was sufficient to enable me to see all that the cave contained. There was quite a stock there. Clothes taken from miners at various times, were piled up in one corner, without regard to order or convenience, and in the next corner were stores, boxes of pickles, wines, and many things which proved that the robbers had an eye to comfort when they took the contents of some storekeeper's team, on the way to the mines.

"What do you think of this?" asked the woman, in a triumphant manner, as she noted my look of astonishment.

"There is only one thing wanting," I answered.

"Name it."

"A rear door, so that a retreat could be made in case of an attack in front."

"And do you think that Keeler is a man to forget sich a thing as that?" asked the woman, in a scornful manner.

"Keeler!" I cried, in astonishment; "do you mean to tell me that Keeler is the leader of the gang?"

"Ay, and a bold leader he is. When his name is mentioned men tremble, and the traps run like sheep."

CHAPTER XIX.

THE UNEXPECTED ARRIVAL. — THE CONCEALMENT. — IN A TIGHT PLACE.

"DID yer hear it?" asked the woman, in a whisper, with every mark of anxiety on her face, "or was I dreaming?"

"I heard a whistle," I replied. "What is the meaning of it?"

"It means that some of the gang is near at hand, and if they find yer, death is your lot."

I picked up my rifle, and examined the cap on the nipple; but the old woman noticed the movement, and whispered, "Don't offer to fight, lad. Keep quiet, and yer may yet escape."

Again the whistle sounded. This time it was nearer the mouth of the cave.

"Under the clothes with yer," cried the woman. "Yes, take yer gun with yer. Don't ye hear 'em? They is impatient for me to answer 'em, and it's a putty cussin' I'll get for not returnin' the signal." As she spoke she tore away the clothes, which had not been disturbed for some time, and motioned me to lie down.

"Some of the stuff is dirty, but divil a bit need yer care, if yer life is safe. Don't yer move a finger arter they is in the cave. Do yer mind me?"

She did not wait for me to answer, but piled the musty-smelling clothes on my person, and would have covered up my head entirely, if I had not avoided it by making a barricade with my hands, and thus left a place to breathe and see what was transpiring in the cave.

"Now, don't yer wink," the woman said, and don't yer move till I tells yer that yer may."

While she was speaking, I heard the shrill tones of a wattle bird some distance from the mouth of the cave.

"They'll bust yet, they is so rampagious. Blast 'em, I

wish they was all pizened. Now yer keep quiet, or yer throat won't be worth a sheepskin."

The latter remark was addressed to me, for she gave the clothes an energetic kick, and then took from her bosom a whistle, and sounded a shrill note. Then she left the cave, and when she reached the open air she once more applied the whistle to her lips, and blew a peculiar blast. Then all was silent for the space of five minutes; and just as I began to think that the visitors had departed, I heard masculine voices, and then two men entered the cave.

"I tell you what it is, old Molly Brown," one of the men said, — and I thought his voice sounded familiar, but I could not get a view of his face, for his back was towards me, — "if you don't leave off drinking gin, and attend to your duties a little better, we shall quarrel."

"Who do yer call old?" demanded Mrs. Brown, in a fierce manner. "And who 'spected yer at this time of the day? Didn't Ben say this mornin' that yer wouldn't be at home afore to-morrer, or the next day?"

"Yes, but you d—d old fool, Ben couldn't tell yer that the traps would push us hard, and send us to cover for a day or two."

"O," grumbled Mrs. Brown, "they is arter ye, is they?"

"Yes, and the rest of the gang will be here before long; so tear around, old woman, and get us some dinner. We are hungry as wolves. Do justice to the eating, and after we leave you may have a glorious drunk."

"Humph!" grunted the woman; "yer is a fool for talking that way. I don't get drunk, but I does drink when I feels bad at the stomach."

"Which is often," laughed the man; and as he spoke he turned his dark face to the light, and I saw the wild, ferocious eyes of the man whom I had seen in the back parlor of Webber's house.

"Look a-here, Keeler," said the woman, "yer has a good deal of jaw to-day, it seems to me. If yer wants me to get somethin' for yer to eat, just yer start to the brook and catch me some fish."

"O, Bob will go," was the reply.

"But I wants water. Here, take this bucket and get me some, and I'll make yer a cup of coffee."

Molly put the bucket close to the man's feet, but Keeler gave it a kick that sent it flying across the cave; and then I saw his dark, ugly eyes flash as he turned them upon Mrs. Brown. But Molly did not appear in the least intimidated at the threats which were uttered. She put her arms akimbo, and looked the robber chief square in the face as she asked,—

"Keeler, am I useful to yer?"

"Yes, when you hold your tongue."

"Then yer keep a civil word for me, or I'll find a way of leavin' yer. I'll not stand much of yer blasted nonsense."

The man did not answer her. Perhaps he knew that he should win no honor in an encounter of words, for at any rate he remained silent while the old woman left the cave, but in a slow and reluctant manner, as though she feared to leave me with such a savage.

"Blast her!" Keeler said to his companion, "she grows more impudent every day. Liquor is raising the devil with her mind."

"But she is still useful," remarked the other. "She knows how to cook, if she is saucy and dirty."

The two bushrangers opened a bottle of brandy, and had a drink.

I could have shot Keeler, or Bob, from the position which I occupied, but I did not want to commence hostilities until the last extremity. I thought that there was a bare chance of my escaping notice, either by the men leaving the cave, or else taking a nap. But while these thoughts were flying through my head, the confounded fleas were taking most unwarrantable liberties with my person. I did so long to squirm and commence a war of extermination on the vermin! but when I looked at the two bushrangers I restrained myself, in hope that something would turn up and relieve me. But in this respect I was disappointed; for, to add to my unpleasant position, I felt something of a more substantial nature than fleas crawling up the leg of my pantaloons, and it was only by a powerful effort that I could command my nerves and keep still.

I have already spoken of the snakes of Australia. They are numerous, and most of them of a venomous nature. As a general thing, the smaller the snake, the more poison its mouth contains. The large, anaconda-like reptiles, called black snakes, bite most ferociously; but their teeth leave no poison in the flesh; while the little copper-colored fellows, with flat heads and bright eyes, such as are found under a stump or a log, or the green and black reptiles, are deadly with their bites, and short are the days of a man who receives one. It seemed to me that the reptile which was crawling up my leg was a small snake. Keeler and Bob still sat facing each other, drinking brandy and water, and apparently enjoying themselves in a moderate way. If they would only leave the cave for a moment, I would make a bold strike for life; but the brutes did not manifest the slightest disposition to stir, and yet the reptile that was on my leg was slowly working its way upward, and would soon be unable to travel farther, and then I might expect trouble, unless I could dislodge the snake by a sudden start. But I could do nothing of the kind without meeting with a speedy death at the hands of the two bushrangers. To be sure, if I had known for a certainty that the reptile crawling up my leg was of a poisonous nature, I should have ended the suspense at once, and met my death like a man, fighting the robbers and inflicting all the damage that I was able to.

But I was hopeful of saving my life, and trusted that the reptile was harmless. Once I moved one of my hands towards the spot where the reptile was travelling, and thought of crushing the animal with a grasp of iron; but then I recollected that I should get a nip from its needle-like teeth, no matter how quick I might be in my movements. But at last Mother Brown shouted from the mouth of the cave that she wanted some help to get dinner.

"Go, and assist her, Bob," said Keeler. "She is half drunk, and needs help."

The young bushranger uttered an oath at the trouble he

was put to, and then left the cave. Keeler turned aside, and commenced removing the earth from one corner of the cave — a place which was covered with boxes. He dug patiently and rapidly for a moment, stopping every two or three seconds to listen to the movements outside, as though fearful of being interrupted; but at last, with much care and some agitation, he drew out a tin box, removed the lid, and his eyes appeared to see something that was extremely gratifying, for a smile spread over the man's dark face, and I saw him thrust in his hand, and remove from the box several bags. He balanced them in his hand, as though to judge if any of the contents had been removed; and after he had gone through with six or eight bags, I heard him mutter, —

"No one has disturbed them — no one knows my secret. A few more captures and I shall have enough to live on in a distant part of the world, if I can make my escape from this country. You go with the rest."

He took from his breast a bag, such as the miners put their fine gold in, and put it in the box, closed the lid, and was about to lay it away in its former resting-place, when Mother Brown, who, I suppose, felt a little anxious about me, entered the cave most unexpectedly. Keeler turned and saw her, and his face assumed an expression of rage.

"What do you want here?" he demanded, in a fierce tone.

"And what should I want," Mother Brown asked, noways abashed or intimidated, "but the bread for the soup?"

"Take it and go, then!"

Mrs. Brown cast an anxious look towards the clothes under which I was concealed, laid her finger on her lips, and then left the cave.

"Curse her! does she suspect what I have here?" Keeler muttered, as he commenced covering the box with earth.

Just at that instant the reptile which was on my leg began to manifest signs of uneasiness, and I could feel its feet as they touched my flesh, even through the flannel drawers which I had on. It seemed as though I should take leave of my senses, I was so nervous and fearful of a fatal termination; and at last I could endure no more. I threw off the clothes, and stood upon my feet. Keeler did not hear my movements. I did not care so much for the bushranger as I did for the reptile, for I was desperate. I stepped upon the hard floor of the cave, and gave my pantaloons a shake; and I had to bite my lips to prevent a cry from escaping them, when I felt something slide down my leg and touch the floor. As the reptile came in sight, I saw that, instead of a snake, I had been frightened at a harmless little house lizard. I uttered a sigh of relief, and that sigh was so heartfelt that it attracted attention. Keeler heard it, and turned, and saw me not ten feet from him.

CHAPTER XX.

FACE TO FACE. — THE STRUGGLE. — THE COMPACT. — THE SURPRISE. — "DEATH TO THE SPY."

I JUST stepped back a few paces, and levelled my revolver. Luckily for me, Keeler had laid aside his fire-arms when he entered the cave. So now I had him at a great disadvantage, and he knew it; for he made a motion for me to lower my pistol, and then asked, in a subdued tone, "Where did you come from?"

"I came through there," I replied, and nodded towards the arch, or entrance.

"And your friends, the traps, where are they?" demanded Keeler, whose voice trembled in spite of his attempts to conceal his agitation.

"You speak too loud," I said, and once more raised the pistol, and pointed it full at his breast.

The man cowered before me, and put up his hands in an imploring position.

"Don't fire," he said, "and I will speak as softly as you

please;" but even while he spoke, I could see the treacherous eyes of the fellow glancing in every direction, as though in search of weapons, or some means of turning the tables upon me.

"We have met before, Keeler," I said.

"Yes, at Webber's."

"You remember me, do you?"

"Yes, for I knew you suspected me at the time I was on the floor pretending to sleep."

"You are right — I did suspect you."

"And why didn't you arrest me at the time I expected it."

"Because I'm not a trap."

The fellow's face assumed a less sullen aspect.

"Then you're on the detective game?"

"No, I'm not. I never belonged to the police department."

"Then how came you here, and how did it happen that you were with the police?"

"I started with the commissioner for the sake of company, to see the country, and see if I could not prospect a little. While the police were in pursuit of you, I got lost, and wandered around until I found this place, but with no intention of meeting you."

"Is that a true statement?" and Keeler looked honest as he asked the question.

"It is."

"Then there is no occasion for us to be at war. Come, let us shake hands and be friends."

He advanced towards me with extended hand, and with such a look of confidence that I lowered my weapon and prepared to shake hands with him; but just as I reached out to do so, the rascal gave my revolver a kick with his foot, and sent it spinning across the cave, and at the same time he threw himself upon me, both hands around my throat as though to garrote me; and he would have done so if I had not possessed sinews of steel, and strength that belied my slight frame. I was rather small but what there was of me was like iron.

"You d—d spy!" he cried, as his hands met my neck, "I'll choke the life out of you."

I made no reply.

"You thought you had tracked the lion, did you?" asked the bushranger, in a sneering manner.

"Jackal, more like," I responded, in a contemptuous tone, for the purpose of exciting his rage, and letting it consume his strength.

"Then I'll eat you, jackal that I am," Keeler cried, and immediately compressed my neck with renewed force.

There was a brief struggle, during which I managed to release one of his hands from its clutch upon my throat, and as I did so, I obtained a firm hold upon his sinewy neck with one hand, while I wreathed the other in his long black hair, coarse and thick.

"D—n you! let go my hair," Keeler yelled, for I had given it an extra wrench while we were struggling.

I made no answer, except by a savage shake, that made him wink. He threw his left arm around my waist, so that we were thus brought side to side — a position in wrestling that rather suited me, for I was accustomed to it, and knew that my agility would nearly, if not quite, counterbalance his terrible strength, even if he exerted it to the utmost, as I had no doubt that he would.

"Now I have you," panted the bushranger, and with a sudden jerk he thought to throw me over his head; but I caught one of my feet around his leg, gave it a twist, and the fellow found that his strength was useless, for while he sought to accomplish his purpose by the most stupendous exertion, he soon saw that his object could not be carried out unless one of his own legs should give way.

All this time I was intent on the man's motions, and I soon saw that he meditated a new trick, and one which I instantly prepared for. While the man was straining and striving to throw me over his head, I felt a slight relaxation of his muscles. It was sudden, so I knew that the bushranger was prepared for the last dodge in his list of tricks; and just as the fellow thought he had me, I gave him a sudden jerk that sent him headlong upon the ground, and I landed on the top of him, much to his surprise and my own satisfaction.

"D—n you! how did you do that?" Keeler asked, after a fierce struggle, in which he found it was impossible to rise.

"O, it was a trick of mine," I replied, improving the opportunity to get a little breath, which I needed, although I concealed the want of it to the utmost.

"Let me up and try that over again," Keeler said. "I'll bet that you can't do it again."

"No, I'm satisfied with what I have done. I have you here in my power, and I can soon end your career if I were disposed to."

"How?"

"You see that I have a knife at my side."

"Yes, I see."

"And I can use it."

The man made a powerful effort to rise, but I held him fast.

"You see that I can kill you at any time," I said.

"D—n you! yes," was the answer.

"And do you think I will?"

"I know what I should do!" and the fellow ground his teeth together.

"What?"

"Kill you." The man looked as though capable of it.

"I know you would, and now you see that I shall return good for evil. I do not intend to injure you, but I mean that you shall listen to me."

"Perhaps I should rather be killed than hear a lecture."

The rascal had a species of grim humor that was rather captivating, and I liked him all the better for it.

"You shall see," I continued. "In the first place, I am here by accident, and not as a spy. Do you comprehend that?"

"O, yes; drive on, for you are hurting my back."

"In the next place, I want to leave the cell, and have the promise of a safe journey to the Lodden."

"Where you can inform the traps of our cave."

"I shall do no such thing. I pledge my word that, if I have a free pass to the Lodden, I will not use the information that I possess. Are you satisfied?"

"Of course I am. Your word is good for that. Now let me up."

"In one moment. Will you promise to allow me a free passage to the river?"

"Yes, and glad to get rid of you. I will shake hands on the contract if you will release me."

I did so. The bushranger slowly arose, stretched his limbs, and then glanced at me. I met his gaze without flinching.

"Come in, Bob," the bushranger said, speaking to his companion, who seemed to have entered the cave.

I turned to look at the man, and that act was an imprudence, for the treacherous rascal threw himself upon me, dashed me to the floor, and then shouted for his comrade. He had played me a bushranger's trick, but it was one that I could not have avoided.

"You fool," he said, when he found that I was too much bruised to struggle or contend with him, "did you suppose for a moment that I intended to release you, so that you could bring a cloud of traps down upon us? You must have thought that I was precious green."

Keeler raised his voice, and shouted, "Bob, come here, and see what I have got."

But no Bob answered to the call; so Keeler was forced to hold me and talk to me; and yet I could read in the man's eye that he was somewhat apprehensive that I would defeat him.

"This time you walked into a hornet's nest, my young spy," Keeler said. "You will go out in a different manner from that in which you came in."

"But remember your promise," I replied. "I had your life at my disposal at one time. Now you have mine at your command. Be as generous as I was. Recollect that I have never done you harm, except when I threw you, a few minutes since."

"You threw me by a foul trick," cried the bushranger, giving me a savage shake for reminding him of his humiliation. "You could not do it by a fair hold."

"Let me up, and we'll see," I answered. "I'll give you a fair trial if you dare take one."

Keeler uttered a savage oath.

"Then you have really made up your mind to kill me?" I asked, in as cool a tone as I could command, at the same time attempting to move one of my arms so that I could gain possession of my bowie-knife, which I still had about my person.

"Swift and sure is a bushranger's vengeance," Keeler replied, and blocked my game in moving my arm. He pinned it to my side, and grinned in a sarcastic manner as he did so.

"No, you don't!" he cried; "I am too old to be taken in that way."

Once more Keeler called to his comrade, and I heard him enter the cave, followed by Mother Brown.

"What's the row?" asked Bob, stopping a few paces from us, and shading his eyes, so as to accustom them to the light. He could not see us at first.

"I've caught a spy," Keeler answered. "Find a pair of bracelets for his hands, and a cord for his feet. Look alive."

"How in the devil's name did he come here?" asked Bob.

"O, he walked in while you were off for water. I didn't see him till he held a pistol at my head."

"Marcy on us!" cried Mrs. Brown, with well-feigned alarm; "we shall all be murdered in our beds."

"Find the bracelets," said Keeler, "and put them on, so that I can get dinner. I've had a tussle with this fellow, and need a little rest."

"I'm arter 'em sharp," replied Bob; and just at that moment he pulled out a pair of rusty handcuffs from one corner of the cave, and came towards us. "Here they is," he said. "They hasn't been used since we put them on that spy purliceman the day afore we shot him."

"And here is another one of the same sort," returned Keeler. "You know I told you of a sharp-looking chap who was with the police?"

"Yes."

"Well, this is the one. He has tracked us to this place. He is a spy, but he will never cross another bushranger's trail."

"I should think not," responded Bob; and stooping down, he raised one of my hands for the purpose of slipping the handcuffs on it. I saw Mother Brown seize an axe which she had in her hand, and with which she had been splitting wood, as though she was determined to give me freedom by smashing the head of one of the villains, thinking that I could take care of the second one; but just as she was prepared to shed blood, a signal outside of the cave announced the near approach of the remainder of the gang.

Keeler heard it as soon as I, for he turned to Mother Brown, little thinking how near he had escaped certain death, and said, "Answer the signal, and tell the boys to hurry up. I have captured a prize for them."

Mother Brown laid her finger on her lips in a significant manner, as though cautioning me to be silent, and left the cave.

"Now, then, my beauty, jist put yer dawley in this 'ere ornament, and then you'll be all right and comfortable. Come, don't be backward, 'cos you must come to it. It is a honor we allers pay to gentlemen what visits us for the purpose of noting our actions."

As Bob spoke I saw that it was useless to struggle. The bushrangers had me in their power, and could do as they pleased. I let them put on the bracelets without resistance; and after they were on Keeler no longer feared me. He suffered me to stand up, and even sit down; but he took good care to deprive me of the last weapon that I possessed. My revolver, especially, was of great value to the fellow, and he stuck it in his belt with infinite zest and satisfaction, while Bob adorned his person with my knife and belt; and after that they took a drink together, and had hardly concluded when six ill-favored, dirty, long-haired, and bloody-minded bushrangers stalked into the cave and deposited their guns and pistols on the heap of clothing,

"By G—d, we've had a run for it," one swarthy ruffian said, wiping his face with his shirt sleeve. "We got the signal just in time, for as we crossed the South Ford we saw the cussed traps stealing through the woods. They didn't sight us, though, and now here we is. Give us some rum, Mother Brown."

The ruffians had not noticed me; but now, after their eyes got accustomed to the light of the cave, they saw me for the first time, and crowded around me, forgetting, for the time being, their love for gin.

"What is he?" demanded the most ill-favored of the ruffians.

"A spy!" replied Keeler.

Every hand was laid on a knife, and every knife was drawn and pointed at me.

"Death to the spy!" was the cry. "Kill him! kill him! Death to the spy!"

Keeler struck up the knives, and waved the men back.

"He is my prisoner," the chief said. "I have a word to say as to the manner in which he shall die."

"Death to the spy!" the sullen bushrangers continued to cry.

"He shall die, men," Keeler said, "but wait until after dinner."

"Yes, let us have some grub first," and just then Mother Brown entered the cave, and announced that dinner was ready.

CHAPTER XXI.

MOTHER BROWN AND HER FRIENDSHIP. — THE DISGUISE. — AN ATTEMPT TO ESCAPE.

Thank God, the bushrangers were as hungry a set of men as could be found in Australia; therefore they did not need a second invitation at the hands of Mother Brown. They rushed out of the cave, and left me alone, the rascals thinking that it was not necessary to leave a guard to look after me, as I could not quit the cave without passing through the gang, most of them being seated at the entrance of the retreat. I heard the robbers, when they gained the open air gather around the respected Mrs. Brown, and express some little indignation because their dinner was not just ready, although the lady had said it was prepared. It was not taken from the fire. And when one public-spirited individual suggested that the gentlemen present could amuse themselves by hanging "that d—d spy" before grub was ready, I feared that the proposition would meet with universal favor; and perhaps it would have done so if Mrs. Brown had not raised her voice in opposition to the project, and when she spoke she talked plain.

"Look a-here, yer rascals," she said; "I ain't goin' to spile my taters and fish to please yer. They is all done, and now yer jist git yer tin plates and squat down. I'll sarve yer."

"But you said that dinner was all ready, Mother Brown," Keeler remarked.

"No, sir, not by a d—d sight," the strong-minded female replied. "I'se got some bitters for yer afore yer takes the wittles."

Suddenly I heard Mrs. Brown's footsteps as she entered the cave. She grumbled all the way through the arch; but the instant that she saw me she ceased her complaints, and whispered, —

"Keep up yer spirits, lad, and I'll do all I can for yer,

'cos yer look jist like my Bobby. They shan't kill yer if I can help it. I wants yer for to live, and marry the blue-eyed Jenny."

She did not have time to utter more, for one of the bushrangers entered the cave, and the old woman left me abruptly, and occupied herself with some bottles which contained different kinds of liquors. The fellow who had followed her in happened to be the sullen-looking bushranger, and the most bloodthirsty of the lot. I don't know but that he was a little suspicious that some collusion was taking place between Mrs. Brown and myself; for he glanced at us in a threatening manner, and then rejoined his comrades outside.

"He's a wiper," whispered the old woman. "I'd like to pizen him."

"And why don't you?"

"'Cos I ain't got no pizen," was the satisfactory answer; and then Mrs. Brown continued to mix her liquors in silence, and after she had concluded, she listened for a moment, found that her amiable companions were all outside, talking of their adventures and escapes, when she cautiously approached me, and whispered, —

"Take a sup of this, honey. It will do yer good."

I just wet my lips with the liquor, which contained sugar in large quantities; and then the woman said, "I'll stand by yer, 'cos yer look jist like my poor Bobby. Them pizen things shan't cut yer wizzen if I can help it. Do yer keep yer weather eye open, that's all."

Her condition must have been remarked the instant that she hove in sight; for one of the brutes, in the most unfeeling manner, roared out, "Hello, Mother Brown! drunk again, and afore we has had our dinner."

All of this the woman denied in most emphatic terms, and while she was thus waging a war of words, she served out the dinner; and then I could hear the men discussing it with infinite relish, like hungry men that they were. I knew that Mrs. Brown was plying them with liquor, and that they drank large quantities of it; but at last she said she must enter the cave, and obtain more.

"Well, don't be all day about it," Keeler said; and in she came, headed towards me, and whispered, "I'll save yer, never fear. Here, hold out yer hands?"

I did so, and she immediately commenced operating on the bracelets; and so smart did she work that she managed to free my wrists, although she swayed dreadfully while about it.

"Now, my dear boy, take yer gun and run for it," she whispered; and as she spoke she made a lurch to port, and would have fallen if I had not caught her and steadied her.

"It's a corn that I have on my foot," she remarked, as an apology for the manner in which she staggered round. "It allers made me walk lame, and it allers will. Sometimes it is wuss than at other times. This is one of the wusser days."

She stooped down to show me the offending excrescent; but, in attempting to lift her dress, she made a plunge forward, and fell upon the pile of clothing under which I had been concealed. She was very drunk, but still she would not own it.

"It's wery troublesome, to-day," she whispered; and then she laid her head upon the clothes, and seemed to be making preparations for sleep, much to my surprise and horror; for I thought that my chances of escape were dull unless I had her assistance. She closed her eyes, and I thought she was about to snore; so for fear that she should, I seized her arm, and shook her rather vigorously.

"Wal," she asked, opening her eyes with a stupid stare, "what is it?"

I could still hear the bushrangers cracking their jokes, and eating their dinner, and I knew that time was precious.

"Come," I whispered, "I thought that you intended to assist me to escape."

She hiccoughed several times, and then stooped down and rubbed her foot in a thoughtful manner, as though to take time and collect what little sense she had left.

"It's wery troublesome to-day," she muttered. "I should think that we was in for a rain. It allers aches when there's a rain."

I once more gave her a shake, and it seemed to do her good; for she passed her very dirty and hard-looking hand over her eyes, and slipped off the pile of clothing.

"I 'members all about it," she muttered. "You wants to cut from this place. You're jist like my own Bobby, and you shall clear. If you don't," the woman continued, after a moment's thought, "them 'ere cusses will rip yer threat open, and think nothin' of it. So, to save your life, I must make a scarafice."

"Why can't I escape by the concealed passage-way," I asked; and I pointed to the place where it was.

The old woman shook her head. "A thafe is watchin' it, and he'd shoot you like smoke if ye stirred that way."

Drunk as the woman was, she noticed the change in my face, and hastened to cheer me.

"I'll save yer yet," she whispered. "We can cheat the divils in more ways than one. Here, see me."

The woman was a terrible spectacle; for she stood before me with only one garment upon her back, and that was of such a color that no man could have told what it was.

"Now then, on with 'em," she said, and pointed to the two articles which she had shed, apparently, by a shake of her person.

"Do you mean that I must on those clothes?" I asked.

"Of course I do. Don't stand there chattering all day about it, or the divils will come in and see me in this terrible state. It's to save yer life I do it."

She made a pitch forward, but I caught her and stood her on her feet once more.

"It's the corn," she whispered; "it aches wuss than ever."

During all this time I could hear the bushrangers drinking and eating, and even cracking their jokes at my expense.

"You hear 'em?" asked Mrs. Brown, with a leer and a drunken hiccough.

"Yes."

"Well, I must save yer for the blue-eyed gal's sake. She'll thank me for what I've done."

She muttered something about the rascality of Sykes and I had to shake her a little to restore her to consciousness.

"Put 'em on," she said, as soon as she was restored. "Put 'em on, or the divils will hang ye. Put 'em on, and pass out of the cave, and no one will notice but yer is old Mother Brown."

I looked at the garments with a feeling of disgust. Mrs. Brown noticed it.

"Ye needn't turn up yer nose at the gown. It's a good gown, and will cover yer up. On with it. It's the only way for yer to cut. I tell yer it is worth some risk; now, mind me."

"But what will they do with you?"

"Never you mind me; I can take care of myself. They won't trouble me; I'd tear their hair out if they did."

I secured the petticoat around my waist, and got my arms in the dress; how it was done I don't know.

"Now mind yer," said Mrs. Brown, "yer must walk jist like me—as lady-like as possible."

She started to cross the cave, but her walk was far from lady-like, unless reeling is a lady-like accomplishment.

"Do that," she whispered, "and take no notice of the thieves. If they talk to yer, don't yer answer 'em, but groan, and put yer hand on yer belly this way, and then steer for the brook with a pail in yer hand, as though yer were arter water."

"In what direction shall I go to steer clear of the bush-rangers who are on the watch?"

"Sure I was about to tell yer that. When yer reach the stream, cross it, and stick close by the edge of the woods. But mind that yer keep out of sight, for there'll be thieves lookin' for yer from every high peak between this and the Lodden. Do yer understand me?"

"Yes."

"Well, then, go, and may the blessin' of old Mother Brown go with yer. It's a bold push I make to save yer life."

The wretches outside had just about finished their dinner,

and were washing it down with liberal libations of liquor, when I appeared.

"Hullo, old lady," shouted one of the men, "what have you been doing with the spy?"

"Making love to him, to be sure," answered Bob; and at this there was a shout, as though something witty had been uttered.

I knew that the old woman would not submit to such an imputation without some remonstrance, so I aimed a playful blow at his head with the bucket, but the young joker dodged me, and put his finger to his nose.

"No, you don't, Mother Brown. I am on the lookout for your back licks; you can't come it."

"Mother Brown is in a ferocious mood," said Keeler.

"Now," I thought, "is my time for an escape."

I had not proceeded far when I heard footsteps behind me. I tried to walk slow, and to show no signs of uneasiness; but when I recollected that I had no weapons for defence, that not even a knife was left me, I must confess that I did not think I could offer much resistance in case I was commanded to return. But I swaggered on, still grasping the bucket, and determined to smash the head of any man who insisted on my return to the cave. The footsteps behind me drew near. I did not turn my head, but I listened most intently, and wondered what the devil the fellow wanted; and just before I reached the foot of the mountain I felt a hand laid on my shoulder, and Bob's voice whispered,—

"Mother Brown, let me make you a present."

I turned and saw the muzzle of my own pistol pointed at my head, and Bob's face looked threatening as he glanced at me under my sun-bonnet. I feared that all was lost—that escape was no longer possible.

CHAPTER XXII.

AN OLD ACQUAINTANCE. — THE PURSUIT. — BUSHRANGERS AND THEIR CONSCIENCES.

As I looked the young bushranger full in the eye, I saw at once that he did not appear very ferocious, or seem very determined, and on taking a second glance I found that my revolver was not pointed square at my head, as I first supposed, so that if he had fired, no great injury would have been done.

"Don't be in a hurry, Mrs. Brown," continued Bob, walking by my side, and attempting to keep step with me, as though he had seen something of military life. "You have time enough to get the water. The day is hot, and I fear you will suffer."

I still pretended to be half drunk, but Bob laid a hand on my arm as if for the purpose of steadying me, and as he did so, he said, —

"Don't attempt to walk so fast, Mrs. Brown. I fear that our friends will think you want to leave them. They might bring you back if such was the case. Keep step with me, and don't be so eager. You are either not drunk enough, or too drunk. Which is the case?"

"What in the devil do you mean?" I demanded, turning on the man and speaking in my natural tone.

He did not manifest the least surprise at the question, but continued to walk by my side.

"I mean," he said, "that if you were so drunk that you had to lay down like a hog, no one would come near you. When half drunk, people offer advice, and are sometimes intrusive. Do you understand me?"

"I think I do."

"Then I hope you will profit by it; for it would be awkward if Keeler should think that his vengeance was not likely to be gratified."

"The fact of it is," I said, "you know me, and would do me a good turn. I thank you for it, and hope to be able to reciprocate some time."

"Of course I know you, Mother Brown. We have been together for some years. You may have forgotten me, but your features are quite familiar to me." I bowed, and walked a little more straight.

"I suppose you remember some years since, Mrs. Brown," continued the bushranger, "a soldier of the English army, stationed at Ballarat, was imprudent enough to get drunk and leave his post. A few paces from the point where he was stationed, two Americans owned a store."

I stole a look at the speaker's face, and began to entertain an idea that I had seen it before.

"Most people would have left the soldier to suffer the penalty of his crime; but not so the Americans. They saw that the soldier had been imprudent, and that he could be saved the penalty of his offence with a little trouble on their part; so they seized on the unlucky dog, stripped him, drenched him with cold water, and then gave him an emetic for the purpose of clearing his stomach of the liquor which it contained. The soldier was awful sick for a few minutes, but the cure was rapid; and before his comrades or officers knew that he had left his post, or had indulged in liquor, he was back to it, with his musket to his shoulder, pacing his rounds."

"I recollect the circumstance," I said; and then I added, with a smile, "if I mistake not, the soldier had to be relieved from his post on account of sickness."

"Yes; but his back was saved from the touch of the cat. I have always recollected the affair, and determined to repay the debt if it was in my power. You see I have gratitude, even if I do belong to a desperate gang. Hold on; not so fast," my companion continued, as I strode forward, anxious to put a wide space between the bushrangers and myself. "Mrs. Brown does not usually exert herself in such a manner. There may be sharp eyes on your movements. Who can tell?"

I checked my pace, and the young fellow continued, still speaking as though I was Mrs. Brown: "You may wonder that I am here; but when I tell you that I struck my commanding officer, and was forced to fly or be shot, you will cease to be astonished. I wish I was out of it; but how can I leave when a price is set upon my head?"

"Perhaps a pardon might be obtained," I suggested.

"Now you are laughing at me, Mother Brown. Bushrangers are not often pardoned."

"I don't know but you might obtain the favor if proper representations were made at headquarters." The young fellow shook his head.

"My crimes are too numerous for such clemency; so don't attempt to inspire me with such hope as that. I must see the thing through, now that I have started."

"But suppose a bold, enterprising young fellow should some day conclude that it would be for his welfare to hand Keeler over to the mercies of the authorities. Such a man could make terms."

"Damnation! Do you think I would commit so mean an act? I can steal, but I can't turn traitor. No, no, Mother Brown, I'll never betray Keeler, for he has proved true to me."

By this time we had arrived at the brook. I looked back, and saw my escape had not yet been noticed.

"We must part here," the young bushranger continued. "Cross this brook, make for yonder woods, keep near the edge, and don't show yourself until after you have passed the bluff which you see on my right. A lookout is stationed there, and he might see you if you crossed the valley near him. Follow the edge of the wood for ten miles, then strike the brook, and it will take you to the Lodden. Once there, you will know how to look out for yourself."

"But do you encounter no danger in thus assisting me? Recollect that your friends will be enraged when they find me gone."

"I'll risk the consequences. No one suspected that you were dressed in Mother Brown's clothes, and I don't know how it happens that you have them on; but I'll risk but that she will clear her skirts, even if she has lost them."

"And how did you discover me?" I asked.

"I did not until I caught a slight view of your face. None of the others noticed you, for your make-up is good"

"Can't I persuade you to leave with me?"

The bushranger shook his head.

"I must stick to Keeler," he said. "I wish I was clear of the business; but I can't see how I can leave. If I could quit the country, I would jump at the chance. But it is useless to repine. Good by. Take your pistol with you; I stole it from Keeler. It will do you more good than him."

He extended his hand, and I shook it most heartily, then threw down the bucket, pulled my skirts up, and with a strong jump cleared the stream, plunged into the tall grass, —so high that it concealed my head when I stooped a little,— and commenced working my way towards the woods. Many times I glanced back and took a survey of the bushrangers; but my absence was not discovered until after Bob had joined them. Then I heard a shout, and saw that Mother Brown, with nothing on but—well, the article that I left on her back—a scant piece of clothing, was out of the cave, and surrounded by excited, disappointed bushrangers. For a few minutes I paused and looked back, listening to their angry voices; for the air was so pure, and the valley so quiet, that I could hear most of the shouting. I saw the men shake their fists at the woman as they surrounded her; but she met them defiantly, and did not appear to shrink from the responsibility which she had incurred.

"Where is the prisoner?" I could hear them roar.

I glanced at the heavens. In one hour the sun would set, and darkness would cover the valley. I had no fear of being taken in the night time; so when the bushrangers ran down the side of the mountain towards the brook, the spot where I was last seen, I turned and entered the woods in a leisurely manner, and commenced my journey towards the Lodden.

But the bushrangers were better woodsmen than I had anticipated. They struck my trail, and followed on through the tall grass; but on entering the Black Forest they found themselves at fault. My footprints could not be easily seen or marked; so the rascals were compelled to follow me at a slow pace, while I pushed on as rapidly as possible; and just at dusk, when it was impossible to distinguish a man from a kangaroo ten rods off, I entered the valley, struck the little stream that meandered through it, took a hearty pull at its waters, and then continued my journey until I found that I had struck dangerous ground; for on every side of me, as I advanced, I could hear the hiss of a snake, or the peculiar noise which the reptiles make when wiggling through dried grass. They were on their way to the brook, either to quench their thirst or to seek for food.

On I went, stumbling over uneven ground, scrambling out of bog-holes, and starting wild dogs from their prey; and at last, just as I thought I should have to give up and rest until daylight, I stumbled against a fence. "Thank God," I muttered, "I am once more near civilization." I climbed over the fence, and walked forward. I found that I was on cultivated land; that trees were set out with some order and regularity; and at last I concluded that I was in an orchard of some kind, and, consequently, could not be far from a farm-house and the Lodden. I walked cautiously forward, expecting every moment to catch a glimpse of a house and outbuildings. I was not disappointed, for through the trees I saw a white building, covered with paint or whitewash; and the instant I caught sight of it a dog seemed to have noticed me; for I heard an angry growl, a deep, loud bay, and then a brute came rushing towards me, as though desirous of making a meal of my precious carcass.

CHAPTER XXIII.

A POOR SHOT. — A FREED FUGITIVE. — AN OLD FRIEND. — THE KISS OF WELCOME.

I THOUGHT what I should do to save my life. If I made a fight it was extremely probable that I should come off second best, for there were at least seven or eight dogs, and I only had six shots in my revolver; and in the hurry of firing I could not kill at every shot, and a miss was death. I thought of all these things in a calm manner, while the dogs were yelling and searching for me; but while I thought I acted, for through the gloom I saw a huge brute leading the pack, bounding along at a pace that proved to me how little show I should have if I attempted to run away, or trusted to my legs for safety. "Ow! ow!" howled the leader of the pack; and the others repeated the cry, and caught sight of me at the same time.

The music they made just at that moment was far from agreeable, and it accelerated my motions. I made a spring for a branch just over my head, and landed in the crotch of the tree. I was none too soon, for the hound which I had noticed made the most savage noise, gave a spring after me, and came very near taking a bite at one of my legs, and all the others followed his example; but I ascended the tree a little higher, and was safe.

There were nine dogs, four of them hounds, and the others mastiffs, all large and all savage; so, when I looked down at them, and spoke to them, the rage which they expressed was fearful. But there was one dog that did not manifest such a desire to tear me to pieces after the first wild spring. It was the huge stag-hound that had led the way towards the spot where I stood, and had made the wild spring at one of my feet. This dog seemed to act very strangely. He sat on his haunches at the foot of the tree, looking up at me, his head on one side, as though he did not hear very perfectly, and wanted a little prompting; and although the rest of the dogs did not relent in their expressions of hostility, this old fellow paid no attention to them, but glanced at me, and even wagged his tail, rather slightly, however, as though not over-confident in his anticipations. After I was securely perched in the top of the tree, — not a high one by any means, — I amused myself by talking with the dogs; but the more I talked, the more enraged the brutes grew, with the single exception of the stately old hound, who uttered subdued growls, stood on his hind legs, and snuffed at my feet, or near as he could reach them. At last the noble animal seemed to be wearied with the continual noise which was heard on all sides; so with a quiet dignity, which was somewhat unexpected, he turned upon his companions, gave two or three of them a severe shaking, and that started the rest in full retreat, although about two rods from the tree they stopped and uttered a chorus of howls at such treatment.

"Why, old dog, what is the matter with you?" I asked. "Do you want to eat me alone? For shame, at such greediness. My old dog Rover would not have served me in that manner. He was a sensible animal, and knew a friend from a foe."

While I was speaking, the animal at the foot of the tree appeared to listen most intently, as though each word that I uttered was of value, and when I had concluded, the brute seemed frantic with rage, or some other feeling, and jumped round the tree in the most astonishing manner, and once or twice I feared that he would find a lodgment in the forks of the tree. But the noise which the dogs made began to attract attention, as I supposed it would. I could see, through the trees, lights flash from the windows of the house, as though the people who inhabited it were alarmed, and about to commence an investigation; and after a short time I heard voices, and then some one took aim at the tops of the trees, and fired a musket. The ball with which the gun was loaded, tore through the branches, and whizzed within a rod of my head, much to my disgust. The dogs yelled with delight at the sound of the gun, and pressed towards my retreat; but the hound, which still remained near me, turned upon them, and drove them back in a savage manner, and lay down at the trunk of the tree, and seemed to wait for further developments. I heard men moving near the house, and I listened to hear what they had to say for themselves.

They were discussing the best means of finding out how the noise originated. I had half a mind to shout for assistance, and make an explanation of my presence; but when I recollected that it would take some time and trouble to clear up matters and prove that I was an honest man, I gave up the attempt, and waited for daylight—and I did not have long to wait, for from the east came a flood of light that gradually rendered objects more and more distinct, until at last I could see house and outbuildings, dogs, and other domesticated animals. The dogs were still near me, silent and sullen, as though perfectly contented to bide their time.

The huge hound lay at the foot of the tree, looking at me with a wishful glance, and wagging his tail every time I moved. The rest of the pack kept at a respectful distance. I heard no more voices until nearly sunrise, and then men assembled in front of the house, and talked over what had occurred an hour or two previous. Two of them still insisted that bushrangers were lurking near, and one of them, to test the matter, came towards the tree upon which I roosted, but in a sly manner. The dogs went to meet him, with the exception of the hound, which stuck to me. I had a good chance to look at the fellow as he came towards me with a gun in his hand. He was a thick-headed Englishman, stout and brawny, with about as much intelligence in his face as a well-trained monkey. When the fellow had arrived within a rod or two of me, I said, "Hello, you, sir!"

The clown started, looked up at the tree, and before I could add another word, he raised his gun and fired. The buckshot with which it was loaded whistled near my head, cut off a limb or two, a handful of leaves, but left me uninjured. The fellow, luckily for me, shut his eyes when he pulled the trigger, and thus I escaped. The clown did not stop to see what damage he had done, for he turned abruptly, ran towards the house, and yelled, "I've killed a bushranger! I've killed a bushranger!"

"Are you sure that he's dead?" asked a voice which seemed familiar to me, although I could not imagine where I had heard it, though I tried to recollect.

"O, dom, I seed him tumble down jist like a calf. I dropped him. But come and see for yerself."

So I could hear the household making preparations for testing the truth of the man's statement. The women declared they would not go, and that the men should not move, and then instantly changed their minds, as a matter of course, and declared that they would not stay behind and be murdered by the rascally bushrangers.

"O, but I killed him dead, mum," cried the confident Joe; and then I heard them approach the tree upon which I was perched. If the dogs had not been within a short distance of me, I would have slid down and run, for I did not want to disgrace the too confiding Joe. But there was no help for it. I must meet the man, and incur his hostility, just because I did not fall when he aimed at me.

"Come on," shouted the valiant Joe. "Here's the body jist at the fut of the tree."

"I think you are mistaken," I remarked; and the instant that I spoke the party uttered a scream, — at least the women did, — and turned towards the house.

"The man's alive," groaned the person whom I took to be the owner of the farm.

"No, dom it, it's another of the villains. I'll hit him. The fust one is down, and the second one soon will be."

"Hold on for one moment," I shouted. "Come near me, and see that I'm no bushranger. Here, look up into the tree."

"How many of you are there in the tree?" asked the leader of the party.

"I'm alone."

"Do you speak the truth?" asked one of the ladies, with a glance at the house as though half inclined to run.

"Do you think I would deceive so amiable a lady as yourself?" I asked.

That little speech settled her business most completely.

"I don't think he's a bad man," the woman remarked to her husband. "Let us go and talk with him. See, the dear old hound does not manifest the least sign of anger."

"Come down," said the farmer, whose voice sounded familiar.

"Call off your dogs, and I will," I answered.

The dogs were called from the trunk of the tree and driven away, and then I descended with as much dignity as I could, considering there were two ladies watching all my movements, and commenting on them. Mother Brown's outer garment was on my head, where I had kept it for the purpose of keeping mosquitos at bay; consequently my face was not seen until I touched the ground; and when I did, the huge hound, whose attention had been marked, made a spring for my neck; and such was his impetuosity, that I was thrown down, and expected to have my flesh torn in a terrible manner; but instead of such treatment, the animal licked my face and hands, and seemed overjoyed to see me.

"Rover, come here," shouted the farmer. "The dog will kill the poor fellow."

At the sound of that name I recollected in an instant the reason of the dog's extraordinary behavior. The animal knew me much better than I did him, and even in the dark he had recognized my voice, although we had not met for several years. At length I was enabled to gain my feet and look around. I saw that the ladies were somewhat surprised at what had passed, and that the bluff, farmer-like person who led the party was staring at me with two gray eyes extended to their utmost dimensions.

"Is it possible?" yelled the yellow-haired, freckled-faced farmer, his eyes rolling as though their owner was in danger of expiring in a fit.

"Husband!" shrieked the lady; "O, what is the matter?"

"Jack!" cried the farmer, with outstretched hand. He smiled as he spoke, and then I knew him.

"Smith!" I exclaimed, and rushed towards him.

The farmer threw his arms around me, pressed me to his heart, raised me from the ground, and then suddenly dropped me, and rushed towards his wife. Seizing her hand, he dragged her towards me, much to the poor woman's surprise, while her companion appeared to regard Smith in the light of a jolly lunatic.

"Wife," cried the enthusiastic Smith, placing her directly in front of me, "put your arms around this gentleman's neck and kiss him."

The poor woman looked a little startled at such a command, and began to think that her husband was hopelessly insane.

"Kiss him," roared Smith.

"But, husband," the wife said, "only think what you are asking me to do."

"Wife," cried the farmer, "you have heard me say that to two Americans I owe all my happiness, all my property, even my life. This is one of the men. Now will you kiss him?"

The woman, with a most grateful look, threw her arms around my neck and kissed me on each cheek. As she was a good-looking woman I just retaliated by kissing her on her lips, and then released her.

"Kiss the other one — my wife's sister," cried Smith.

I had no objections, not in the least, for the girl was a splendid specimen of English blood, with blue eyes, brown hair, clear skin, and plump form. I advanced a pace for the purpose of saluting her; but the gypsy, with a coquettish laugh, turned on her heel and fled towards the house.

"Stop!" roared Smith.

The girl paid no attention to him.

"If you don't stop you shall never have a husband!" cried the farmer.

At this terrible threat the young lady suddenly stopped, looked at us with a saucy glance, and then turned and ran towards the house, laughing in a jolly manner, as though she would like to see me kiss her, or any other man attempt it.

"Come to the house," said Smith. as soon as he could gain breath after his welcome. "You need some breakfast, and a change of clothing. Come."

CHAPTER XXIV.

AN AUSTRALIAN FARMER'S EXPERIENCE. — HIS WIFE AND FAMILY. — BUSHRANGERS IN PURSUIT. — BARRICADED.

As we walked towards the house, it seemed as though Smith could not control his joy; while his wife looked a little thoughtful as she witnessed the demonstrations of her husband.

"To think that we should see you of all persons in the world," Smith said.

"But tell me how it happens that you are in such a plight? Why are your clothes soiled, and how came you in a tree instead of the house? You knew where I lived."

"No, I didn't," I answered, with a laugh. "I hadn't the slightest idea that you were residing within a hundred miles of me. I was shaping my course for the Lodden as fast as possible, when I tumbled against your orchard fence, and from the fence I went to a tree to escape from the fangs of your dogs, for all appeared desirous of tasting my flesh, with the single exception of Rover, and his conduct was so strange that I did not know what to make of it."

"Ah, he's a noble dog," remarked Smith; "but I suppose, now that you have returned to the country, that I can no longer claim him as my own."

"We will settle that question by and by," I replied. "Ah, here is the house. Why, what a pleasant place you have secured for yourself and family! This is indeed a home, and has the comforts of one. A man must be happy here."

"We should be," Mrs. Smith said, "if the country was free of bushrangers; but the wretches bother us to death. They rob our orchards and gardens, kill our sheep and wound our cattle, and if we venture to remonstrate, they threaten to burn our house and murder us. What can we do?"

"In our day," Smith cried, rubbing his hands at the recollection of such stirring times, "we never gave the rascals a chance to threaten; we chased them from point to point, and gave them no rest. Ah, those were glorious days, were they not? If Murden had a command, we should soon be free from the presence of bushrangers."

"He has a command," I answered, "and is near us; but where I can't tell. I got separated from him a few days since, and that separation nearly cost me my life. I am in hope of meeting him and his command in the course of a few hours, and then we'll sweep the bushrangers beyond the Lodden."

"And will you give me a chance with you?" demanded Smith, in an earnest tone.

I glanced at his wife's face, and saw that it expressed her heart's fears.

"No," I said, "we want no married men. They should remain at home and attend to their families. You have done your share of work. Leave us single men to complete it."

"Perhaps your friend would like to change his clothes," Mrs. Smith said to her husband. "I am sure you can furnish him a suit, such as it is."

"To be sure I can. Come this way."

While I was dressing, my old friend told me all that had transpired during my absence from Australia; and we were still conversing when Mrs. Smith interrupted us with the information that breakfast was ready.

As I entered the room I saw that both women looked at me quite sharp, to see what effect clean clothes and soap and water had on my appearance. Although my garments were far from fitting me, yet I looked well enough in them to please the ladies, for they exchanged glances, as much as to say, "He'll do;" and then it struck me that Mrs. Smith was more than ever convinced that I would make a suitable match for her sister. I thought that the latter, as she took her place at the breakfast table, was more attractive than the married lady, for she looked fresh, plump, and young, not being more than eighteen years of age. It must be confessed that Smith knew how to entertain his guests with genuine English hospitality. He had on the table broiled duck (the creeks and streams of Australia abound with water fowl), fried eggs, cold chicken, toast, and excellent coffee, while the butter was as fresh and hard as the best that comes from Vermont.

"I tell you what," said Smith, as we took our places at the table, "this is different fare from what we used to get when we were stalking bushrangers."

"Pray don't allude to those days," said the wife; "I have heard enough of them. I expect every hour that you will start off on a tramp."

"Well," replied Smith, "I don't know but I should like it. There was some life and excitement in the danger, after all. Don't you think so?" and he nodded his head towards me.

"We never understood how much real danger there was until after the excitement was over. Now, for instance, we often —"

I was interrupted by the entrance of Joe, the genius who had fired at me and missed while I was perched in the tree. The fellow was laboring under some excitement, for his face was flushed, and his eyes looked as large as saucers.

"They is comin'," he cried. "I seed 'em."

"Who are coming?" asked Smith.

"The bushrangers."

We all jumped from the table, and the ladies began to scream, as was to be expected from them.

"We shall be murdered!" they cried, and then commenced kissing the baby's nose; and as they were under some excitement at the time, of course it was communicated to the child; so the young one joined his lungs to the women's, and for a moment we had lively music.

I led the way to the piazza, where we could command a view of the valley, the same one which I had stumbled through the night before, and there we saw ten horsemen approaching the house at a gallop. At first I thought it was Murden and his party, and I was delighted at the idea of meeting the commissioner and Hezekiah Hopeful, my New Hampshire friend, who, no doubt, thought me dead; but a careful scrutiny did not reveal the blue coats and bright buttons of the police.

"Smith," I said, "those fellows are bushrangers, and they are in pursuit of me."

"Well," answered Smith, with a touch of the old times in his air, "let 'em come on. We'll show 'em that we hasn't forgot how to shoot."

"But there are ten of them."

"And we can muster but four," answered the farmer. "The odds ain't so much, arter all. Bob, get the rifles out of the bedroom, and muster all of the ammunition. Where's Moloch?"

"He's set the natives to drivin' off the stock. He'll be here in a minute."

"Is it not better," I asked, "that I should leave the house, and take to the bush? There's yet time for me. By that means you will escape all trouble and damage."

"You stay here, beneath the shelter of my roof," cried Smith, "and as long as I has one, you is welcome to it. We will make a stand if they is disposed to fight, and see which party can hit the hardest. Do you mind that?"

Just at this moment Moloch made his appearance. He had been running, and was out of breath.

"Have the natives driven off the horses and cattle?" asked Smith.

"Yes; they is all in the bush by this time."

"Then come in."

"First close the doors of the stable, and fasten them," I said.

"That can be done on the inside. We can reach the stable from the house."

"So much the better. You have outside shutters to your windows, have you not?"

"Yes, of course. During some of our gales glass stands no show in keeping the wind out."

"Then close the shutters, but do it carefully, so that the bushrangers will not notice the act."

"And the women and baby, what shall we do with them?" asked Smith.

"Put them down cellar, and tell them to keep as quiet as possible."

Away went Smith to conduct his wife and her sister to a safe place, while Moloch closed the shutters, and Joe brought me the rifles and pistols found in Smith's bedroom. As soon as I had examined the firearms, I looked for the bushrangers, and saw that they were near the orchard fence, had halted, and were consulting together, as though devising the best means for capturing the house and contents.

"Good," I thought. "Only give us a few moments to prepare, and we'll be ready to receive you in a becoming manner."

"Shall I load the guns?" asked Joe, as he laid a pile of ammunition on the table near me.

"Yes, and be sure that you aim better than when you fired at me. We must waste neither time nor shot in case we are attacked."

"Then I won't shut my eyes when I pull the trigger," Joe remarked, with a grin that showed his capacious mouth to its fullest extent. Just at this moment, Smith joined us.

"Here comes the devils," he cried, "and that big devil of a Keeler is at their head."

I looked out and saw that such was the case. They had thrown down the fence, and were galloping through the orchard.

"Shall I give 'em a shot?" whispered Smith. "I can hit one of 'em as easy as I could take a drink."

"No; let them commence hostilities. We shan't have to wait long."

CHAPTER XXV.

A SKIRMISH WITH THE BUSHRANGERS. — OUR DEFENCE. — ATTEMPT TO BURN THE HOUSE.

As the rascals dismounted, I saw, to my intense disgust, that among the horses were the four which Keeler had stolen from the police, near Webber's station, a few days before. There was but one loop-hole in the shutter, and my eyes were applied to that, watching the motions of the bushrangers, and calculating our strength and the strength of the robbers, when Smith whispered, —

"What is they doin' now? Can't you give me a chance at 'em? Let me see what they is up to."

"Keep quiet," I replied, "or you will spoil all my plans;" just as though I had a plan, which I had not, for I intended to be governed by circumstances.

This kept all of them quiet until Keeler reached the door. He tried to open it, but found that it was fastened on the inside; and although the brawny robber put his shoulder to the door, yet he could not move it in the least, for three good oak bars were across it in addition to a bolt.

"You d—d mean Englishman," roared the fellow, "show your red face, and tell us where that rascally spy is concealed. He's in your house; so you had better give him up. It will be all the better for you."

No reply was made to this demand, although Smith expressed a wish to shoot some one in short order.

"They have all run for it," said the young bushranger, who had assisted me to escape.

No," replied Keeler, with a terrible oath, "they are in the house. Do you not see the smoke from the chimney? They are in there, and must come out." And then the fellow raised his voice and shouted, "Smith, you beer-drinking vagabond, if you don't give us that spy, I'll take your pretty wife and sister and —"

"Give me a chance at the devil," cried my old friend, rendered perfectly frantic at the threat. "He shall never live to repeat those words!"

"Keep cool," I whispered. "Go into the next room, and get ready for a shot. Pick your man, and make sure of him. Let Joe and Moloch do the same. We can't touch Keeler, for he is screened by the house; but we can reach his gang. Now, then, be lively, and let me know when you are ready."

"I am ready," cried Smith, a few minutes afterwards.

"Aim carefully," I said; "but don't harm that young, careless-looking fellow with the red shirt. He has shown me a kindness, and I'll repay it."

"Why, that is the one I was arter," cried Joe, in a tone of surprise.

"Then keep aimin' at him, 'cos he'll be safe enough," chuckled Smith.

Just then I had a fair mark, and I gave the word to fire. Four guns were discharged; but only two men fell, shot through the breast. I had no doubt that Joe and Moloch had missed; for I was certain of my aim, and Smith, I knew, was a fair marksman.

"We have waked 'em up," cried Keeler, in a calm tone, as though nothing unusual had happened; and then the fellow gave a bound, and took shelter behind a tree, while every bushranger disappeared from sight as suddenly as though swallowed by the earth, leaving the two bodies of the dead exposed to view, lying upon their backs, with their glazed eyes glaring at the sun.

"Have we licked 'em?" asked Smith, as he entered the room where I was reconnoitring through the loop-hole.

"No, the rascals will seek for revenge. They have not yet got enough of it."

At that moment I saw one of the bushrangers leave the shelter of the orchard, and advance towards the house, waving at the same time a white flag.

"What is wanted?" I asked, and opened the shutter a little, so that I could converse more freely.

"The captain of our gang," the bushranger replied, "is anxious to save blood and respect the property of the stockman who lives here. He has, therefore, directed me to make this proposition: to throw open your doors and admit his men, and surrender the spy who has taken refuge under your roof. By complying with these demands, you will be left in peace."

"And in case of refusal?" I asked.

"Then your buildings will be burned, and your stock driven off, your wife and sister outraged, and your grounds laid waste."

"These are hard conditions," I remarked.

"We have no others to give."

The bushranger was about to turn away, but stopped and asked, "Can I remove these two bodies?"

"Yes, take them away. You will have to remove others if you make an attack."

The bushrangers were too shrewd to dash against the house and end their lives without accomplishing certain results, and I knew that Keeler was too able a chieftain to expose his men in an unnecessary manner. Although he cared nothing for their lives, or how much blood was shed, still he knew that it was hard work to recruit his gang with proper men; so he had no desire to lose what he had. But I had hardly closed my shutter and stepped back, anticipating what would occur, than a shower of bullets struck the window, and sent a number of splinters into the apartment. For fifteen minutes the bushrangers remained so quiet that Smith began to think they had gone; but I knew better.

"Moloch," I said, "go to the other end of the house, and see if you can discover what the bushrangers are doing in that quarter. Mind and not let them obtain a glimpse of you."

"No fear of that," responded the man, and left me.

"Joe, you make your way to the stable, and bring me word if anything is transpiring in that quarter. Now, look sharp."

"Smith,' I said, — for I saw that he was shaking for the safety of his wife, — "I will leave the house, and run for my life. You can then say that I am not here, and permit one or two of the bushrangers to search the buildings to verify the statement. Perhaps that will satisfy them, and they will leave you in peace."

"Jack," said the stockman, "I really believe you'd do as you say; but I won't hear of it. We is in the same boat, old boy, and we'll sink or swim together. That's what we'll do. We has seen too much of life together to falter now You has allers stuck by me, and now we'll all stick together.'

He extended his hand as he spoke, and we shook hands most heartily.

"Yes," I said, "we'll die together or defeat the rascals. As long as I have life, I'll protect the ladies. We have been in worse positions than this, and escaped."

Just then Joe returned from his inspection of the field near the stable.

"I could see 'em," he said, "in the orchard; but they wasn't doing nothin', except cuttin' off the branches of a tree what they has tumbled down."

"Ha! now I understand their game, and will prepare to check them. Come with me, and tread softly," I said.

Connected with the stable and the house was a passage-way, covered, to protect those who passed from one building to another from the heavy winter rains. Down stairs we went, through the passage-way, to the stable, not making the least noise in our progress; and after we had reached it, we crept to the loft and looked out.

"What do they mean to do?" asked Smith, after a brief survey of the bushrangers' proceedings. "They appear to be amusing themselves in some way."

"And they will amuse us in a few minutes, or I'm much mistaken. Now, then, look to your rifles."

I saw the rascals raise the tree which they had been trimming, and direct their steps towards the stable door.

"Smith," I said, as I cocked my rifle, "you take the man on the right, and I will take care of the chap with the ferocious whiskers, on the left. Moloch and Joe can fire at whom they please."

"All right," was the cry, and we poked our rifles through the mud openings, took deliberate aim, and fired.

The two foremost bushrangers plunged forward, let go their hold of the piece of timber, and fell upon the ground, face downward. The joist fell from the hands of the other four; for, of course, Joe and Moloch missed, as we supposed they would. The uninjured men turned, and, with a bound, took shelter behind the trees in the orchard.

For half an hour I remained in the stable, watching for the bushrangers to make another dash; but they did not. I could neither see nor hear them. They appeared to have left the orchard, although it was impossible to tell if such was the case, for they were as crafty as North American Indians, and about as savage. I had sent Smith and his men to other parts of the buildings, for the purpose of keeping me informed if any demonstration was intended in those quarters, and it was lucky that such was the case; for Smith rushed into the stable with the information that the bushrangers had appeared at the back of the house, and that they were piling up dry branches against the building.

"That means," I said, "that they intend to burn us out. Now comes our real danger. Do the windows command a view of the robbers?"

Smith scratched his head as he answered, "There ain't no windows at the back part of the house. A carpenter who built that portion said that I'd better not put 'em in, 'cos I'd find the light too strong for my eyes."

"And you listened to such advice?" I asked.

"Of course. I s'posed he knowed better than me."

"Your indifference will cost us dear," I remarked. "If we had windows to use —"

"But as we ain't got 'em we'll have to do as well as we can," replied Smith, with more spirit than I ever gave him credit for.

"Right; so come with me, and show me the danger. We must try to overcome it."

He led the way to the back part of the house, but there were no windows for us to look through. All of those useful contrivances were in front. I glanced around the apartment, and saw that it had been used as a store-room, that it was adjoining the kitchen, and on the first floor. My mind was soon made up, and I decided upon my course of action. Although I could not hope to save the building, I could prevent the fire burning very briskly. In the kitchen was a pump, and around the pump were half a dozen wooden buckets, great clumsy things, of Australian manufacture.

"Set Joe and Moloch to pumping water," I said.

"For what purpose?"

"Ask no questions, but work. Here, out with your bowie-knife, and enlarge this crack. Don't spare the wood-work of your building; for your exertions may be the means of saving the house itself."

Where we commenced cutting a hole, the bushrangers had piled up brush so high that our operations were covered. Smith and I were working hard at our tasks, when bang, bang, went two muskets in front of us, and the balls struck the wood-work of the house, after tearing through the brush, and entered the room where we were engaged. The rascals had heard us operating, and took that method of letting us know that they were awake. No sooner was our work completed, than smoke commenced circling through the opening.

"Bring on the water!" I cried, and dashed bucketful after bucketful on the brush, and by this means was enabled to keep the flames in check; but I saw that unless we could work from the outside, we should have to give up all hope of saving the house.

"Throw on the water, Smith," I said; "I will return in a few minutes."

I took a rifle and ascended the stairs, dashed open one of the windows, in hopes of reaching the fire or the bushrangers; but I found that it was impossible, and for a moment I allowed my eyes to wander over the valley through which the Lodden flowed, and then I saw something that made my heart beat fast, and I could not repress a shout of joy as I put my cap upon the ramrod of my rifle, and waved it in token of recognition.

CHAPTER XXVI.

ARRIVAL OF MURDEN AND HIS MEN.—GREAT JOY OF HOPEFUL.—THE FIRE SUBDUED.—CHANGE OF MIND.

My expressions of joy were answered by some ten or twelve men on horseback, who were advancing towards the house. Yet they did not quicken their pace when they heard me cheer, simply because they supposed that it was a salute of welcome on the part of Smith; for the men I was prepared to greet with open arms wore the uniform of the Melbourne police, and I strongly suspected that I saw Murden and his party, although I could not be positive of it. Most of the police knew Smith, and stopped at his house when they passed near it. This I knew, but I was in despair at the slow manner in which the men moved, knowing as they did what a generous welcome they would receive; so I waved my cap, and yelled for them to hurry along, all of which they answered by one or two yells, but walked their horses as before.

"Confound them!" I muttered, in a tone of intense bitterness, "why don't they dash up to the door and capture the bushrangers who are in the rear of the house? We shall be burned out before they reach the yard."

Once more I yelled and gesticulated with my hands, pointing to the smoke, which began to curl around the roof of the house, a sure indication that the fire was making headway. At last my cries seemed to attract some attention. I saw one of the party point with his hands to the smoke, and then I saw Murden,—for I could now make him out,—turn in his saddle, and give an order, and then strike his horse with his spurs; and although the animal did not respond very readily, yet a rather tame sort of gallop was the result, and all came limping towards the house, as though the brutes were knocked up with a long journey, and were foot-sore in consequence. Not till then did I leave the window and run to the room where Smith and his stockmen were at work. The apartment was filled with smoke, and the men were rubbing their eyes and damning, instead of pouring on water, as I had directed when I left the room.

"Why ain't you at work?" I demanded, as soon as I saw the state of affairs.

"Work!" repeated Smith, rubbing his eyes, and coughing as though likely to burst a blood-vessel; "what in the devil is the use of working when we are smoked like a ham, and shed tears like whipped schoolboys? We can hardly breathe, much less work."

I knew that it was useless to talk with a man who had made up his mind that the house must burn down; so I seized a pail of water, ran to the door, slipped the bolt, and was just about to step into the yard, when Smith threw his arms around me.

"Don't go there!" he cried; "you'll be shot if you do. Let the house burn and be d—d, but don't you let the bushrangers kill you. My wife has made up her mind that you will make a good husband for her sister, and I darsen't disappoint her."

"Let him do it," growled Moloch, "and then he won't crow no more round here," while Joe offered to go out and "pitch in," if the fight was a fair one, and he could be assured of meeting man for man, and no underhanded cutting with knives, which he didn't consider the true English style of fighting.

I dashed at the fire, and by the aid of a stick was enabled to tear some of the brush down; but still the flames burned brightly, and threatened to give trouble unless I had help and a few buckets of water. But there was no time to lose.

"Bring me some water;" I yelled, and the shout was the means of arousing Smith to a sense of his duty.

"I won't see my old friend perish without help," he cried, and sprang into the yard, ran to the back part of the house, saw how I was engaged, and after one ejaculation of "O, what a d—d fool I am!" ran back for water.

In the mean time the police had arrived in the front yard,

and dismounted, but found, to their surprise, that the door was closed and locked, and that the window shutters were securely fastened. Murden did not know what to make of it, and just as the men were about visiting all the outbuildings in search of the folks, they heard me shout for Smith and men to "come on."

"Forward!" shouted the commissioner, suddenly turning to his men; and at the word they struck their horses and tore through the yard, over flowers and garden beds, the pets of the women, without the slightest regard to damages.

I was busily engaged in raking down the brush, when Hez turned the corner of the house and saw me. He gave one yell, and threw his arms around my neck.

"You is alive and well!" he cried; and then he saw at a glance the work which I had before me. He released his embrace, and dashed at the fire like a madman, to the intense astonishment of Smith, who gazed at the poor fellow with wide-expanded eyes and open mouth.

"If I had only time," muttered Hez, as he threw the flaming sticks to the right and left, "I could make a machine what would squash the whole thing in the waggin' of a dog's tail; but as I ain't got time, why, I must make my boots do."

Just as he had arrived at this wise conclusion, around the corner came Murden and his troop. The commissioner comprehended matters at a glance.

"Dismount!" he yelled; and off tumbled his men, and rushed towards the fire.

"Bring water, some of you!" was the next order the police received; and without the least confusion or delay the men separated, some for water, and some for long poles to rake the fire from the house.

Somehow or other I was edged away from the flames, as though I had done enough, while the police took my place, but said not a word respecting the strange meeting. They were too well drilled for that. They knew that with them it was duty first and questions afterwards.

Leaving the crowd to trample out the last vestige of fire

I entered the house, and found my way to the cellar. Down the steps I went, feeling my way, for the place was rather dark, but when I had reached the foot of the stairs I felt a pair of arms thrown around my neck, and Miss Amelia's face was laid close to mine as she exclaimed, —

"O, brother, is it all over with us?"

"Not quite," I replied; "but I wish it was, if you would only keep your arms around my neck. I think that it is very pleasant to have them so near me."

The young girl uttered a little scream, and withdrew her arms.

"O," she said, "I thought it was John. Pray forgive me."

"With much pleasure. Any time you wish to repeat the affair, I shall submit without a murmur. Don't feel ashamed on my account."

"Thank you for your kindness," she said in a tone that betokened the least degree of offended pride, and by the little light that streamed down the stairway I could see her toss her pretty head as though she would never commit another such act.

"Do not be angry, Amelia," said Mrs. Smith, coming forward with her child in her arms. "The gentleman is not to blame for the embrace. But he comes to us with news. Is my husband well? Do not tell me that some accident has befallen him."

"I am happy to inform you that Mr. Smith is uninjured, that the bushrangers have fled, that a large police force is near the house, and they are hungry and need some refreshments."

"Heavens! they will eat us out of house and home," cried the impetuous Amelia. "I never saw such gluttons as those officers are; and so impudent, too. They always look at me as though they would eat me."

"You must regard that in the light of a compliment," I said. "It is not often that the poor fellows see such a fresh-looking face as yours; so they can't help staring a little. But this time they are really hungry."

"Yes; I never saw policemen who were not hungry. But I suppose that I must endure the men's staring, although I wish they wouldn't look at me in such a manner. Is that odious commissioner with them?"

"Yes, Mr. Murden is with the force."

"Then there won't be much peace for me. He's an awful tease. I wish he wouldn't come here. I suppose I must see him."

"Of course," I replied, knowing that she was only talking for effect, as many young girls do. "We are indebted to him and his men for house and life. Had he not come to the rescue just as he did, we should have fared badly."

"But I thought that you were to beat the fellows off," Miss Amelia said.

"We were doing all that we could towards it," I answered.

"O!" and the young lady sighed, as though resigned to her fate: "if that is the case I suppose that I must endure the presence of that Murden and his men. But I hope he won't pay me any compliments."

At the door I met Hez and Murden. The fire was extinguished, and they were wiping their heated faces after their late exertions.

"Only think," said Hopeful, almost blubbering with joy at the meeting, "I thought you dead. I'll be rammed, jammed, and hung up to dry, ef I didn't. I s'posed the cusses had killed yer, and then what would have come of our partnership?"

"O, we should have re-formed in the other world," I answered.

"Yes," laughed Hez; "but darn ef I want to go to t'other world jist yet. I want to see Martha fust, and marry her ef I can."

"And I hope that you will accomplish your designs, for I am sure they are honest," I remarked, as Murden came forward and gave my hand a hearty shake.

"I knew you would turn up," the commissioner said. "I did not give you up, although Hez told me that he was certain you were lost to this world. But where have you been, and what is the occasion of this fire?"

"It means," I answered, "that a few minutes since Mr. Keeler and his gang were near the house, and had extended a pressing invitation to us to come out. We declined; consequently the rascals fired at us, and then fired the house. If you had not come up just as you did, we should have experienced hot work, and perhaps been browned like roast ducks."

"Keeler near us?" cried Murden, in a state of intense agitation. "The very cuss I'm after. Why did you not say so before?" and the commissioner put his silver whistle to his lips, and blew a shrill blast, which brought his men around the corner with a rush, Lieutenant Maurice at their head, pistol in hand, as though some great danger threatened.

"What's the matter?" gasped Maurice.

"Keeler! that d—d Keeler!" shouted Murden.

"Where?" roared the men, looking in all directions, and cocking their pistols.

This question Murden was unable to answer; so he had to look to me for the information.

"The bushrangers," I said, in a slow, deliberate tone, "are about three miles from here, and galloping like mad towards the Black Forest."

"To horse!" yelled Murden; "we can overtake them."

The men rushed for their animals, which were tired, and almost unable to move without the influence of the spur. I let the police mount, and did not utter a word in opposition. I sat and looked at them, and just as they gathered up their reins, Murden noticed that I had not joined them.

"You'll come with us, won't you?" asked Murden, in a tone of surprise.

"No, not to-day."

Not a man of the squad but looked disappointed. They had anticipated a different result.

"And why not?" asked Murden, apparently a little vexed at my refusal.

"Because I'm a Yankee," I answered.

"But, d—n it, man," cried the commissioner, "Yankees are not cowards, and that's no reason why you should not go with us."

"As you say, Yankees are not cowards, but when they undertake anything, they wish to win. They study all the chances, and never start on a chase unless they can see successful results."

"And you think that our pursuit will amount to nothing?" asked the commissioner.

"Just so."

"And will you please give me a reason for such a sage conclusion?"

"Half a dozen, if you desire them."

"One will do."

"Well, then, look to your horses. How many miles have you travelled within the last twenty-four hours?"

"Between sixty and seventy."

"And you think they are in perfect condition to overtake bushrangers who are mounted upon fresh horses, and the best ones to be found in the country? Remember they never steal poor animals."

I saw the commissioner's face change. He began to comprehend me.

"Let your horses rest for a few hours — let your men recover from their fatigue, and then we will start on an expedition that will result to your satisfaction."

The police looked their gratitude, although they did not dare to utter a word. But they thought I was right, nevertheless.

"Be content, for the present, to know that we have killed four bushrangers, and recovered the four horses stolen from the police, and a fifth that belonged to some one else."

The commissioner opened his eyes to their widest extent, and then shouted, "Dismount!" and as the men touched the ground, I led them through the orchard to the spot where I could see horses, and where I knew the dead bushrangers were lying.

CHAPTER XXVII.

DEAD BUSHRANGERS. — HOPEFUL AND AMELIA. — A WARNING. — OLD LOVE FORGOTTEN.

When we were defending the house from the murderous attack of the bushrangers, and had succeeded in killing four of them, I knew it was not a peculiarity of the rascals to care for their dead or wounded, time being too valuable to stop and bury the defunct or succor the injured; so when I saw the bushrangers drag the dead bodies away, I knew they would leave them near the house, or just beyond the reach of our fire. I was therefore pretty confident that my statement would prove true, for I had seen that four horses were in the orchard, and I knew our troublesome visitors would not take those which the dead men rode, as speed was something of a consideration with the fellows in their retreat, not knowing how hard the police would pursue them.

"If you have killed four of Keeler's gang," said the commissioner in a tone that showed he had some little doubt of the statement, "and have saved our police horses, you have done us an immense benefit, and redeemed our name. But lead the way, and let us have a glimpse of the bodies."

I led the way through the orchard, all hands following close to my heels, while Rover stalked by my side, the noble hound refusing to leave me even for a moment; and he also declined the friendship which the rest of the pack proffered in my behalf, as though he had no notion of sharing my affections with any other dog. We stopped for a moment to examine the horses which the bushrangers had left behind. As I expected, three of them belonged to the police, and the other was an animal stolen from White's farm, on the Murrumbridgee, judging from the brand on the brute's flank. All four of the animals were exhausted, and that was why they were left behind. A few yards beyond the horses we came to the dead bodies of the bushrangers, their faces covered with flies, which hovered around them in countless numbers.

"Well, get some spades, two or three of you," said the commissioner, "and make a hole and tumble them in. We'll give them a burial at any rate, and thus disappoint the vultures;" and with these words we turned and walked towards the house.

"Where have you been? Why didn't you join us?" resumed Murden. "Give me a history of your adventures, while I have time to listen to them without interruption."

"One question first," cried Hez, who had listened to our conversation with breathless interest. "Did you see any gold *specimens* durin' your tramp? We come here for the dosh, you know, and not to kill people."

"I have not thrown away my time," I answered. "Be content with what is to come."

"That depends upon what *is* to come," returned Hopeful. "I'd ruther fight gold-bearin' quartz rock than those sneakin' thieves what jumps on you before you knows it, and cuts yer throat jist as though yer was a pig instead of a human bein'. Now I—" He stopped suddenly, and stared with open eyes towards the house.

I followed the direction of his glance, and saw the coquettish Miss Amelia Copey near the door, with red ribbons on her dress and several flowers in her hair; and altogether she looked much better than when I first saw her, or when she made a slight mistake, and threw herself into my arms, and gave me several very sisterly kisses.

"By Jehossephat! what is that?" Hopeful asked.

"A woman, of course. What should it be?" I replied.

"Wal," he answered, with a sigh, "she's a rusher, now I tell you, and she's almost as purty as my Martha, of Hillsborough county, New Hampshire. I tell you, ain't she got the hair and the face?"

The little coquette must have known that Hez was complimenting her, for she smiled in a most benignant manner, and flashed a glance at him that made him shiver, so well directed was it; and as I noted the damage, I felt a little apprehensive for my friend's peace of mind.

"She looks good enough to eat," muttered Hez, his mouth watering; and to tell the truth, Amelia, as she stood on the steps of the piazza, with bare arms and neck plump and white, was enough to entice almost any man into forgetfulness of wife or sweetheart.

"Remember Martha," I whispered in Hopeful's ear. "Steel your heart against the girl before you, for she will but lead you on a wild-goose chase. Remember, show no evidence of admiration, or she will take advantage of it."

"You want her yerself," cried Hez, in a blunt tone, and with more temper than I ever saw him exhibit before.

A woman's smile or frown can make the best of friends enemies. I laughed at the remark, and laid a hand on his shoulder, and then looked into his white eyes and freckled face while I asked, —

"Hopeful, if I wanted the girl, and you wanted her, which do you think would stand the best chance of obtaining her?"

"You," he answered, and looked upon the ground, and pawed it with his foot like a restive horse.

"Why?" I asked.

"O, 'cos you is better lookin' than me. You has dark, curly hair, black eyes, and a handsome face — or the women all say that it is, and they know."

"Anything else?" I asked.

"Yes; you has lots of money, and I ain't got much."

"And with money and good looks you think I would stand the best chance with yonder little flirt?" I asked.

There was a sullen "yes." It is terrible for a man to acknowledge that in the eyes of a woman another is superior to himself.

"And do you think that I should succeed in preference to yourself with Martha?"

"Gol darn it, no!" was the hearty exclamation.

"Even with my wealth?"

"No, I tell yer!" and the man showed signs of impatience.

"Then don't you think the affections of such a girl are worth more than the passing whims of yonder flirt, who would jilt you to-day and me to-morrow?"

"Yes; Martha is a noble girl," answered the man, as though thinking over the subject.

"I know she is, and on her account, and on your account, I want you to escape the net which yonder girl will weave for you."

"And you don't want her for yourself?" asked Hez, his face clearing up a little.

"I assure you that I do not."

"And you don't want to crowd me off?"

"I have no such idea, I assure you."

"I believe you;" and the honest son of New Hampshire extended his hand and grasped mine.

"Let me prove it," I said, without a thought of the consequences. "In her company, and while I am at the house, I'll pass for a poor man, and you shall be known as a rich one. You shall quote your wealth, and I'll laugh at the loss of fortune. Now are you satisfied?"

"Yes;" and Hez drew a long breath, as though he felt relieved.

While we were conversing Murden had approached the house, and was chatting with Miss Amelia, who tossed her head and flaunted her ribbons as though she knew her value in that part of the world, and was determined to be appreciated.

"O, you odious thing!" was the first salutation which the commissioner received. "I was in hopes I should never see you again. The last time you were here you nearly pestered my life out of me — you know you did."

"I shall never do that until you marry me," was the laughing reply; and Murden extended his hand, which the young girl took, and then threw away, while a blush mantled her face as she said, —

"Impertinent! I'll never shake hands with you again, for you always squeeze my fingers."

"And how can I resist such temptation, when that soft

white hand is laid in mine? Come, let us kiss, and be friends."

"I would not kiss you to save your life;" and the little coquette tossed her head and looked her scorn. Murden laughed.

"And this gentleman,"— he pointed to me, —"he has a better looking face than mine; it is not so red, and his beard is not so stiff. Would you kiss him?"

"No; for I hate him worse than I do you;" and she pouted her red lips, while I laughed at her antics.

"Well, we wish to accommodate you," continued the provoking commissioner; and he laid his hand on Hez's shoulder and said, "What do you think of this man? He is rich, while we are poor. He can make a lady of you."

Murden uttered the very words that Hopeful desired him to; but the commissioner was unconscious of it. He meant that as far as brains went, Hez had the advantage of us, for he could make a fortune by their aid, while we should starve. I watched the young lady while Murden was speaking, and saw the sudden sparkle of her eye, and the quick glance which she threw at my New Hampshire friend. His freckles, in her eyes, were covered with golden scales, and his sandy hair was shaded by the siftings of gold dust. Hopeful assumed a new light in her eyes. He was rich — wealthy enough to give her station and all the luxuries which a young girl supposes are her due and right if she condescends to accept of a husband. From that time Hez assumed a prominent position in her mind, and much unhappiness was the result, all because I did not see the bearings of certain idle expressions and suppositions.

"Come," said the commissioner, with a hearty laugh, while Amelia was looking us over, "won't you kiss one of us?"

"No, Mr. Impudence."

"Well, which one would you kiss if compelled to?" Murden asked.

"This one."

She pointed to Hez, much to the man's delight, and then

vanished, sending back a ringing laugh as she disappeared; and as she was lost to sight I looked up and saw the clownish features of Moloch, who had overheard all that had taken place, and expressed his feelings through his face. I read love, jealousy, and hate, but which of us merited his anger I could not tell; but it was evident to me that the clown dared to lift his eyes to Amelia — that he loved her; worshipped one who would have killed him with a look, had she supposed he was serious in wishing her for a wife, although, to tell the truth, she did not object to his admiration. That she could tolerate, but no familiarity must result from it. He must keep his distance, and treat her like a princess, or bow down to her, as the natives of the East bow to the sun. But if he had dared to talk of love and marriage, she would have crushed him with a torrent of scorn and reproach for his presumption.

"That fellow will occasion trouble in the family," I thought. "He is already crazy with jealousy if a man but exchanges a word with the girl. I will speak to Smith about it."

After we had finished breakfast we lighted cigars and walked out to see if the horses and men were properly cared for. We found the latter under the shade of trees, contented with their present ease.

CHAPTER XXVIII.

A COQUETTE AT WORK. — A JEALOUS LOVER. — AN ATTEMPTED MURDER. — AN ALARM.

AMELIA was assisting to perform some household duties when I returned to the house. Hez was watching her motions as she flitted to and fro, staring at her with a species of loving, longing expressions upon his face that would have made me laugh at any other time. I could not help sighing as I noticed the scene, and I wished that I was the victim instead of Hez. I thought I could stand the pressure better than my friend. Besides, the girl was handsome, and I have a weakness for pretty girls.

"Come, Hez," I said, "let us go and take a nap. We need rest, for there's no knowing how soon we shall be called to the saddle."

"I am sure it would be very impolite in Mr. Hopeful to leave me just at this time," cried Amelia. "I have many things for him to do. But go if you want to — don't let me detain you;" and the jade threw a glance at the victim that made him almost ready to fall down and worship her.

"Miss Amelia," I said, following the young girl into the dining-room, and speaking in a low tone, so that Hez could not hear me, "do you think that it is right or honorable to coquet with that young man? He is not accustomed to the ways of the world, and knows but little of woman's heart."

"So much the better," answered the pert jade, and pursed up her red lips and balanced herself on her toes, took one or two dancing steps, and lifted her dress so that I could catch a glimpse of as neat an ankle as man could desire to see.

"Will you listen to me for a moment?"

"No, not if you intend to be serious, for I can't bear such people."

"Well, let me tell you one thing that will interest you. If you want to test your power, just try it on me."

The little gypsy laughed while she made a mock courtesy, and replied, "But I prefer my present subject. He is much more interesting than you." She turned away with a laugh, while I wiped the perspiration from my brow and retired in as good order as possible, considering the rebuff which I had met with.

As I left the room I saw Moloch standing at the open window. He had been listening, and had heard every word of our conversation. I saw a most diabolical grin upon his face, and that maddened me; but I did not show signs of it. I pretended not to notice the man, but passed up the stairs to the room which Smith had assigned me, and saw that the dirty water in which I had washed had not been removed from the wash-bowl. The window was open; an excellent opportunity was presented for punishing an eavesdropper. I walked softly to the window, and emptied the slops upon Moloch's head. I heard a roar like that produced by an enraged bull, and, looking down, I saw Moloch gasping for breath, and spitting the soap and water from his mouth. and rubbing it from his eyes.

"Hullo! you there?" I asked.

"Yes, and damn it, you knowed I was!" the victim shouted.

"Well, the next time you listen to my conversation, see that you are some distance from the window, for sometimes I act without thinking."

"You is a d—d good-looking feller," the clown said; "but you can't make love to Miss Amelia;" and with these words off he went, muttering some threats which I did not heed, or deem of the slightest importance, for I had heard many of them in my day.

I lay down on a mattress which was on the bedstead, and with Rover on the floor, I went to sleep in less than five minutes.

I must have slept soundly, for when I awoke it was dark, and for some minutes I could not recollect where I was, or anything that had occurred during the past twenty-four hours. At last I heard some one ascending the stairs, but the step was so quiet and light that I could not tell who it was; and I came to the conclusion that the person had removed his shoes for the purpose of not awakening me. I remained perfectly still; and then I heard my door open, and some one looked into the room. I knew it could not be a stranger, for I heard Rover's tail beat the floor. I was just about to speak, for I supposed that it was Smith, when the door closed, and the sound of footsteps informed me that my visitor had departed.

"Rather singular," I thought, and rolled over, and intended to go to sleep again; but I no longer felt sleepy, so

I rolled back and forth on the mattress, and wondered what time of night it was, and where the deuce the matches were; and just as I thought that I would get up and hunt for some, — and, in fact, I had sat up in bed, — I heard a slight noise at the window, and on looking in that direction I saw a man's head and shoulders. He was standing, apparently, on a ladder, and seemed to be peering into the room and listening at the same time. There was a low growl from Rover, as though warning the intruder to be cautious.

"Good doggy," I heard a voice whisper; and then Rover beat his tail upon the floor in response to the compliment.

"This is rather singular," I thought. "Perhaps the man desires something from the room, and don't care to wake me. He is very considerate, at all events. I'll lie still, and see how he operates."

I kept my eyes upon the window, and by the light could see the dark form of the man motionless and silent, as though resolving upon what course he should pursue. He seemed afraid of the hound, for he whispered, —

"Come here, pup;" and Rover went towards him, and was rewarded by a pat on the head. "Now lay down, good dog," my nocturnal visitor said; and this time he spoke rather louder than he intended, for I recognized Moloch's voice.

"Ho! ho!" I muttered to myself; "the rascal has a design in visiting me. I will wait and see what his intentions are;" and after I had arrived at such a conclusion, I felt quite comfortable, and remained quiet.

Obedient to orders Rover lay down, for he did not think it remarkable to see a man whom he knew as well as he did Moloch. He had been accustomed to obey the farm hand, and he still remembered it, although he had found a new master. As the dog lay down Moloch put one foot over the window-sill, and prepared to step into the room, and as he did so, I saw, by aid of the starlight, that the fellow held a knife between his teeth; and I instantly came to the conclusion that the weapon was intended for me, and that he was prompted by jealousy to attempt my assassination. A word would have explained that his ill feeling was all thrown away — that Amelia did not love me, nor I Amelia; but then I did not deem it worth while to say a word, for I thought that my good luck would get me out of the scrape in some manner, in spite of the fellow's cat-like movements, and long, sharp knife.

After Moloch had swung his leg over the window, he rested for a few seconds and listened. I remained quiet, and even gave utterance to a snore, to assure the listener that I was asleep; and it appeared to be convincing, for he stepped into the room, and came towards the bed, stealing along on tiptoe, and making not the least noise. I watched all of his motions, for I could see them by the aid of the window, and he kept between it and the bed; and when I thought he was near enough for comfort, I just uttered a slight yawn, as though I was waking up. Instantly the fellow dropped to the floor, and remained in a crouching position, waiting for me to go to sleep again, or become composed; but with one eye on the rogue I commenced a noiseless retreat from the bed; and I had this advantage in so doing — I could see all his movements, but he could not notice mine; and so quietly did I work that I was on the floor, and the bed was between us, and yet Moloch knew nothing of the matter; and by the time he had regained his feet, and advanced, knife in hand, towards the bed, I had changed the pillows so that they represented my form, and covered them with a sheet.

The clown would have noticed the change if he had not been blinded with passion; he would have observed that the form on the bed did not breathe, did not move, and that its face was covered — an unusual thing in a hot climate. He did not stop to remark these things; he was so full of spite that he was thirsting for blood, and when he raised his knife he let it fall with the full force of his arm. Of course the blade entered the pillows, and I uttered a deep groan, and then slyly jerked the pillows in such a way that the would-be assassin supposed that I was struggling in the agonies of death; and so did Rover, for the dog all at once seemed struck with an idea. He appeared to comprehend that Moloch was not exactly doing the fair thing; and when I uttered a groan the noble hound made a spring for the assassin, and seized him by the seat of his pants, and shook the rascal, and tore out whole mouthfuls of cloth and some flesh, for the fellow uttered a subdued howl, and started for the ladder, Rover hanging on as though determined never to let go; but he altered his mind when Moloch reached the window, for, after giving the fellow one or two nibbles, which elicited suppressed cries of pain, he released his hold, and down the ladder the clown tumbled, too excited and alarmed to reach the ground the way he ascended. I stole to the window and glanced out. Moloch was picking himself up, cursing and muttering in a subdued tone, too fearful of attracting attention to express all that he desired to. But I saw him hobble off and disappear around the corner. I concluded to dress in the dark, to wash, and to brush my hair; and then, after feeling for the stairs with much caution, I managed to descend them with safety, although I had some doubts about the security of my neck, owing to the peculiarity of the stairs, which were built by a man laboring under *delirium tremens*. As I reached the foot of the stairs I heard a confused clatter of knives and forks, and smelt the odor of roast ducks and boiled onions.

"It's devilish mean in them not to call a fellow," I muttered, and then opened the door, and entered the dining-room.

I saw at the table Murden, Smith, Hez, Maurice, and a neighboring farmer named White.

"You are smart!" roared the company.

"Why did you say you didn't want any supper? and now you are here," demanded Smith and Murden in a breath.

"I have not had a chance to answer that important question," I replied, a little sulky at what I supposed was their fun.

"Not had a chance?" repeated Smith. "Why, I sent Moloch to call you, and he returned with word that you were tired and sleepy, and didn't want supper. So on that ground we let you rest."

"Moloch said that, did he?"

"Yes."

"Well, I'm much obliged to him, and have to thank him for favors. You shall see whether I am hungry or not;" and down I sat, and took half a roast duck on my plate, and commenced eating it with hearty relish.

"By the way," I said, in an abrupt manner, as though the thought had just occurred to me, "it is a little singular that Moloch should have returned such an answer as he did. I don't understand it."

"The man is not yet awake," laughed Murden.

"I think that I have given evidence that I am not only awake, but tolerably hungry," I answered. "But, seriously speaking, did Moloch say that he called me?"

"Of course he did," they all cried in chorus.

"Would you mind sending for Moloch?" I asked, turning to Smith.

"Of course not. Why should I?"

"Just humor me in my whim," I said. "Call in Moloch, send him up stairs, and tell him to wake me at all hazards. While he is absent I'll just slip into the closet, and wait for developments."

Smith went to the door and called Moloch, using for the summons a peculiar-shaped sheep-whistle, which hung near the entrance. It brought Joe in the course of five minutes.

"Where's Moloch?" asked Smith.

"In the barn, sleepin'."

"Send him to me. I want him to do an errand."

"Yeez, zur;" and Joe went in search of his comrade.

He was gone a long time, and then returned and said, —

"Moloch be wery sleepy, and say he won't get up."

This aroused all the ire of Smith's nature.

"The rascal?" he exclaimed, and snatched his stockman's whip.

Joe knew what Moloch's punishment would be; so he threw himself in front of his master, and cried out for him to hold his hand, and that he would make Moloch come to the house, even if he had to carry him.

"Very well," returned Smith; "if he is here in five minutes, I shall not use the whip; if not—"

Within the time specified, I could hear the two coming towards the house; and when Moloch presented himself before his master, his countenance bore all the evidences of supposed guilt, for I could see it through a crack of the closet door.

"Did you vant me, zur?" asked the clown, with a tug at his foretop.

"Want you? Of course I wanted you. Did you call the man who is up stairs?"

"Yeez, zur."

"What did he say?"

"That he would not come down."

"Well, we want you to call him again, and tell him that he must get up. Don't leave him till he turns out."

"Must I go up there, zur?" and the rascal pointed overhead.

"Yes; and be lively about it."

"Can I take a light, zur?"

"A light! What do you want of a light? Are you afraid of ghosts?"

"No, zur, I'se not; but you see the man is quick with his pistol, and he might shoot I."

"Then knock at the door and make a row. Come, don't be all night."

"Can't Joe go with me, zur?" Moloch asked, as he edged towards the door.

The farmer made a movement towards his stockman's whip, and at this stage Moloch retreated at a rapid rate, but left the door open behind him. I listened, and so did the company present, for any demonstration on the part of Moloch. I heard him knock at the door, and call me; and then, after some hesitation, as though it took a long time to make up his mind, he entered the room, still shouting my name, as if to keep up his courage. Then there was a moment's silence, and the yell which I had expected came at last.

"O, zur!" the man shouted, and plunged down stairs as though he was closely pursued by a whole army of ghosts He dashed into the room, and manifested the utmost consternation as he closed the door, and then faced the company at the table, all of whom were sufficiently startled to manifest some little alarm.

"What in the devil's name is the matter?" roared Smith, and once more reached for his whip; but this time it possessed no terrors for Moloch.

"O, maister!" he shouted, "the poor man up stairs is dead."

"Dead!" exclaimed the company, with well-affected surprise.

"Yees, zurs. I put my hand on 'im, and he's cold as mutton in winter. But you come and see for yourselves."

The company arose from the table, as sober as so many undertakers, and prepared to move up stairs.

CHAPTER XXIX.

MOLOCH IN A FIT. — HIS DISAPPEARANCE. — A CLOSE SHOT. — PREPARATIONS FOR A TRAMP.

Of course I saw the whole of the scene; for the door of the closet stood ajar, and I had one eye close to the crack, and could take in all that transpired in the room. I saw the pretended horror of Moloch at the supposed discovery of my death, I saw the well-played consternation of the company at the table — and they acted their several parts in an admirable manner; and then I saw Smith seize the trembling Moloch by the arm, and heard him ask, —

"Be you sure that Mr. Jack is dead?"

"Yees, zur, I is sure of it. I put my hand on 'im. He vas stone cold."

A few moments previous to this, Amelia and Mrs. Smith

had entered the room, startled by the noise which Moloch had made in descending the stairs.

"O, my goodness me!" cried Amelia; "what is the matter with you men that you make this noise?"

"Matter enough," returned Smith, still keeping his hold on Moloch. "Mr. Jack is dead."

Amelia threw up her hands, and then dove for her sister.

Mrs. Smith led her sister from the room, and soothed her, while Smith still kept a firm hold of Moloch, and urged him towards the stairs which led to the room I had occupied.

"Let's have a light, maister," cried Moloch, who still manifested symptoms of alarm. "I don't want to go in that 'ere room without a light."

He took a candle from the table, and led the way up the stairs, followed by the rest of the party; and no sooner had they disappeared than I left the closet, and once more seated myself at the table. Up the stairs stamped the party. I heard them when they gained the door of the chamber. I heard them pause for a moment, as though deliberating or gaining courage, and then with a rush enter the apartment. For one moment there was silence, and then I heard a loud cry from Moloch, and a laugh from those with him.

"Where is the dead man?" they shouted. "Come, show him to us."

"He was here, zurs;" was the reply; and then there was a pause, as though the men were confounded at the sudden disappearance of the body.

"If he was here, where has he gone to?" asked Smith; but Moloch could not answer.

"There has been some foul play here," cried Murden, whose eyes had not been idle while he was in the room; and as he spoke he lifted the sheet and pillows, and exhibited the cuts which the knife had made when my body was supposed to occupy the place where the pillow was lying.

"I don't know nothin' about it," said Moloch, with evident symptoms of alarm. "If somebody has been usin' a knife, I don't know who done it, so there's a end of it;" and the fellow turned away

"Well, let's go back and finish our supper," Smith cried, and the proposition was accepted without a dissenting voice. Down the stairs they came, and took their seats at the table; but, according to agreement, not the slightest notice was taken of me.

Moloch crawled into the room, his face very pale, and his eyes cast down to the floor. In one hand he carried the candle, and he held it in such a careless manner that the mutton tallow of which it was composed dripped over the floor, looking like hail-stones.

"Put the candle on the table," said Smith, in a sharp voice.

Moloch advanced to the table without looking up, and it so happened that he attempted to reach the table over my shoulder; but just as he was about to place the candlestick he glanced upward and saw my face, prepared especially for the occasion.

"'Tis he!" the clown yelled; and giving the candle a flirt he just missed my nose, and set fire to Hez's red hair which had been greased with tallow, for the purpose of concealing its fiery character from Amelia. "'Tis he!" yelled Moloch; and he pointed with trembling finger at my face and let the candlestick drop with a crash, while his knees shook with terror.

"What's the matter with you?" roared Smith, pretending great indignation.

"'Tis he!" was all the man could utter.

"Who, you fool?" Smith asked.

"Mr. Jack," stammered Moloch.

"Where?" asked all the company, with pretended amazement, and glanced around the room as though in search of me.

"*There!*" cried Moloch, in trembling accents, not daring to withdraw his gaze from my face.

"We see no one," Smith and Murden exclaimed.

"No one!" stammered the wretch; "and yet the man is in a chair, and at the table; and now he turns his eyes upon me, and looks — O maister! how he do look at me — jist as though I killed him!"

"You did kill him!" thundered Murden, while I slowly rose from the table and took a step towards the fellow

"Yeez, I done for him," confessed the wretch; and then with foam upon his lips he fell to the floor, frightened into convulsions, and convinced that a ghost stood before him.

Smith took the man by his heels, and dragged him out of the door, and threw him on the grass in the front yard; and there he left him to recover as he pleased, or die if nature should so direct. After this feat the farmer returned to the table and called for coffee, and Miss Amelia brought it in; but as Hez had slipped out of the room and informed her that it was all a mistake, that I was not dead, the amiable young creature dried her eyes, told her sister that it was all a joke, and that she was rather sorry than otherwise that I was not an inmate of the other world, and then insisted upon carrying in the coffee, so that she could make faces at me, for she assured Hez that she hated me above all earthly things, which Hopeful believed, and was comforted thereby very much.

"This affair is no joke," said Murden. "The rascal has attempted to kill our friend, and only missed because Providence was on his side. Now, the question is, what shall we do with him?"

"Send him to Melbourne for trial," Smith answered. "I only wish that we had the power — we'd hang him within an hour, the rascal! What could have possessed him?"

"Love," I answered. All at the table re-echoed the word, and laughed at the idea.

"Who in the devil's name is he in love with?" demanded Smith.

"Your wife's sister."

"Are you sure?"

"Yes."

"Then I'll go and kick the cuss; you see if I don't."

He jumped from the table and rushed to the yard. We followed him as close as possible; but when he reached the place where Moloch was left a few minutes before, found that the man had disappeared.

"D—n him! let me find him," roared Smith; and he cracked his stockman's whip and ran round looking for the fugitive in all the dark corners in the barn where Joe was sleeping, and who was bewildered at the visit, and then through the outbuildings; but no Moloch could be seen. "If I had found him," Smith said,—and he handled his whip in a menacing manner,—"I would have skinned him as sure as you live. To dare to fall in love with that lass! D—n him! what impudence."

I could have set Rover on his trail and found the scamp, but then I reflected that loving a girl was not a serious crime; and, looking at my watch, I saw that it was past twelve o'clock, so informed Murden of the fact.

"That means that we must mount and be off," he said.

"Not exactly," I replied. "I have altered my opinion respecting the expediency of an attack. We will wait."

"And for what length of time?" asked the commissioner, in a tone as little removed from a sneer as it could be, and still remain a sneer.

"O, say for a day or two."

"I shall do no such thing," was the commissioner's answer, in his usual impetuous manner, headstrong as ever.

"Very well, then, I shall remain behind. You can cross the valley, and see if you can find Keeler's cave."

I lighted a cigar and walked towards the house. I had taken but a few steps when Murden overtook me.

"D—n it, man, don't go off in that manner. Tell me your plans, and if I like them I'll agree to them, so that we can work together. Come, what have you on your mind?"

"Well, listen. While I was awaiting the attack of that rascal Moloch, it struck me that Keeler was too shrewd to go near his cave to-night, or even to-morrow."

"There's something in that," muttered Murden.

"One thing more," I said. "Let me whisper it in your ear." And as the commissioner bent his head, I said, "In the cave Keeler has his whole stock of gold and silver, the result of one or two years' robberies. Do you think that he would allow it to remain there while expecting a visit, and half suspecting that I know the place where it was buried?"

"Of course he would remove it," muttered Murden.

"To be sure he would. He is no fool. But he must do it carefully, for he don't care to let his companions suspect the treasure which he possesses."

"I see, I see," Murden said. "There's reason in every word you utter. Of course the men don't share with us in case we lay hands on the spoil."

"Why should they?"

"To be sure, why should they?" briskly responded Murden, as he rubbed his hands and thought how he would like to handle the gold.

We entered the house, and announced to Smith and his family that we should remain with them for some days, at which news the stockman was delighted, and Amelia pretended a little petulance.

"O, dear!" she said; "have I got to endure the company of you men for such a length of time? I hope that none of you will speak to me."

"Unless we offer a proposal of marriage," laughed the commissioner.

"You might offer in vain, Mr. Policeman," the little beauty said, with a flash of her blue eyes and a toss of her well-formed head.

Murden laughed as he replied, "Don't be alarmed; I have no idea of asking such a butterfly to become my wife. I want a woman for a companion, not a bread-and-butter school-girl.

"I won't remain here and be insulted," she said, "although I should like to sit up an hour or two longer, if any one was here to protect me;" and with these words she swept from the room, and we saw no more of her that night.

Hez smoked his pipe in silence for a few minutes, and then knocked out the ashes and betook himself to bed, while Murden and I commenced an official despatch, and before daylight we had finished; and I think a neater thing never went to headquarters. It told of deadly peril; of ambushes in the Black Forest; of sharp skirmishes; of burning house and rescued women, and property saved, and closed by hoping to annihilate the whole of Keeler's gang, upon whose trail we were.

"There," said Murden, as he signed the document, after paying a compliment to Hez and myself, "I think that will make the government open its eyes to my merits, and crush all who were opposed to me. I'll call up one of the men and send it off at once, for we shall have daylight in an hour's time."

He stepped to the door and blew a whistle, and one of the sentinels came running to see what was wanted.

"Who has had the most rest?" asked the commissioner.

"Martin, sir. He has not been called as yet."

"Rouse him out, and tell him to saddle his horse and get ready for a trip to Melbourne."

"Yes, sir;" and the man vanished.

In ten minutes Martin reported himself as ready, received the despatch and orders to return as soon as he could, and then started on his journey; and we went to bed and slept until noon, when we turned out, found something to eat, joked a little with Amelia, and received scornful, withering replies, and then Hez and I took our rifles and wandered off towards the hills. As we strolled along, Hopeful manifested some little impatience at the time which he had wasted while in the country, not having made a dollar, as he expressed it; so he was a little peevish in consequence.

"Why, Hez," I said, "what do you care for money? You no longer have the noble ambition which actuated you to visit the country. You have forgotten Martha, and her constancy and truth, for a fresh-faced, coquettish English girl. Tell me that you will still remember the New Hampshire maid, and that you want gold but for her sake, and I'll go to work in earnest in the course of a few days."

Hez plucked the grass up by the roots, — we were sitting near a bank, and in sight of Smith's house, — and did not reply for some time: but at last he looked up and asked, with a cunning leer, "Jack, don't you want the little English gal for yourself?"

"No, I assure you that I don't."

"And you ain't sorry that you told her that I was a rich man and you a poor one?"

"No: why should I regret it?"

"O, 'cos I see that arter all the gal likes you better nor she does me."

"A pretty way she takes of showing her favor. She stuffs you for the sake of showing her love for me."

"You may laugh, but it is so," growled Hez, in a sulky tone. "I'd marry her if I could."

"You shouldn't do any such thing," I replied in a quick tone, and without a moment's thought.

Hez sprang to his feet, defiance in his eye and mien. As he came towards me I arose to my feet, for I saw that he was not sane, and for the moment capable of committing some rash deed, which he would regret in his cooler moments.

"Hopeful," I said. But he made no reply, and just as I was about to speak the second time I heard a sharp report; and the next instant my broad-brimmed hat fell from my head, knocked therefrom by a musket ball; and then the lead passed between us and touched the earth some thirty rods beyond. The expression of Hez's face changed in an instant from jealous rage to deep anxiety. He sprang forward, clasped me in his arms, and asked,—

"You're not hurt? Don't tell me you are hurt! I won't believe it. Will you forgive me?"

"Yes, on condition you will help me find that skulking rascal."

He released me, and both of us seized our rifles and rushed up the bank in the direction from whence the shot proceeded; but although we looked in every direction, and hunted in tree-tops and behind bushes, no sign of a human being could be seen, nor even the trace of one. Hez was frantic at the idea of the villain's escaping; but after a search of fifteen minutes we gave it up, and retraced our steps towards Smith's ranche, the best of friends, all past jealousies forgotten and forgiven; for I knew that Hopeful felt ashamed of his conduct, and was dejected in consequence. I made no allusion to what had occurred, nor did he; but during the three days that we remained at the farm, I noticed that my friend still looked with loving eyes at Amelia, and that she wrung his heart more than once; so, to end the farce, I told Murden that we would start in search of Keeler and his gang, and he joyfully gave the orders to get ready for the march.

CHAPTER XXX.

AN EXPEDITION. — CROSSING THE VALLEY BY NIGHT. — A CONFESSION. — POINT LOOKOUT. — THE SENTINELS.

"What time shall we start?" asked Murden, when I announced that I thought the hour had arrived for action.

"Soon after twelve to-night. We must get close to Point Lookout by daylight, and see if we cannot seize the bushrangers who are acting as sentinels."

"I will order the horses to be ready, and will start at any hour that you will name;" and with these words Murden went to the stable, leaving me with Hez.

"You will go with us?" I asked.

"No, I shall stay here," was the sullen response.

"As you please," I answered, and left him.

We cleaned our arms that evening, loaded them, and at one o'clock in the morning mounted our horses and started on our expedition. We all shook hands with the stockman, and left the farm, filing out of the yard by the way of the orchard, and then gaining the valley which stretched for miles north and south, and ended at the edge of the Black Forest and Point Lookout. By the side of my horse trotted Rover, henceforth destined to be my inseparable companion.

At last, as we progressed, the travel became precarious

and we were compelled to walk our horses, for the bog-holes were numerous, and sometimes our animals sunk into them up to their girths, and were extricated with difficulty. Such being the case, Murden and I rode ahead of the troop, and with the men, like a miserable lover that he was, came Hopeful; for when the hour of departure had arrived, he had concluded to go with us, and not remain in Miss Amelia's company any longer.

As Murden reined his horse alongside of mine, he said, "Miss Amelia is a sprightly sort of lass, and to tell the truth, I rather like her. I need a wife to look after my house, and comfort me a little, and why shouldn't I take her?"

"I know of but one reason why you should not," I replied

"And what is that?"

"Why, will she have you?"

"How should I know till I have asked her?" the policeman retorted, in a tone of surprise. "I never spoke to her about love or such nonsense, because I was always busy with my chaff; but she seemed to take an interest in me."

"How so?" I asked; and I attempted to obtain a look at the man's face, but it was bent close to his horse's neck, on the lookout for "sink-holes," so I could not tell if he was in earnest.

"O, she always tells me that she hates me, and gives me as much chaff as I give her."

"And you think she means esteem when she scolds you?" I asked.

"Well, it ain't indifference, for you know young girls say they hate you, when at the same time they have some little love for you; and I've watched Amelia —"

Here his confession was interrupted by his horse making a plunge, and another narrow escape from a "sink-hole" was the result. I was rather glad of it than otherwise, for I could not do my duty with two men and one girl, where both of the former loved the latter, and while I was not entirely free to act as umpire, for the red lips and saucy eyes of Miss Amelia were tempting to a young man not more than — Ah, well! what are ages when love is concerned?

But at last we left the vicinity of "sink-holes," and were close under the lee of Point Lookout, where Keeler kept one or more of his men for the purpose of sweeping the valley for miles in extent, and giving timely notice if enemies approached.

"We must dismount here," I said, as we reached the base of the mountain, and could proceed no farther on horseback.

"Leave three of your most careful men with the horses," I said, "while the rest of us climb the mountain, and pounce upon the robbers in case they are near us."

The commissioner selected three of the oldest men in the troop, and gave them their instructions, and then turned to me for further advice; for on this expedition he relied entirely upon me for guidance.

"Tell the men that they must not exchange a word when they commence the ascent — that our success depends upon silence and caution. Now, then, are you ready?"

Murden spoke to the officers, cautioned them about their movements; and then we commenced the ascent of the mountain, about a quarter of a mile in the rear of Point Lookout, so that we could cut off all retreat in case we gained the summit of the mountain without being discovered.

We were within fifteen rods of the point which commanded a view of the valley, and yet not a sign of a bushranger was to be seen; and I began to think that Keeler had withdrawn his sentinels and fled towards the Great Murray, or concealed himself and gang in the fastness of Mount Macedonskirt, where a regiment of soldiers could not have found him, had they hunted for a week; for the mountain is full of deep gorges, dark caves, and terrible precipices, where a false step would send a person flying through the air, and land him, a mass of jelly and broken bones, on the rocks below. I was about to rise from my recumbent position, and boldly advance, when Hez said, "Hist!" in as low a tone as possible; and at the same time I heard the peculiar serpent-like hiss which the police use, when they communicate with each other, in localities where the human voice is not to be trusted. I looked up and saw Murden signalize to me. He was in a better position than myself for commanding an observation, and as I caught his eye, I saw quite plainly that he had news for me.

"What is it?" I telegraphed; and an answer was returned that "some one was in sight."

I edged away from the quartz rock behind which I was sheltered, and at last obtained a position where I could see some distance, and note all that was going on. The first thing that met my view was the sturdy form of a bushranger, who was standing near the point, his back towards us, and his eyes scanning the valley which lay at his feet, covered with mist. The fellow seemed to have just "turned out," for he was yawning and stretching his arms like a man who had enjoyed a good sleep, and was rather regretful that daylight had appeared. The bushranger, after a good hearty stretch, pulled out a black-looking pipe, filled it, and commenced smoking with much apparent relish. After a few whiffs he took his pipe from his mouth, and shouted,—

"Bob, come out of that; you have slept long enough."

"What in the devil's name do you want to rouse me out at this hour for?" growled Bob; and then he cast his eyes over the valley, and continued: "Ugh! the fog is so thick that you couldn't see a regiment if marching towards us. I say, Alf, what a fine time this would be for the traps to steal towards us. They could get up to Point Lookout before we knew it; and then wouldn't we be dashed?"

"Don't mention traps to me," growled Alf. "The name makes me tremble. I never wants to see one of 'em, or hear of 'em. They is our enemies, and we is theirs."

I was anxious to save Bob, for I believed him capable of better things than a bushranger's life; so I signalized to the men, as we arose from our crouching position, to be careful how they handled their weapons, and to spare Bob if it was a possible thing. The dry grass on which we stepped gave forth no sound as we advanced, and it was not until we were within ten paces of the bushrangers that their sharp ears detected our movements; and then they sprang to their feet.

CHAPTER XXXI.

AN ATTEMPT TO EXTORT A CONFESSION. — THE PERILS OF TRAVELLING IN AUSTRALIA. — A SURPRISE.

SURPRISED although the robbers were, they did not seem so much intimidated as we expected; and as they surveyed their enemies, I could see that they were calculating all the chances, and considering which one was the best.

"Surrender, you sons of the devil!" roared the commissioner. "Drop your pistols and knives, or I'll bore you through and through with cold lead."

The bushrangers glared at him as though they would like to be on equal terms; but they did not drop their arms, as requested. They appeared to be too much surprised to do so; but I noticed that they were gradually retreating, and it struck me that they were attempting to reach their cave, or place of concealment, and then bid defiance to our arms. No sooner did I note the movement than I determined to defeat it.

"Stop!" I shouted. "If you take another backward or forward step you are dead men. Now, move at your peril."

In an instant they were like statues, immovable. Suddenly Alf, a stout, broad-shouldered fellow, with a cast in one eye, so that it was impossible to tell the direction in which he was looking, spoke in the slang of the bushrangers; and although he did not turn his head, we knew that he was talking to Bob.

"Sligo the sling," he said, "and stalk the lags," which meant that either he or his companion should manage in some way to give warning to Keeler and his gang that the traps were at hand.

"No, you don't," said Murden, who understood all the vile slang of the bushrangers; "if you do, you are dead men. We are not to be trifled with."

The cross-eyed bushranger seemed to lose all hope after

this remark. He held his arms up over his head in token that he surrendered unconditionally.

"Put your irons on," he said, "or else in mercy shoot me in my tracks, and save the courts all trouble. I've run my career."

"And I mine," returned Bob, imitating his companion. "The traps have got the best of us. Our time has come; so we may as well fall in, for our drill is over."

At a sign from Murden two of the officers advanced with irons in their hands, and secured the men, and after that was done we went forward to inspect their place of abode. It was a small cave, with plenty of blankets in it to keep the sentinels warm during the night, a lot of provisions, a few books of a low order, and that was all. As I left the cave, I saw that the young bushranger was looking at me in a wishful manner; so I approached, and sat down near him.

"Well, sir," he said, "luck is in your hands this time. You has us, and no mistake. I don't s'pose we can expect a bloody bit of mercy from the traps."

"I shall do what I can for you through the authorities; but it will depend in a measure upon yourself as to the result."

"I know what you would ask," he said.

"What?"

"That I should betray Keeler."

"No; I don't ask that in so many words. I want you to just hint as to his present position, and how many men he has with him. You can do that."

"No, I can't," was the candid answer; "I will not turn traitor even to save my life. I should despise my bloody self if I did, and so would you despise me. I can't do it, and you know it. I've been a tough cove, and desarve what I shall get; but I can't betray Keeler and my old comrades."

"Come, old feller," cried the commissioner, "give us some information, or you will find your neck in danger. Tell me this instant how many men Keeler has with him."

"I can't answer the question, and I shan't answer it," was the sullen answer; for Bob saw that he had a Tartar to deal with.

"O, you won't, hey?"

"No."

The men looked like two bull dogs ready to spring at each other's necks.

"Maurice," said the commissioner, addressing his lieutenant, "just rig a gallows. We will see if that cove won't answer."

Bob did not seem in the least intimidated at the order, but sat in sullen silence, with his eyes fixed upon the ground. Although I knew that Murden would not dare to hang the man, yet I knew him well enough to be aware that he would not scruple to choke the bushranger just a little, for the purpose of obtaining information; and the authorities of Melbourne would have winked at the matter, even if poor Bob's life had gone with the experiment; for the fellow, in the eye of the law, was only a desperate villain, after all, and the sooner he was out of the way the better for those who travelled to and from the mines. Maurice, who had no more feeling for a bushranger than he had for a snake, deliberately produced a cord, and looked around for a convenient tree to which he could attach it; but Alf, the old robber, who had watched all the movements with an eager eye, now thought that it was time to interfere.

"You have no authority for hanging a man," he said. "I dare you to do it."

Murden was so surprised at the man's impudence that he could not answer him for a moment. At length the commissioner managed to find his voice.

"Who in the devil's name are you?" he shouted.

"I'm a pal of Bob's, and I won't see him abused if I can help it. No, sir, much as I should regret to appeal to legal tribunals, — for I confess that I don't like them, and I have avoided them when I could, — yet I warn you that I shall do so if a hair of my pal's head is injured. Now, d—n you, do your worst."

It was amusing to witness Murden's face while the captive bushranger, heavily ironed, and at the mercy of the police, was speaking.

"By the Lord Harry!" he said, "I must flog that fellow or burst. The law permits me to do so, and I will. Don't say one word to prevent me."

"Nonsense," I replied, in a tone which I knew would calm him; "do you mean to take notice of such trifling matters when events of importance are about to transpire? You don't intend to injure either of these men. I owe my life to one, and the other is a captive, and entitled to some consideration. Come, look around. It is almost daylight. If we are to surprise Keeler, we had better be about it."

"So we had. We'll move at once. I didn't mean to harm the prisoner, you know. It was only to frighten a little information from him."

"The rope is all ready, sir," cried Maurice, as we once more neared the spot where the bushrangers were lying.

He had thrown it over the limb of a tree, and made a slip-noose with one end.

"Nonsense," returned Murden; "you didn't think I was in earnest, did you? I only wanted to frighten the men."

"Well, then, what is to be done with the prisoners? We must secure them, for we cannot take them with us."

I thought of the matter for a moment, for it was an important subject. We could not take them with us, for they would impede our advance. We could not leave them behind, for we should have to detail men to guard them; and men we could not spare just at that time, when it was uncertain how many bushrangers composed Keeler's gang.

There was no help for it. We must detail "Fiery Tom" in charge of the prisoners until our return; and so I told Murden, who jumped at the suggestion, for Tom could not fight, although he could burn.

"Yes," said the commissioner, "we'll put irons on the fellows' legs, and leave Tom to take charge of them."

I saw a dangerous light in Tom's eyes as he heard the suggestion, and I knew what the villain was thinking of. He imagined that he would have a nice time all to himself, flourishing lighted grass in the faces of the bushrangers; but I cut short his happy thoughts by laying one hand on the butt of my revolver, and the other on Tom's arm.

"Look here, my chicken," I said, "if you but hurt a hair of those men's heads, I'll send a bullet through your body, even if I never shoot another man during my life."

"So help me God, Mr. Jack," the fellow cried; but I interrupted him.

"None of your blarney, Tom, for you know I won't stand it. But you understand me, I hope. That young fellow"—and I pointed to the deserter from the English army—"saved my life; so I mean to save his in return. If you play any of your pranks with him, I'll pay you for it with compound interest."

"To think that you should doubt my word!" returned "Fiery Tom," with a reproachful look.

"You'll have no occasion to doubt mine," I answered; and then we separated.

The policemen shackled the limbs of the bushrangers so that it was impossible to move hand or foot, and then we gathered up our arms and prepared to depart; but while the men were getting ready, I stooped and whispered to the young bushranger.

"No, sir," he said, in answer to my question, "I don't know as there's anything that I want. You has been very kind to me, and I'm much obliged. If you had a drop of liquor about you, I could sup it, I suppose, and it wouldn't make me sick."

I raised his head and put my flask to his lips. He took a good swig, and then he whispered to me that his pal would be thankful for a sup; so I accommodated him, and was called a "real gentleman" for my kindness, it was so unexpected. We returned to the valley, where we found our horses. We mounted, and galloped along the base of the mountain, using as much speed as we dared, considering the uncertainties of the road, which we were entirely unacquainted with. But as the mist rose, slowly circling over our heads, but still clinging to the sides of the mountain, as though reluctant to part after a night's close embrace, I was enabled to take an observation of my position, by the aid of certain marks which I had well observed the day I made my escape from the cave.

"Near here," I said to Murden in a whisper, — for we had checked the speed of our animals for fear the sound of their hoofs would be heard, — "is the small stream I told you of. If I can find it, there will no longer be any doubt on my mind. I can lead you to the cave without the least hesitation."

Murden turned in his saddle, and spoke to his lieutenant. "Send men to the right of us, and tell them to keep a sharp lookout for a stream, the banks of which are concealed by tall grass. Let me know as soon as they discover it."

Obedient to a sign, the men started in different directions, and then we walked our horses for half a mile, expecting to come upon the stream every moment.

"D—n me if I believe there is a stream within ten miles of here," the commissioner cried, and turned to me as if daring me to deny it.

I smiled at his warmth, and that smile seemed to make the officer more and more excited. He struck his horse, and the animal suddenly plunged forward, and down he went, out of sight; but Murden's head could be seen above the grass.

"I think you have found the stream," I said, in the coolest possible manner. "Can you tell me how deep it is?"

I heard the policemen titter, as though they would like to laugh if they dared to; but as they did not, they only smiled, and allowed an audible snicker to escape them.

"Yes, I have found it," was the sullen answer.

"And how do you like it?"

"None of your business. By ——, if I don't believe you knew it was here;" and Murden touched his horse for the purpose of climbing the bank, but found the task a difficult one, for the earth was soft, and easily gave way beneath the horse's feet.

"I knew it was near here; but as you were positive that it was not within ten miles of us, I began to doubt if I was correct. However, I am glad to see that you have cleared up all doubt on the matter by personal observation."

"O, blast your preaching! Help me out of this, and I'll make a solemn promise not to doubt your word again."

I dismounted and approached the stream, so that I could examine his situation. After a brief survey I found a place where cattle had climbed up the bank, and to this point I directed the commissioner's attention. He headed his horse down stream, and after a while landed on firm ground, and then commenced grumbling, as is customary with Englishmen.

"Do you mean to hunt bushrangers, or stand here and growl all day?" I asked.

"When I am unable to growl, I am unable to stand," was the reply; and I believe the remark holds good with all his countrymen.

"And while you are growling the mist is rising. In a short time the whole of the valley will be exposed to the jealous scrutiny of the bushrangers; and if they once catch sight of us, we might as well attempt to capture so many eagles. Come, give the word to march, and scrape the mud from your person some other time."

The mist still clung to the mountain side, as though to facilitate our movements; but already had the sun appeared above the horizon, and it would soon scatter the thin, haze-like web that hung over us. We left the horses in charge of two men, and then commenced ascending the mountain, leaving the beaten path for fear we should be observed sooner than was desirable. We crept up, making not the least noise; and it was well for us that we were so quiet, for while we were in the mist I suddenly found myself face to face with a burly bushranger, who was seated on a piece of quartz, smoking in a complacent manner, and probably meditating on the evil deeds which he had committed.

"Ugh!" he growled, when he caught sight of me; but he had no chance to sound an alarm, for I sprang at his throat just as he was rising, and bore him to the earth.

CHAPTER XXXII.

THE ROBBER'S DEATH. — BUSHRANGERS SURPRISED. — THE ATTACK AND FLIGHT. — MURDEN'S ALARM.

"You scoundrel!" I whispered, as the man fell upon his back, and I placed my knee upon his breast, "tell me where Keeler and his men are, or I'll blow your brains out!"

He made a motion for me to release his throat, so that he could speak, and I complied with his wishes, thinking that the muzzle of a pistol which one of the men placed at his head would deter him from giving an alarm; but the swarthy villain was not intimidated in the least. Perhaps he thought that the threat was a vain one, and that he could really serve his comrades; for as I released his throat he uttered a shrill yell that could have been heard for half a mile. I knew what it meant. It was the signal that danger was near; but the prisoner did not have time to repeat it, for my hands once more clasped his throat, and at the same moment the policeman, who held the pistol, discharged it, for he was a man who knew no mercy when bushrangers were arrested. The ball entered the poor fellow's head, and as it struck it sent a shower of brains all over me, and for a moment I felt so sick that I thought I should faint; but I recovered in an instant, and then turned on the policeman who had fired the shot.

"Who told you to do that?" I asked, horrified at the murder, and at the cool manner in which it was performed.

"You did, sir," was the calm answer.

"You lie! I told you nothing of the kind."

"You threatened the man, and said that you'd kill him if he made a noise. I s'posed you was in earnest; so I jist put a ball through his head."

"This is no time to settle the question," I cried. "The bushrangers will be on guard if we remain here a moment longer. Forward!"

We all charged up the hill on a run, and just then the

mist suddenly dissolved and revealed some eight or ten men standing at the mouth of the cave, apparently listening for a repetition of the warning signal which their comrade had given a moment before. They were not more than fifteen rods from us, and among the group I recognized the tall form of Keeler. But the leader of the bushrangers was not a man to run without good cause. He was a bold fellow, and would have made an excellent soldier; but he did dread the sight of half a dozen blue uniforms, for he knew that no mercy would be shown him if the law once laid hands on his person; so when he heard the commissioner's voice, he replied, with a rallying war-cry, —

"Death to the traps! Stand firm and give it to them."

I think that about four or five out of the ten bushrangers raised their muskets as though to fire; but the others glanced over their shoulders, and that I knew was a sure sign that they were slightly demoralized, and decided to change their base as quick as possible. In the meantime we were advancing at double-quick time; but I was not in such a hurry that I failed to watch all the motions of the enemy, and when I saw them raise their guns, I just shouted for a halt.

"Halt be d—d!" roared Murden. "What for?"

"Ready — aim — fire!" I yelled; and at the last word the police poured a volley into the ranks of the bushrangers, and at the same moment the villains gave us a few scattering shots, one of which was aimed at me, and by Keeler's hand. It passed within a few inches of my scalp, raised my cap as though to take it from my head, and then the bullet sped on, and struck a poor fellow who was just behind me, knocking him down with a ball in his shoulder. A second bullet passed through the breast of a young fellow who was on the left of the line, and down he dropped dead. In addition to this, there were some narrow escapes similar to my own. Our own discharge was more destructive. Four of the bushrangers fell, killed or wounded; but Keeler was uninjured, for I heard his deep, sonorous voice cry out, —

"Kill the d—d traps! down with them!" advice which was not followed by his men; for they gave one look at our advancing columns, a second glance at their own dead and wounded, and then turned and ran for their lives, throwing away their guns as they dashed down the mountain, springing from rock to rock like a flock of scared goats.

Keeler paused at the foot of the mountain, shook his fist at us in a threatening manner, and then ran across the plain that skirted a piece of woods. But just before he disappeared he stopped, and insulted us with a gesture, the meaning of which we comprehended without the aid of a dictionary.

"D—n him!" muttered Murden, who seemed to think that the gesture was intended for his especial benefit; "if I had him in my power I'd kill him, or I'd know the reason why."

"But as he was too quick for us this time, we shall have the pleasure of meeting him some other day," I remarked.

"Humph! yes, I suppose so;" for, Englishman-like, Murden was not quite satisfied with his victory. He wanted the glory of saying that the last man of Keeler's band was dead, and that the roads were free.

"I think we have done enough," I said, "to satisfy you and the government. We have destroyed one half of a desperate band, and I think you can glorify yourself and your men, and with ample ground for all that you say."

The mouth of the cave was so well concealed that none of the men had as yet discovered it; so, after a brief survey of the country, so as to be satisfied that none of the bushrangers were lurking near, I led the way to the entrance, Murden following close to my heels.

I pulled aside the brush, and exposed the mouth of the cave; but, for fear of a trap, I sent the hound in to explore. He obeyed me without the least hesitation, and while he was absent we listened with much attention. All was quiet; but at last we heard a movement, and then a voice exclaimed, in querulous tones, —

"Ah! be aisy wid yer kissin' an old woman. I'd be ashamed of meself; that's what I would. It's liberties yer takin', and I an honest woman. Go way wid yer, and don't come blarnyin' round me, or ye'll feel me fut in a place ye won't like. Do ye mind, now, ye divil on airth."

CHAPTER XXXIII.

RESCUE OF AN ENGLISH BARONET. — HIS ADVENTURES. — A STRANGE SIGHT.

The sight which met our gaze as we entered the robbers' cave, revolvers in hand, was so peculiar and extraordinary that we stopped upon the threshold, and surveyed the scene before us, uncertain whether to laugh or assume a serious mien. In one corner, where I had found protection under a lot of old clothing, was stretched the fat form of Mother Brown; and, to my horror and dismay, she had upon her portly person but one garment, and that one such as ladies usually wear next to their skin. The woman was stretched out upon her back, apparently sleeping most soundly, while standing over her, with a puzzled expression upon his face, was Rover; and, as though to waken her to life, he was slobbering her tanned face with his huge red tongue.

"Be aisy, ye divil!" she murmured. "Don't take any more liberties wid a woman what ain't got more clothes on than a leedy like meself. If ye is honest in yer intentions, ye can take me afore the priest, and then ye can have the right to do as ye plase, honey."

This was too much for Murden. He laughed until the cave seemed full of echoes; but it had no effect upon Mother Brown, who continued to sleep, and the dog continued to mop her face as inclination prompted him. But hardly had our laughter died away, when we heard a deep groan in the darkest corner of the cavern, in a quarter where the light did not penetrate sufficiently for our eyes to reach.

"Who is there?" I asked, and took a step forward.

"If you are men and Christians, help me," said a feeble voice.

"Who are you?" I cried, as I advanced, followed by Murden, while the dog left his prey, and trotted towards the new applicant for aid.

"A poor, unfortunate man, who has been made a prisoner by a cursed band of highwaymen. I pray Heaven that you don't belong to it."

"Have no fear of us," I answered; and by this time I had reached the prisoner, and was kneeling down by his side.

The person who claimed our help was lying on his back, heavily ironed, and chained to the wall of the cave; so that escape was impossible.

But in spite of his gray hair and age, the prisoner was one of the best looking men that I had ever seen. His face was stamped with such a noble expression, so full of dignity and kindness, that I knew he was no ordinary person, and I was determined to know more of him before we parted.

But those eyes — where had I seen them? They were so handsome, dark blue, with long eyelashes, and seemed to recall to my mind some one's face, and yet I could not think whose. I taxed my memory to its utmost, but was unsuccessful. At last I spoke to the prisoner, thinking that his memory might help me.

"Your face appears familiar to me," I said. "Where can I have seen you?"

"I am sure I cannot answer the question," was the careless answer. "You policemen often note faces — it is your trade."

The reply nettled me, it was delivered in such a peculiar manner — as though it was not of the slightest consequence whether we had ever met before or not.

"My trade is not that of a policeman," was my reply, and in as haughty a tone as I could assume.

"O, isn't it?" and then the prisoner glanced at his irons, and continued: "Well, I wish you were a machinist, or a locksmith, or could pick the locks which fasten these irons, for they are galling my flesh, and I should be grateful if they were off."

"I am neither," I answered, and was about to walk off when Hez came forward.

"Let me see them 'ere locks," he said. "P'aps I can do somethin' with 'em."

"Then you're the man for me," returned the dignified-looking prisoner; "and if you free me I will amply reward you."

"Don't want no reward for work like that 'ere," was Hez's answer, with all of a Yankee's independence. "I'll be gol darned if I can't snake 'em off! You jist wait a minute."

The New Hampshire born man searched his pockets, and produced a stout wire, a file, and a miniature vice. He put the wire into the latter, filed it to a point, bent it in a peculiar manner, so that it bore some resemblance to a skeleton key, and after he was satisfied that it was all right, he thrust it into the lock, worked it about in a cautious manner, and at last had the satisfaction of seeing the lock fall off, and the irons removed.

"Well done, my friend," cried the stranger; "you have as much ingenuity as a Yankee."

"Wal, ain't I a Yankee?" retorted Hez. "You didn't go for to suppose that I was a pig-headed, beef-fed Englishman, did ye?"

The stranger laughed, as he answered, —

"You are complimentary to my countrymen, I must confess; but I suppose they will forgive you. If they don't, I will."

"He is not so prejudiced against our women as he is against the men," retorted Murden, — a remark that made Hez blush, and look as silly as a sheep.

"O! but few can withstand the influence of our ladies," responded the stranger in a gallant tone, as he rubbed his limbs, and tried to restore the circulation to them.

"And the Americans are especially susceptible to the tender passion," Murden remarked, and cast a sly glance at me, which the stranger noted.

"Ho, ho!" he said, with a pleasant smile, "we have another American in the person of that gentleman, have we? Well, I like them, and wish there were more of them in this country. But how does it happen that I find two persons from the United States in the police service in this country?"

"I have already told you that I am not in the police service," I said.

"O, so you did; I had forgotten," the stranger replied, in a careless manner, and continued to chafe his wrists; and while he was thus employed, I took a second survey of the man, and in spite of the dirt which covered his garments, and the general neglect of his toilet, I could not help feeling that the stranger was a gentleman — one who had moved in good society, and had been accustomed to respect and deference.

But Murden soon set all doubts at rest; for after he had directed that the bodies of the dead should be searched and buried, and our own wounded attended to in as comfortable a manner as possible, he asked the stranger, in his usual business-like, policeman style, a series of questions.

"Pray, sir, what is your name?" the commissioner demanded, taking out a book and making a note.

The stranger stopped chafing his wrists, and looked up.

"O, my name you want, do you?"

"Yes."

"Well, it is Byefield."

"Have you either trade or profession?"

The stranger laughed.

"To tell you the truth, I regret to state that I was not brought up to either. My parents had some vague idea that I should play the part of a gentleman."

"As this is not a country in which gentlemen flourish, I shall have to require a statement more definite," the commissioner remarked. "The fact of it is," he continued, "it is for me to determine whether you belong to the gang, or was a prisoner, as you state."

"I think that I have proof enough of the latter;" and Mr. Byefield pointed to the irons which had been removed from his hands and feet.

"Ah, but those amount to nothing. Keeler would have served any mutinous member of his gang in the same way."

"True, I did not think of that;" and the prisoner began once more to chafe his wrists, as though that was all the work he had in his mind at the time.

Murden winked at me, as much as to say, "We have a queer customer here," and then continued the interrogations:

"I must have direct answers to all my questions."

The prisoner looked up, as though surprised at the remark.

"If such is the case, I am bound to answer them:" and Mr. Byefield smiled in a quiet, subdued sort of manner, as though he had no secrets from the police.

"Well, sir," contiuued Murden, making an effort to write in his note-book, "be pleased to give your name in full."

"Well, sir, I did hope to escape such a necessity, for I have no relish for notoriety. I came here to attempt to accomplish certain objects, and I fear that if my name is known my purposes will be defeated."

"Ah," cried Murden, with a sniff like a war-horse, "you are a London detective; I know you are."

A smile, but rather a contemptuous one, passed over the sunburnt face of Mr. Byefield; but Murden did not notice it. He was too much excited at the thought of having met a brother officer. He held out his hand, but Mr. Byefield did not seem inclined to take it.

"Perhaps I can help you," Murden continued. "The whole force of the police shall be at your disposal if necessary."

"Thank you; but before you make many promises, let me undeceive you. I am not a London detective."

"The devil you ain't!"

"No, sir."

"Then who in thunder are you?"

Murden was so much disappointed that he was growing impolite.

"I am called," the stranger said, in a calm tone, and with all the dignity of a thorough-bred gentleman, "Sir William Byefield, of Lancaster, England, where I have estates which have been held by my ancestors for the past six hundred years."

O rank, what charms thou hast for an Englishman! How the sons of Great Britain will humiliate themselves before thee, and kiss the ground on which thou walkest! And Murden, into whose mind I had endeavored to instil the principles of republicanism, and a most hearty contempt for all the extravagant forms of royalty, felt the influence of rank and a name, even as announced by the individual before us, dirty as he appeared to my eyes. The commissioner stepped back and raised his hand to his hat, in token of respect, — for titles were not so plenty in Australia as in London, — and then asked, in a tone that was the very essence of respectfulness, —

"Sir William, can you give me any proof that such is your rank? You will excuse me for asking; but recollect I am a police officer, and feel compelled by duty to make inquiries."

The stranger laughed a frank sort of laugh; such a one as he would have uttered if his butler had asked if he would have ten pounds until the next quarter day.

"The proof of my statement will depend very much upon the contents of my valise, which I believe the bushrangers deposited in the cave. I do not know but they have destroyed all my papers. If they have not, you will find ample evidence that my report is true. At any rate, the bushrangers seemed to know my worth, for they offered to ransom me for the sum of one thousand pounds sterling; and, faith, they would have got it if you had not rescued me, for I had at length concluded to send an order to Melbourne for that amount. The courier left yesterday, but the order was not payable until ten days after date. Now, Mr. Commissioner, if you will send for my valise, I'll see what there is in it."

Murden despatched a man without delay, and he returned with the article. The baronet opened his valise, and found some of his papers unmolested, while others appeared to have been removed, which caused him to utter expressions of impatience and annoyance.

"Nothing lost, I hope, Sir William," cried Murden. "If

the rascals have dared to steal any of your important documents, I'll follow them all over the country, but I'll bring them to justice."

"Yes, I have no doubt but you will, Mr. Officer," returned the baronet, in a careless tone, as though such homage was his due; "but there is one paper which is of no value to any person excepting myself. It was simply a description; and yet, strange to say, it is gone."

"Look around, men, and see if you can find it," the commissioner cried; and in obedience to the order, the men commenced peering into every bush and through the cave; but they were not successful. In the mean time Sir William had gathered up a handful of letters and thrust them into Murden's hand.

"If you will take the trouble to read some of those, you will be satisfied that I am the person I represent myself to be."

"These papers are perfectly satisfactory, Sir William," the commissioner said, "and I feel glad to be able to offer you any assistance in my power, although your visit to Australia is a —"

"Secret, sir," was the answer. "I did not come here for gold. I did not come here to examine the country; but what I did come for must remain unknown to you, for the present, at least, although the time may come when you will be able to help me."

"I hope so, Sir William," was the reply. "I should be proud to render you some assistance. You can depend upon me."

"I have not the least doubt of it, sir," the baronet replied, with a wave of his hand, as though it was an honor to serve a man of good blood, even without the hope of reward; and then Sir William, as though he had performed his duty in acknowledging Murden's offer of assistance, turned to me, and said, —

"It is a little singular, Mr. American, that I did not recognize you when first we met. I am sure Lady C—— described you in the most accurate manner. She has a nice sense of gratitude, and each time that she looks at her diamonds she blesses your name."

"I hope that she still recollects me, Sir William," Murden said.

"Yes, I suppose so; although she did not appear to revere your name. I have no doubt that Lady C—— is profoundly grateful to you. Egad! a woman should be."

"By the way, Mr. Commissioner," the baronet cried, "will you send one of your men to the city and stop that draft? I'll write the order immediately."

"Certainly, Sir William."

The baronet was about to do so, when we heard a roar of laughter from the men; and on looking up we saw so strange a spectacle that we could not help joining in the merriment. The cause of it was Mother Brown, who had slept through the din and racket, and had just awakened to consciousness, and staggered into the open air, minus a dress, but clothed in an under-garment, none too clean, and none too long. For a moment the woman looked around with semi-sobriety and semi-drunken gravity, and then, as her glance fell upon Sir William, she uttered a shrill shriek, and tumbled to the ground; and so heavily did she fall that the earth shook when she touched it.

CHAPTER XXXIV.

MOTHER BROWN'S MYSTERY. — A SEARCH FOR GOLD. — A TERRIBLE SURPRISE.

I DID not understand why Mother Brown should shriek and tumble to the ground. She certainly had seen nothing to alarm her, with the exception of the police uniforms; so I was forced to conclude that her illness was produced through strong drink. In the mean time she was lying on the ground like a log, and in a most uncomfortable position; and the men, instead of lending her some assistance, were laughing at the sight, for they considered her beyond the scale of humanity, and were too much accustomed to such sights to care for them. But I was determined that she should not suffer, so I ran towards her, straightened out her limbs and neck; and then threw cold water upon her face, and sent one of the officers to the stream for more; but before he returned Mother Brown gave some evidence of life, and at last sat up, and stared at me in a wild sort of manner, as though she did not recollect to have seen me before.

"Where's Keeler?" she asked.

"He's fled. The traps have driven him away, after killing some of his men. He won't come back again."

She looked at me for a moment without uttering a word; but at last her mind seemed to comprehend something, for she said, "Where's the clothes ye stole from me? It's naked ye left me, taking the only frock I had in the world. Ah, it's scandilous the way ye trated me. Give me the frock, so I can cover me nakedness, and not put me to blush afore all the men."

"Have patience, and you shall have the best frock that I can purchase in Melbourne. Don't think that I have forgotten the manner in which you saved my life."

"Ah, yes; now I remember. I saved ye on Jenny's account. Had it not been for me, divil a bit would she have knowed ye for a husband. Yes, lad," the old woman chuckled, "I know the blue-eyed lass, and I'll help yer with her. Ah! ye may smile, but I can do more than ye think for. Time will come when ye will say so."

While she was speaking, Sir William approached the group. I saw Mother Brown's eyes rest upon the baronet's face, but only for a moment; but that brief time was sufficient to satisfy me that she had met him at some period of her life, and was now desirous that he should not recollect her. I don't know what made me think so. I am sure that Sir William did not appear to regard her in the light of an acquaintance, for I saw on his aristocratic face only an expression of deep disgust, but no sign of recognition

Mother Brown turned her head as soon as she met the earnest gaze of the baronet, and I saw her pass her hands over her eyes, and heard her murmur, —

"Indade, then, I did not drame it. It is himself."

Just at this instant Sir William happened to pass near, when she shuddered as though she had seen a ghost. She turned abruptly away, so that he did not notice her face, and then retired to the cave in a precipitate manner. No one, excepting myself, noticed her movements; so there was no remark made by the men. As Mother Brown gained the entrance of the cave, she turned and motioned for me to come near her. I obeyed the summons; and when I was within whispering distance I saw her face had undergone a great change. She appeared to be perfectly sober, as though she had experienced some shock of an unexpected kind, which had driven the liquor entirely from her head. Her face, naturally red, was pale; and her limbs trembled.

"My boy," she whispered, "I must lave this place. Can I go?"

"Yes; but where do you wish to go to?"

"Divil a bit do I know. But I must lave, though, for all that. I can't stay here another hour. It would kill me."

"Can you ride?" I asked.

"Yes."

I tore a leaf from a note-book, and wrote to Smith, asking him to let his wife see that Mother Brown was properly dressed and cared for until my return. This I gave to her, and to prevent her losing it she pinned it to her — well, call it under-garment.

"Do you know the way to Smith's farm?" I asked.

"Sure I do. It's in the valley."

"Yes. Go there and wait for me."

"I will. Anywhere, to lave here."

"And mind that you keep sober."

"Divil a drop will I touch, even if whiskey is offered me."

"That is right. Now follow me."

I led the way down the hill, no one excepting Murden and Hez noticing me. We reached the place where the horses were tied. Two men were with them, and they were somewhat astonished at our appearance.

"Which horse belonged to Jones?" I asked.

"This one, sir;" and the policeman pointed to a stout cob.

"Poor fellow! he will never want him again. Lead the animal this way."

After Mother Brown was mounted, and her garment adjusted in a satisfactory manner, I turned the head of the horse in the direction of Smith's house, and told her to hurry on and wait for me. I saw her disappear, and then I once more rejoined my friends.

"Where is the woman?" asked Murden.

"I have sent her to Smith's house for a fit-out of clothing," I replied.

"The devil you did! Why, she's a prisoner!"

"Well, you'll find her when you want her company."

The sun was beating down most intensely, so that the men were glad to seek shelter under the shade of the bushes and stunted trees, where they could smoke their pipes or sleep, just as they pleased. But Murden and I did not care for a nap just at that time, although we pretended that we needed one. We had other business to look after as soon as the men had closed their eyes and lost consciousness. We were anxious to solve the mystery of the cave. We longed to stir the earth in one corner, and see if Keeler had removed his treasures, and mentally I was calculating how much they would amount to. While I was indulging in such a reverie, Murden poked me with his elbow.

"Come," he whispered; "we'll visit the cave, and see if anything turns up. Softly, now; don't make a noise."

We walked towards the cave in a quiet and cautious manner. No one noticed us, nor was a single head raised. We entered the cave, listened for a moment to see if any one had followed us; and when we found that no one had, we commenced removing the clothes which covered the spot where I supposed the treasure was buried.

"The earth has recently been disturbed here," whispered Murden, as he felt with his hands, and discovered how loose the ground seemed. "I wonder if that cunning cuss has carried off his plunder. If he has, I'll never forgive him."

While Murden was speaking, he was scraping away the earth, digging it up with a stick which he found near the pile of clothes.

"Can't you find a shovel for me?" the commissioner asked. "It's such deuced slow work with a stick."

"I think so. At any rate, I'll see what I can do;" and I crossed to the other side of the cave, and searched around, but found nothing excepting a large spoon. Just as I was about to stoop and pick it up, I heard some one breathing hard, as though laboring under considerable excitement, or else under much fatigue. I thought it was the commissioner; so I said:

"What in the devil's name is the matter with you? Have you found the gold?"

"No; but I'm hard on to it. Hurry up something for me to dig with."

I tossed him the spoon, and he recommenced work, throwing out the dirt with much eagerness.

"Thunder! I wish that I had a shovel," muttered the commissioner.

I was standing, looking over my friend's shoulder, when the remark was made, and to my intense astonishment a deep bass voice just back of me said, "How will this suit you?"

I turned and saw, within two feet of me, with a cocked revolver in each hand, the vigorous form of Keeler.

CHAPTER XXXV.

A VISIT FROM KEELER. — HE IS URGENT FOR OUR COMPANY. — DOINGS AT POINT LOOKOUT.

I DON'T think I was ever more surprised in my life than I was when I turned so suddenly and saw the villanous features of Keeler. I couldn't help staggering back a pace or two; and in this operation I stepped upon Murden's feet, which provoked from him an oath.

"What in time are you about?" demanded Murden, who, strange to say, such was his eagerness in searching for gold, had not heard the bushranger. "Hang it, man, can't you keep off of my feet, when I'm near one of the boxes?"

I could not respond to that subdued shout of congratulation.

"Do you hear me?" demanded Murden. "I have found something. It is heavy, and I'll wager it is full of dust." As he spoke, he got up from his knees, holding the can in his hands, and so intent upon examining it that he did not even notice Keeler. "I shall claim one third, old feller," the commissioner continued. "You know the bargain we made."

"And I shall claim the whole!" said the deep bass voice of Keeler.

Murden looked up, and for the first time saw the bushranger and his threatening attitude. Of course the commissioner was surprised, but he did not quail. He was an Englishman, and I will give them the credit of being brave in the presence of danger.

"Hullo!" said Murden; "where in the devil's name did you come from?"

"Speak in a lower tone," cried Keeler, in a hoarse whisper; "and while you speak, remember that I am armed, that I am desperate, and that I expect to lose my life; but I will take yours in return."

"That's devilish considerate on your part," the commissioner replied; "but before I die, I'd like to know how you passed my pickets, so that after I'm dead I can haunt the men who neglected their duty."

"Your men looked sharp enough," Keeler answered, "but they did not happen to see me when I passed them. I am well acquainted with the neighborhood, and thought that I would return and secure the treasure which I had buried for future use. It appears that I arrived just in time."

"So it seems. Now take your money and be off;" and Murden rolled the can towards the bushranger, and spoke in such a cool tone that I thought the fellow would leave us; but I was mistaken.

"When I go, you will go with me," was the quiet remark of the robber.

"But suppose I decline your invitation?" Murden said. "I have no desire for your society, unless you yield as a prisoner."

"That I shall not do. You are mine, and I shall hold you. When I leave this cave, you and your spying companion will go with me. If either of you make the least noise, I shall end your days in short order, although my own life pays the forfeit of the act. Now be warned in time. My revolver is loaded, and never failed me. If you resist, and raise an alarm, waking your companions, they will rush in only to find two corpses. I shall escape."

"How?" demanded Murden, in a sullen tone.

"No matter how. But I give you my word that I can disappear with wonderful rapidity."

"I'd like to see you do it," the commissioner remarked.

A grim smile passed over Keeler's face. He relished just such coolness.

"When I go, you will go with me. My men are thirsty for revenge. They have lost comrades through your pursuit, and they will feel better if they can see you experience some of the tortures which their friends have suffered."

"Thank you kindly for your good intentions, but I don't choose to leave the cave in your company;" and Murden folded his arms, and looked determined.

A flush of anger passed over Keeler's face. He raised his revolver, and seemed determined to blow out the commissioner's brains; but a better thought restrained him.

"No," he said, "I'll not kill you just at present. I came here for my dust. There is more of it in that hole. Dig, and take it out."

"Suppose we divide it, and call it all right?" the commissioner asked. "You can take your share, and go to the devil with it if you like."

"I shall take the whole, and two devils with me," was the

cool rejoinder. "But we waste time in arguments. My comrades are waiting for me. If I remain much longer, they will think that some misfortune has happened to me, and possibly venture upon a rescue."

"I wish they would," cried the commissioner. "My boys would handle them in such a lively manner, that they would be glad to run a second time. Can't I persuade you to let them come?"

"Dig," replied the ruffian, who did not relish such joking; and as he spoke he raised his revolver and looked most threatening, as though his will was good enough; but prudence restrained him from firing, for he knew that he would endanger his own life.

"O, you want me to dig, do you?" the commissioner asked, in a sullen tone, as though just awakened from a deep sleep.

The bushranger stamped his foot with impatience. "Time is precious — dig!"

The pistol was pointed at Murden's head. He did not offer to resist its threatening influence, but dropped on his knees and re-commenced removing the dirt from the hole where the treasure was buried. Keeler remained at a convenient distance from us, and watched all motions with the sagacity of a tiger. Murden had not thrown out more than half a bucket full of dirt, when his iron spoon struck upon some solid substance.

"Here it is!" cried the commissioner, in his enthusiasm forgetting the presence of Keeler. He threw out a few more spoonfuls of earth, and then lifted a large tin can, such as preserved meats are put in. The can was nearly a foot long, and so heavy that it required most of Murden's strength to raise it from the hole.

"The devil, but it is heavy. There must be nearly fifty pounds of dust in that can," Murden cried, and then stood up and faced the bushranger.

"There is all of that in the can," was the quiet reply. "And now that you have brought it to light, just pick it up and lead the way out of the cave."

"Faith, I'll do that very readily;" for Murden thought there was but one entrance to the cave, and he was about to make a bolt for the outer world, when the bushranger stopped him in his cool, determined way.

"Excuse me, but you don't pass out in sight of your men. I should be green to permit such a course. There is another passage-way which we can take."

Murden said, "O, is there?" and looked a little disappointed.

"The one by which I entered. Come, follow me, and I'll show it to you."

"I'll be hanged if I go!" was the commissioner's rough exclamation. "I've followed you far enough. Now shoot and be blessed, for I go no farther!"

"You'll follow me, sir," Keeler said, and once more raised his revolver, and brought it to bear upon the commissioner's head — an act that did not alarm me much, for I had learned to read the bushranger's face.

Murden hesitated. He did not want to yield too soon, because he had said that he would not leave the cave. He wanted the privilege of arguing for a moment, partly in hopes that some of his men would enter the cave and rescue us, and partly in hopes that Keeler would take his treasure and run with it. We were just opposite the front entrance, or rather the bushranger was there, and we within two feet of him. Keeler could notice if any one offered to enter the cave, and take measures accordingly. But of that there was not much danger; for the men were tired, the sun was hot, and it was probable that they would sleep or doze until the air was cooler. Therefore, as we stood, Keeler's back was towards the secret entrance, while we faced it. He was for retreating into it step by step, drawing us along; and we should have reached it in a few seconds if Murden had not grown rebellious, and declared that he would not move — a remark which caused the argument, in the shape of a revolver, to be once more raised and pointed at my friend's head.

As I said before, Murden's English-like obstinacy delayed

as for some time, — that is, when we count seconds as hours, — and enabled a very pretty little diversion to be made in our favor, but from a quarter that we least expected, and by a man whom we thought a prisoner. But to understand the matter thoroughly, we will leave our party standing in the centre of the cave, in no pleasant position, while we return for a short time to Point Lookout, and see what had taken place there.

It will be remembered that we left the two bushrangers, Bob and Alf, whom we captured on Point Lookout, in the charge of Tom Spitman. Well, after we were gone, Tom began to feel lonesome for the want of amusement. He forgot, in a measure, his promise and instructions; and as he sat looking at the two bushrangers, he imagined what a chance it was for roasting them; and then he laughed as he thought how they would squirm when the flames reached their bodies. In fact he approached Bob, and felt of his ribs and stomach, which caused the robber to ask, —

"What in thunder do you want to do that for?"

"Never you mind what I'm doin' it for," was the reply. "You jist keep still, and don't make a noise."

"Do you want to see how fat I am?" asked Bob.

"Well, such is my intentions;" and Tom once more poked his victim's ribs, and then turned his attention to Alf, which caused that grim old bushranger to utter the most fearful oaths and imprecations upon the head of his guardian.

"Keep still," said Tom, who found that owing to the restlessness of the man he could not detect the condition of his ribs. "If you don't keep still," Tom continued, in a tone that indicated a resolution to do him some damage, "the worse for you."

But the grisly old bushranger had no notion of keeping still; and as Tom continued to feel of his ribs, and punch him in various parts of his body, Alf lost all patience. He managed to draw up his feet, manacled though they were, and firmly planted them in Tom's breast; and the effect was to send the fellow rolling over and over for some distance.

"Blast you," Tom muttered; "I'll make you sweat for this, you see if I don't."

"Let me help you," cried Bob, who pretended to have espoused Tom's cause, and knew too much to laugh when Tom was knocked over by Alf's huge feet.

"Ah, how's that?" asked Tom, a new idea seeming to strike him.

"Why, you just let me out of these 'ere darbies, and then we can have some fun with the old feller," Bob said, in an insinuating tone.

Alf uttered a horrid oath, and growled at his comrade for deserting him.

"But you'll run away," said Tom, who appeared to think favorably of the scheme.

"No, I won't. On my honor, you know."

"I was told by that bloody young swell," Tom said, after a moment's thought, "not to hurt you; so I won't; 'cos if I did, he'd come down on me like bricks. He's the devil when he's riled. I heard the commissioner say so. He'd shoot me like a mice if I burned you."

"What do you mean by burning a cove?" asked Bob, who had wit enough to see that he was making an impression.

"I'll show you in a minute. Jist roll yourself out of the way, so that I can come at this feller," meaning the grisly old bushranger. Bob complied with the request, and Tom commenced gathering leaves, dried branches, and grass. With these he surrounded Alf, — the bushrangers watching proceedings in a state of profound astonishment.

"Blast you, and your arrangements, too!" shouted the old bushranger; and he rolled himself outside of the circle which Tom had built around him.

"It's the worse for you, old cock," cried Tom; and he commenced rebuilding the magic circle; but no sooner was it completed, than Alf, in the most ungrateful manner, rolled out of it, and swore horrid oaths at the man who had so patiently constructed the whole thing.

By this time Tom began to grow angry.

"Hang you!" he said, "you do that again, and I'll roast you like a goose; you see if I don't. I only intended to scorch you; but if you spile my work once more, I won't leave a pin-feather on yer."

"Come here a minute, sir," said Bob, "and I'll tell you how to manage him."

Tom went to him, when Bob whispered, "Just take me out of these irons, and I'll hold him until the fire is under way; and then what fun it will be to see him roll through!"

Tom thought of the matter, and then asked, "Won't you attempt to cut and run?"

"No, indeed; and if I should, haven't you got pistols? Couldn't you shoot me?"

The temptation was too strong. Tom unlocked the irons, and took them off.

"Now you hold the old cove, while I get the things ready for a fire."

"No; you do that," replied Bob, who dreaded the maledictions of the old bushranger.

Tom complied, and in a few minutes Bob had built up a circle of stuff, and then set fire to it.

"Hurrah!" yelled Tom, leaving the body of the bush ranger, and dancing outside of the circle for very joy. "This is jolly," he continued, as the old robber began to squirm under the influence of the fire.

"So it is, but I'll make it more jolly," said Bob; and with the words he gave Tom a vigorous push—one that sent him on top of the bushranger, where Alf held him with his teeth until both were pretty well scorched, Tom's hair being all gone, and Alf's beard entirely destroyed.

When the fire went out they separated, and then it was discovered that the honest Bob had taken advantage of the confusion, and left the scene.

CHAPTER XXXVI.

AN UNEXPECTED VISITOR, BUT A PLEASANT ONE. — THE TREASURE. — A GREAT SURPRISE.

Tom was aware that it was useless to follow the fellow, for he knew all the mountain paths, and could easily elude all pursuit; so he sat down, and looked at the bushranger, who was still lying on his back, smoky, grim, and sullen, and wondered how he should lie himself out of the scrape, and so escape severe punishment. And Alf looked at Tom, and thought how his old teeth did bite, but could not imagine where the fun was in being burned and smothered like a rat. In the mean time, Bob was bounding from rock to rock, leaping across chasms and over dead logs, leading in the direction of the cave, but knowing that he could not reach that place before the police force, as the latter had had two hours the start. But some inward feeling urged him to take that course, although he knew that it was dangerous to do so.

When Bob was within half a mile of the cave, he stopped and rested, and thought of the matter. It was not safe for him to approach the cave without reconnoitring, so that he should not be surprised and recaptured. He had no doubt that the traps would either capture his comrades or drive them off, and perhaps kill one half of them. If Keeler was out of the way, he no longer had a motive for remaining in the band. He would make some efforts to reform, and escape from the country as soon as possible.

Bob started for the cave; but he worked his way through the brush and trees in such a manner that he escaped the observation of the pickets which Murden had thrown out, and soon found himself in the secret passage-way. He crawled along on his hands and knees until he arrived at the cave, and then stopped and listened in astonishment, for he heard the low, threatening tones of Keeler, and after a few words had passed, knew that the robber chief had managed to get hold of his treasure and capture two prisoners at the same time.

"Keeler will kill that young swell," Bob muttered, "and he has saved me many times. I will lend the young cove a helping hand."

As Bob muttered the last words he sprang from the mouth of the passage-way, just as Keeler had pointed his revolver at Murden's head, and, with an angry scowl, intimated that we must accompany him or die a sudden death.

"Hullo! cap'n, don't be violent," cried Bob, whose appearance had caused me the most intense surprise.

As the lively young bushranger spoke in a careless tone, it was so sudden and entirely unexpected that Keeler lowered his arm and turned half round. I had expected such a result the moment Bob spoke, and was prepared for it; for while Murden was gathering his wits, and wondering what the devil it all meant, I had bounded forward, thrown my arms around the robber captain, and, with a twist of my right foot, knocked his feet out from under him, and down he went with a crash; and as he struck the earth his revolver went off, the ball just grazing my arm, but doing no damage. The next instant I had wrenched the pistol from his grasp, even while he was attempting to cock it, so that he could take a second shot; and with the butt of the weapon I struck the prostrate man a violent blow upon his temple, and so well delivered was it, that the bushranger did not make any more resistance, but just dropped his head and uttered a deep sigh.

"Gently, young swell," cried Bob, who had not moved to assist his captain. "Don't be violent, sir, if you please. He is human, sir, although I should judge you thought him made of iron. He can't stand sich blows, and live."

Before another word of remonstrance had been uttered, the police officers, awakened from their naps by the report of the pistol, came rushing into the cave pellmell, sabres in hand, and revolvers ready to do instant execution.

"What's the row?" asked Lieutenant Maurice, who was at the head of the men.

"O, nothing remarkable," answered Murden, who had

fully recovered his presence of mind, and thrown the two cans of treasure behind some clothes which were lying on the floor, so that his officers should not see what we had been searching for. "These two men thought they would surprise us; but we rather got the best of it, and astonished them."

The policemen did not know what to do or say; so they stared at Keeler and at Bob.

"I'm blessed if this isn't the feller what we left in charge of Tom," Maurice remarked, giving Bob a whirl round, which the bushranger took in good part, and grinned an acknowledgment of the charge.

Murden started, and would have rushed forward for an investigation; but I stopped him by a sign.

"Put the irons on these men," I said. "We *must* secure them and keep them."

"Egad! I think we will," Murden exclaimed, in a triumphant tone. "Put on double irons."

Bob looked at me as though wondering if I would consent to that, but I pretended not to notice him; and while the officers were securing him I walked out of the cave, so that I could compose my thoughts, and manage some plan for Bob's relief. I passed on to the fire, lighted my pipe, and sat down under the shade of a balsam tree. While I sat smoking, the men brought out Keeler and Bob. The former had recovered consciousness, but did not look in the least humbled. His eyes were as bright, and his face as threatening, as they appeared in the cave but a few minutes before. A small stream of blood was trickling down his temple from the effect of the blow which I had given him; but it only added to the robber's determined look and fierce appearance. The police officers surrounded the bushranger, and examined the features of a man whom they had heard of so often, and who had always managed to elude their closest pursuit.

"Look a-here," Maurice said, addressing the lively young bushranger; "how did you manage to slip the darbies off your feet and hands, and escape from Tom's custody?"

"Why, he wanted me to assist him," was the reply.

"In doing what?"

"O, in getting up a little bit of fireworks on his account."

The officers all laughed. They knew Tom's predilection for fire.

"Tell us all about it," Maurice said.

Bob told the story in his own peculiar manner, which elicited shouts of laughter from those who listened to him; and when he concluded with a humorous description of the manner in which he had sent Tom heels over head into the circle of fire, right on top of Alf, even Murden and Sir William were compelled to join in the laugh, and to acknowledge that Bob was smart, and had obtained a decided advantage over the fire-loving servant.

"But I'll thrash him within an inch of his life when I next see him," Murden said. "He has disobeyed orders."

"I rather think he's smarting enough. He'll look like a singed cat. I don't suppose that he'll forgive me, but I can bear it if he don't."

"That man was never intended for a robber," remarked Sir William, as we turned away from the scene. "He is too jolly for a bushranger. I believe that he is the most decent of the gang."

"I know that such is the case. To him I owe my life; and I'm not one to forget a debt of gratitude."

"Then why not obtain a pardon for the fellow?"

"The task is no light one."

"I know it. But, to tell the truth, the rascal did befriend me when I was captured on my way to Ballarat, and through his aid I was enabled to save some papers of value; and, as you are grateful, why, so I'll prove. I'll join you in obtaining his pardon, or, at least, a probation order."

"Agreed; and, if we succeed, let us hope that our efforts will not be lost on the fellow. It's his last chance for life."

"And he should understand that it is," remarked the baronet, in an impressive manner.

We then separated—I to consult Murden as to the next move, and Sir William to stretch himself under the shade of a tree. I put my arm through Murden's, and led him a short distance from the men.

"How shall we manage to carry off Keeler's hoard?" I asked.

"I have been thinking the whole subject over," the commissioner replied, "and have concluded that the best course we can adopt is to call Hopeful into our councils, and see what advice he can offer. He is good at suggestions."

"So he is. Let us enter the cave, and lay the whole matter before him."

We went in, called Hez, told him what we had found, and showed him the cans. At first he would not believe us; but after we had convinced him that the cans were really filled with dust and gold coin, his joy was extravagant and most heartfelt.

"Why, there's thousands of dollars in them 'ere!" Hez cried, his eyes opened to their widest extent.

"We are aware of it. We want the money for our own use; and, to enable us to keep it, you must help us."

"Am I to share in all that?" asked Hez, with trembling eagerness.

"Yes; provided you do your part of the work in securing it."

"I have it," said Hez, in an eager tone. "We will wrap our blankets around it, and strap it on behind our saddles."

"It's our only chance," replied Murden. "If we leave it behind us, we shall never set eyes on it again. We must carry it off with us."

"Yes, even if I have to swaller it, and then heave it up," cried Hez.

"Go and get your prisoners on horseback," I said to Murden, "and leave Hez and me to look after the cans. We will manage, in some manner, to blind the eyes of your men."

The commissioner left the cave to give the necessary orders; to secure the prisoners, each one was strapped to the back of a burly police officer. Of course this caused some trouble, and took some time; and while attention was directed towards Keeler and Bob, Hez and I slipped down the mountain with the valuables under our arms, secured them to our saddle-bows, and then gave the signal to Murden that we were ready. He took the hint, and shouted out, —

"Why won't you escort Sir William across the valley, and tell Smith that we shall want some supper and breakfast. It will save time, and help us."

We started on our journey, followed by Rover, who had just returned from a hunt without leave on my part, and therefore felt a little ashamed of himself; for had he been in the cave when Keeler appeared, the career of that adventurous robber would suddenly have terminated, for the dog would have thought no more of taking him by the throat, than he would of taking a kangaroo. He might have lost his life by so doing, but the bushranger would not have lived to tell the story.

"A fine dog that," remarked Sir William, as we crossed the brook, first allowing our horses to drink.

"Yes; and I esteem and value him," I replied.

Just at this instant Rover sprang towards a clump of tall grass, or hummock, near the edge of the Black Forest, and as he bounded along, he uttered a deep bay. I knew his calls too well to class it among his expressions of rage.

"Holloa!" cried the baronet, "your dog has started something. A kangaroo, perhaps. Let us give chase."

"Rover does not bay like that when he meets a wild animal," I answered, confidently.

"Well, let's see what it is, at any rate;" and the baronet touched his horse and galloped towards the spot.

When we arrived at the hummock, Rover wagged his tail, and looked as much as to say, "Well, this is a pretty go. I don't understand it."

I jumped from my horse, pulled the grass one side, and then found, to my intense astonishment, that I was face to face with Jenny Sykes, the handsome blue-eyed daughter of the Manchester Pet, the ex-prize-fighter.

CHAPTER XXXVII.

MISS JENNY AND HER POSITION. — AS HANDSOME AND VULGAR AS EVER.

As I pulled aside the bushes, Jenny looked up startled and frightened; but when she caught sight of my face, I think that she was as much astonished as myself, for I started back, and exclaimed, "Good heavens! Jenny, how came you here?" and before she could answer, or even rise from the sitting position which she had assumed for the purpose of concealment, Rover walked up to her, gave a snuff, and then with his huge red tongue licked her face, as though he really liked it.

"I can answer none of your questions," was the haughty reply.

"Jenny," I cried, in more humble tones than I thought it possible for me to use towards a bar-maid, even if she were as handsome and virtuous as an angel, "why can't we be friends, and trusting ones at that? I do not deserve this coldness and reproach, and you know it."

"You know that's a lie. You can't come the blarney over me, Mr. Spy," the plain-spoken girl replied; and I sighed when I heard such words issuing from a mouth that looked sweeter than the one that kissed Paris and Troy to destruction, for I don't believe that fair Helen could have shown such white, even teeth and red lips as the bar-maid of Melbourne.

I heard a sigh, a deep, painful one, at my side, and I turned to see who uttered it. Sir William was standing near, regarding the haughty face of the girl with so much attention that I felt a little jealous of his glances; but I soon saw that it was not admiration for her beauty that caused that look of interest, for the baronet turned away after a moment's silence and stern gaze, with the remark, —

"Such a jewel, and such a setting!" and just as he spoke

Miss Jenny, who had not relished Sir William's ardent gaze, said, with an impudent toss of her pretty head, —

"Don't eat me up with your eyes — or didn't you ever see a woman like me afore?"

"Hush, Jenny," I said. "The gentleman meant no offence."

"Well, don't let him stare at me in that way. I ain't one of that sort."

"Tell me, Jenny," I said, as Sir William turned away, "what brought you into this part of the country?"

"My legs," was the answer.

"You know what I mean, Miss Jenny," I continued. "How happens it that I meet you in this lonely spot?"

"The meeting ain't none of my seekin'. It ain't likely that I would run towards the cove what jugged my dad."

"You grow worse and worse," I exclaimed, in a pettish manner. "Do for Heaven's sake leave off uttering such slang."

"Why should I? 'Tain't to please you that I is here. I comes here for —"

She stopped short, and tossed her handsome head like a well-bred racer when in the company of a cart-horse. She was determined to treat me with contempt at all hazards, and I was equally determined that she should not disgust me or anger me in the least.

"You saw us coming, and so concealed yourself," I said. "Do you know the danger of this valley?"

"Yes."

"That it is surrounded by bad men, who would not care the least for your beauty or your haughty ways, but would —"

"Stop!" she said. "If a man talked slang to me, I'd spit in his nasty face."

"He'd care but little for that. On every side of you there are bushrangers, desperate men, who would treat you in a vile manner, and laugh at your tears. Come, Jenny; confide in me, and, believe me, I shall prove a kind protector."

She curled her lip in scorn at the offer.

"I ain't afeard of men," she said. "If they come near

me they'll catch it. I'd scratch their eyes out in no time No, sir; you look arter yerself, and let me alone."

"I shall not leave you here alone," I remarked, in a firm tone. "You would be stung to death with snakes before morning. See; there is one gliding through the grass and heading this way."

I had touched her on a tender point. All women have a horror of snakes, and I don't blame them for entertaining such a feeling; for to encounter a reptile in the woods, or in a valley, is far from being agreeable to most people. Jenny was no exception to the general rule; so, when she turned and saw a black snake with a white ring around its neck, with head erect, gliding towards us, the handsome bar-maid changed color, trembled for a moment, as though uncertain what to do, and then sprang towards me, and threw herself into my arms.

"Kill that blasted thing," whispered the terrified maid. "I don't want it round me."

I heard a suppressed laugh, and I knew that Sir William and Hez were enjoying themselves at my expense.

"The lioness is conquered by a python," Sir William said.

"Then I'll be darned ef it ain't the fust time she ever took pity on 'im," cried Hez, who misunderstood the meaning of the word python.

I encircled the graceful waist of the girl with my left arm, and drew my revolver with my right hand. The snake continued to advance, not in the least intimidated by the firm stand which I had assumed. As it neared us I saw at once that it was not a poisonous reptile — that its bite was not dangerous, although painful, owing to the length of its fangs.

"Don't tremble so, Jenny," I whispered, placing my lips as near her cheeks as I dared. "I will protect you from all harm. The snake shall destroy me before it touches you."

Now there was not the slightest danger of my being destroyed, or of Jenny's being harmed, unless she provoked the reptile to hostilities; so when I told her that I would die for her, she just clung a little closer, and then I took a deliberate aim and fired; and I was fortunate enough to put a ball through the neck of the snake, which caused it to tie itself up into hard knots, to lash the grass with its powerful tail, and then to stretch out and die.

"The danger is over, dear Jenny," I whispered. "The snake is dead."

"Well, I'm bloody glad of it;" and with these coarse, vulgar words upon her lips, the girl twisted her form from my arms, and once more her lovely face assumed a cold, disdainful look, as though she hated herself for the momentary weakness which had got the better of her nature.

"You see, Jenny, what you would be exposed to, if you remained in the valley over night," I remarked.

"I see," was the cold rejoinder.

"And you will go with us to some place of safety?" I continued.

She hesitated, and looked up and down the valley with a perplexed air.

"Let me speak with her," cried Sir William, coming forward. "Perhaps the girl will listen to the words which a gray-haired man utters."

There was something in the voice and manner of Sir William that caused Jenny to look up with a face that was frownless; and as my eyes wandered from her countenance to that of the baronet's, it suddenly flashed across my mind, that the mystery was at last solved. I had puzzled my brain for some hours to determine where I had seen face and eyes that resembled Sir William's. The question was answered at last, and as the girl and baronet stood opposite to each other, the likeness appeared to be marvellous — one of those accidental coincidences which cannot always be accounted for.

For a few seconds the parties looked at each other, Jenny apparently as much surprised at Sir William's face, as he was at hers; but at length the baronet recovered his self-possession, and said, —

"Young lady, you had better take advice, and such advice as my friend here offers. You can't go forward, and you can't remain here, without danger. This is no place for one like you; so go with us, and we will see that you are taken care of."

"Miss Jenny," I said, "I know your errand, and can tell you that it is a useless one. The bushrangers, whom you were sent to communicate with, are dispersed, and those who did not escape were either killed or taken prisoners. They will not venture in the vicinity of the cave for some days, so you can understand how necessary it is that you should go with us."

"I didn't want to see no bushrangers," pouted Jenny, with her finger in her mouth, and a frown on her brow.

"You know that your father sent you here," I continued, making a bold guess.

She did not answer, but continued to suck her finger, and to frown at me. I knew I was on the right track, so I continued: "Keeler is a prisoner, and in the hands of the police; and Mother Brown, the only one who would be likely to protect your sex, is gone."

"And where has she gone to?" asked Jenny, with a start, and at the same time removing her finger from her mouth, and staring at me with her clear blue eyes.

"Across the valley;" and I pointed in the direction of Smith's house.

She turned and looked in the direction I indicated, and I saw that her resolution was shaken. She did not know what to do, or which way to turn. For a few moments I enjoyed her perplexity, for I knew that she must ultimately confide in me, or endure terrible hardships; and I am sure I wished to save her from the latter. I was too sincere in my friendship to wish that she might suffer on account of a little wilfulness. After a long pause, during which Jenny had stared at the ground as though it would solve some of her difficulties, she raised her head, and asked,—

"If I go with you, can I see Mother Brown?"

"I am not certain on that point, but I think you will be enabled to. I will do all I can to bring you together."

"Then I will go with you; but I won't stand any gammon, mind you."

"If you is goin' to take the gal along, you had better do it," said Hez; "'cos the purlice will overtake us, and then all hands will have questions to ax, and all will want to see her ride. I'd hurry if I was you, and cared for the gal."

For the first time I began to wonder how I was to transport Jenny across the valley. She could not walk, for her shoes were nearly gone, and her feet were bleeding where she had torn them in the brush, and with the rank grasses which grew near the small streams that ran through the valley. There was no help for it — I must take her on my horse.

"Will you ride before or behind me?" I asked.

She pouted, and made no reply. I saw that a little urging was necessary. I took her hand and led her to my horse, and then lifted her to the saddle, adjusting her clothes around her small feet and delicate ankles; and before she had recovered from her surprise, I had sprung up behind her, put my arms around her waist, and started the horse in the direction of Smith's house. Jenny only uttered one word of remonstrance; but I silenced her.

"Take your arms from my waist," she said.

"And allow you to fall? I shan't do it;" and I tightened my embrace.

Few were the words which we exchanged on the route, for Jenny seemed to be meditating on the failure of her mission, while I was thinking what it was about, and wondering if she would not enlighten me. Once I spoke to her on the subject; but she rather cut me short, as though to intimate that it was none of my business, and that I had better hold my tongue; and, like a sensible man, I did. As soon as we reached the orchard, Smith and his family, Mrs. Brown and the dogs, came out to meet us, and gave us a warm welcome; but no sooner did Mrs. Brown catch sight of Sir William, than she waddled back to the house as fast as her fat limbs could carry her; while Miss Amelia appeared to be struck dumb at the sight of Jenny, whom I assisted to alight, and introduced to Smith and his wife; and I would have done the same thing to Amelia, if she had not tossed her head and turned her back upon us, as though disdaining such company.

CHAPTER XXXVIII.

A COQUETTE'S CONTEMPT.—THE DISAPPEARANCE.—AMELIA AND MOLOCH.

When I lifted Jenny from her seat on the saddle, and introduced her to Smith and his wife, they extended their hands and treated the fair stranger like an equal, in spite of her shabby appearance and the accumulation of dust and dirt on her person. Miss Copey, however, just turned her back and skipped towards the house. But she first made up a face at me, expressive of disgust at my conduct, although what there was to be disgusted at I could not imagine; but girls are whimsical at times, and hard to understand. I stole a look at Jenny's face as Amelia walked off; but I did not see manifested any of the indignation which a high-bred girl would have exhibited at the insult. Her large blue eyes followed Amelia's form; but there was no anger in those heavenly orbs. I saw a different kind of emotion, but one that was quite womanly. It was a feeling of envy, to think that Amelia was so much better clothed than herself—was cleaner looking in every respect, and had on a pair of neat-fitting shoes, which showed a small foot and ankle to much advantage; while the shoes which Jenny wore were loose, broken, and entirely unworthy of the small treasures which they covered.

Jenny had not been educated in the forms of polite society, and therefore did not know that she was insulted; but Amelia had received a fair English education, and should have known better than to treat a poor sister in the way she did, and I determined to tell her so the first time I had a chance, even if she did not relish my remarks. But I did not manifest the least emotion as I turned and introduced Sir William to Mr. Smith and wife; and it was amusing to see Smith's eyes when I made the announcement.

"A baronight in my poor house!" ejaculated the stockman. "Good Heavens, what an honor for me and my children! Run, wife, and have the best room in the house prepared for Sir William. Cook everything you can lay your hands on."

"Shall I prepare some mutton?" whispered the wife.

"Mutton for a baronight!" cried the excited stockman. "Hang mutton! no."

Mrs. Smith saw that her husband was in earnest; so she became as excited as her lord. For the first time in her life she saw a man of rank, and when she met Miss Amelia, who was mentally abusing my impertinence in introducing such an ill-dressed woman to her consideration, she exclaimed, —

"O, Amelia, only think of it! that strange gentleman is a knight, and he's come on a visit!"

"I don't care if he's Mr. Day," pouted the young lady. "I don't want to see the tribe. To think that that hateful monster should bring a woman here. She's none too good, I'll warrant you. I wouldn't have her in the house; I'd send her a trooping, I tell you."

"You won't understand me, you little flirt," cried the married lady. "The strange gentleman is a Sir William — a nobleman of much wealth, and he must have something to eat."

"Hey?" cried Miss Amelia, pricking up her pretty ears.

"A real nobleman, child. A baronet."

"Good Lord!" Amelia said, with a little shriek, "is it possible? Is he married? I had better put on my new muslin, hadn't I?"

"You'd better help me with the housework, you silly child," the married sister replied; and then Miss Amelia pouted, and said that was just the way — she never had a chance to show her accomplishments before people who could appreciate them.

"O, you provoking girl!" suddenly exclaimed Mrs. Smith; and with the words she pounced upon her sister, shook her in a brief manner, and then dropped her and ran to the kitchen to give directions to the cook.

"Well, of all things in this world!" cried the indignant girl; and then she relieved her feelings with a flood of tears, and they flowed the more freely because she thought that she was an ill-used woman.

But while Amelia was wishing that she was married, dead, or some other dreadful fate, she heard our party approaching the house.

Out of the window she went, just before we entered the room, then ran round to the orchard, and threw herself under the shadow of a tree, and went to sleep, where we will leave her for the present.

Smith preceded us as we entered the house.

"Welcome, most honored sir," he cried. "Beneath my humble roof I hope you will find repose and shelter. Never was I more honored, never —"

He stepped back, hit his heels against the stairs, — which were built out into the room, — and over he went, to the intense delight of Hez, who roared and stamped with joy, while Sir William suffered a smile to pass over his face, but it was only a transient one. Our host speedily recovered his feet, cursed the stairs, and then rushed out of the room to see how his wife was progressing with the supper, while Sir William sauntered to the window, looked out, and then turned suddenly, and asked, —

"What do you intend to do with that girl?" pointing to Jenny.

"Take care of her until she is returned to her home in Melbourne," I answered.

"Humph! A young man is not exactly a proper companion for a girl like her."

"There is where we differ. I think that any man who will protect a girl's honor is a companion that no woman need blush to have near her."

The next instant in rushed Smith, in a state of great excitement and perspiration.

"Your room is all ready, Sir William. Sorry that it's no better. I've done the best that I could. Plenty of water in the room to wash the dirt from your face, Sir William; and if you want to change your clothes, I've laid out a suit of mine that you can put on. Walk right up stairs, Sir William, and turn to the left."

The baronet, like a gentleman as he was, smiled and bowed, and expressed his thanks in a few words. Then he left the room, and navigated up the stairs, which were built on entirely new principles; and those who ascended them often found, unless warned, that no sooner had they arrived at the top than they were transported to the bottom, to the great danger of neck and limbs. Sir William, however, had ample warning. He passed the Rubicon in safety, and entered his room. As soon as he had locked his door, I intimated to Smith that I wanted an apartment and clothes for my *protegée.*

"Mealy's about her size," the stockman replied, with a scrutinizing glance. "Maybe this one is a little higher than t'other. If she has a room it must be the one that you had."

"Let her have it, then. I will find a place to sleep."

"Well, as for clothes, I don't know as Mealy's will fit; and, if they did, she'd make a rumpus if we took 'em."

Smith scratched his head, and looked a little serious. He knew the temper of his amiable sister-in-law, and rather stood in awe of her on account of her education and beauty. But I had no such feeling, although I was a little tender on the latter point; so I said that I would stand between him and Amelia, and that satisfied the stockman that his shoulders were safe. He knew that Amelia would not dare to show much of her temper to me, while she had not the least conscientious scruples against giving her brother-in-law, who supported her, a piece of her mind.

"Come, Jenny," I said, "let me show you to your room."

The girl drew back, and a blush of indignation mantled her brow.

"No, you don't," she said. "I ain't one of your kind, if you come to that."

I thought that Hez would kill himself, he laughed so heartily.

"I'll send my wife up with the lass," Smith remarked,

seeing that Jenny was suspicious of us men. "You won't be afeard of her, will you?" and the stockman laughed as though he had uttered a good joke.

"I ain't afeard of no woman," the inhabitant of Mud Lane replied; and I think she spoke the truth, for there was a calm confidence in her eyes that would have repelled most vicious men.

Smith called his wife, and that amiable lady soon led Jenny up stairs, gave her such clothing as was needed,—all from Amelia's wardrobe, which I intended to restore in so liberal a manner that she would have no cause to complain,—saw that the young girl was washed in a thorough manner, and that her poor, wounded feet were attended to, and then returned to her company, and glanced around the room as though expecting to see some one; and when she found that she was disappointed, she asked her husband if he had seen Amelia.

"No; I s'posed she was up stairs with you."

"I have not seen her for at least two hours," Mrs. Smith remarked, in a tone of alarm.

It was now dark, and we were expecting the police squad every moment, supper having been cooked and kept waiting for them. The stockman looked a little wild at hearing such a report from his wife; but if he seemed alarmed, his better half more than shared it, for she feared that some accident had happened to the girl—Amelia not being in the habit of absenting herself from the house, especially just towards evening.

"She can't have gone to White's, can she?" asked Smith.

White was a farmer, their nearest neighbor, and lived one or two miles farther down the road.

"She wouldn't have thought of such a thing," Mrs. Smith replied. "You know she is very timid."

We looked through every room in the house, and in every closet and chest; but Amelia, the pert, fair-faced, laughing Amelia, was not to be found; and so our anxiety quickened into fear that she had wandered out in the valley and was lost, or that some accident had happened to her. In the mean time, while the search is going on, we will return for a moment to the young lady whom we left asleep under a tree in the orchard — a very imprudent act on her part, and one that she would not have committed if she had not been grieved and angry at the sight of a face that rivalled her own in point of beauty. Well, perhaps the young lady slept ten minutes, and was dreaming that a box containing half a dozen dresses, all trimmed with ribbons and point lace, had just arrived from Melbourne, and that she was to have five of the best and smartest dresses, and her sister the remaining one, when a hand was laid on her white, graceful neck; and opening her eyes, and attempting to start up, she found a man leaning over her, and that man was one whom she had no desire to see, for it was Moloch. Of course the young girl was startled to wake up and see that ruffian's repulsive face close to her own; and as she struggled to rise, she said, —

"O, is this you, Moloch? Have you come back?"

"Yees, I'se come back;" and the ruffian grinned, but never offered to release his hold of her throat, as though he feared she would utter a cry that might attract attention.

"Mr. Smith will be glad to see you," Amelia remarked, although she knew she was uttering a falsehood.

"Yees," grinned the brute; "but I don't vant to sees Mr. Smith, and he don't vant to sees me."

"O, but he does."

The ruffian chuckled, and looked at her flushed face with an admiring glare, more like the glance of a satyr than a man. Amelia noted the look, and her little heart trembled; but she kept up an outward show of composure, even if she did not feel it.

"Do take your hand from my throat, Moloch," the young girl said. "You hurt me with your rough fingers."

"Yees; and if I does take it away you vill jist yell, and that I von't stand."

"No, I won't cry out," the girl said, although she meant to do so the first opportunity.

"Vot men is in the house?"

"Why, the same ones who were there when you attempted to —" She nearly said "murder," but checked herself in time, and continued, "when you left us."

"The traps ain't there, is they?" demanded the fellow.

"No; but they will be here in a short time. Supper is being prepared for them, and I must go and help set the tables."

But Moloch had no notion of losing such an agreeable companion. As she started towards the house, he put out his hand and seized her arm, and held her fast.

"No, lass, you don't leave me in this vay."

"Release me, Moloch," the young lady cried, attempting to throw off his hand; but the man held her fast, and did not seem to quail under her indignant looks.

"You be a beauty, lass," the fellow said, "and I likes you Ve don't part just now; it vould break my gizzard if ve did."

"You mean wretch, if you don't leave me I'll scream, and then Mr. Jack will come to my assistance, and beat you as you deserve."

"No, you von't do no sich thing. If you but open them purty lips of your'n, I'll take care to shut 'em."

She tried to shake him off, but could not; and then she uttered a yell; but before she could repeat the experiment, Moloch's hard, dirty hand was placed over her mouth, and the other paw grasped her white, slender neck.

"If you does that agin," whispered the desperate villain, "I shall have to choke the life out of yer. I don't vant to, 'cause I loves yer."

"O, Moloch, if you love me, please let me go to the house. I'll never say one word to Mr. Smith about this; you see if I do."

"I'll see that you don't, my purty lass," was the reply; and the fellow grinned as he spoke, while he still held her in his rude grasp, so that her screams would be instantly checked in case she attempted to utter any; and then, as her face showed the disgust with which she regarded him, he continued: —

"I loved you, lass, long afore you thought of it, or afore you vould look on one like me. I vanted you for a vife, but

I knew you vouldn't have me till I vas rich; so I used to think, day after day, how I should get money, and you at the same time; and vile I vas thinkin', along come this 'ere young feller with the kinky hair, and ven I saw him I knowed that you vould love him, 'cos he's handsomer than me."

"But I don't love him," cried Amelia; "I hate him."

"I vish you did," replied Moloch, "but I know better than that; so ven I saw you smile on him, I determined to take his life, and I vould have done it, lass, if the devil hadn't stood his friend."

"You attempted to murder him, and got frightened into a fit for your pains," Amelia remarked, in a tone that was a little malicious.

"Vell, I thought it vas the feller's ghost; but no live man can make Moloch afeard;" and then after a pause he continued: "I had a shot at the fellow the next day, ven he vas in the bush, but I missed 'im. Dom him, I think he be hard to kill."

"If you do not release me," Amelia cried, growing impatient, "you shall suffer for it."

The words made Moloch angry. He threw one of his brawny arms around the girl's waist, placed a hand over her mouth, and then bore her towards a horse which was concealed in a clump of palm trees, the huge leaves of which completely hid the animal. And all this time we had never missed her.

CHAPTER XXXIX.

THE ABDUCTION. — A NATIVE ON THE TRAIL. — THE PURSUIT.

In the mean time, at the house, we had searched every part of it, from cellar to attic, and found no trace of Amelia. Then we looked through the outbuildings, the orchard, where fruit trees were growing which had been brought from England, — for, strange as it may seem, Australia does not boast of fruit indigenous to the soil,—and at last we called her name, but there was no response.

"She may have gone to White's," Smith said; and he looked at us in hopes that we should agree.

"Let your stockman ride over there and inquire," I said.

Joe was instantly despatched, on the back of the fastest horse that was at hand at the time; but hardly had the sound of the animal's hoofs died away, than Hez picked something from the ground near the grove of palm trees. He ran with it to a light, and then cried out that he had found a ribbon, one which Amelia had worn in her hair the last time he had seen her. None of the rest of us recognized it, but love had made Hez's eyes sharp; so we had no reason to doubt his word.

"Hold on a bit," cried Smith. "Don't you move and destroy the trail. I'll soon know if she's been here."

He ran to one of his barns, where several natives were sleeping, having been employed during the day in tending sheep, seized one of the long-haired fellows by his greasy and matted locks, dragged him out of the barn, and to the spot where we were standing with lighted lanterns, and pointing to the ground, said, "*Teazy mouki.*" The fellow understood the words, and his dark, eloquent eyes surveyed our anxious faces with an appearance of sympathy that assured us that his best services were at the disposal of his master. He was counted the best "tracker" within a radius of ten miles, and his deeds were known from the river Murray to the Lodden. The fellow was tall and straight, and better formed than most natives, and for his quickness with his eyes was called "*Kalama,*" or the "Ox-eyed."

Kalama took a lantern and commenced examining the ground and grass, both so hard from the effect of the drought, that a footstep made no impression upon them, as far as our eyes could note. But our examination was superficial as compared with the native's; for I never saw such patient industry as the black displayed. He seemed to note the manner in which each blade of grass turned, even lifting some of them from the ground, and then allowed them to fall, so that he could tell if they had recently been pressed by a heavy foot; and after he had spent some time in such an examination, he arose from his knees and said, in broken English, "No girl goey dis way."

We looked at each other in astonishment.

"Are you sure that the girl has not passed this way?" Smith asked.

"Yese; no goey dis way. Man foot all time."

We pricked up our ears at this information.

"What maney goey dis way?" Smith asked, imitating the native's language, so that he could comprehend him the more readily.

The question was a test of the native's thoroughness of examination; but he did not hesitate to answer it, not even for a moment, for his bright eyes were raised to our faces as he said, —

"Moloch go;" and he pointed with his fingers to show that he had passed from the orchard towards the palm trees.

"Moloch!" we all exclaimed; "why, it is impossible. He would not dare to venture near the house."

"Moloch," repeated Kalama, in a firm tone, as though his eyes were not to be deceived.

"If he says it's Moloch, and sticks to it, then we must believe him," Smith remarked. "But Moloch ain't the lass. She's the one we want, and she's the one we must find. Can't you tell us somethin' about her, Ox-eye?"

"*Num*," replied the native, and, taking up the lantern, renewed the search, following the trail towards the palm trees, apparently without an effort, until at last he led us to a tree where a horse had been tied; the marks of its hoofs were distinctly visible, where he had stamped to shake off the cloud of insects that always hover around animal life beneath a warm Australian sun.

"The bloody villain has been here," Smith remarked. "But he couldn't have taken the lass with him, could he?"

Ox-eye soon answered that question. He had examined the grass and ground, and now a smile of triumph passed over his face, as he said, —

"Lass go Moloch."

"Are you sure?" we demanded, eagerly.

"Go Moloch," was the only answer, and he pointed to the ground.

"I have it," cried Hez, who had been in a fever of excitement during the whole of the search. "The tarnal villain carried the gal in his arms to the hoss, and then, jist afore he lifted her up to the saddle, stood her on the ground for a moment. I tell ye that audacious cuss has got her, and is off to the mountains with her, and we shan't see no more of her."

Ox-eye could not understand all that was said, but he comprehended enough to nod his head, showing that he indorsed all that Hez had uttered; and the rest of us were forced to think Hopeful correct in his supposition. Just at this moment, Smith's assistant stockman rode up in hot haste from Farmer White's. He reported that no one of the family had seen anything of Amelia, and offered all assistance in case she was lost in the bush.

"It's no use for us to stand here gapin' at each other," Hez cried. "The gal is gone, and we must find her. Let's start in chase at once."

"How in the devil's name can we trace her in the dark?" roared Smith.

"Why, by the aid of the nigger," answered Hez, quite confidently.

"But he can't see in the dark;" and as Smith spoke he wrung his hands and looked as though he would like to lay his brawny paws upon the neck of his treacherous servant.

"No, no more he can't," Hopeful answered; and he began to look wild, for he knew, and we all knew, what kind of treatment the young lady would receive at the hands of Moloch, unless he was closely pursued and prevented from carrying out his designs.

At this instant, as though to remind me that an important friend was at hand, ready to afford any assistance in his power, Rover, the noble hound, whose scent was superior to the native's eye, poked his cold, damp nose in my hand, and uttered a low whine, which no one noticed but myself.

"Hopeful," I said, "you and I will start in pursuit of the lady. Give us the best horses on the farm, provisions enough to last us three days, and we will see what can be done."

"I'm with you, old fellow," replied Hez, in a hearty tone.

"But I'll go too," Smith cried.

"No, you must stay at the house and look after your visitors. We do not need you."

"But I'll be d—d if I don't go," Smith roared; "you can't find the way through the bush without me."

"Then we shall get lost. But I am not fearful. Give us the horses and we'll start."

"But you can't track 'em in the night, I tell you," remonstrated Smith.

"We can't, but Rover can," I answered, in a quiet tone.

"The devil! I never once thought of the hound. If he takes the scent you'll have hard work to keep up with him. The dog is quicker than Ox-eye;" and then Smith renewed his argument in favor of going with us; but we would not listen to him, for we did not need his services, Hez and I thinking that we were quite competent to take care of Moloch, in case we were fortunate enough to meet him.

At last we convinced Smith that his place was at home, and then he gave orders for saddling the horses, and returned with us to the house to pack in our knapsacks a blanket, some bread and cheese, a flask of wine, dried beef, and some other things which were needed for our welfare during our absence.

"Down with yer, and put some of that 'ere supper into yer insides," Smith said, pointing to the table which his wife had suddenly loaded with the best that the house contained, in spite of her grief at the abduction of her sister. "It won't take but a minute; jist while I'm gittin' a few things put up for yer."

We knew that the advice was good; for we did not know how long we should be absent; so down we sat, and ate most heartily. By the time we had finished, the horses were standing at the door, and Rover was full of anxiety and doubt. I threw a few scraps to the animal, just enough to whet his appetite.

"All ready," said Hez, who had employed his leisure time in loading our revolvers and putting up a stock of ammunition.

I rose to go, when Mrs. Smith threw herself into my arms.

"You will bring her back to me if it is a possible thing?" she said, in tones that could hardly be heard for stifled sobs.

"I will save her or avenge her," I answered, and then placed the poor woman in her husband's arms, and was just turning to leave the room, when Jenny met me face to face.

"I must leave you for the present, Jenny," I said, as I took her hand and pressed it warmly, to which she made no objection. "You will remain here until I return, and then I'll see you safe to Melbourne."

"Don't want no one to see me there. I can go alone. I can find the way. If you leave the house now, you won't see me again, not soon. If you want to run after women I shan't wait for you." She jerked her hand away, and walked towards the window.

"What do you want me to do, Jenny?" I asked, as I followed her.

"I don't want you to do nothin'," the girl said, in a petulant manner. "You jist clear out from me."

I was indignant, and stepped back the quicker, because I heard Sir William and Hez attempt to smother a laugh by the aid of a cough.

"I'm ready," I said, and without another look at the handsome girl, I left the room.

"We'll look arter the lass," Smith whispered, as I crossed the threshold.

"I don't care whether you do or not," I answered, for I was angry with Jenny, and at the manner in which she had treated me.

"Don't be angry with the poor child," Sir William remarked. "Remember, she is not a lady."

He extended his hand as he spoke, and pressed mine, and after a moment's silence continued:—

"When you return, it's quite probable that I shall be in Melbourne. May I not hope to see you there before long?"

"I trust so."

"If we should not see each other there, do not be surprised, for my mission to this country is of an extraordinary nature, and I must go where even a trace of information may lead me."

The baronet uttered a deep sigh, as though his heart was touched; and without venturing another word he retreated into the house, and resumed his old position by the window.

"Now leave us," I said, as all the members of the farm gathered around; "I want to put the dog on the scent. Good by, all of you. We will return with Amelia or Moloch's head."

The crowd retreated to the house and outbuildings, while Hez and I led our horses towards the grove of palms, and then called Rover, and pointed to the marks which Moloch's horse had made, and bade the hound look around. He put his nose to the earth, snuffed a little, first in one spot and then in another, moving round in a circle at the same time, until at last he raised his head and uttered a low bay.

"No noise," I said. "We must follow them without giving an alarm."

Rover wagged his tail, waited until I had mounted my horse, and then, with his nose close to the earth, started in the direction of the Lodden; and just as we galloped off I heard the police squad arrive in front of the house.

CHAPTER XL.

THE PURSUIT.—BRIDGE OF SALT.—MYSTERIOUS SOUNDS.—ALLIGATORS AND THEIR ATTACKS.—AN ESCAPE.

Rover followed the trail without faltering. He ran along with his nose to the ground, keeping just ahead of us, so that we did not lose sight of him for a moment; and in this manner we dashed over the prairie, sometimes checking our horses for the purpose of avoiding a bog or salt spring, the latter to be found in all parts of the country, and sometimes in the most unexpected places; and, confound them, they have caused more blaspheming to men on horseback than even the Australian insects, which fill your nostrils, your ears, and your mouth, unless you keep it shut; for in the night time, when near a light, even if you undertake to swallow a "drink," unless the neck of the bottle fills your mouth, insects will creep in and take their chance with the liquor. And sometimes, in the dark, such an event occurs; for Hez. who had been nervous and eager ever since he had learned of the abduction, and had only kept up his spirits by the aid of a pocket "pistol," while trotting along by my side, drew his bottle and threw back his head; but the next moment, with a strangling cry and a terrible fit of coughing, he exclaimed, —

"O, darn! I've swallowed a bug bigger than my fist, and the cuss is gnawing at my vitals. What shall I do?" and the poor fellow commenced pounding his stomach, which sounded like a badly strung bass drum.

"Drown him with liquor," I exclaimed, laughing so that I could hardly sit my horse.

"I'll do it;" and once more the bottle was applied to his lips, and a long pull showed that Hez was determined to have satisfaction.

"Ah, I guess I've fixed him," Hopeful remarked, as he removed the "pistol" and took a long breath; "I don't feel him now."

He had hardly ceased speaking when Rover halted, and manifested signs of having lost the scent. We waited a few minutes in hopes that he would recover it; but as he did not, I rode forward a few steps, and saw that we were close to a deep bog, and that if we had rode into it we should have lost our animals, for we could not have got them out of the black mud, most of it encrusted with salt, showing the nature of the water that flowed into the marsh. Moloch had crossed the bog — that was evident; but he knew the path, while we did not, and it was rather difficult for Rover to find it on account of the water, which destroyed the scent, and caused us to lose much valuable time. I dismounted, and commenced an examination on my own account. There were thousands of sheep tracks in the vicinity, for the animals had visited the marsh for the purpose of licking the salt; and there were the tracks of cattle, some of the latter having wallowed deep in the mud, as if for the purpose of enjoying the luxury of a bath, and escaping from the persecuting flies and mosquitos. As I stumbled around, sometimes up to my knees in mud and water, Rover wagged his tail, as much as to say, "I'll see how you succeed where I fail; but if you find the trail you'll do better than I anticipate."

At last, by some sort of accident, I crossed a little sheet of water, where I found hard and firm bottom. A short distance from the water, not more than one or two inches deep, was a white crust of salt, so substantial that it felt under foot like quartz. It was about ten feet wide, but the length I could not judge of on account of the darkness. I could see that it led in the direction of the river; but I hardly dared to hope that it was a natural bridge, and one strong enough to cross to firm land. But in a moment all doubts were set at rest, for Rover joined me, gave one sniff, and with a bay announced that the lost trail had been found. With his nose close to the salt he started to follow; but I stopped him, and compelled him to wait until we were ready to continue the pursuit. I shouted to Hez that we were all right, and to lead the animals towards me, and then I stooped down and saw the marks of a horse's hoofs on the hard salt; so there could be no mistake but that we had hit on the right trail; but the fact that Moloch had made use of the bridge was sufficient to convince me that he was rather a cunning sort of a genius, and knew more than I had given him credit for, and that if a capture was to be made, much discretion must be used on our part.

"Wal," growled Hez, as he rode up, "you don't go for to tell me that the cuss has gone this 'ere way?"

"It seems that he has," I answered.

"Wal, blast the feller! who'd a s'posed it? I'd never have thought of looking for a bridge like this, would you?"

"Yet you see that I found it," I answered, with a little self-complacency, that I considered pardonable under the circumstances.

"So you did; I'll give you the credit of it, Jack, and tell everybody I know arter we return."

I spoke to the dog, and he started forward, we following. Then commenced one of the most peculiar phenomena that I had witnessed for many months; and even for Australia, that land of wonder and extraordinary occurrences, it was something remarkable. As soon as we started our horses, the salt bridge upon which we stood commenced shaking and swaying back and forth, so that our animals could hardly keep their feet; and they were so terrified at their novel position, that they trembled in every part, and the sweat started from every pore, and covered their hides with a dampness that felt as though they had just come from a swim in the river.

"There's an earthquake," roared Hez; and he was about to slip from his horse, when I checked him and requested him to remain quiet.

He complied with my demand, and the instant that we were quiet, the bridge was the same; but if our animals moved but a foot, the frail structure quaked like a jelly, with regular undulations similar to the waves of the ocean, while at the same time, from all parts of the quagmire issued sighs and groans like those uttered by a human being in terrible pain, or the regular moan of a high-pressure steam engine.

With some difficulty we soothed our horses, and induced them to remain quiet. The sighs and groans which they heard, human-like in their agony, had frightened the brutes as well as ourselves; and with their long ears thrown back close to their heads, and their eyes restless and dancing in all directions, it was with much trouble that we were enabled to prevent their backing off the bridge into the mud, or else turning and retreating the way in which they came.

Our hound, apparently imbued with no superstitious ideas respecting the noises, finding that we did not follow him, returned to us, wagging his tail, as though wondering what we meant by not continuing the chase.

Hopeful, whose eyes had protruded to an unusual extent, while the sighs and groans were prevailing, now managed to speak.

"Gol darn it, Jack, what's the meaning of these 'ere noises? I don't understand 'em."

"Neither do I," but I began to have a faint glimmering of how the sounds were produced.

"I tell you it's jist enough to make a man's hair stand right up on an end. It sounds jist as when old uncle John kicked the bucket when he didn't want to, and he tore all aunt's sheets to bits afore he would straighten out and shut his eyes."

"Pshaw! you don't suppose that the sighs and groans which we heard were produced by unnatural agencies, do you?"

"No, but I wish I was out of it, I do."

"Then we must make a start," I replied. "We only waste time here."

As I spoke, Hez uttered an exclamation of alarm.

"Look!" he said. "We shall be swallered up as well as frightened to death."

I looked down, and noticed for the first time that water had overflowed the bridge where we stood, and was already some two inches deep.

"Let's get out of this," cried Hez. "I've had enough of swamps. Gol darn 'em, say I."

I grasped my horse by the bridle, and led him forward a few steps; but the instant we advanced, the sighs and groans came from all parts of the swamp, more terrible than ever, until it seemed like a hundred fiends near us, and laughing at us. The animals manifested their terror by snorting and rearing, and making desperate efforts to break away from our grasp.

Suddenly, within a few yards of Hez, who was on the right, came a snort and a roar that sounded entirely different from anything we had yet heard. Hopeful started, and exclaimed in astonishment, —

"Jehosaphat! what in the devil's name is that?'

If Hez did not know, I did; and I was well aware that more danger was near us, unless we made tracks or showed fight. As Hez asked the important question, there was a loud splash on the left of the bridge, a shower of water was dashed into my face, and as some of it reached my eyes, nearly blinded me for a moment, burning my flesh like caustic.

"O, darn!" yelled Hopeful; "I've got some of the blasted stuff in my mouth. Bah!"

"Jack, what is this thing near me?" asked Hopeful, when he had cleared his throat, and was able to speak. "It looks like a blasted log, but it ain't, you know, 'cos logs don't throw water at a feller."

"Hez," I said, in as calm a tone as I could command, "we are surrounded by alligators."

"What?" asked the New Hampshire genius in a tone that was loud enough to awaken all the alligators in the swamp.

I repeated my remark.

"Wal, this is the cussedest country I ever heard tell of," was the response, for Hez seemed to care less about the slimy brutes, than he did for the sighs and groans.

I saw at once from Hez's remark that he knew but little respecting the habits of alligators.

"Jack," he said, in a light, bantering tone, as though the subject was rather a laughable one than otherwise, "I'm blamed if that old log ain't comin' for me, jist as sure as you live."

"If it comes too near," I said, "aim at the mouth and fire."

"How do you call too near?" Hez demanded. "The cuss is so near now that I can see that he's got a very open countenance, and rather good teeth. Blast him! I guess he's cleaned 'em lately."

I glanced to the other side of the bridge, and saw that Hopeful was confronted by an alligator at least twelve or fifteen feet long.

"Jack," said my friend, while I was watching the slow

movements of the alligator, "this cuss keeps comin' nearer and nearer. What shall I do?"

Hez was a short distance behind me, on the near side of his horse, holding the animal by the bridle, and with one hand on the pommel of the saddle, ready to leap into it in case it was necessary to ride for his life. This explanation is desirable to illustrate what followed, and how Hopeful escaped from what was intended as a death-blow. I had told Hez, in a low tone, to take certain aim and fire at the monster's head; while I looked after the alligator on my left, which had as yet shown no signs of animation or hostility.

"I'm all ready," said Hez, cocking his revolver.

"Then fire."

There was a sharp report, a terrible splash, and showers of mud fell upon us. My horse made desperate attempts to escape, but I managed to hold him fast; and while I was thus engaged, I heard Hopeful exclaim, —

"Wal, I'm blessed if that ain't a go!"

As soon as I could clear my eyes I saw Hopeful's horse off the bridge, struggling in the mud, and half a dozen alligators wiggling towards it.

"Did you see that?" asked Hez, in a cool, unconcerned tone.

"No. What has happened?"

"Why, that blasted brute jist put up his tail, rapped my horse on the head, jist clearing me, and thar the poor cuss 's up to his neck in mud, and no hope of gittin' him out."

"Forward," I shouted. "We have not a moment to lose. We have aroused all the alligators of the marsh, and they are pushing towards us."

"Forward it is," returned Hez. "I'm ready."

CHAPTER XLI.

PERILOUS POSITION. — ESCAPE FROM ALLIGATORS. — ON FOOT. — A WESTERN MAN IN AUSTRALIA. — HE JOINS US.

But we encountered an unexpected obstacle; for when I attempted to lead my horse, he refused to budge an inch.

"Jack," said Hopeful, "what shall we do? Hadn't we better leave the brute and cut stick — hey?"

I was almost resolved to do so, for the roaring and splashing around us began to assume such proportions that we thought of Daniel in the lions' den.

"If the cusses would only give me time," muttered Hez, as he surveyed the black-headed monsters encircling the carcass of the horse, with snapping jaws and limber tails, "I'd make a trap that would catch a dozen in twenty-four hours, and then we could go into the alligator-skin business, or start a shoe-shop, on our own account. Thunder! couldn't we make money!"

"Curse your shoe-shops!" I exclaimed. "Help me with this frightened beast, will you?"

"Chuck him in with the other," Hez remarked, in a good-natured tone, as though he stood on one of his granite hills, instead of on a treacherous bridge with monsters on each side of him.

Just as he spoke, an alligator nearly fifteen feet long commenced crawling on the bridge with the intention of crossing it. It was not more than two yards from us, and seemed to care as little for our presence as it did for its comrades. I suppose that to this monster we were indebted for the manner in which we escaped; for the alligator inspired my horse with such unbounded terror that he ceased trembling and endeavoring to retreat. He gave a snort, reared, broke from my grasp, and, to my surprise, dashed ahead, regardless of the quaking bridge, the slime that covered it, or the devilish roars of the alligators, disturbed in their feed by the racket.

"There goes your hoss," yelled Hez.

"Yes, and here I go in pursuit," was my answer; and forward I went at a rapid rate, followed by Hez, and soon left our musk-smelling acquaintances far behind us.

The instant I struck dry and hard land I paused to take breath and consult with Hopeful as to the next movement. We could hear my horse crashing through the bush half a mile distant, and we knew that he would not stop till entirely exhausted, and unfit for further service; so it was useless to pursue the animal. Even if we succeeded in catching him, he could not aid us in continuing the pursuit; so we resolved to follow Moloch on foot, and let the horse go, knowing quite well that the animal would be picked up by the shepherds and returned to Smith at no distant day, the peculiar brand upon the horse's flank proclaiming the ownership without question or doubt.

As soon as we had rested we called to Rover, once more put him on the trail, and started over a broad prairie. On we went across it, skirted the river near the ford, and approached a clump of palm trees that stood just at the edge of the plain; and when we were within gunshot of them, Rover uttered a peculiar bay, and bounded forward.

"By darn," cried Hez, "we has 'em."

But I knew better, for Rover never uttered such a sound as that when in the vicinity of an enemy; and a minute later proved that I was correct in my surmises, for a gruff voice cried out, "What in thunder's name do ye mean a settin' a dog on me? I'll be darned if any western man will be put on in this 'ere style by Britishers or 'Stralians, niggers or boomerang throwers. Call off yer dog, I say."

"Don't be alarmed," I cried. "The dog won't hurt you unless you provoke him."

"Provoke him!" repeated the man; "why, I ain't doin' nothin' to provoke him. I'm just settin' down 'ere smokin' to keep off the skeeters. But you just wait a minute till I stir up the fire, and then we'll see who you is, and what you is arter."

As the stranger spoke he threw on the smouldering fire

some dry, resinous sticks, and they instantly blazed up, revealing a man about thirty years of age, as near as we could judge, with long hair and immense beard, neither of which had been trimmed for some months. He was a tall, thin individual, with round shoulders, long arms, and not a spare ounce of flesh on his body.

"Wal, strangers," cried the long-haired individual, "you is on a late tramp to-night. Where might you be from? Bendigo or Ballarat?"

"Neither," I answered.

"Be you from the new diggin's up at the Devil's Elbow? I heard tell that it's mighty rich dirt up thar. But they lie so like —— in this kintry that a decent man don't know what to believe."

I shook my head as I pulled out my pipe and commenced lighting it.

"Strangers," said the long-haired individual, in an impressive manner, "you don't mean to say that ye are on the bushranger lay, do yer? 'Cause if ye do, jist let me say to yer that I ain't got a darned dime, and the only thing I'm worth is this old rifle, and if ye want that ye must fight me for it."

"Why do you think we are on the bushranging lay?" I asked.

"Yes, jist tell us that," broke in Hez, speaking for the first time.

"By the Lord Harry, strangers, if you ain't Yankees, then darn me!" shouted the long-haired individual.

"And you are —"

"A native of the Great West, sir, whar the big rivers is found, and the wide prairies, and the rich sile, and the great crops, and the handsome women-folks."

As the western man spoke, he extended his hand, and we had a fraternal greeting beneath those palm trees.

"From your description, I should say that you were from Illinois," I remarked.

"Yes, sir, from Illinise, Washington county, whar I was born and brought up, man and boy, till this 'ere darnation gold fever took me and carried me off to this place, whar I ain't made shucks for months past."

"Sorry to hear it. I hope you will have better luck in future."

"Hope so, too, stranger; but I'm a little doubtful. I wan't one of the kind what come into the world with a silver spoon in my mouth, and a pair of silk stockings on. But Bill Hackett don't grumble at that; he takes things jist as he finds 'em."

While Mr. William Hackett, of Washington county, Illinois, was talking, he also was working, and in some mysterious manner had managed to put a little tin coffee-pot on the fire, to fill it with water from a tin canteen, and in a few minutes presented Hez and myself with about a pint of very fair coffee, which was quite acceptable to us after the fatigues of the night.

"Drink, strangers," said Hackett, who appeared to have all the liberality of the western people. "I know men must feel a little puckery in the mouth after a long tramp. Do yer want a bite of somethin'? I've got a little bacon, and a few cakes of bread; but ye're welcome to 'em, as all my countrymen would be if they was hard up, and I should meet 'em in this blasted country, which don't make whiskey, raise corn, and precious few hogs. What do they know here about bacon? Nothin'."

Mr. Hackett took his pipe from his mouth, and expressed his disgust by spitting at a burning knot. He aimed so accurately that the flame went out with a sudden sizzle; and the spitter remarked, with a complacent snort, —

"I knowd I could hit it. I never misses my aim. I can hit anything within two yards. You can bet on that. Now, strangers, I've told you all about myself. I've given you a whole history of my doin's. I ain't kept back nothin' at all. Now, let's see if you can enlighten me a little about yerselves. Yer see I am all in the dark about you fellers."

"To tell you the truth, my friend," I said, "we are in pursuit of a man who has committed a great wrong, and so anxious are we to overtake the fellow that we must instantly part company."

"Sorry for that, strangers;" and then, as we finished our coffee and rose to go, he continued: —

"Might I ask what the cuss has been doin' that starts you on his trail?"

"He has abducted a young woman."

"He has done what?" roared Hackett.

"He has carried off a young woman much against her will."

"O," growled Hackett, with a sigh of relief, "I thought he'd done somethin' else. He's only carried her off. Wal, you must get her back agin."

"That's what we intend to do."

"Wal, then, I'll jist pack up and jine ye. I tell ye, I'm tired enough of sinking shafts, and findin' nothin' but sand and water. A bit of a tramp won't hurt me, nor nothin'."

"Perhaps you had better leave some of your traps behind," I said, as the Illinois gentleman threw his knapsack over his shoulders and fastened it in front.

"What for?" demanded Hackett.

"We may have a long tramp, and your load will feel heavy before we have time to rest."

"O, that is it?" and Mr. Hackett did not appear to feel as though the advice was worth taking.

"I ain't much on a tramp, stranger," Hackett continued, as he threw his rifle over his shoulder; "that is, compared to some of the Illinise folks; but when I cry baby, you jist sot me down as a poor coot, and unworthy the great state that I represent. Now, then, shall we start arter the mean cuss what took the gal? or shall we stand here all night and look at each other jist as though we was beauties, and had fallen in love with each other?"

"We will start," I said. So, calling Rover, I directed him to once more find the trail — no difficult task, for the dog was impatient to start. We then went forward, heading this time towards Mount Macedonskirt, the top of which we could see, looking dark and sullen as the clouds settled around its rugged sides. So all that long night we tramped on in silence, over prairies, across dry gullies, through brush and grass, and patches of wood, straight on towards the mountain, which began to show its seared sides as daylight came stealing over the plains, revealing in a deep valley on the right a flock of sheep, numbering thousands, huddled together for warmth and protection from the wild dogs, and guarded by some half a dozen shepherds.

Just as the sun rose I was glad to call for a halt, and to acknowledge that I was too tired to proceed farther until after a brief resting spell and a cup of coffee.

"Pooh!" cried Hackett, as he removed his heavy knapsack; "you don't call this 'ere walkin', do you? Sakes alive! I don't begin to feel tired. Won't somebody run a race with me, just so I can get my blood sarculating?"

I thought this was western bombast, at first; but a look at the man soon convinced me that he was as fresh as when he started upon the trail.

But while Hez and I threw ourselves down to take that rest which we so much desired, Hackett was busy unpacking his traps, making a fire, and preparing a pot of coffee. After the beverage was ready, we broke our fast with a keen relish, and then lighted our pipes, and called a council of war to deliberate on future proceedings.

CHAPTER XLII.

A TEDIOUS TRAMP. — AN UNEXPECTED ENEMY. — A STRANGE SIGHT. — SERPENTS IN PURSUIT. — A FIGHT.

As we lighted our pipes I looked for Hackett, and asked his opinion as to our future course; for I knew that he was a man whose word could be depended upon. He had resided two years in Australia, knew the country, and the trails of bushrangers, had starved in the mines, and suffered on the prairies for the want of water, was bold and active and in fact just such a man as I desired to be associated with in hunting for Moloch and Amelia.

"Wal, if you ax me what I think of it," Hackett said, as he puffed out volumes of smoke, "I shall tell you right plain that we shouldn't stop here no shakes of time, 'cos if you do we shall miss the cuss just as slick as greased lightning. His hoss can't go much further without rest; so now is our time to push him."

I looked at my poor feet, which began to feel like blistering, and sighed as I thought how much I would give for three horses, just at that time. But Hopeful cared nothing for blisters or fatigue. His whole thoughts and anxiety were centred on Amelia, and fear that the villain Moloch would do her some injury before we could overtake and rescue her. He was impatient at the least delay, although he was more tired than myself.

"Yes," said the Illinois chap, "if we mean to find 'em we must put arter 'em, 'cos the best hound that ever followed a trail can't keep on the scent many hours arter this hot sun has laid on it. The dog is a good dog, I won't deny that; but he can't do unpossible things like. No, you hadn't ought to expect 'im to."

"Let us start at once," cried the impatient Hez. "I shan't feel satisfied till I've seen the gal safe, and the mean cuss what took her dead. Come, I'm all ready."

"So is I," replied Hackett; and he collected his traps, and stowed them in his knapsack in an expeditious manner.

There was no excuse for me; so I pulled on my boots and started, skirted the base of the mountain — the side which we approached being too rugged and steep for a horse to ascend. Of this fact Moloch appeared to be aware; for he had made no attempt to pass up the deep gorges, down which the winter's rains poured in torrents, flooding some of the low valleys with water and sand; and even huge rocks were sometimes carried long distances from their native beds, the mountain sides and summit.

At length we passed through a grove of trees, and at one place we saw where Moloch had halted for the purpose of resting his horse; and we could even note how the rascal had struggled with the girl when he wanted to resume his journey, and Amelia had refused to be lifted on horseback. Perhaps I should not have noted the signs if it had not been for Hackett, whose eyes were like a hawk's. He pointed out the marks of the young girl's feet, and showed us how she had been dragged some distance by the ruffian.

"Don't you see that the hoss was kind of uneasy like. See how he sorter stepped around and kicked up a dust. That shows that the gal resisted, and the cuss had some work to get her near the animal. Of course while they was a fighting the hoss wasn't quiet. Come on — the scent is warm. We'll come up with 'em."

We pressed on with renewed ardor. Hez led the way at a slashing pace, and he never slackened his gait until we left the woods and came upon a sandy plain, where, for the first time, Rover seemed unwilling to lead, and acted in the most unaccountable manner.

"What is it, good dog?" I asked, as I came up.

He looked up with a whine, and, when I urged him forward, declined to go, as though fearful of encountering some unknown danger. I knew Rover too well not to be aware that something threatened us; but what it was I could not imagine, and although my companions would have pressed on regardless of the hound's warning, I was not disposed to do so, having been taught to confide in the animal's sagacity and fidelity.

"What is it, Rover?" I asked.

He looked up with his bright, intelligent eyes, as though wishing that he could express his thoughts in words, and uttered a subdued howl; and at the same time the hair upon his back began to bristle and his tail to stiffen, while his lips were drawn back, showing his white fangs, long and sharp, and capable of doing good service in a close encounter.

"Push on," cried Hackett. "The dog is growling at his own shadow. We can see danger if any is near. Jist trust to me, stranger, and you'll come out all right."

But I knew better; and it was well for us that I was willing to trust to the instinct of the hound, for hardly had Hackett ceased speaking when the sand, not more than a rod from us, and directly across the trail, commenced moving, agitated like water boiling in a huge pot; and while we looked on in astonishment, wondering at the cause, a huge, dark head, with a circle of white around the neck, was thrust out of the sand, raised some two feet from the ground, and with glittering eyes and huge mouth commenced hissing at us; and while the fiendish sounds were continued, a second head was thrust out, and then another and another, until I counted some twelve different snakes, all of mammoth proportions, and all with white rings around their necks, like ministerial neck-ties, but more terrible than any white choker ever encountered by evil-doers during puritanical days, when it was unlawful to kiss a wife on Sunday. The sight was not a pleasant one, and I think that I recoiled a few paces, still facing the reptiles, whose heads were twisting and squirming in every direction, as though attempting to obtain an unobstructed view of the gentlemen who had ventured to obtrude their presence upon such distinguished company; and when I add that the movements were all accompanied by shrill hisses, each reptile using a different key, it will be considered that the concert was most infernal in every respect, and one that a man could not listen to for any length of time without going mad.

"Wal, if that don't beat all that I ever seed in Illinise, Californy, or in this blasted kintry," exclaimed Hackett.

"Nothin' in Hillsboro' county can come up to that for ugliness," ejaculated Hopeful, who seemed to think that the honor of New Hampshire required him to utter some words to keep the state prominently before his audience.

"Darn me if they ain't comin' arter us," cried Hackett, in a subdued whisper; for the scene was well calculated to affect the boldest.

I was so much absorbed in watching the antics of the snakes, that I did not realize that they were advancing towards me, with heads a foot or more from the sand, each black devil striving for the lead. as though in such company there was a post of honor; and very frightful, yet interesting they looked, as they bobbed their white, curved necks to and fro, like a flock of black swans in search of food. I could not help laughing, the sight was so novel; for it did not enter my head that it would be wise on my part to retreat as fast as my legs would carry me. But I was aroused from this stupor — I can call it nothing else — by the voice and action of Hackett, who probably comprehended my position at a glance.

"Darn me!" I heard the man say, "if them 'ere black reptiles ain't charming the cap'n. They've got their eyes on him, that's sure!"

"Jerk him away," cried Hopeful; "he mustn't stay there. If he does he'll be swamped."

The next instant I felt a hand on my shoulder. I was rudely jerked back; and then as though some spell was broken, I awakened to a sense of my danger.

By this time the snakes were within a rod or two of me, and their hissing was terribly distinct — a spur sufficient to make me resolve to get away from it as soon as possible; so I don't mind confessing that I turned my back upon the enemy and ran as fast as possible, just looking over my shoulder, to see if they followed me. The brief glance that I obtained showed that the snakes redoubled their exertions when they saw me run.

"This beats anything I ever heard of in Illinise," Hackett muttered, as he dashed along close by my side, while Hopeful was a little in advance, where I wished I was.

"Can't we knock over two or three of the reptiles?" I asked.

"I can answer for some of 'em," returned Hackett; "but won't what remains tackle us, and give us fits?"

That was a question I could not answer, much as I desired to. But we soon had to make a decision, or else leave a companion to his fate; for Hez struck his foot against a vine, and plunged headlong to the ground; and so severe was the fall, that it seemed as though the breath had left his body, never to return. At the same moment we turned and faced the reptiles. Perhaps they were a little surprised at the movement; for I noticed that the leading snake — the one that had held the advance during the chase, a fellow more than fifteen feet long, with a collar three inches wide, and of a dull cream-color — suddenly relaxed his speed, so much so that the snakes behind him ran over his body before they could check their headway, and a very pretty knot was the consequence.

"Fire!" I yelled; and although I was so much blowed with my run that I could hardly hold my revolver in a horizontal position, I managed to aim and discharge the pistol three times in rapid succession, while Hackett poured in the contents of his rifle, and Hopeful struggled to his feet, and did the same with his six-barrelled weapon. There was a mighty flash of long and flexible tails, a gleaming of white throats, dark streams of blood that flowed from ragged wounds, and, above all, clouds of fine sand that soon enveloped the reptiles, and almost hid them from view. The sight was one of the most terrible that I ever saw or heard of; and long afterwards did it remain impressed upon my mind, so that even in my sleep I would dream of the matter, and awaken to find myself in a cold perspiration, and trembling in every limb.

We maintained our ground when we found that the reptiles no longer pursued us, reloaded our weapons, and watched the heaving, struggling mass, hissing and biting each other, and lashing out with their flexible tails like young whales tortured by harpoons.

"Blame me, if they ain't fightin' each other!" exclaimed Hez, who had recovered his wind and good nature at the same time.

It did seem as though such was the case; and the longer we regarded the struggle that was going on, the more convinced we were that the reptiles had turned their weapons upon each other, and were fighting among themselves with a ferocity that I never saw equalled. I suppose that the snakes which were wounded imagined that their companions had injured them, not being aware of the powers of lead and gunpowder; consequently they had turned upon those not hit, and attempted to retaliate by striking to the right and left; and when their sharp teeth did inflict a wound, it was serious. The sight was a wonderful one, and we stood and looked at it, as well as the dust would permit us, until the struggles in a measure ceased, and the view became less obstructed. Then we saw that most of the snakes were dead, that only the larger ones were alive, and they were desperately wounded. One of the reptiles — the largest of the number, and the fellow which had led the pursuit, and shown the most vindictive rage — had received a large gash on the white ribbon around his neck; and as the thick blood trickled from the wound, and dyed the cravat-like mark, it resembled a throat that had been cut with a razor.

"By thunder! but they is suckers, ain't they?" said Hackett, who now spoke for the first time. "Never did I see anythin' in Illinise equal to that 'ere; and yet that state can produce some of the greatest sights of any state in the Union; now, you had better believe."

"You ain't got no snakes like them 'ere, have you?" asked Hopeful, who was jealous for the reputation of New Hampshire.

"Wal," answered Hackett, after a short pause, "if we ain't got 'em as big, we've got 'em twice as furious; now, I tell you that; and we has got 'em twice as fast. Some of 'em will run as fast as a horse. We has 'em of that kind what will jist put their tails in their mouths, and roll arter you like a hoop; and when they strikes yer with that tail, yer a gone sucker, unless ye has plenty of whiskey to pull at."

"That accounts for so few of your folks dyin' from the effects of the reptiles' bites," remarked Hez.

"What?"

"'Cause ye see every one carries whiskey in his pocket, as though expectin' a snake bite;" and Hez laughed.

It was just four o'clock when we entered a dark and silent gorge. On each side of us were rugged precipices, with huge masses of rock almost suspended in the air, and wanting but a touch to send them crashing into the vale. As we picked our way over the rocks, Hackett remarked, —

"Wal, stranger, this ain't much of a place for raisin' corn, is it?"

"No," returned Hopeful, after a critical glance around: "but what a place for a water-power dam! See, you jist throw it up here, and you has water enough to last six months, and power enough to carry all the mills that could be jammed around the outside. What a chance for a feller! Eh, what's the matter? Give me that?"

Hopeful's remarks were caused by Hackett suddenly stooping and picking up a handkerchief stained with blood. Hez sprang forward, and snatched it from his hand, and commenced examining it.

"It's her wiper," the young man said, pressing it to his lips. "See, here's the first letter of her name. She's dead, and that ugly cuss has killed her."

He uttered a howl of grief; but Hackett checked him with a few words.

"She's had the nose bleed," the western man said. "Young women allers has it. She's used it all she wanted, and then threw it away, and took her apron and frock, like the good gal that she is. Thar ain't no use for cryin'."

Under such mild treatment, Hez speedily recovered his composure, and was able to follow in our wake. At length we reached the head of the ravine, and then turned to the right and commenced the ascent of the mountain. The path which we pursued was narrow, and would admit but one man at a time; and the course was most tortuous, walled on each side with rocks, dead trees, stunted palms, and balsam wood. While we were slowly pursuing our way, Rover suddenly recovered the scent, and dashed on ahead of us.

"We are close to them," I said. "A few miles more and we shall have Amelia safe."

At that moment, some little distance above us, we heard the loud report of some kind of firearm, and then a bay, a fierce howl, as though Rover was deeply incensed at an affront, and wanted to get hold of the person who fired the shot.

"Was that a rifle shot?" I asked, turning to Hackett.

I knew that it was not; but I thought I would strengthen my opinion with one from a man who was accustomed to all kinds of firearms.

"That a rifle shot!" Hackett repeated in disgust. "I should think not. No rifle sounds like that. I'll bet a glass of whiskey with any man that a hoss-pistol did that work."

I bounded up the steep mountain side, stumbled over a piece of quartz that was slippery with moss which clung to its sides; and, as I fell, a shot whizzed past me, and struck a tree on my right, cutting off a small branch, and dashing it into Hackett's face.

"Wake snakes!" roared the western man. "Hurrah for the fust smell of powder."

"To cover!" I cried, and sprang into the nearest clump of bushes, so that I was entirely concealed from observation.

"Bury!" returned Hackett, and plunged under the shadow of a tree, and took refuge behind its trunk.

Then we peered out and took observation, but could see nothing of our enemy, although it was very probable that he saw us; but if we could not see him, Rover did, for the dog kept up a continual baying, and yet he was but a few feet from us. I was fearful that the hound would bring bush-rangers to the spot if he continued his cries; so I called him off. He obeyed me, but still manifested a strong desire to tear some one with his teeth.

"Where is he, Rover?" I whispered, and patted the dog on his head.

He looked upward, and continued to manifest signs of uneasiness. I followed the direction of his eyes, but could see nothing excepting a ledge, with thick-leaved balsam trees on each side; and they seemed to be just over our heads, growing on what appeared to be a shelf of the mountain.

"What is it, old dog?" I asked; and just then I had a most emphatic answer in the shape of a pistol shot, the ball striking a piece of quartz by my side, then bounding off and grazing the skin on Mr. Hackett's nose, causing that earnest gentleman to utter several oaths in succession.

In an instant I rolled over and pretended to be shot; but

as I turned, I managed to keep my eyes on the shelf overhead, so that I could note all the movements that took place. I was repaid for my trouble, for as I fell back and pressed my hand on my side, as though fatally wounded, I had the satisfaction of hearing a triumphant laugh issue from the thicket overhead; and the next instant the repulsive features of Moloch were thrust through the branches of the trees, and he seemed to enjoy the appearance which I presented.

"Bah! you fools!" cried the rascal, in a mocking tone, "do yer think that yer can take me? I vos too quick for yer. Had yer come an hour sooner, yer might have caught me nappin'. But now I jist spits at yer. Ah, fools, I has the voman, and I means to keep her."

I seldom miss with a revolver, especially when the object at which I aim is within reasonable distance; but I must confess that I was nervous and full of revengeful feelings, or perhaps I was too hasty; for I suddenly raised my pistol and fired at the fiend who was grinning at me from amid the branches of the balsam trees. I missed the scoundrel, and yet I would have given a thousand dollars to have sent a bullet crushing through his brain, and killed him on the spot.

"Ho, ho! yer didn't come it," laughed the fiend. "Vait a minute and I'll make yer see somethin' that'll open yer eyes."

He disappeared, and while he was gone I changed position, so that he could not single me out for another shot, in case he desired to test his old horse-pistols.

"You ain't hit, is you?" whispered Hackett and Hopeful in anxious tones.

"No," I answered.

Before they could congratulate me, Moloch, the devil, appeared, bearing in his arms the almost lifeless form of poor, dear Amelia Copey, whose dress was torn and soiled, and whose hair was hanging down in tangled masses, neglected and uncared for.

"Look!" yelled the fiend, in a triumphant tone; "'ere's the gal vot I loves, and she vill love me afore long, or I'll know the reason vy."

As he spoke he held the fair form in such a manner that

if we fired we should be more likely to injure the lady than the brute who clasped her in his arms.

"Darn me if I stand that," roared Hackett; and with revolver in hand, he sprang to his feet, and rushed towards the shelf on which Moloch stood.

I was about to follow Hackett, when I saw his head disappear; and then I heard his body strike among the trees and bushes as it fell, down, down the precipice on the very edge of which we stood, unconscious of our danger. I drew back with a shudder, and at the same moment I heard a mocking laugh from Moloch. He had seen Hackett fall, and was enjoying the misfortune.

CHAPTER XLIII.

MOLOCH AND HIS VICTIM. — HE EXPLAINS MATTERS. — NEGOTIATIONS. — FAILURE. — WE RAISE THE SIEGE.

SEVERAL times did I raise my revolver for the purpose of taking aim at the rascal; but the rogue was cunning, and sheltered his body with that of the lady's, holding her form before his own, so that I did not dare to fire for fear of injuring Amelia; and Moloch knew very well that I was not rash enough for any such business as that, much as I might desire vengeance on the fellow. The cowardly conduct of Moloch almost drove Hopeful mad; and if I had not restrained him, and kept him within bounds, he would have rushed forward and attempted to reach the cliff on which the fellow stood, in defiance of the chasm just before us, and the huge horse-pistols which he had discharged at us and the dog so often.

"Do you see the blasted scoundrel?" cried Hez, with chattering teeth and flushed face. "He's got her in his arms, and is hugging her like all possessed. Cuss him, how I wish I had my self-regulating choke-all screw around his neck! I'd twist the life out of him in no time."

"Be calm," I whispered, in reply, although I did not feel calm by any means, for I was burning to revenge the poor girl's wrongs.

"Calm!" repeated Hez, in a tone of contempt; "how can I keep calm when that cuss is a huggin' and kissin' the gal, and I never dared to even touch her hand, much as I wanted to?"

"Hush," I said; "Moloch is shouting to us. Let us hear what he says."

"Vill yer listen to me for a moment, yer Yankee dogs?"

"Talk on, you British hound," I responded.

"Vell, I vill, but don't yer play none of yer tricks on me, 'cos if yer does I vont stand it. Now listen, and hear vot I has for to say. Vill yer?"

"Yes."

"And yer vont shoot at me?"

"Not while you are talking with us."

"Vell, then I vont bang at you; so come out of the bush, and hear me."

We left our places of concealment, so that the rascal could see us; and then for the first time Amelia turned her face and stretched out her hands towards us. Poor thing, we could see by her eyes how much she had suffered during the past twenty-four hours. All her little playful, coquettish airs were gone, and in their place were dejection and unhappiness, such as a young girl feels when she first meets with trouble.

"O, Mr. Jack," Amelia said, in trembling tones; and then words failed her, and she commenced crying as though her heart was broken.

"She is veeping for me," grinned Moloch. "She knows that if she don't mind her eye ve vill have to part, she goin' one way, and me another. That's vot she knows, don't you, deary?"

"Tell the coves," Moloch continued, "how much ve loves heach other, and how ve intends to live here on the mountain jist like two blessed lambs. That is," the wretch continued, "if she minds me and cooks my mutton to a turn

If she don't, down a gulch she goes, and I shall be left all alone."

The fellow paused for a moment, took a look at Amelia's face, clasped her still more closely to his breast, as though fearful that our wrath would prompt us to fire at all hazards, and kill him at any risk.

"Come, speak up," the fiend cried, and gave her a little shake to enforce attention. "Knock off yer sobbin', and tell the coves that ye is in love with me, and means to make me 'appy."

"I cannot speak," Amelia replied. "My words seem to choke me."

"Yer vords vont choke yer, but I vill if yer don't talk up Come, let's have none of this gammon, or I'll pitch yer off into the gorge." He made a motion as though to throw her from the shelf; but the girl clung to him with desperate energy, as though to prevent such a fearful fate. But as Moloch made the motion, I glanced down the gorge over which we were standing, and then understood how it happened that Hackett fell so suddenly. The edge of the precipice was covered with short brush, which concealed the danger until a person had entered it. Then a false step would be fatal; for the gorge, or canon, was at least two hundred feet deep, and appeared to have been caused by some terrible convulsion of nature — some upheaving of the earth, that rent the mountain asunder, so that the distance across, from the top of the gorge, where we stood, to the other side, where Moloch was, measured at least twenty feet, and could only be crossed by a bridge of some kind, so that the cunning rascal had Amelia completely in his power, and we could not help ourselves, although she was almost within our grasp. We were in a peculiar position, and Moloch knew it. We could not descend the gorge, for it was too steep; and if we had made the attempt, we ran much risk of losing our lives, provided the bushes to which we would have to cling gave way. Even if we had succeeded in descending, a more difficult task was yet before us. We would have to scale the opposite side — an undertaking of no slight account, when it is understood that the precipice was perpendicular, and the brush upon the sides was not of a vigorous growth. If we retraced our steps, and ascended the mountain from a different point, we would still be at fault, for we might wander about for days, and not find Moloch, even if he did not once more cross the bridge as soon as we left, and seek shelter at some of the shepherds' huts which were scattered along the plains.

The longer I pondered over the matter, the more discouraged I felt at the task before me. I think that Moloch must have comprehended some of the thoughts that passed through my mind, for he grinned in a most malicious manner as his eyes encountered mine, and he had the impudence to shout out, —

"Vell, Yankee, vot do yer think of it? Can yer fly? If yer can, yer can reach me; if yer can't, jist valk back to the farm and tell old Smith that I has the lass, and that I means to keep her till I's tired of her. She loves I, and I loves her; so ve means to be 'appy 'ere in my kingdom. Now go back, or yer von't be able to find yer vay out of the gulch. Take my vord for it, I ain't to be reached by the likes of yer."

"Listen, Moloch," I said, commanding my temper as well as I was able, so that I could talk to the scoundrel in a convincing manner; "you know that you are in our power, as well as we know that the girl is in yours." The fellow uttered a shout of derision.

"Hear me patiently," I continued; and the scoundrel seated himself on a rock, and drew the struggling girl to his lap, and held her so that only a small portion of his head was exposed. He was determined that he would not be taken by surprise. All this time Amelia's face was concealed in her hands, and I could hear her sob; and every one that she uttered went to my heart, and almost unmanned me.

"Drive on," Moloch said. "Say vot yer've got to say, and don't be long about it, 'cos I've got to have a little rest. Yer know I vos up all night, don't yer?"

"You know," I continued, "that you are in our power; that you can't leave the mountain without our consent. We can remain here on the watch, and starve you, or else compel you to go into the valley for food. Now don't you think that it would be better to give up the girl, accept a large sum of money for so doing, and then go where you please, unmolested by any one?"

"How much money, Yankee?" Moloch demanded.

"One thousand pounds."

"Now yer begin to talk. More money, Yankee; the lass is worth it. If yer loves her as well as I does, yer won't think of a few pounds. I must have somethin' to pay me for a broken heart."

"What do you think, Hez?" I asked. "The fellow will demand two thousand pounds. Can we pay as much?"

"Yes, yes," answered Hopeful, eagerly. "Three thousand, if he insists upon it; any sum, so that we get the gal safe in our power. She's worth all we give for her. I'll stand my share of the blunt; now yer see if I don't."

"And so will I," was my response, in a hearty manner; for I felt a little rebuked at the liberality of Hopeful, who wanted to acquire a fortune in such a short time.

"Wal," shouted Moloch, with a vigorous squeeze of the young girl, who still sat in his lap, held there by force, "vot does yer coves think about it? Don't be all day, 'cos me and the lass has been up all night, and ve vants a little rest. Don't ve, ducky?" and the brute pulled the girl's head back so that he could obtain a view of her fair face; but Amelia struggled with him, and managed to turn towards us.

"O, Mr. Jack," she cried, "if you have the least pity in your heart, do save me. Pay the money, and I will work like a slave until I give it all back to you. Save me from this man, and I'll bless you forever and ever."

"Amen!" cried Moloch, with a brutal shout of laughter. "Yer see, Yankee, the lass ain't quite at home vid me; but she vill be afore many days."

In reply Amelia held out her arms in a beseeching manner, and then her head fell, and she appeared to have fainted. Hopeful would have raised his revolver and fired if I had not restrained him. He was almost crazy with rage, and forgot all consideration or thought of the danger which the young lady would incur in case his hand trembled and the bullet chanced to strike the wrong person. Quick as the movement was, Moloch saw it, and took the alarm.

"You coves mean trickery," he shouted; and he sprang to his feet, and appeared disposed to beat a rapid retreat.

"No, no," I answered; "you are mistaken; we mean fair."

"If I see any signs of that 'ere game," Moloch said, "I'll jist quit this palaver; now mind your eye if I don't."

We saw the danger that we encountered; we knew that the devil who stood opposite to us, only a little higher up, would, in a moment of rage, murder Amelia, and then chuckle at our grief; so I determined to temporize with the rascal, and buy her if possible.

I assured the fellow that we had no thought of harming him, and at last calmed him so completely that he once more seated himself, and pulled the almost insensible girl into his lap.

"Vell," he said, "vot is it about money? Can yer talk big about the shiners? The lass is worth all yer'll give for her. Now, then, Yankee, speak up like a man, and let's hear you."

"Your demands are excessive," I said; "but we have considered the young lady's situation, and are disposed to be liberal."

"Vot do yer call liberal?"

"One thousand nine hundred pounds, all in gold, and to be paid you in two days' time."

"It won't do," was the ruffian's response. "I must have more dosh. I vant enough to last me through life. Give me three thousand."

"I'll see you hanged first," I answered. "I'd sooner cross over and take the girl by force."

"I'd like to see yer do it," was the complacent response

"You know it can't be did. I'd murder yer both afore ye could do it. Go back to the farm, get the dosh, and bring it here. Then I'll let yer have the lass. Now start yerselves, 'cos I'm sleepy and vant rest."

He caught Amelia in his arms, and retreated to the bush; but as he retired we could hear one agonizing scream, that told of lost hope and deep despair on the part of Amelia. Then all was quiet, and for a moment Hez and I stood looking at each other with white faces and trembling limbs, hardly realizing all that had passed before us, and almost willing to believe that we had dreamed what we had witnessed; and while we stood thus I was surprised to see tears trickling down Hopeful's face.

"We've lost her," he said; "we shan't see her no more."

"I think we shall," I returned with more confidence than I felt. "She is not lost to us."

"She wouldn't have been if you'd offered all the money the feller wanted. Why didn't you give him the three thousand pounds? She's worth more'n that. You didn't want her to get clear; you know it."

"Hopeful," I said, in a faltering tone, "Moloch would have required his three thousand pounds in hand; you know that we have no money with us. I did the best that I could in negotiating."

"I don't believe it," he cried. "I could have done better; I know that I could. You didn't want the gal, 'cos she cares nothin' about you. I know it."

"Go and see what you can do in the way of a trade," I said, losing a little patience. "If you can buy the fellow, I've no objection to furnishing the money. Try him, and don't waste time; for we must descend the mountain, and look for poor Hackett's body, and give it suitable burial. We must not leave it for the wild dogs to feast on."

Hopeful turned from me abruptly, and walked to the edge of the precipice.

"Hallo, you sir," he said, in a loud tone. There was no response.

"Moloch, you rascal, come out and listen to me."

There was a stir in the bushes on the shelf opposite to us, and the next moment a loud report and a ball cut the air close to Hez's head. As usual, Moloch had missed with his antique horse-pistol.

"Darn yer," growled the brute; "if yer wakes me up agin I'll hit yer harder next time."

Hez made a movement to draw his revolver; but Moloch saw the motion, and dodged back to his shelter, out of sight, and the son of New Hampshire joined me, indignant, but remarkably silent. I did not utter a word at the man's failure, but commenced descending the mountain, so that I could find the gorge in which Hackett's body was lying. After I found it, I determined to renew my efforts at recovering Amelia, unless I had to retreat on account of the want of provisions, our stock of which was very low.

CHAPTER XLIV.

GLOOMY PROSPECT.—A BRIGHT LIGHT.—FRIENDS OR FOES?

I MUST confess that the prospect before us was not promising. We were miles from the nearest shepherd's station, with but a mouthful of food in our pockets, and but a sup or two of brandy in our canteens. As far as I was concerned, it did seem as though I could not walk five miles, without a long rest, to save my life; and I know that Hez was full as lame as myself, for as soon as he recovered from his passion, disappointment, and vexation, and while we were descending the mountains, he admitted that such was the case, and hinted that a long halt was necessary on our part, so that he could take some of the stiffness out of his legs, which he declared were like ramrods.

We reached the foot of the mountain an hour or two before sunset, and then commenced a search for the gorge. Already were the dark shadows stealing along the side of the mountain, and shutting out the sunlight from the crevices which we had just left. We searched a long time, or until the sun had entirely disappeared; and then Hez found that it was useless to look any further for the gorge in which Hackett's body was lying. He threw himself down upon the hot sand, through which we had waded, and confessed that he could go no farther.

"I must rest," he said, "until morning, for all life is out of me. If I should even hear Amelia's voice, I don't believe that I have the strength to answer it. Poor girl; do you think that the wretch will dare —" He did not finish the sentence, for it seemed too terrible to talk about; but as he buried his face in his hands, I could hear him sob as though his heart was nearly broken at the dreary prospect before the young and handsome coquettish girl, who had stolen his heart in spite of the claims which a New Hampshire beauty had upon it.

No sooner did daylight vanish than we felt the cold air sweep down the side of the mountain, attracted by the burning sand which covered the plain. We felt it, and anticipated an uncomfortable night; but suddenly I recollected the lesson which the serpents had taught me, and resolved to follow their example. I commenced scraping away the hot sand, scooping out a large hole capable of holding our bodies. Hez watched me at work, but did not offer to help until he saw the object which I had in view, and then he lent a willing hand. Poor fellow, it was rather tough experience for him, and I did not much blame him for his low spirits.

"Rover," I said, "go and find something to eat and drink. Kill a lamb if you can't do better."

The brute understood me, for he wagged his tail in token of assent, and then trotted off, and was soon out of sight.

"This is not so bad, Hez," I remarked, in a cheerful tone.

There was no response. Hopeful had forgotten his troubles in sleep. I remained awake for half an hour or less, thinking of poor, dear Amelia, and the unfortunate Hackett, and then I dropped off, and dreamed that I was crossing the chasm on a tight rope, and that Moloch was endeavoring to shake me from the same, and while I was striving to hold on he flung a snake at my head. It struck me on the nose, and so great was the shock that I suddenly awoke, and found something cold pressed against my face. I started up, and a dozen wild dogs scampered off, alarmed at the movement of what they considered lawful prey. I once more nestled in the sand, piled it around my shoulders as well as I was able, and was asleep in less than a minute. This time I dreamed that I saw Hackett's body, terribly bruised, lying in the gulch, with face dark and swollen, festering under the hot sun, and that one of the arms of the corpse was raised, as though to remind me that I must not forget to inter the body as soon as it was found.

"I will not," I said; and I must have spoken in a loud tone, for the sound of my voice awoke me.

I started up, and found Rover near my head, licking his jowls, as though he had feasted, and was indulging in the remembrance of the same. As I sat up, I patted his head, and glanced towards the mountain. To my surprise, I saw, not more than a mile from us, a bright fire; and it appeared as though I could distinguish forms moving around it. For a few minutes I sat and looked at the unexpected sight, so as to be certain that I was not laboring under some delusion; and then I punched Hez in his ribs — a proceeding that produced an oath or two on the part of that young man.

"Go to the devil, and let me alone," he said.

"You would soon go to him if I should let you alone," I replied, and once more touched his ribs with no light hand.

"What in thunder is the matter?" Hez asked.

"Clear your eyes of sand, and then look under the shelter of the mountain," I said.

Hopeful complied, but he had slept so sound that the effort was rather a laborious one; and half asleep as he was, he muttered, "I don't see nothin'."

"Will you never awaken?" I asked. "Look, and see what is near us. Think of Amelia and revenge."

In an instant he had shaken off all his drowsiness, and was looking at the fire with as intent a gaze as myself.

"What is it?" he asked in a whisper, as though fearful that his voice would be heard by those around the fire.

"That is what we must find out," I replied. "If there are bushrangers around that fire, we must avoid them; if natives, hire them for a few days; and if Moloch is there we must—"

"Kill him," Hez cried, springing to his feet.

"Act cautiously," I said. "Remember that we tread on dangerous ground—that we are surrounded by enemies, and—"

But Hez did not hear me. He was walking towards the fire at a rapid pace, and I found that I had as much as I could do to keep up with him; so between restraining the dog and my friend, I had as much as I could attend to for the first five or ten minutes of our movement. A few blows with a strap brought Rover to his senses, and caused him to keep by my side; and then I darted forward, and seized Hopeful by his collar, and held him fast.

"What do yer mean?" he demanded, in an angry tone.

"That I am determined to save your life and my own Now, just be guided by me. We are near danger. I don't want my throat cut by a party of bushrangers, nor to be knocked over by a boomerang from the hand of an excited native. We must approach that fire cautiously, and not as though we had a regiment of traps at our back. Be guided by me."

The distance was too great to distinguish the party clustered around the fire. Neither could we hear the sound of their voices; so we loosened our revolvers, saw that they were capped, that our bowie-knives were handy, and then dropped on our hands and knees, and crawled towards the fire. By and by Hopeful put his mouth close to my ear, and whispered,—

"Bushrangers, sartin—I know it."

"How do you know it?"

"'Cos one does all the talkin' and swearin'. You don't hear but one voice. Listen."

I did listen, and was so much interested that I concluded

to crawl nearer the fire and examine the face of the man who talked so much, and to whom the others listened so respectfully. It was not a bushranging custom. Men of the bush had but little respect for each other, and were not fond of what they called "blab."

I waited patiently for ten minutes; and then a particle of sand got into my nostrils, and caused me to sneeze.

"What in the devil's name is that?" cried the voice, which somehow sounded familiar to me.

I saw two or three forms rise from the ground, and glance around, while at the same time some one stirred the fire, and a bright flame started up. By its light I saw that the men were Australian natives, and that they were armed with spears and boomerangs.

"Squat down, you black fellers," some one cried in English. "Don't you be afeard as long as I'm here. Down with yer, and let's have another slice of kangaroo."

"Here, you black imp," the voice said, after the natives were seated, "cut me off a big junk of meat, and then pass the coffee. Ah! don't put yer dirty mugs in it afore I'm done. White men first, the world over."

I could not be mistaken — that was surely the voice of Hackett, my Illinois friend. And he seemed remarkably lively, just as though he had not fallen from a three hundred feet precipice, broken his limbs, and generally disarranged his system.

"It's him or the devil," muttered Hez.

"Illinois, aho!" I roared, making a speaking-trumpet of my hands.

"Hello!" was the instant response.

"Is that you or your ghost?"

"Me, a-stuffin' of kangaroo meat and coffee. Heave ahead, and have some."

We rushed towards the fire, and there saw Hackett, the man whom we supposed dead, seated on the sand, roasting meat and drinking coffee, and surrounding him were a dozen natives.

"Glad to see yer, old feller," cried Hackett, as we shook

hands. "Knew I should come across yer somewhar afore long."

"Why, we supposed you dead," I remarked.

"Dead be darned. What in thunder should kill me, I should like to know?"

"The fall from the precipice, to be sure."

"Yes, I went over; but that's no reason why I should knock my brains out, is it?"

I saw that Hackett was determined to take his own time in relating his experiences; so, as we were hungry, we brushed the natives aside, and sat down near the fire, first helping ourselves to a junk of kangaroo flesh.

"Help yerselves," cried Hackett, who had lighted his pipe, and approved of our actions with a nod.

"Tell us your experience," I said.

"Wal, 'tain't much, now I've gone through with it; and although I'm a little sore, I ain't got no limbs broke. I made one of these nigs rub me down with kangaroo fat, and I think it's took some of the soreness out of me. That's the worst bit what I got."

As he spoke he stripped up the leg of his trousers, and exhibited a shocking bruise, one nearly a foot long, and black and blue.

"Come here, you black cuss, and rub it. Kinder begins to feel a little stiff, like."

The native understood more by motion than he did by words. He commenced rubbing the bruised part with a careful hand, and then Hackett finished the account of his adventures.

"Ye see, when the British cuss, the one what had the gal in his arms, kinder got me riled, and I jist made a rush for him, and that's whar I made a mistake. I had ought to have played Injun; but ye see I didn't, and I suffered for it. The fust thing I knowed, I was a goin' down that gorge head fust; and then the next thing I felt was, that I struck a tree, and bounded off to another one. I caught at that, but it was no go. On I went, like an express train; and then I slipped from tree to tree, and at last landed in the centre of some bushes; and thar I laid for a while, wonderin' if I was in heaven or on 'arth; for it didn't seem as though I had much breath in me jist then. I kinder think I went to sleep, for I didn't know much for some time; and when I woke up, it took me half an hour to move and get out of the bush, whar I was lodged pretty fast."

"Why didn't you call for help?" I demanded.

"What for? Didn't I know you was busy, and that the gal was of more importance than me?" He then continued: —

"I waited a little while, and then I began to pick my way out of the gorge. I was some time a doin' it, but I seemed to get strength as I moved along, and at last I found the plain; and then who should I meet but these black cusses! When they seed me, they would have cut, but I stopped 'em by jist pintin' my rifle; and then I made 'em build a fire while I knocked over a kangaroo that came near us. And that's the end of my yarn."

I did not ask any questions, because just at that moment the Illinois gentleman was writhing under the influence of pain, the native using the palm of his hand in an active manner, in attempting to reduce the swelling which disfigured the poor fellow's leg.

"Yes," said Hackett, as soon as he could speak, "I must use that leg to-morrow, 'cos if I did tumble it was for a good purpose. While I was down in that 'ere gorge, I jist saw a trail what will take us right up to the Britisher. Thar's no mistake about it. I seed it with my own eyes."

Hopeful started to his feet.

"Let's go for that trail now," he said. "Perhaps we can find Amelia to-night."

"You'd have sharp eyes, then, let me tell yer. We must wait till daylight."

We went to sleep, and did not awaken until aroused by the roar of Hopeful, a sand bug having fastened to his leg, and he labored under the impression that a snake was biting him.

CHAPTER XLV.

ON THE TRAIL. — A YOUNG GIRL'S DISTRESS. — A RUFFIAN'S THREATS. — FORWARD TO THE RESCUE.

Our friend was too seriously bruised to think of walking. His leg presented such an appearance of discoloration that I seriously feared he would lose it, unless he had medical treatment. I took what little brandy I had left, and rubbed the limb as gently as possible, for each touch of my hand caused him intense pain, although the poor fellow declared that it was a waste of good liquor, and that it would do him much more good if taken internally. And the natives seemed to think the same thing; but they had a slight difference of opinion as to who should imbibe it. They contended that their stomachs were well calculated for a dose, and Hackett thought the same thing, and begged me to give him just a wine-glass full; and so urgent were his entreaties, that I consented.

As Hackett raised the canteen to his lips, the natives uttered a howl and danced around him, the victims of despair. But we calmed them with promises and threats; and then I suggested that Hackett should mount on the shoulders of one of the blacks and accompany us to the gorge, so that he could show us the trail which led to the mountain. In this position our western friend could move without much pain or trouble. It was tough on the natives, but their reward was to come; so we did not spare their feelings as much as we might have done. With some little trouble we made the blacks comprehend what we wanted, and then mounted Hackett on the shoulders of the stoutest man of the party; and as the western gentleman clasped his arms around the neck of the fellow who bore him, he remarked, —

"This 'ere cuss won't run as long as I'm on his back. You see if he does. Now, then, go ahead, old fellow

We has no time to lose if we wants to breakfast with the young lady."

Our course was blocked with stones, mounds of earth, and trunks of dead trees, which had been washed from the mountain side during the winter rains, and then lodged in the gorge until the next spring freshet drove them to the plains, where the sand, wood, and stones mingled, and in the course of time formed soil suitable for the growth of such grass as sheep and cattle feed upon when nothing better is to be obtained. Here the natives had hard work, as they were compelled to spell each other very often, their load was so heavy, and the road was so rough. More than once I caught the rascals looking over their shoulders, as though they were disposed to run for it; but a touch of my revolver changed their minds, and they would do the best they could to carry Hackett over the route.

"Dump me here," said Hackett, after we had penetrated the ravine about a mile, and the difficulties of locomotion steadily increased.

"Curse the leg," he said, as we laid him down on some sand, the softest place that we could find; "how it does jump! just as I want to use it, too."

We offered to rub it, but the man declined.

"You ain't got no time," he said. "You must start on the trail; thar it is, close to them bushes. You can't see it unless you pull 'em apart. It is jist opposite whar I come over. That's the tree I lighted on. Kinder shook me up, didn't it? Now, then, jist pick yer way up that trail, and you'll find the gal and the Britisher. But be kinder keerful how you go, 'cos the bushes is thick and the path narrer. Leave me here; I'll look arter the natives, and see that they don't cut stick. Take care of yerselves, and come back as soon as possible, 'cos I shall feel kinder lonesome, with no one to talk to but these black fellers, and they can't understand me much."

It was rather ticklish work, walking up the side of that mountain, unable to see if enemies lurked on either side. There were some points in our favor, which we were to make the most of. Moloch would not suspect our presence, and therefore would not be on the watch. He would not have the least idea that we were so near him, and unless he had friends we could count on an easy victory. All was quiet as we worked our way along, and after an hour's toil we suddenly left the trail and the bushes on each side, and found that we were close to the rock on which Moloch had defied us the day before.

"Down!" I whispered; and at the word Hopeful and myself dropped to the earth, and crawled behind a clump of bushes, where we could not be seen unless some one was close to us.

"The villain is near us," I said. "Perhaps he is asleep.'

"And p'haps he's watching us," suggested Hopeful.

As I had no facts that such was not the case, I remained silent, and listened.

"Let the dog lead us to 'em," remarked Hopeful; "it will save time."

I called Rover to my side, and told him what I wanted, and I spoke just as though I was addressing a human being with good reasoning powers. The brute understood me, and with his head to the earth he walked slowly on towards a grove of palm trees, that stood just above us on an elevated part of the mountain. We followed him on our hands and knees, sheltering ourselves as well as we were able, and, after some moments of excessive toil, gained the edge of the wood, and found Rover lying down and awaiting us, with an expression upon his intelligent face that seemed to convey a great deal of meaning.

"What is it, good dog?" I whispered.

He manifested an inclination to bound forward, and by the bristling of his hair I knew that an enemy was near.

I kept him back by a motion of my hand, and then crawled forward until I suddenly stopped to listen to a sound that was strange to my ears. It was a woman weeping.

I changed my position, moving a little to the left, so that I could remain sheltered by the bushes, and yet see all that was going on just ahead of me. The advantage of this movement was soon apparent; for while we were wondering if those sobs came from Amelia, we heard the harsh voice of Moloch.

"Vill yer stop that 'ere snufflin'?" he asked. "Does yer s'pose I can 'joy my breakfast ven yer is makin' that kind of noise?"

The only response to this was a fresh torrent of tears and sobs. Hopeful began to look wild.

I found that it was only by a powerful effort that I could command my feelings. But I remembered the fate which the abductor deserved; so I replaced my revolver, and determined to wait, and learn as much as possible before we acted.

The sobbing continued. I could not see the young lady, neither could I see Moloch. They happened to be behind a bush that stood just in front of us. We continued to listen.

"Vill yer stop that 'ere?" the brute asked. "Vot is the use of yer makin' that noise? It von't do yer no kind of good, and yer knows it; yer only hurts yerself for nothin'. I don't vant a vife vot has red eyes all the time — does yer s'pose I does?"

"O, take me home!" we heard the poor girl exclaim.

"Not a bit of it," was the reply. "I has yer fast, and I means to keep yer."

Here the ruffian chuckled in an audible manner, and the sobbing was renewed.

"Yer didn't think yer'd have me for a husband, did yer," the wretch cried, "ven yer used to turn up your nose at me?"

A fresh volley of sobs and cries was the only response, and that seemed to provoke Moloch.

"Don't I tell yer that I vill marry yer some time if yer is good and minds me? Vot more does yer vant? Jist make the most of it, 'cos thar's no one to help yer. The poor coves vot follered us has gone home, 'cos they knowed they couldn't reach me; so now vot has yer to hope for?"

"Nothing but God's mercy," was the almost inaudible response.

"Vell, that may do for another vorld, but it von't do for

this; so jist put yer trust in me, and I'll treat yer kindly till I gets ready to sell yer to some of my bushranging chums."

At this threat the poor girl renewed her lamentations, and in such a loud tone that Moloch was enraged.

"If yer don't stop that I'll jist lay hands on yer," he said; and we could hear the fellow walk towards her.

While he was moving, we shifted our position, and managed to obtain a view of the parties. I saw Amelia, her dress torn, her hair down over her shoulders, lying upon a bed of leaves in an arbor-shaped hut constructed of trees and branches. This was the place which Moloch or some one else had prepared with some little patience. By the time the wretch had reached the girl, we were enabled to gain our new position, and see all that transpired. He laid his hand upon her shoulder, not in a gentle manner, and raised her to a sitting position.

"Stand up," he said; "I vant to talk to yer. Now, if yer don't jist shut up, and smile on me, and kiss me when I vants yer to, yer vill go over the bank, and never know vot hurt yer. Do yer hear?"

He shook her in a fierce manner, as though he had lost all patience with her, but the next moment softened, for when she turned her eyes upon the man, he spoke more gently.

"Come, be a good lass, and love me, and then I'll treat yer vell."

"Love a wretch like you!" she cried. "No! I hate you! and if it were possible to give you to the hangman, I would do so."

She spoke as though her wrongs had made her desperate, and reckless to her fate. For one moment the scoundrel quailed before her; but the next instant he sprang forward with his huge, black fist upraised, as though to strike her to the earth; and he would have done so, if I had not spoken to the dog just in time to save her. With a growl that sounded savage and threatening, Rover bounded over the bushes, towards Moloch, while Hopeful and I followed the animal, pushing on through the brush as fast as possible, and with such success that we were close upon his heels, when the rascal, who was threatening Amelia, turned, his attention being attracted by the noise which we made. He saw us, and comprehended all at a glance. His hand sought the handle of his heavy knife; and if the hound had not been close to him, he would have been enabled to draw it, and we should have had to content ourselves with simply shooting the villain, which we did not want to do, such a death being too easy for crimes such as he had committed. The dog was too quick for him. He went over the bushes at a flying leap, just touched the ground, and then bounded forward straight at the throat of the shepherd, whose right hand was on the hilt of his knife. The fellow saw that he would not have time to draw it; so he suddenly adopted a new plan. He thought that the dog would not attack a person who was well known; so he managed to stammer out:—

"Good doggy."

He had no chance to utter more. The hound did not appreciate his endearments, for the noble animal dashed at the man's throat, and down he went.

"Take him off," the scoundrel yelled; and then we broke through the brush, and stood before the half-distracted girl and the struggling, groaning, panting Moloch.

"Saved! saved!" cried Amelia; and down she tumbled upon her knees, and up went her hands, raised towards heaven in token of gratitude to Him who had directed our steps, and sustained us during all our hardships and troubles.

"Take the brute off, vill ye?" roared Moloch, who saw us, and desired aid even at our hands.

"Which one is the brute?" asked Hopeful, who really seemed to enjoy the sight before him.

"In the name of the devil, take off the dog!" howled Moloch, who still struggled with the hound.

"In one moment," I said; and then, stooping down, I removed the knife from his belt, so that he could not use it.

"Now don't you move," I remarked. "If you do it will be all the worse for you. Release him, good dog."

The hound let go his hold, and the instant he did so, Moloch struck him with his clinched fist. The animal avenged the insult in a savage manner, for with one snap of his mighty jaws, he tore a huge piece of flesh from the rascal's face, causing it to present a most shocking spectacle, for the blood spurted out and dyed his red beard and breast one mass of carmine. The fellow uttered some frightful curses, but I did not heed them; and then without opposition I strapped his arms behind his back, secured him so that he could not run away, or do any mischief, and then turned towards the lady, whom I found on the ground, and once more weeping most bitterly.

CHAPTER XLVI.

ON THE MOUNTAIN. — AMELIA'S GRIEF. — SHE DEMANDS VENGEANCE. — PREPARATIONS FOR HANGING.

It was a great triumph to stand over such a scoundrel as Moloch, and know that he was a prisoner, and was like to be punished as his crimes deserved. When I left Smith's station I had pledged my word to return with Amelia — to save her, if such a thing was possible; and now, when I looked at the villain, as he was lying at my feet, securely bound, I could not help feeling that I had sustained, in a measure, the reputation which I had enjoyed, and which I was so anxious to maintain during my residence in Australia, simply because I desired to show the pig-headed Englishmen that Americans were full as clever as themselves in all that makes a man adventurous and noble.

Of course Moloch's tongue was not idle while I was tying him. He blasphemed in the most outrageous manner, and swore that we did not dare to give him fair play in a free fight — just as though such a wretch was capable of comprehending anything that was just or honest.

"If my hand hadn't viggled," he cried, "I'd have popped yer over the mornin' arter I was turned out of the house.

I came near puttin' a ball through yer head, and I'm sorry I didn't. Cuss yer for a downey cove."

The ruffian kicked at me with his heavy shoes; but the blow fell short, luckily for me, for the brogans were armed with iron nails of monstrous size, and if he had touched my skin I should have been lamed for some days.

Rover understood the movement as a challenge, and he did not fail to accept it. He dashed at the prostrate ruffian, gave him a severe nip, and then looked at me, as though waiting for commendation for the act.

"Do yer want the dog to murder me?" asked Moloch, with some manifestations of alarm.

"I don't care what he does to you," was my answer; and then I turned towards Amelia, who was seated on the ground, her face covered with her long, thick hair, as though to shut from her sight the presence of two of her best friends, or as if the light of day was hateful to her.

The stockman continued his abuse until it was so bad that Hez stopped his mouth with a stick, putting it in until the fellow's tongue was forced aside, and incapable of movement. Then Hopeful compelled him to rise, and move down the trail to the gulch, where Hackett was awaiting us, leaving Amelia and me alone.

"Come, Amelia," I said, "summon all your resolution, dry your tears, and be prepared to meet the world with calmness, if not with happiness. You are saved, your life is spared, and you have so much to be thankful for that your present despondency should not be lasting."

She clung to me closely as I spoke; but she did not look up, nor cease to sob. Her face was buried in my bosom, and still covered with her long hair, once so bright and shining, and in which she took so much pride when I first knew her, in her coquettish days, when life seemed full of pleasure, and was of a rosy hue.

"Death would have been better than this disgrace," she managed to murmur; and then she broke down, and commenced moaning, and it was a long time before I could calm her so that she was prepared to listen to reason.

"O God!" she said, at length, "how can I return home and meet my relatives, with this terrible disgrace hanging over me? I shall die with grief."

"Grief seldom kills, and there are many days of happiness in store for you. Come, let us return to your friends, whom you will meet and inform that your injuries are avenged, that death has settled the account."

"You promise me that he shall die?" she asked, in an eager tone.

"I promise. If you wish to witness his fate, you shall. You can feast your eyes on his last struggles, and think how dearly the wretch paid for the outrages he committed."

Then, for the first time, she brushed back the hair that had concealed her face, and I was enabled to catch a glimpse of her eyes, swollen and red with weeping. How different she looked from the time when she had "made mouths" at me, because I had crossed some of her whims, or laughed at some of her vanities — girl-like and innocent, but still sufficient to cause me to smile and ridicule what I really liked.

"You — you — will tell sister that I did not come — come here — here of my own accord?" she asked in a low whisper.

"Why, of course she knows that such is the case. We all know that the villain forced you to go with him. They all understood that before I left your home. You need not fear but that your reception will be all you can desire, cordial and tender."

"O, I have suffered so much!" she moaned. "It seems as though I had grown old within the last two days."

"But in a short time your sufferings will cease. Make one effort, and then you will reach home."

"I will try," she said, and partially dried her tears; but when she attempted to walk, I found that her feet were badly cut with stones, her shoes worn out and hanging in strips. Every step she took was accompanied with such expressions of pain that I at last determined to take her in my arms, and carry her to the foot of the mountain, difficult as I knew the task would be. When I suggested it to her, she disapproved of the plan; but a few steps convinced her that her feet could never take her form down the trail, rocky and rough as it was; so she made no strong objection when I raised her in my arms, and commenced picking my way down the side of the mountain.

"You are real good," she whispered, as her arms were thrown around my neck, and her head rested on my bosom.

"Of course I am," I replied in a cheerful tone, glad that she had found some theme to divert her thoughts.

"I used to think you were hateful," Miss Amelia continued.

"I have no doubt of it; but I never entertained such an opinion of you. I knew that you were a little coquette; but all young girls have that failing."

"Now rest a moment," Amelia said, when she found that I began to feel her weight.

I never saw a girl more tender and considerate than Amelia, even under such trying circumstances as she was placed in. Suffering as she did, ill treated as she had been, overpowered by grief as she was, the poor child still found time to condole with me on account of the burden which I had assumed.

"Are all Americans like you?" she asked, as I once more resumed my precious load.

"Well, yes, I think they resemble me in some respects," I answered. "For instance, my countrymen like to look at a handsome face, and if a lady possesses one, all her faults are forgiven."

"And is that the reason why you paid such court to the young girl you brought to the house? Jenny, I think you called her."

For the first time since we had met she raised her eyes to mine; but it was only for a moment. They dropped in an instant, and were blinded by tears. I was just about to sit down with my precious load, for the purpose of resting,—and I have no doubt but that I should have uttered some nonsense,—when I heard steps ascending the mountain; and the next instant Hopeful stood before me. His presence prevented the words which I should have spoken, as much under the influence of pity as of passion.

"Give her to me," my friend said, in an ungenerous tone; and he made a grab at her, as though he would tear her from my arms.

She clung to me for a moment, closer than ever; and then her arms were loosened, and she whispered, "You are tired; let me go."

I was tired, and my arms ached; but I could have endured the fatigue, for the sake of being kind to the poor child, had I not known Hopeful's jealous nature, and how sensitive he was; therefore I relinquished the girl to Hez. I followed him down the side of the mountain, and although it was some distance to the gorge where William Hackett kept watch and ward over the natives and the prisoner Moloch, yet the enthusiastic and strong-limbed Hopeful disdained to stop and rest until he had reached the foot of the mountain. As I appeared in sight, Hackett received me with a cheer and a flourish of the pipe which he was smoking, and his rifle, which he had laid across his knee for the purpose of using it in case of disaffection on the part of the subjects who were under his charge for the time being. After the Illinois gentleman had exhibited his pleasure at my return, he commenced rubbing his bruised leg, and consoling Amelia after a style that was far more original than elegant.

"Don't cry, young woman," he said; "sich is life. We must all come to it, you know. Don't think nothin' about it, and then you'll be all right. A cup of tea, strong, and plenty of sugar in it, will put you on yer pins agin. Look at me."

I knew that Hackett only needed a hint to hold his tongue; so, as I slapped him on his back, I whispered to him that the lady was not in a mood to listen to advice, however good. He took the hint, and turned his attention to Moloch, whom Hopeful had bound to a tree in so secure a manner that the fellow could not escape. I expected that Hackett would not be over choice in his remarks, or that Moloch would remain silent under his taunts. Whatever he said in extenuation of his crime, would grate harshly upon Amelia's ears, and render her more miserable than she was at the present time; so, as soon as Hackett turned his batteries upon the prisoner, I led the young girl away, so that she could neither see nor hear what was going on.

"Do not move from this place," I said as I turned to leave her, "until I return."

She nodded her head in token of her acquiescence, and then, to my surprise, said, "I have been most terribly insulted by that villain Moloch. Promise me that my injuries shall be avenged; that he shall not live to boast of his inhuman treatment."

"Amelia," I said, taking her hand and speaking as calmly as I could, "when I left your home in pursuit of Moloch, I determined that I would avenge the outrage if I could overtake the villain. He is in our power. Rest assured that I have not forgotten my vow."

"But I cannot appear in a court-room," she remarked. "I could never bear to meet the eyes of a gaping crowd. It would kill me."

"You shall not be called upon for any such trial. Trust to me for that."

"I will," she answered, and pressed my hand, and would have kissed it if I had not jerked it away.

"You will not remain long?" she asked, as I was leaving her.

"No, not long," I answered; and I thought how many minutes it would take to choke the breath out of the brute who had made two attempts upon my life, and then committed a foul crime because he suspected the young lady cared more for me than she did for any one else.

When I joined my comrades I found them engaged in reviling Moloch. The wretch did not suppose for a moment that we would dare to injure him, excepting as far as a few slight kicks or cuffs were concerned. He did not once imagine that we would take his life. It was in consequence of false hope and expectations that Moloch was rather lively when I returned.

"Say, Yankee," the scoundrel asked, "how did yer find me out?"

Instead of replying to the remark I began to look around for a tree that could boast of a strong limb.

"Vot is it?" he asked. "Vot do you vant?"

"A rope and tree strong enough to hang you," I answered.

"Yer don't dare to do it; it ain't lawful. I defy yer."

"Here's fun," cried Hackett; and from his knapsack he took a stout rope and threw it towards me. "Hang the cuss, and give me the end of the rope to hold when he swings off. Blast him! no mercy."

The prisoner saw the preparations with dismay, and uttered protests, prayers, and angry howls, of which we took no notice; while I quietly made a slip-noose, and addressed Moloch as soon as he would permit me.

"Say your prayers, for you have but a few moments to live," I remarked.

"You don't dare to do it," he cried, although his teeth chattered as he spoke, thus belying the air of courage which he assumed.

I nodded to Hez. He sprang forward and unbound Moloch from the tree, and then dragged the wretch towards the place of execution. At last the natives began to comprehend the meaning of the preparations, and they danced around the prisoner with demonstrations of joy at the proposed treat; and the two stoutest willingly lent Hopeful a helping hand in dragging the fellow forward towards the rock from whence he was to take his final leap.

CHAPTER XLVII.

THE HANGING.—AN INTERRUPTION.—THE TABLES TURNED—ESCAPE OF AMELIA.—A TABLEAU.

At length Hopeful and the two natives, who worked with much zeal, as though they would have been willing to help hang every Englishman in Victoria, dragged the prisoner to the rock, and put the rope around his neck. The instant it touched him he yelled to the extent of his voice, and began to realize his situation. He saw that we were in earnest, and really meant to hang him; and as he was not quite prepared to die, and was a coward at best, he made considerable trouble for us in the way of noise and struggles.

"Look a-here, you coves," he cried, "yer ain't in arnest; yer know yer has no right to do this sort of a thing. I must be tried afore one of the big vigs, and found guilty, and sentenced in reglar ship-shape fashion. I don't understand this kind of vork."

"Pray," I answered. "If you have prayers to utter, now is the time to use them."

"You can't frighten this cove," was the answer. "I'm game; I knows vot my rights is, and I'll stick to 'em."

"When I drop this handkerchief," I cried, "you will be pushed from the rock. I give you five minutes in which to repent."

"You don't mean it," the wretched man exclaimed; "you is only jokin' vid me. Let me off this time, and I von't do so no more. I von't, on honor; I'll live like a decent cove; you see if I don't."

"Your time is nearly up," I remarked.

"O, no, it ain't; yer don't dare to do so. Vere is yer varrant for all this 'ere? Let me go; I vant more time; I has lots of sins to confess; you don't know one half of 'em."

"We know enough," growled Hackett. "In Illinise we'd hang you long afore this. We values young women in that state, we does, and we don't allow nobody but their husbands to talk sass to 'em."

"You be —"

I looked at my watch and saw that the five minutes had passed. There was no mercy in keeping the man longer in suspense; so I shut my eyes, and dropped the handkerchief. I heard a brief struggle, a rush, a fall, and then I was knocked down in a very energetic manner; and as I fell I heard the report of Hackett's rifle, heard the yell of the Illinois gentleman, the screams of the natives, the vigorous exclamations of Hez, and then all was a blank; for I seemed to sink into a painful slumber, from which I did not awaken for some time; and when I did open my eyes it was after a painful effort; and then I found that there was a ringing in my head and ears, and on putting up my hand I discovered that there was blood on my face, and that Rover was licking it off, and uttering a mournful whine at my condition.

"What the deuce is it all about?" I asked myself, after trying to collect my thoughts. "What has happened to me? I am injured, and yet cannot tell how it was done. Let me think."

Soon I heard voices, strange voices, and then harsh oaths; and on looking around, as well as I was able, without raising my head, I saw some half dozen rough-dressed men sitting on the rock from which Moloch was to take his leap, eating the few provisions which we had saved, and drinking the last drop of brandy which I had in my flask, and which the inhuman wretches had robbed me of while I was lying insensible. The natives had disappeared. Hopeful and Hackett I could not see or hear, and I feared that they had met with speedy deaths at the hands of the bushrangers during the *mêlée*. I lay quite still, and listened to the conversation that was going on; and by this means I was enlightened on some points.

"Old pal," said one of the ruffians, addressing Moloch, "you had yer neck stretched a little that time. If we'd been a few minutes later, the devil would have had you or his coals long afore this time. Yer old friends stood yer in good need this once, and ye must recollect 'em the next time they comes round the station. If they wants a few bones, give 'em, and don't be mean about it."

"You won't see me near the station agin," answered Moloch, speaking with an effort and a terrible twist of his face, as though the words hurt him.

"Come, old pal," cried the rough-voiced villain, "tell us how it happened that you is here hangin' by the neck, when you should be at the station."

"I left Smith's —" was the answer.

"With the lass? I know you did. Ah, you rogue, she's here somewhere, unless you've put her out of the way. Now where's the gal?"

"Yes, show us the lass," was the cry of these ferocious men.

Moloch knew that it was impossible to conceal Amelia. Do the best that he could, her presence would be known, and if he lied about the matter, the worse for him; while, if he told the truth, would not those desperate men claim the prize and keep her, paying no attention to his fancied rights? Here were questions which the ruffian asked himself. The bushrangers noted his sullen looks, and the voice, that sounded familiar, remarked, —

"I say, old feller, you don't appear to be satisfied with us. We've saved your life, yet you don't seem kinder grateful. What is the matter?"

Moloch replied, with an oath, that he was a "dummy cove," and he was "ever so much agag," which meant in plain English, that he was indeed grateful, and would like to show his gratitude.

"Then tell us where the lass is; come, my fine covey, she is near us; now show us the place."

Moloch did not dare to resist the pressure, much as he would have desired to. The bushrangers were too powerful for him. As he led the way, the ruffians were compelled to pass within four yards of me. Through my half-closed eyes I could see them, six rough, ugly brutes. As they approached me, Rover prepared for hostile demonstration; but I soothed him with a word. The hound understood me, for I had trained him to obey my glance; and no matter how savage he might feel, he knew that I would direct him right. I was well aware that the bushrangers would shoot the animal if he even growled at them; and as I did not wish to lose the dog, I thought that it was best to compel him to remain quiet, and manifest no sign of hostility. As the bushrangers passed me, they laughed; and one of them remarked, —

"The pistol ball was too much for that cove. He don't seem to move readily. Even the dog can't bring him to life."

"'Im is the best dorg in the country," muttered Moloch. "They wouldn't have found I, if it hadn't have been for the dorg."

"I thought you said the dog was savage," one of the men remarked.

"Weel, 'im is; if you don't believe I, jest you go near 'im;" and Moloch chuckled at the thought of the reception he would receive.

"If he be so good, we'd better not kill him; he may be of use to us some day."

The men passed on, too impatient to see the girl to pay much attention to me or the dog. I listened to the sound of their voices as they swore and laughed, and often raised my head and looked around as well as I was able, though I seemed rather dizzy at first, and felt a little faint: these weaknesses soon passed away, and I was able to notice Hopeful and Hackett, both bound hand and foot, and lying on their backs near the rock from which Moloch was to take his leap. The natives were not to be seen. They had disappeared at the first sound of strife. I called the names of my two friends, and they answered me.

"We is in a tight box this time," Hackett said; "but I have known sicker children than we is to live! The cusses may kill us, but we will die game at any rate."

As for Hopeful, he was too much cast down to talk. Suddenly a loud shout reached my ears, and then I heard curses mingled with blows. I listened, and found that the bushrangers had fallen upon Moloch, and were beating him in their usual savage fashion, simply because Amelia had left the place where I had told her to remain, and disappeared. In a few words I communicated the state of affairs to Hopeful and Hackett, and they were as pleased as myself at her escape, although they knew she would suffer and die on the plains or in the gulches. Suddenly Rover put his face to mine, and manifested his sympathy by a howl. I patted the dog on his head, and thought what a pity it was that he should die, when he could easily make his escape, and could not be of the slightest use to me.

"Good dog," I said, "go home and tell Smith that unless we have help here within an hour we are lost, and Amelia with us. Do you understand?" He uttered a low whine.

"On your way," I continued, talking to the animal just as though he were a human being, "if you should see Murden and his police, tell them to come to our rescue."

I never saw a dog look so intelligent as Rover did while I was speaking. He listened with the most respectful attention, as though to carefully weigh each word and treasure it in his memory. When I ceased talking he waited for a moment to see if I had any more commands; and when he found that I had not, he gave my face a lick, uttered a mournful whine, trotted towards the woods, looked back for a moment, saw me wave my hand in token of a long farewell, and then, with a howl expressive of pain and sorrow, disappeared in the woods.

"Wake up here!" shouted one ruffian; and as he spoke, he kicked me with all his might, and hurt me most outrageously.

"Blast your eyes!" I said, as I looked up, knowing that timidity was of no account, "don't you do that again."

The ruffians laughed in a jovial manner at the words, and one of them said that it was a shame to hurt such a game chicken.

"He'd make a good bushranger," one of them remarked. "If he'll jine us we'll save his life."

"Say, cove, will yer go with us?" one or two of them asked.

"Don't yer take him," yelled Moloch, struggling to the front, so that he could command immediate attention. "He's a cove vot is down on bushrangers, and is in vith the traps."

"How do you know it?" asked the voice that had sounded so familiar to me.

"'Cos I'se seen 'em as thick as two thieves at Smith's. They treated him jist as though he vos von of 'em."

"Let me see the man's face," the familiar-voiced bushranger said, and came towards me.

I knew the man at once, in spite of his rough appearance, so entirely different from what it was when I met him at Melbourne, in the saloon of the Red Lion, when he was concocting with his pal how they should leave the country with the diamonds which they had stolen from the lady of the governor-general. In fact, before me stood Patrick Doland. The fellow looked at me rather hard before he decided that he recognized me. The blood on my face rather disguised my appearance; but after a while Mr. Doland began to assume a ferocious look, as though he was growing mad very fast, and then he said, —

"Blast him! I know him. It's the cove what diddled me out of the diamonds. This is a happy meeting, sir."

I made no reply, because I knew that I could say nothing that would please him or appease his anger. As soon as Doland had stated that he knew me, the bushrangers uttered a shout of wrath, all of which was directed towards me They had a trap in their midst, and he must die.

Suddenly my friend Moloch, the amiable creature, shouted out, "Hang him! jist as he vas goin' to do vid me!"

"That's it!" was the exclamation, as if they all comprehended it. "Where's the rope? Drag him to the jumping-off place. String him up."

"Don't you do it, you darned thieves!" roared Hackett, as the bushrangers dragged me past.

"Let him up!" shouted Hopeful; but he might as well have talked to the winds; the rascals paid no attention to either of my friends. A rope was put around my neck and I was pushed off the rock.

CHAPTER XLVIII.

AN UNEXPECTED TUMBLE. — THE RESCUE. — A PRIVATE CONVERSATION.

According to all calculations, made by romancers and men of a scientific turn of mind, I should have broken my neck, and then died quite easy, after the bushrangers pushed me from the rock with a rope around my neck; but, fortunately for me, as it afterwards happened, the rascals had neglected to fasten one end of the rope. Not the one that was around my neck — that was all right, and rather tight — but the end that belonged to the limb of the tree was not secured, and by this little mistake I tumbled to the ground entirely uninjured.

"The trap has more lives than a cat," remarked Doland, who was inclined to laugh at the exhibition which I made, as I landed on the sand and gravel.

"If he has fifty lives they shall all be tried," one of the scamps remarked. "Up with him, and then down with him."

One of the robbers came towards me and jerked me to my feet.

"You was born to be hung," he said. "I see it in your face. You has got thief stamped all over it, like the small-pox."

"Hang me in welcome," I replied, "but don't say that my face has any of the peculiar characteristics of you gentlemen of the bush and chain-gang."

The fellow did not know what I meant, for he had never heard such language. He stared at me for a moment before he muttered, —

"What kind of chaff is you throwing at a cove?"

Before I had time to reply, some of the impatient ones had jerked me to the top of the rock; and one of the most active climbed the tree and recovered the end of the rope.

"Now, then, pray, trap, pray!" yelled the crowd, manifesting the most intense delight at my position.

"Do you wish me to pray aloud?" I asked, anxious to gain time.

"Yes, yes, spit it out;" and the wretches laughed at the novel sensation which they were likely to experience.

I don't know how long I continued praying; but I do know that I exhorted for such a length of time that my audience grew tired, and more than once intimated that I had better shut up, and be hanged in peace and quietness. But I would not be advised; so at last one of the brutes sprang upon the rock, and advanced towards me, for the purpose of throwing me off; but as they had neglected to secure my hands, I determined to give the rascal a warm reception; so, when he got near enough, I raised my arm, and struck him just between his eyes. He fell off the rock as though he had been shot, and rolled at the feet of his companions. I saw Doland draw a pistol from his belt, and then I suspected that death was near. I closed my eyes, expecting to hear the report of his weapon every moment; but other sounds caught my ear, and for a moment hope revived within my breast. I opened my eyes, and looked at the bushrangers. They were listening, as much astonished as myself, and unable to comprehend the movement. What could it mean? I thought that I could save myself by a bold stroke. I threw from my neck the rope, and shouted, "The police are upon you. The traps are here." Doland raised his pistol, and fired at me. I noted his aim, and threw myself from the rock just as he drew the trigger. The ball passed near my head, but left me uninjured.

"Kill the spy!" they shouted. "Don't let him escape!"

I shouted in return. In fact I yelled like a fiend. "Come on!" I cried, speaking as though I was addressing a party of burly police officers. "Here they are. Down with them."

To my surprise, I was answered with a cheer and a loud howl that spoke of joy and rage. I turned, and looked down the gorge, and saw half a dozen police officers, mounted on horseback, spurring towards me as fast as the nature of the ground would admit; and just in advance of them was Rover. The bushrangers, who were on the other side of the rock, heard the cries, and saw the advancing force. They knew their fate if they remained; for they could not hope to oppose in a successful manner the well-disciplined officers.

"Take away!" yelled the leader of the gang. That meant scatter as soon as possible.

But a new obstacle was suddenly presented to the notice of the bushrangers. It seems that while the robbers were making preparations to hang me, and while I was praying for their welfare and my own safety, Hopeful, a worldly-minded youth, and at all times ungodly, not caring to listen to my exhortation, set his mind to work devising ways for freeing his limbs from the bonds that confined them. In this he was successful, as by some squeezing and a little work he got one hand loose, and then the other; and no one looked at him, or watched his motions, still intent upon my execution. He crawled towards Hackett, cut the ropes which secured his arms and legs, and then made for the spot where the robbers had stacked the weapons.

Hopeful picked from the heap, sheltered in his operations by a ridge of sand, Hackett's rifle and revolver, his own pistol, and the one belonging to me, and then emptied the pans of the muskets, pulled out the flints, and crawled out, just as I knocked over the fellow who was anxious to see me hung before I was quite ready for the operation. Hopeful and Hackett were about to pull trigger, and try their luck at saving me, when I tumbled the bushranger from the rock. Then they thought they would wait for a few minutes, and see what would turn up. As soon as the police appeared in sight, the bushrangers turned to run; but, as I said before, they were opposed by an obstacle that they did not count on. Behind some trees that stood near the mountain trail were posted Hez and Hackett; so, as the bushrangers dashed that way, they were met with the sharp cry of, —

"Stop, blast yer eyes, or yer dead men!"

The bushrangers stopped, astonished at the sight of two resolute men armed with revolvers.

"Surrender!" roared Hackett, "or we'll blow yer to thunder."

The bushrangers glanced over their shoulders. The police had dismounted, and were advancing as skirmishers. The robbers saw the danger that threatened, turned suddenly, and dashed to the other side of the gorge, meaning to escape up the mountain by the aid of brush, long grass, and tree trunks. But they did not carry out their plans; for at this moment the police emptied their carbines, while Hackett and Hez fired at the same time, and then volley after volley was poured in until every man had fallen, killed or wounded. Not one escaped to carry the news of the disaster to the gangs of bushrangers who still infested the mountain.

"Hurrah for our side!" roared Hackett, making an effort to stand; but the swollen condition of his leg prevented him from using his feet.

The police responded to the shout, and then reloaded their carbines and pistols as calmly as if they had been firing at a mark.

"Well, old boy, I was just in time," the commissioner cried, as we shook hands. "A few moments more and the rascals would have laid you out. Thank fortune I arrived just as I did."

"You can't be any more thankful than myself. But tell me how you happened to arrive at such an opportune moment."

"In one minute. Let me tell the men to look after the wounded, and see if they can be assisted. We must be humane, you know."

But the police did not need such orders. They were already examining wounds, and binding up such as required immediate assistance if life was to be saved. Moloch was dead, shot in the back with three balls; for it seemed that Hackett and Hopeful aimed at his person, determined that he should not escape, at any rate. Doland was wounded, a ball having crushed the bone of his right arm, so that amputation was necessary if his life was to be spared.

"I can tell you in a few words how I happened here," the

commissioner continued, on his return, after he had examined the wounded. "You know you left Smith's without waiting for me or my men, which I don't think much of. It was an act of imprudence that should have cost you dear, and as soon as I heard that you had started I felt uneasy; but thinking that you would return by morning, I secured my prisoners, and told the men to take that rest which they needed so much. In the morning you did not make your appearance. I grew impatient, and determined to seek you. I divided my squad, sent Maurice to the city with six men and the prisoners, and then took the best tracker that Smith had at the station, and followed your trail. We met Rover, and you never saw a dog so delighted as he was. He almost talked; for I understood him sufficiently to know that you were alive, and that you had sent him to find assistance. He led us here, and you know the rest."

"Now let one of your men look after Hackett," I said; "you will find him a trump;" and I led the commissioner forward and introduced him; and then an officer was set at work rubbing the western man's leg.

I whispered to Murden that I was going in search of Amelia, and asked him to keep his men occupied until my return; then, calling Rover, I started for the place where I had last left the girl. I had no difficulty in finding it, or in putting the hound on the trail. I hurried on as fast as possible, and at last found the object of my search lying upon the ground, and nearly insensible. I knelt beside her, and called her by name; but at first she only shuddered, and seemed to think that Moloch was addressing her.

"Spare me, Moloch," she moaned, "and I will forgive you. Let me return home. My head aches so badly, and I feel cold and tired."

I took her fair head in my lap, and bathed her face and forehead with brandy, and forced a few drops between her lips. The liquor seemed to benefit her; for she ceased to moan and sob, and at last opened her large blue eyes, and fixed them on me with a terrified glare that soon gave place to a look of pleasure. She started up, and clasped my hands, and commenced kissing them, although they were not in a kissable state, for they had not seen soap and water since we left her brother's house. For a moment I feared that her mind was unsettled; but she soon convinced me that such was not the case, for she whispered,

"You have escaped them. Are you safe? Are we both safe from pursuit? If we are not, I can walk;" and she showed me her poor wounded feet, with the blood soaked through her stockings, or the remnants of stockings, and only the uppers of her boots left.

"We are both safe, Amelia," I remarked, in a quiet tone.

"Are you sure? You will not deceive me?"

"Thank Heaven, there is no occasion for deception. There is a squad of police in the gulch. They came just in time to save us."

"And that devil?" she asked, with a fierceness that was unnatural.

"He has paid the penalty of his crimes."

"Is he dead?" and in her joy she would have started to her feet; but I kept my arms around her, and prevented her from doing so.

"He is dead."

"Thank God!"

She laid her head on my bosom like a tired child, anxious for rest. Her eyes were closed, and she seemed to be engaged in deep thought. I did not disturb her meditations, for I could imagine what they were. At last she opened her eyes.

"Take me home," she cried. "My head aches, and I need rest."

I had just raised her in my arms, when my friend burst through the bushes and joined us.

"This ain't jist the thing!" he exclaimed. "She don't belong to you. Give her to me; I'll carry her down the mountain."

Even before I had time to remonstrate, he put out his hands and took her from me, and then turned and dashed down the mountain like a madman. When I reached the gorge, I found that the police were burying, as well as they could, the bodies of the dead bushrangers. Doland was alive, and so were two other members of the fraternity, but so badly injured that it was hardly possible for them to recover. As for taking them on horseback, it was not to be thought of; they would not have lived an hour. The commissioner, as soon as I was at leisure, asked my advice on the subject, and I gave it promptly, as usual.

"We must press the natives into our service," I said. "We must build litters, and compel them to carry our wounded. Some of your men must walk, and see that the blacks do not desert, while we ride to the station and send out ox-teams. Hackett can ride, and so can Amelia — both of them need immediate attention and rest."

Murden liked my plan so well that he instantly resolved to carry it into effect.

CHAPTER XLIX.

A TIRESOME RIDE. — ARRIVAL AT THE STATION. — DEPARTURE FOR MELBOURNE.

When we left the gulch, Murden gave the officers, whom he left in charge of the natives and the litters, a few directions about the route, and the place where they might expect to meet the ox-teams, sent from the stations, and then he joined me at the head of the cavalcade, and we plunged into the desert. For an hour or two we toiled on, too much occupied with our thoughts to exchange words; but at length the darkness made us more companionable, and I asked the commissioner a few questions which I had longed to be enlightened upon.

"I hope that Smith is taking care of the gold I left with him," I said, as a feeler for conversation.

"O, of course, I saw him stow it away in his cellar. That is all right, I'll warrant you. Smith is not the man to neglect such trusts."

"Did you leave Sir William Byefield at the station?" I asked.

"No; he left the morning that I did, bound for Melbourne."

"What became of Jenny, the young lady whom we met in Mud Lane several times?"

"Ah! now your conversation is getting interesting, to you at least, if not to me. You mean the girl with the blue eyes?"

"Yes; you know whom I mean."

"Well, the young lady started for Melbourne when I sent my prisoners to the city, under the charge of Lieutenant Maurice. She would go, in spite of Smith's protestations and my entreaties. The fact of it is, Maurice is a devilish good-looking fellow, and just the sort of a man to suit a girl like Jenny."

"If you talk any more such nonsense, I'll desert your company," I replied; "you know I don't like it."

"To be sure I do; but the quicker you are ridiculed out of your passion for that girl, the better it will be for your peace of mind and happiness."

I did not answer him, for just at that moment I heard Amelia calling me; so I turned to see what she wanted. Her had rode by her horse's head ever since we left the gulch. As I drew up by her side, much to Hopeful's disgust, she leaned over and whispered, —

"I am nearly dead with fatigue, and can hardly keep from falling from my horse. Do remain near me and support me, for my eyes close of their own accord."

I looked at my watch, — for I had recovered it from the hands of the bushrangers after their defeat, — and found that it was twelve o'clock, and that we were some ten miles from the mountain, having made fair progress in spite of the condition of the roads and the fatigue of our horses. I saw that the animals could hardly wade through the sand without rest, and it was singular how quick I made the discovery after I found that Amelia was almost exhausted. I rode forward and spoke to Murden.

"We must halt until daylight," I said. "The horses are ready to drop from exhaustion."

"Let 'em drop," was the answer. "We can find others."

"Not in this desert. Besides, think for a moment; Miss Amelia is nearly dead for the want of rest."

"Why didn't you say so in the first place? Of course we'll halt and rest;" and in a few minutes we were on the sands, while I speedily prepared a bed for the girl, and spread over her and under her blankets which we found strapped to the saddles.

"You're very kind," Amelia murmured, as she closed her eyes. "I shall never forget such kindness — never."

Hopeful took up his position near her head, but did not speak. I left him, and went in search of the commissioner, who was smoking his pipe, and suggested that he should induce Hez to take the freshest horse, and push on for the station, and obtain relief, which we should need the next day. Murden approved of the idea, and at length induced Hopeful to undertake the mission, although he wanted to know why I couldn't go as well as he; but the commissioner hinted at attacks, and how much I was needed to resist them, so that on the whole my comrade took his departure in pretty good spirits.

We wished him success, and off he went, to my great relief. We were up at daylight; but while we felt refreshed, the animals did not, for they had eaten nothing but the tops of the bushes, and attempted to quench their thirst with the dew that settled upon the same — rather scant diet for horses accustomed to better fare. We turned from the trail, which was over a country composed of sand, bush, and dried grass, and went in search of water, which we had been informed could be found near at hand.

At last we caught sight of a stream, not more than a yard wide, and a few inches deep, a tributary to the Great Murray in the wet season, but lost in the sand long before it reached that river during the dry months. Our animals were too impatient to slake their thirst to be restrained after they caught sight of the stream. They plunged down the sand hills, and did not stop until they were standing in the hot, shallow water. We dismounted so as to allow the poor brutes a chance to drink. I assisted Amelia to alight, and then helped Hackett to the ground, for his leg was so much swollen that he could not use it or move it without excessive pain. I made the lady as comfortable as possible, screening her head with a brush tent; and was thanked for the same in so sweet a manner that I almost forgot the dear child's misfortunes. At one o'clock we were up and off, shaping our course for the bridge of salt, where I thought we could cross without much trouble from the alligators, and save time and many miles of travel. All turned out as I anticipated, to my joy and Murden's disgust. We saw evidences of the struggle that had taken place when Hez and I had crossed, some few nights before; but all traces of the horse, which the alligators had knocked into the mud, were lost. We had but a few miles to go to reach Smith's station; and, by urging our animals, we were enabled to arrive at the farm in the course of the afternoon. Smith was in the yard, in front of his house, when we galloped up. The poor man, who had been almost dead with anxiety during our absence, neither able to work nor rest, rushed towards us with outstretched arms, ready to give us the warmest welcome that it was possible to bestow.

"You have brought her back!" the stockman cried. "O, how glad I am she's here! How shall I thank you for this? Here, Mary!" and he ran towards the house to tell his wife the good news, shouting all the way; but just before he reached the door he altered his mind, and came tearing towards us, too confused to utter a half dozen words in a grammatical manner.

"What did yer do with the rascally cove what Amelia ran away with? No — I mean — well, I'm glad to see you all. Come to my arms, lass, and don't you do it agin. Wife has been sick about yer all the time yer was gone; but I told her you'd be here when you come, and yer see I'm right."

The honest and enthusiastic fellow did not wait for a word, or even note the girl's appearance. He snatched her from her horse, and carried her in his arms to the house, and gave her up to his wife; but when he rushed out again he did not know that he left the brave and heroic girl insensible. All her noble resolution and courage had failed when she found that she was once more at home and in her sister's presence. Mrs. Smith, her eyes blinded with tears, laid the poor child upon a bed, and then came to the door in search of help.

"I am glad that you have come," she said; "for I fear that Amelia is dying. What shall I do?"

"Call your servant girl, and let her assist you to undress the young lady. Before you do so, wash Amelia's face and neck with cold water, and when she is able, let her take a bath. It is a critical period of her life, and her reason depends upon your management. She must be treated as carefully as a child."

"You were not in time?" asked Mrs. Smith, as she turned her agitated face upon me, with tears streaming from her eyes; for she began to surmise the worst.

"The one who ill-treated her is dead. Let that suffice for the present. If she recovers she may tell you all, or bury the secret in her own breast. Do not seek to force it from her."

"I will be guided by your advice; but it is a cruel blow to one so young and ambitious as she was. I did hope at one time that you and she would — But never mind now; that is all passed."

I did not know what she meant; neither did I stop to ask for an explanation. There was no time to waste in words. I left the room, and hurried to find the servant, and when I found her, sent her to her mistress's assistance.

"Where's Amelia?" asked Smith. "I must go and see her. I suppose she's dying to talk with me."

He started towards the door; but I laid a hand upon his shoulder and detained him.

"You had better not see her for a few days," I said. "She needs rest after her escape."

"Well, can't she rest while she's talking to me?"

"Not in this instance. After you have heard how much she has suffered, you will think so."

I saw that Smith looked surprised and inquisitive; so I led him aside, and imparted to him as much information as I pleased respecting the results of our trip. In the mean time, Murden had retired to the house for the purpose of sending a despatch to Melbourne announcing his successes, and asking for a strong squad of officers to join him and take charge of the prisoners. I helped with his despatch, and put in the romantic touches when he felt a little at fault. The day after the police arrived, and took charge of the prisoners. Lieutenant Maurice came with them, and reported that the whole city was in an uproar of rejoicing at the brilliant successes which Murden had met with. The lieutenant brought several newspapers, which contained flaming accounts of the commissioner's doings, furnished by an eye-witness, and about as reliable as some of the reports which found their way into the American papers during the late rebellion. As soon as Maurice had rested, I managed to exchange a few words with him on a subject that interested me.

"To tell you the truth," the officer said, "Jenny returned to the Red Lion as soon as she reached Melbourne, and I have not seen her since. Deuced pretty girl, but rather airy for one who don't know more than she does."

"Where is her father, the Manchester Pet?" I continued. "You recollect we left him in jail for that murderous assault on me in his crib at Melbourne."

"O, the Pet was held for a week by the beak; but as no one appeared against him, after continuing the case for three or four times, he was discharged."

I was about to leave my friend when he continued: —

"Sir William is in Melbourne. I saw him the morning I left coming from the direction of the Red Lion. Look out, old fellow, or the baronet will get the best of you. He is rich, and has a title, and women like titles. By the way, Sir William has something on his mind. I wish I knew what it was."

I smiled at the honest frankness of the police officer, and had no doubt but that he would soon have found out if he had had a clew to work on.

"I suppose you know that Mother Brown is in Melbourne?" Maurice continued. "I saw the old hag, drunk as a lord, in a station house; and she asked me to let her out, on the ground of old acquaintance."

"And she is still in custody?" I asked.

"Yes, and will remain in prison for a month or two, or until she has worked out her fine. She's a miserable old drunkard, ain't she?"

That she knew something of importance about Jenny and Sir William Byefield, I had not the least doubt; but she had managed thus far not to lisp a word of it to me, saying the time would come when I should know all. I was now quite anxious to reach Melbourne as soon as possible; so I left Maurice, and hurried to find the commissioner.

"Let us leave this place at once," I said.

"You've changed your mind rather quick," Murden remarked, with an expression of surprise.

"Of course I have, and you shall know the reason why. Maurice has brought news that the city is in a ferment about your successes. To keep alive the excitement, you had better reach Melbourne before the prisoners, and then give your own version of the matter."

"And the gold? You know Smith has all of our plunder in the cellar."

"Smith starts for the city in a few days to obtain his winter supplies. He can bring the money concealed in one of his ox teams."

"And your friend Hackett — what will you do with him?"

"Let him remain here until his wounds and bruises are healed; then I will find something for him to do. He is too valuable a man to part with."

Murden revolved the matter over in his mind, and then agreed to start at once for the city, leaving Maurice and his strong corps of police to bring in the prisoners next day. I entered the house, saw Mr. Smith for a moment, and found that Amelia was doing quite well, having slept for nearly twenty hours, with occasional wakings, and had ceased to sob during the latter intervals, although she did moan, while sleeping, in a wild and random manner.

Smith made some serious objections to my moving, but withdrew them when he heard that we must go on important business, that would admit of no delay. We shook hands and started on our journey, and did not draw rein until we stopped at Webber's. We roused the old Dutchman with some difficulty, made him give us a "spider," or some brandy and beer mixed, the best drink that he had, fed and watered our horses, and were off at full speed before the host had time to comprehend that we had arrived. We reached Melbourne at sundown. I changed my clothes, had a bath, and then stole from the commissioner's house, while he and Hez were at table, and walked rapidly towards Mud Lane and the Red Lion, for I longed to take one look at Jenny, and to know that she was well before I slept. I pulled my hat over my eyes, and walked down the lane in a careless manner, and at length stood before the open door of the saloon. I glanced in, and saw Jenny sitting at one of the tables, and opposite to her sat a man who appeared too respectable for such a place, and I wondered who he could be; but the instant he raised his cap, I saw it was Sir William Byefield in disguise, and that the old wretch was quite attentive to the girl, while the Manchester Pet did not appear to regard them in the least, as she dispensed beer and "spiders."

CHAPTER L.

A ROW AT THE RED LION. — A BARONET IN DANGER. — TO THE RESCUE. — THE PET KNOCKED OUT OF TIME.

I don't know how long I remained standing at the door, looking at the couple; but at last I was aroused from my reverie by some one driving his elbow into my ribs. I looked up and saw a rough, weather-beaten man-of-war's-man, who was steering for the bar of the Red Lion, determined to get rid of his money as soon as possible. I drew back from the door, so that the sailor could pass, and declined his invitation to drink.

"Well, my hearty, if you won t, some one else will. But you're a tough one not to drink when you're axed. No offence, you know;" and in the tar rolled, and was greeted with a grunt of profound satisfaction by the Manchester Pet.

"Gin," said the sailor; and then turning to the crowd of loafers and customers who were congregated in the room, he invited all to drink at his expense — an offer that was not long in being accepted.

The sailor swallowed his liquor, and then glanced around the saloon. His eyes fell upon Jenny's fair face, and lingered there for a few minutes with much pleasure. Thinking that he would like to kiss the girl, he rolled towards her, put one arm around her waist, before she knew what he meant, and then gave her a hug that must have made her ribs ache, and bent his head to kiss her red lips; but instead of encountering anything so soft, he met the hard fist of Sir William, sent out straight from his shoulder. The blow fell upon the sailor's face with much force. Jack released his hold of the girl and staggered back, but did not fall, as I thought he would. He rallied in an instant, and then made a rush for Sir William, two or three of the vagabonds going forward to assist him. Miss Jenny, like a well-disciplined girl, or one brought up in a porter-house, did not utter a shriek or yell. She merely swept out of the room as quick as possible. I was at first inclined to bound forward and lend the baronet some assistance; but jealousy kept me quiet. So I remained at the door, and looked on. But this indifference was speedily changed to admiration at the pluck of the baronet, and the coolness of the Manchester Pet. The former repelled the three or four men who came upon him, striking at his head and face, and the latter did not seem to care whether there was a fight or not. Presently the Pet said, "Close the door," and I knew what that meant. One of the bar-room loafers rushed forward for the purpose of closing it and obeying the orders of the Pet. Just as he laid his hand on the door I determined to act.

I sprang forward, seized the loafer by the collar of his coat, and hurled him into the street, and with such force that he fell his whole length. Then I put a silver whistle, which I carried in my pocket, to my lips, and blew a shrill blast. For a moment I listened; then away off, on the corner of a street, still near the purlieus of Mud Lane, came back an answer. Satisfied that the signal was noted, and that my retreat would be secured, I entered the Red Lion. As I did so, the Manchester Pet caught a glimpse of me, and left his position behind the bar. "The spy," he said, in a low tone, but full of passion, that meant mischief. He came straight towards me, his huge fists doubled up, and vengeance in his eyes. I glanced around the room, saw that no one was near me, so that I could not be taken at a disadvantage, took one step nearer a table stained with slops of beer, and then awaited the onslaught of the giant, whose strength I had felt once before. But this time I determined not to be caught in a trap, and if the worst should come, to use my revolver to some effect, and kill the brute.

"O, you —" It was a terrible oath that the man uttered when he came within striking distance of me; and he aimed a blow at my head that would have crushed my skull, had it hit me. But it did not, for I avoided it by a quick motion of my body, and consequently the Pet swayed one side, and reeled like a drunken man. I had expected this, and made preparations for it; and before the giant could recover his upright position and self-defence, I seized a heavy pewter pot that stood on the table near my right hand, and with all the strength that I could muster, struck the brute full upon the nose, just between the eyes. I saw the blood spirt out of the wound, and then the Pet reeled, and fell with a crash that jarred the room, and made the bottles on the bar shake as if with fear. For a moment I stopped to look at the fallen brute, and the next I rushed towards the crowd that were pressing on Sir William, whom I found down, and receiving much punishment, without a cry for help or a murmur.

"Let the man alone, you scoundrels," I roared.

At this stage of the proceedings, the sailor, and the loafer who was assisting him in pommelling Sir William, turned and made a furious assault on me. I disdained to use the beer pot against them; so I threw it at the Pet's head, for the giant was beginning to show signs of life. It hit him, and down went his cranium with a crash.

"Board the land pirate," roared the sailor; and at me he came, his companion a little in the rear.

I dodged the first onslaught, but did not have time to do more, for I suddenly found a stout hand upon my collar; and turning I saw that I was in the hands of half a dozen police officers, while at the same moment the sailor and loafer were secured.

"Put the darbies on 'em," said the sergeant of police. "They has had a precious fight, and must pay for it."

The officer attempted to slip a pair of handcuffs on my wrists, but I resisted.

"O, it's no sort of use; you must wear 'em," he said.

"Let me alone, and look to the gentleman who is on the floor. I fear that the ruffians have injured him."

I spoke in so authoritative a tone, that the man was confounded, and turning to the sergeant, remarked, "Here's a queer sort of a cove. I wish you'd see what you can make of him. He talks like a big wig."

The sergeant came bustling towards me, full of importance, and all ready to condemn the officer for his want of zeal.

"Who are you, sir?" he asked. "A student on a lark?"

"No."

"Does any of you know the cove?" asked the sergeant, pointing to me.

Not one of the officers knew me.

"We must take you to the station house. Put the irons on 'em, lads;" and the commanding officer lighted a cigar.

"One moment," I said. "I do not desire to go to the station house, and I also wish to keep my friend out of it."

The police consulted together for a moment, but I saw that they were like to act against me unless I was prompt. I did not wish to send for Murden if it was possible to avoid it, for I did not desire to have the laugh against me, and I knew that he would quiz me most unmercifully if he was aware of my visit to the Red Lion. This I meant to avoid; so when the sergeant had followed me to the other end of the room, I said to him, in a confidential manner, —

"Sergeant, you must get me out of this, you know. Take the rest of your prisoners to the station house; but the gentleman whom I saved from a bad beating must go with me."

"Why, you know that it ain't exactly regular to take hush-money," the sergeant said, with a wishful look.

"I am aware of it. I don't intend to injure your feelings by offering money."

The fellow's mouth began to open, and a frown gathered on his brow; but I chased it away in an instant, by producing the small silver whistle which I carried in my pocket. It was an emblem of authority, used only by those of high rank in the department. I continued: —

"I gave the signal which called you hither. I should not have done it if I had not thought the danger imminent."

"Yes, but your name — what is it?"

I mentioned it to him, or rather the name by which I was known in the department, and in many parts of Australia. The man was astonished. He raised his cap and saluted me in the most respectful manner.

"Am I at liberty to go?" I asked.

"Certainly, sir; and your friend also, or whoever you wish should go. You have but to say the word."

"Thank you."

I crossed over, and put my arm within Sir William's.

"Come," I said, "the path is clear at last."

The people assembled outside saluted us with a yell, for they thought we were prisoners; but when they discovered their mistake, they wanted to injure us, and for that purpose threw mud and stones at us. They were indignant to think we were not dragged to the station, as some of them had been during their eventful lives. The police, who had mustered in large numbers, beat the rascals back, and enabled us to escape from Mud Lane, the only injury inflicted being spattered with dirt, and a torn coat.

CHAPTER LI.

TEN MINUTES IN JAIL. — A BELLIGERENT CABMAN. — A FIGHT AND KNOCK-DOWN.

As we walked along the well-lighted street, the baronet's arm still within my own, I determined to press him and discover the meaning of his visit to the Red Lion.

We entered a hotel, the Nugget House, where the prices charged were fabulous, and where Sir William was quartered during his stay in the city. He led the way to his suit of rooms on the second floor, overlooking the street, rang the bell, ordered a bottle of wine, invited me to a seat, gave me cigars from which to take my choice, and then induced me to talk of the expedition in which I had been engaged, and kept me so well employed that it was late before I had concluded my yarn, and then I found that I had learned nothing concerning the baronet's visit to the Red Lion. As I lighted a fresh cigar, and arose to go, I asked, with American bluntness, —

"By the way, Sir William, how did it happen that I found you at the Red Lion, in such a disguise as you now wear?"

"O, I suppose that I went because my feet took me there;" and the baronet laughed in such a genial manner that I could not feel offended.

"The answer is not so direct as my question," I remarked.

"No, it is not." And then the baronet looked at me, and I returned his gaze.

"The next time you are attacked at the Red Lion," I remarked, "I shall not be near you to render assistance; so I would avoid it, if I were you."

"Perhaps I am as reckless of danger as yourself."

"You should not be, for the fire of youth had ought to be quenched when Time has shaken a dredging-box over your head."

"I see that you are curious, and a little jealous. Don't deny it, for I have felt it all along. Acknowledge that when you saw me talking with Jenny, you were at first inclined to let me suffer at the hands of those bar-room loafers; yet while you entertained those hard thoughts, I was doing all that I could to improve your standing in the girl's estimation."

"And did you succeed?"

I was so eager in asking the question, that the baronet smiled in a tantalizing manner.

"Well, perhaps I did. How can I tell? Who can fathom a young girl's heart? It is too deep for man's understanding. I will not tell you all that transpired at our interview, but your interests did not suffer, and I think that you stand in a better light than ever."

I bowed and smiled, and then the baronet looked more serious than I ever saw him look as he continued: "Do not let what I have said induce you to take advantage of the girl's position in society. I have an interest in her welfare, and shall watch over her personally, or else by agents."

"And may I ask what that interest is?"

"Certainly, you can ask, but I am not yet prepared to answer. But you can rest assured on one point, and that is, that I have not been making love to the girl, and that I have no such intention."

I took up my hat, and made signs of departing.

"If you must go, let us shake hands before we part. Good night. I shall see you to-morrow, for I have business that will detain me in town for some days. I will call for you in the afternoon, and I hope that you will dine with me."

I hesitated for a moment, and Sir William continued: "Your friends, Mr. Hopeful and Mr. Commissioner Murden, are included in the invitation. I should be delighted to see them."

"I will deliver your invitation, and promise that it shall be accepted;" and with these words I left the baronet, and walked home, as much mystified as ever.

Hopeful and Murden exchanged significant glances when

I entered the house, but said not a word as to where I had been. I simply informed them that I had seen Sir William, and that he had requested the pleasure of our company at dinner the next day, at the hotel; but I did not inform my friends under what circumstances the invitation was issued, or relate the conversation that had taken place between us.

The next morning, as the sun was out hot and strong, I called a cab, and told the driver to carry me to the prison. The governor of the prison was a large man, bald-headed, red-nosed, as though beer and brandy were favorite drinks during his official career.

"Well, sir, what is it?" he asked, as soon as I appeared, as though already tired of my company.

"You have a woman, called Mother Brown, confined here on the charge of drunkenness?"

The governor did not commit himself by a direct answer; he merely said, "Well?"

"If she is here, I desire to pay her fine and release her," I continued.

"For what purpose do you want the woman?" the governor asked, after a few moments' silence.

"Is it necessary that I should answer all your questions?" I demanded.

"It is, sir."

"Well, go on and ask, and soon have an ending, for I have business elsewhere," I replied.

"What kind of business?"

The question was so blunt that I was entirely taken by surprise; and before I had time to think, I replied, with some little arrogance, "That is none of your affair, sir."

The governor started back, horrified at the reply. At first he could hardly believe his ears, and he was compelled to polish his nose to collect his thoughts; and when he had found them, he roared, —

"Out of this, you gallus-bird, afore I locks yer up."

I did not move or look frightened, although the governor expected me to.

"Out with him," roared the governor, and pointed at me. "Chuck him out," he said.

"Wait one moment," I cried, just as the men were about to rush on me. The ruffians paused, and looked at the governor, and the latter looked at me.

"What is it?" the red-faced official asked.

"I demand the right to leave this place unmolested. If I am assaulted, I shall defend myself in the best way that I can, and you must suffer the consequences."

"Why, you cursed —"

I did not stop to hear the remainder of the sentence; for I suddenly stepped backward, touched the spring of the door that led to the court, threw it open, and passed out in as dignified a manner as I could. I had proceeded but a few steps when I heard the door open, and the governor shout after me, —

"You scoundrel! the next time you come here I'll lock you up."

"We shall see," I answered in a confident manner, and entered the cab that was waiting for me.

"Yes, we shall see;" and the governor slammed to the door.

"Where to, sir?" asked cabby.

"The city hall."

"O, you vants to go among the big vigs, do you? Vell, recollect I ain't done nothin' vot calls for a fine. Now, you knows it, don't you?"

"Drive on," I said; "I don't want to talk so much. You bother me with your slang."

"Vell, if this ain't high old times, then I'm blowed!" and muttering his disgust, he mounted his box, and lashed his steed into a run.

As I left the cab at the hall, the driver looked particularly disgusted and puzzled at the same time.

"Look a-here," he asked; "is you goin' to complain of me. 'Cos if ye is, I'll fight yer for the beer, and no favors axed on either side; or I'll fight yer for half a crown, money up."

All this display of ill-temper was on account of my refusing to furnish him with drink-money.

"How much is your bill?" I asked. "I will pay it, and let you go. You are too excitable for me."

"Ten shillin's," was the answer.

I knew that was just double the legal charge.

"Here are six shillings," I answered. "Take them or go without your pay."

He dashed the silver to the sidewalk, and called me a thief and a swindler, and all that was vile and hateful; and, as I turned away from him, he construed the action into cowardice; so he sprang forward, and laid his hands upon my shoulders, thinking that he could give me a lift, and sprawl me on the sidewalk. I swerved a little, turning so quickly that his plans were frustrated. This brought me face to face with the fellow, and for the space of one second we glared at each other. Then I made a sudden blow, and down the rascal went. He struggled to his feet, roaring and swearing like a fiend. On he came, thinking that this time he would demolish me; but he was never more mistaken, for I stepped one side, out of his course, and then planted a crushing blow just under his left ear. He went over with a rush. I don't know how it would have fared with me at the hands of the cabmen who were in the vicinity; for it is probable that they would have avenged their comrade's injuries, had not Murden run down the steps of the city hall, and placed himself at my side.

"Yes, sir, that's him; that's the cove vot done it," said the injured man, sitting up on the sidewalk, thinking I was under arrest. "I'll take my oath of him. He's the cove."

"I saw the whole of it, Barney," the commissioner replied. "You can't blind me. You commenced the assault, and for it I take away your license."

"Come in and see us," said Murden, passing his arm through mine; and up the steps we went.

CHAPTER LII.

MOTHER BROWN'S PARDON. — HER CONFESSION. — MY ASTONISHMENT.

We entered a room where there were officials of high and low degree, who had congregated for the purpose of hearing the commissioner's account of his doings during his absence. We were congratulated on our exploits, and asked innumerable questions; but at length I remembered Mother Brown, and the object of my visit to the city hall, and then I related the particulars of my interview with old Harry, the governor of the prison.

"I'll tell you how to spite him," said one of the upper secretaries to a cabinet officer. "We'll have the woman pardoned out, and then old Harry will lose his regular fees. That will worry him in the most fearful manner."

All in the room shouted out their approval of the plan, and the secretary started off to find his chief and obtain a pardon.

"Old Harry," a young man said, "will tear his hair out when he reads the order. He won't be able to relish his beer for a month. Ha, ha! I'd like to see him when he fully comprehends the meaning of the discharge."

In the course of an hour the secretary returned, with the order in due form. It was handed to me; and then two or three of the young men offered to accompany me to the jail; but I declined their services, because I knew that I had much to say to Mother Brown, all of a confidential nature. In ten minutes I was at the gates of the prison, and the next moment I had entered the gloomy building.

"You 'ere agin?" asked one of the turnkeys, with a look of surprise.

"Yes, I am here again," was my quiet answer.

"Vel, you'd better not let the hold man see yer. No, I should think not."

As I did not manifest the least alarm, the turnkey looked up from the stone floor, which he had appeared to regard in the light of an enemy, and asked, "Ain't you goin' to cut and run for it?"

"For what reason?" I demanded.

"O, 'cos if the hold man should see yer, he might pitch in, you know."

"I'm not in the least alarmed. In fact I mean to wait here until I see him."

Just at this instant the door opened and the governor entered. He had been refreshing himself with beer; but the extract of hops had not modified his temper in the least, for he uttered a roar and a growl when he saw me.

"Out with him!" shouted the enraged governor. "Knock him down, somebody."

As "somebody" didn't make his appearance to carry out the behest, I was enabled to call the governor's attention to the paper which I held in my hand.

"It's a begging petition," the red-faced man said. "It's no use. It won't change my opinion in the least."

"If you will have the kindness to look at the paper," I said, "you will see that it contains the governor's signature."

"Hey! what is that?" and the official snatched the paper from my hand, and glanced over it in a rapid manner.

His red face paled at the signatures which met his eye. He could hardly believe his own senses; and, as he read, he muttered, —

"A full — pardon — no — fees — no money — no chance to make — even expenses. It's a d—d outrage."

"I shall have to report such language to the governor," I remarked, hardly able to keep from laughing.

"I'm sure you're too much of a gentleman to do that," the man said, changing in an instant from the rude barbarian to the grovelling snob, which I disliked as much as I did the tyrant.

"Will you release the woman?"

"Of course I will. Here, Sam, make out Mother Brown's discharge."

I did not care to encounter Mother Brown in the presence of the governor and his officers; so I asked them to send her to the carriage. In ten minutes' time Mother Brown waddled from the doors of the prison, stared around as though still laboring under the influence of liquor, appeared undecided which way to turn, and at last saw my face, and came towards me, grinning from ear to ear.

"Ah, it's yer, is it?" she said. "I might have knowed that no one but yer would do it."

Without waiting for an invitation, she entered the carriage, and planted her substantial form on the seat opposite me, and then, taking one of my hands in both of her own, kissed it, in spite of my resistance. Suddenly she dropped my hand, and snuffed the air, which was impregnated with the odor of tobacco.

"Ah," she cried, "that smells something like. You haven't a pipe?"

"No."

"Then a weed will do. I hope they is strong. Give me the blackest one you has."

I handed her a cigar that would have made a Dutchman sick in less than five minutes. She lighted it, and puffed away with perfect content for a while.

"That prison's a cussed hole," she said at last. "They won't allow smokin'."

She puffed in silence for a moment. I saw that the turnkeys were grinning at us through the bars of the prison; so I told the cabman to drive on at a slow pace.

"You sent word that you had something which you desired to communicate to me," I remarked, as soon as she had become a little calm.

"Yes; I want to talk to yer. I want to tell yer how wicked I has been, and what I has done."

"And I don't want to hear it. I am not a confessor."

"Ah, what things you men is! You can't wait a moment, unless a pretty girl is in the case; then yer smile and bow, and scrape and cringe, and kiss the ground on which she walks. O, yes."

"You old fool," I said, losing all patience, "you must recollect that you are neither young nor pretty; so you cannot wonder if I show a little restlessness."

"Ah, but I knows a lass what is young, plump, and pretty."

"Well, what has that to do with me?"

"It depends upon yerself to say. I want yer to marry her. Ah, that word makes the blood mount to yer cheeks, and yer heart go pitapat."

I was silent, for I knew whom the old woman meant. Why did she want me to marry Jenny? What interest had she in the business? I could not comprehend her and her mysterious ways. I lighted a fresh cigar, and obedient to the woman's motions, handed her one. She was rather fond of tobacco, I thought, judging from the manner in which she rolled the weed about her mouth; but I pardoned the fact when I recollected that she had lived for so many years in the midst of reckless men.

"Now," said Mother Brown, as soon as her cigar was fairly lighted, "I suppose that yer want to know my great secret."

"If you have one."

It was an unfortunate answer, for she commenced a tirade of abuse for my suspicions, but calmed down when she found that I did not take any notice of her words. As soon as she had run down, I said, "Now for the secret, Mother Brown."

"Yes, now for it. But fust tell me one thing — do yer love the blue-eyed Jenny?"

I stammered over the question.

"I mean, well enough to take her for a wife; that's what I mean."

"Under some circumstances, I think that I should."

"Yer as proud as the divil!" the old hag remarked, in a blunt tone. "Yer men must have all the accomplishments as well as money, or yer turn up yer noses. Yer know it's so, man that yer are. But answer the question, and look alive about it; 'cos on yer answer depends the secret I'm about to tell yer."

"Well, then, if Jenny was accomplished and intelligent, I should love her well enough to take her for a wife, even without a cent of money; as she is not, I shall have to think the matter over for some time before I act."

"And in the mean time attempt to make her yer mistress. Bah! Yer can't do it."

She chewed away at her cigar for some time, and seemed undecided what to say, but at last burst out with, "I know yer love her; so I'll tell yer all about it. Stop the carriage under the trees out there where there's some shade, and I'll begin."

I shall not give Mother Brown's words in this chapter, because she will have to repeat them in the presence of other people, and then I will introduce them. At length the old woman ceased, and then I had time to ask, —

"Is this true that you have told me?"

"Do yer s'pose I'd tell yer a lie, when I knowed yer could prove it was a lie? I has spoken the truth, and yer shall acknowledge it afore many days."

"You must acknowledge it at once," I cried. "This very day you must prove to Sir William and me that you have uttered true words."

"So soon?" The woman shuddered.

"Why do you hesitate?"

"I dread the anger of the Pet. He will kill me if he can lay his hands on me."

"But we will take care that he does nothing of the kind. We will look after him, and see that you are not hurt."

"But what shall I say to Sir William?" The woman put her face to her hands, and I saw tears stealing down through her fingers.

"Tell your story just as you have told it to me. Tell him how you were tempted, and fell, and perhaps even he will forgive you, although I should not blame him if he did not."

"I has wronged him, and I will do what I can to right him," Mother Brown said at length. "Just tell me what to do, and I'll do it."

"Then promise that you will not touch liquor until I offer

it to you. When you appear before Sir William you must be sober and truthful."

She gave a reluctant promise, and then I recalled the driver, and told him to take me to Murden's place, where I could keep the woman under lock and key until I wanted her.

In a short time, Murden and Hopeful returned to the house to dress for dinner. Both of them were in good spirits, but to neither did I say one word about Mother Brown and her presence in the house. I thought I would surprise them when the proper moment arrived, and I think, all things considered, that I did. We made our toilets, dressing like gentlemen, not gold-diggers, with gloves, patent-leather boots, white shirts, and black coats (terrible uncomfortable things in Australia), and then rode to the Nugget House, where we were shown to Sir William's room without delay, and welcomed by the baronet in the most hospitable manner. But as we passed into the room, there glided from it one of the most desperate characters known to the Mud-Laners it was the "Brazen Boy," a ticket-of-leave man.

CHAPTER LIII.

THE BARONET'S CONFESSION. — A COMPARING OF NOTES. — THE LOST CHILD. — A TABLEAU.

I SAW that Murden gave the ticket-of-leave man a sharp look as we entered Sir William's apartment, at the Nugget House; but the Brazen Boy returned the glance without manifesting the least confusion or guilt. He seemed to say that he had a right in the room, and cared nothing for the police of Melbourne, even if the leading commissioner did scowl at him. As the Brazen Boy (named thus for his impudence by those appreciative people, the Mud-Laners) passed down the stairs, Murden said to Sir William, —

"Beg pardon, sir, but of course you haven't lost anything, have you?"

"O, no," returned the baronet, with a slight expression of annoyance.

"Sure your gold watch is in your pocket?" persisted Murden.

"Quite sure, sir."

"And no bank notes missing? If they are gone, now is the time to let me know."

"O, no, nothing is lost; I am positive."

Murden would have insisted upon running after the Brazen Boy, and searching him; but I stopped him by an emphatic pinch, for I saw at a glance that Sir William had some secret connection with the ticket-of-leave man, and did not want it revealed even to the police commissioner, or his friend who had saved him the honor of a beating in the Red Lion. Dinner was soon served up, and for an Australian hotel dinner, it was a fair one, although a Boston host would have cried for very shame, if such a jumble of food had been displayed on his tables. The liquor unloosened Murden's tongue. He commenced talking as I feared he would.

"It is a peculiar thing, Sir William," he said, "to find a man like you, of wealth and influence, in such a helter-skelter country as this. There's nothing to be seen here that's worth seeing. No racing, no prize-fights, no boating, but little cricket, no nothing that rich men take to. In fact we are not celebrated for even possessing handsome women. There's only one real beauty in all Melbourne, and she's low, although I am fearful that Mr. Jack will feel angry with me for saying so."

I made no reply.

Murden continued: "Come, Mr. Jack, acknowledge that you like the girl — that you have run some risks to see her, and that you will do so again."

"I have a high opinion of the young girl's virtue and fair face," I remarked. "Let that satisfy you. She has beauty enough to grace any station; but she is certainly deficient in one thing — her education."

"Yes, she's ignorant, that is true; but she could be

learned. Take her for a wife, and see how you could train her. Be quick about it, or you'll lose her."

"I will think of your advice," I remarked, "and the more seriously, because I, this day, heard something in relation to the girl's history that surprised me."

Sir William was about to raise a glass of wine to his lips; but I saw his hand tremble, and he put it down untasted.

"You're allers hearin' somethin' about the women," growled Hez.

"What is it?" demanded Murden. "Has she left her father, and eloped with a ticket-of-leave man?"

I knew that this was torturing Sir William; so I hastened to relieve him as much as possible.

"Listen to me," I said, "and don't interrupt me."

"A romance is coming," said the commissioner, and filled his glass.

"Or a mighty tough yarn. He's the greatest man for adventures," muttered Hopeful, and lighted a fresh cigar.

"What should you think," I remarked, "if I told you that a young girl was in this city whose parents rank among the aristocracy of England?"

The commissioner uttered a scornful sniff.

"The girl whom I allude to has no respectable station in Melbourne society. She has no rich and influential friends that she is aware of; she is constantly surrounded by all that is vile, and yet she is of good birth."

Sir William was terribly agitated, yet managed to conceal it from my friends. He listened with avidity to all that I said, and appeared impatient for me to continue.

"Bah! a romance," said Murden.

"Bah! two or three of 'em," Hopeful remarked.

That young man was growing intoxicated very fast.

"Gentlemen," said Sir William, in a low, trembling, yet earnest voice, "I am interested in our friend's remarks. Will you be kind enough to allow me to listen to them? Perhaps what he says is not such a romance as you think."

"O, certainly, Sir William," the commissioner replied, with all an Englishman's deference for rank and wealth. "I did not for a moment suppose that you cared to hear the yarn. We will keep silent, Sir William — never fear."

"Two or three fears," muttered that wretched Hez.

The baronet motioned for me to continue.

"How I became acquainted with the young girl does not matter —"

"O, but it does, though," muttered Hopeful. "Make a full confession. He always was the devil among the petticoats."

"Perhaps," said Sir William, "we had better talk this matter over in another apartment. Will you follow me, if you please?"

I arose and left the room, leaving the commissioner chagrined at Hopeful's interruption. The police officer wanted to hear the communication that I had to make. As soon as Sir William had closed the door, he said, his voice no longer firm, —

"I suspect that you have obtained some knowledge of my secret, although in what manner I cannot comprehend, for I have not lisped a word to you."

"I am aware you have not; but perhaps it would have been better if you had," I responded.

"Tell me what you know," the baronet said, in an imperious tone, as though I was bound to obey him.

"If you speak in that style I shall decline to answer you, or hold further communication with you on the subject."

"I forgot you are an American — pray excuse me;" and the Englishman held out his hand, which I took, and was reconciled.

"Now, let us talk this matter over in as calm a manner as I can command," Sir William said. I had no objection to that.

"In the first place," he continued, his dark-blue eyes looking tender and appealing, "you will tell me all you know on the subject."

"Provided we exchange confidences," I replied.

"Agreed." We looked at each other in silence, each waiting for the other to begin.

"Well," said Sir William, seeing that I did not speak, "let me state, in the most frank and reliable manner, that I have visited Australia for the purpose of finding a lost daughter."

"And you think that you have found her?"

"I think that I have."

He uttered a deep sigh, as though he was not fully satisfied in his own mind that it would not have been better never to have discovered any trace of her existence.

"I am certain," I remarked, in a confidential tone, "that the young girl called Jenny is your daughter, and that she is not in the least related to the Manchester Pet, although he calls her his child."

It was some moments before the baronet could recover from his agitation. At last he raised his head, and asked,—

"How have you made your discoveries? Tell me all the circumstances, so that I need not grope in the dark."

"Do you recollect, twenty years ago, at your residence in Lancaster, England, that among your domestics was one named Mary Brown?"

"Yes, I have a distinct remembrance of her. She was a pretty, rash, headstrong thing, and did not listen to the advice which I gave her. She left my service years ago, and is dead, I suppose."

"No, she is still alive, but so changed that you would not know her. The old woman whom you saw at the cave, hideous, repulsive, and dirty, was the same one who left your service twenty years since."

"Yes; but what has she to do with me?"

"Much. You recollect that you attempted to give her some good advice, do you not?"

"I think that I did caution her against the advances of a ruffian known as a prize-fighter, and called the Manchester Pet. The girl was infatuated with the brute, although she knew that he was a married man."

"You have a good memory, Sir William. What you have stated is correct."

"O, yes; it is not difficult to recall such things to my mind."

"And you would remember the prize-fighter if you should see him again?"

"Of course; a man of his stature and peculiar looks is not easily forgotten. I have seen the fellow several times since I have been in this country. He keeps the saloon called the Red Lion, where you saw me last night in conversation with the girl, Miss Jenny."

"He does not recollect you?" I asked.

"No; and I don't mean that he shall, just at present. If he should hear my name he would know me immediately. Twenty years have changed me, making an old man out of a young one."

"Before I relate to you what I know, will you be kind enough to tell me the relations which existed between yourself and the Pet?"

"Certainly, although it may cost me a blush to do so. At one time, before I was married and settled down to be a devoted Benedict, the Pet and I were great friends, and devoted to each other; that is, I backed him in his fights, and he backed me in all the rows and nonsense into which I entered. Of course he was often at my house, and there saw Mary Brown, and took a fancy to her; and the wench was captivated by his bruised face and giant form. She knew that the Pet was married, but it made no difference to her; and at last I had to order the prize-fighter from the house, for the purpose of saving the girl. Shortly afterwards I married, and then dropped all connection with the Pet; but Molly Brown did not, for she met the man quite frequently, unknown to me and to the rest of my family. I had a daughter born to me — a beautiful child; and when she was two years of age the Pet met with some misfortunes. Then he sent for me, and wanted money. I declined to see him, but forwarded a hundred pounds for his relief; and the next that I heard of him he was sentenced to transportation. Once more he appealed to me; but his appeal was useless. I did not answer it; and that was the last I heard of the prize-fighter until I saw him in Melbourne."

These few words had unravelled the mystery, and corroborated Mother Brown's statement. But I was cautious, and determined to proceed step by step.

"Your daughter, when she was two years old, disappeared, did she not?" I asked.

Sir William was so agitated that he could not speak for a moment; and, while he was struggling with his feelings, I saw tears stealing from his eyes and mingle with his beard.

"Yes, she disappeared; but in what manner we could not tell," the baronet answered, after a long pause. "We supposed that the gypsies had taken her; but a large reward, and a careful examination of every tribe in England, failed to produce her. Then I feared that she had been drowned; but every stream was searched, and we failed to discover her body. At last we gave her up. From that time until within a year we have mourned her as dead."

"Can you recollect whether Molly Brown left your service before or after the child was lost?"

"Some two weeks before."

"Are you positive?"

"Quite so. I remember that she expressed the greatest regret at leaving the child, and asked permission to kiss it before she quitted the house."

Here was more and more startling confirmation. I could only command my feelings by a powerful effort, so that I could continue the conversation. Sir William noticed my agitation, and extended his hand.

"You feel this as keenly as myself," he said. "I thank you for the interest you have taken in my affairs. It shows that you have a sympathetic heart."

"Yes," I muttered, in a tone that he could not hear, "I am fearful that my heart is more deeply concerned than you are aware of."

"Do you recollect where Molly Brown went after she left your house?"

"I heard that she emigrated to Australia, and that was the last information concerning her until, a year or two ago, a returned Australian called at my house, and, while waiting in the drawing-room, saw a portrait of the child, taken when she was two years of age. He expressed his astonishment to my wife and myself, and declared that he saw the original on board a ship, twenty years before, with steerage passengers, bound to Australia. He was the more particular on this point, because he had often played with the little girl on board the ship, and did much to amuse her and make her comfortable. She was then named Jenny Sykes; but what was singular, the child did not seem to know her own name, and acted in a confused manner when called Sykes. She was in charge of two women, one of whom said that she was Mrs. Sykes, and the other did not give her name, although she was a good-looking, smart-appearing girl, and was always called Mary."

"Those two women," I said, "were Mrs. Sykes, the wife of the Manchester Pet, and Molly Brown, your domestic. They went in one ship, an emigrant vessel, and the Pet went in a convict transport. The little girl whom they had — "

"Was who?" demanded the baronet.

"Your daughter!" Sir William uttered a groan, and dropped to the floor as though struck by lightning.

CHAPTER LIV.

EXPLANATIONS. — MOTHER BROWN AND TOM. — AN INTERVIEW WITH THE BARONET.

When Sir William dropped to the floor on my announcing that Jenny Sykes and his long lost daughter were one and the same person, I opened the door leading to the room where Hopeful and Murden were still at the table, smoking and drinking with the air of lords.

"What's the row?" the commissioner asked, startled at the noise that the baronet had made.

"Yes, what's the row?" repeated that miserable Hopeful; "don't you know any better than to disturb us with your noise."

"Sir William has fainted," I replied. "Bring me a glass of water."

The two men started from the table. Murden with a glass of water in his hand, and Hopeful with two pitchers — one containing hot water, with which to mix punch, and the other iced water. I bathed the baronet's head and face, while at the same time I loosened his cravat, and unbuttoned his shirt collar. Sir William opened his eyes.

"You are better, Sir William," the commissioner said. "Shall I call a surgeon? Can I do anything for you, Sir William?"

"Yes, hold your tongue," was the brief rejoinder.

"Certainly, Sir William," was the abject reply of the Englishman.

Sir William raised himself up and looked around.

"Bring me a glass of wine," he said to the commissioner.

"Give him two glasses — one might make him sick," muttered that wretched Hopeful, who cared no more for a baronet, unless he was a good mechanic, than he did for any man.

The wine was brought and drank. Its influence was reviving, for the baronet arose and took a chair.

"Leave us for a few minutes, my good fellow," the knight said; and at the words the commissioner bowed and retired.

"Now, my kind friend," said Sir William, as soon as the door closed, "tell me all that you know on the subject."

"But first inform me if you had not some suspicion that the girl was your daughter?"

"I have strongly suspected it, ever since I met her, after my release from the custody of the bushrangers. Her appearance, her eyes, face, and hair resemble my wife's so much that I was confounded at the likeness, and determined to investigate and learn all the particulars that I could respecting her history. I was engaged in that business last night when you saw me, and saved me from a terrible punishment at the Red Lion."

"Yes; and for being there I was almost resolved to let you do the best that you could, all alone."

"A little jealous of an old man like me. Fie! where is your pride?"

"It seems that Miss Jenny does not think much of me," I answered, a little bitterly.

"To be sure she don't, and with reason. She supposes that you are in some manner connected with the police department, and that you are ashamed or fearful of acknowledging the same. Recollect that she has been reared in the midst of people, who, by their habits and instincts, are taught to hate law, and those who support it. In time, her mind will become disabused of all such nonsense, and then she will estimate you at your proper worth."

"I fear not," I sighed.

"Have no fear on the subject. If she is proved to be my own flesh and blood, she will know by instinct her friends. None from my house are ungrateful. Now," he continued, after a moment's reflection, "will you lay before me all the particulars of the plot by which I lost a daughter?"

"Perhaps you had rather hear the whole matter from the lips of the woman who stole your child."

"Certainly. Who is she?"

"No less a person than Mother Brown, whom you saw at the bushrangers' cave."

"What!" cried the baronet, starting up; "do you mean to tell me that that old hag was once the good-looking domestic in my family?"

"The same, sir."

"The old she-devil! I will have her beaten to death for the crime she has committed! I will tear her limb from limb!"

"Sit down, and listen to me for a moment," I said; and at length he did so, although he still fumed and raved. "I have promised Mother Brown that if she would make a full confession, and undo the wrong that she has helped to do, that you will forgive her in the fullest manner, and institute no proceedings against her."

"I shall do no such thing," he cried, in a hasty manner, jumping up, and making the house shake with his firm tread as he walked up and down the apartment.

"As you please," I answered, and remained quiet. Presently the baronet became more calm; and then he once more resumed his seat.

"Well," he asked, "why don't you go on?"

"I have finished my story," I said.

"No, you have not. You have failed to give me the particulars of that hag's confession."

"Yes; but, nevertheless, I have said all I intend to."

"What do you mean?" spoken most impatiently.

"Just what I say. If you can't bind yourself to keep the pledge that I have given the woman, not another word passes my lips on the subject of your child."

"Do you mean what you say?" he asked.

"I do, most emphatically."

"I can open your mouth only by means of a promise?" Sir William said. I bowed.

"Well, then, take it; but I tell you it is with great reluctance that I give it. She should be hanged for what she has done."

"I have no doubt of it; but that same woman saved my life at the risk of her own. I owe her a debt of gratitude for what she has done for me. It is natural that I should be her friend, and while thinking me one, she confided to me the secret of her life — the abduction of your daughter. But first she extorted from me a promise that I would see that she was not punished for her offence. Now you know all." The baronet extended his hand.

"You are a noble young fellow," he said, "and I am proud to call you a friend. If you had lost a child in the manner that I did, you would feel as anxious for revenge as I felt a few moments since. But go on with your story. You have my promise."

"And you will speak kindly to the old woman?" Sir William smothered his rising choler, and said yes, and motioned to me to proceed.

"Mother Brown made a full confession this morning, telling me the reason why she stole the child, and at whose dictation."

"Who could have asked her to perform so mean a part?"

"Do you think of no one who had a spite against you at the time?"

"No, for I had offended no one. I did not have an enemy in the country, that I was aware of."

"But still you had an enemy, and a most unscrupulous one. He was enraged at your refusal to use your influence to have his sentence changed from transportation to a light fine or imprisonment at home."

"You refer to Bill Sykes, the Manchester Pet?"

"I do. He could think of no other manner in which he could be revenged, than by stealing your child. He did not do it himself — but he employed Molly Brown; and such was the influence that he possessed over her, that she consented to do his bidding, and leave the country for Australia. But I had better let the woman tell her own story, provided you will listen to it with patience."

"I will," the baronet answered. "But I must have vengeance on that scoundrel, Bill Sykes."

"With all my heart; I am willing," I answered. "Shoot him or hang him, imprison him or pardon him, it is all one to me. I have no love for him, I assure you."

"You are not so indifferent about my daughter?" asked the baronet, with a sly glance of his eye.

Of course I blushed, because it was impossible to do otherwise on having such a pointed question put to me. Sir William noticed my embarrassment, and said, —

"Well, well, don't look so distressed. I noticed, on the day that we met the girl on the plain, that you had a fancy for her. Let me say that I honor your taste. Just such a looking lady was her mother at Jenny's age. But what nonsense I am talking, when I have work of so serious a nature before me! About this old woman, Mother Brown — where is she to be found?"

"You will see her without delay, will you?"

"Yes, the sooner the better."

"But are you strong enough? Remember, you gave evidence of some weakness."

"Pshaw! do you think me a school-girl, ready to faint at the sight of blood, or on hearing an emotional story. I am an Englishman, sir, and have a heart like a rock."

"I want you to remember your promise. The woman is to escape all punishment, except in the shape of words. Scold her as much as you please, but nothing worse."

"A Byefield does not forget or forfeit his word. I have said what I would do; now let me see the old —" He meant to have used a strong expression, but a glance silenced him.

"I think it is better that you should see her here in your own rooms; do you?"

Sir William nodded his head, and asked, "When can I see her?"

"Within half an hour."

The baronet breathed hard, and his eyes flashed; but in a moment all evidence of rage had passed away.

"Remember that you boast of being a Byefield," I said.

My companion laughed, and once more extended his hand.

"I wonder if you can subdue your own passions as easily as you do those of others?"

"I am afraid not," I answered. "But the roaming life I have led for so many years has taught me coolness and audacity at the same time."

"I believe you," was the reply, but spoken in a tone so low that it was not intended for my ear.

"But the woman, the woman! let me see her as quick as possible, and thus solve all my doubts," Sir William said, a moment afterwards.

I obtained a carriage at the door of the Nugget House, and entering it, was soon in front of Murden's home. Ascending the stairs, I found that I was none too soon, for Mr. Tom Spitman was attempting to pick the lock of the door leading to the room in which Mother Brown was confined.

"You rascal!" I said, "what do you mean by trying to open that door?"

"O, sir," the fellow replied, with a squirm to escape from my grasp, "the old voman is dry, and I vants to relieve her."

"And if you had gained access to her, you would have supplied her with liquor, would you not?"

"Yes, sir."

"And what then?"

The rascal grinned as he replied, "I should have sperimented with her a little."

"How?"

"Jist seen if she could stand fire. She's so jolly 'ily, you know."

I took the young man by the neck, gave him a sharp turn to the left, and headed him down stairs. He picked himself up, and said, —

"You'll be the death of me some day, if you don't mind. You seem to think that my neck ain't good for anything, don't you?"

I shook my fist at the wretch, and he vanished in the direction of the kitchen, and commenced some of his useful labors, interspersed with torturing and threatening the cook, so that the lower atmosphere was rather hot on that eventful afternoon. Mother Brown had heard my voice, and subsided immediately. There were no more calls for liquor. She appeared to recollect her promise, and kept sober; but I was not deceived in the least. I unlocked the door, and walked in.

"O, my child," she said, "how I have wished you to come."

"For what reason?"

"I'm so dry," was the reply.

"Ah! you want water. You shall have some, as much as you can drink."

"Well, I'm not at all particular. If there ain't water, you can give me the fust thing that comes handy — gin or beer; one or both will do," Mother Brown said.

"Do you remember your promise?" I asked.

"What promise?"

"That you would not drink until this mystery was all cleared up."

"Well, ain't it cleared up. Haven't I told you my story, and ain't that enough?"

"No; you must do more than all that; you must now go with me to the Nugget House."

"For what?"

"To see Sir William."

"They won't let me see him. They'll turn me out. They wouldn't even trust me for a glass of gin that I asked for one day."

"No matter for that. Sir William is at the Nugget House, and will see you."

"And have you told him all?"

"No, not all. I leave it to you to make a full confession."

"And won't he punish me?"

"He has pledged himself not to."

"The dear old master! O, how he must feel towards me!"

"He is calm now, and will listen to what you have to say. Come."

"Not a step till I has a 'spider' to keep my courage up."

I saw that the old woman was resolute; so I went to my room and poured out a fair dose of gin. She took it at once, and then declared that she was ready. She trembled violently as I opened the door and led her into the presence of Sir William, who was standing up ready to receive her. No sooner did she catch a glimpse of the baronet than she uttered a cry, broke from my control, and threw herself at the feet of her former master.

CHAPTER LV.

MOTHER BROWN'S CONFESSION. — THE STOLEN CHILD. — THE LOCKS OF HAIR.

For a few moments there was silence in the room, broken only by the sobs of the woman. That wretched Hopeful who did not comprehend the meaning of the scene, managed to mutter some maudlin stuff; but no one paid the slightest attention to him.

"Stand up," said Sir William, stooping down, and attempting to raise the woman; but she shrank from his touch, and continued to sob and beg for mercy.

By some exertion we managed to get the woman into a seat; but we found it necessary to hold her there. In the mean time the scene was so confounding to the police commissioner that he could only gaze at the old woman and at the baronet, and then turn his gray eyes upon me, as though asking for an explanation. I had schooled myself for the scene, and was prepared for it. Not so Sir William. In spite of his firmness, he trembled, and looked pale and haggard. I went to the table, and poured out a glass of wine, and handed it to him. He thanked me with a smile, and then noticing Mother Brown's wishful look, he said, —

"Will you give her a glass? It will do her good at the present time."

"More blessed and truthful words yer never said afore or will agin," whined Mrs. Brown, with a gasp, and a clutch at her throat, as though to convey the impression that it was dreadfully parched.

"It is many years since you left my service, Mrs. Brown," the baronet said.

"Yes, sir, and it was a sorry day for me that I did leave it. It would have been better for me if I had stuck by the old hall."

"You know why I have summoned you here?" the baronet demanded.

"Yes, Sir William; I knows, and am sorry for what I knows."

"If you are truly repentant I shall forgive you, provided you make a full and candid confession."

Hez began to grow interested. He reached towards a bottle, but suddenly altered his mind, and turned his back upon the table and contents. As soon as Mother Brown had recovered from her agitation, Sir William motioned for her to go on.

"I was a contented girl, Sir William," she said, "when I lived in yer household, till I met that 'ere Manchester

Pet, or Bill Sykes, — that was his name, — the prize-fighter what yer allers had hangin' at yer heels, and followin' round arter yer like a dog."

The baronet winced a little, but did not interrupt her.

"Well, sir, as he was allers in the servants' hall, a drinkin' and a guzzlin', and tellin' us women-folks that he could whip most every one, and not more'n half train at that, I kinder took a likin' to him, 'cause I was a young and foolish woman at that time, and didn't know what was best for me. The Pet appeared so brave, and could lick men so easy, that I thought that he must be somethin' more than a man; and so I just took a fancy to him. He read it, and took a likin' to me, and told me that when his wife died he would marry me; and I lived on, hopin' that she would pop off; but she didn't; she lived, just to spite me, I used to think. But the Pet was just as pleasant, kinder, to me, as though she was dead, and I used to give him all the best pickings from the first table, and steal wine from the butler, so that he could wet his lips with the best that the house afforded. Yer didn't know all that was goin' on in yer house, Sir William."

"No, I suppose not," groaned the baronet.

"We used to be awful extravagant, Sir William, in the servants' hall, 'cause we had no missis to find fault and check the accounts. But arter a while yer brought home a wife, Sir William; and a bonny thing she was, and she loved yer very much, and spoke pleasant to all of us; but I hated her, 'cause Bill Sykes told me to. Yer turned a cold shoulder to him after yer was married, 'cause yer didn't care so much for prize-fights, and dog-fights, and rat-terriers, and horse-racing, and sich like sport, arter yer had sich a handsome wife to love."

The baronet blushed at having the secrets of his early life exposed; but he did not interrupt the old woman.

"All of yer people rejoiced at the change, 'cept Bill Sykes and me. Yer was colder and colder to Bill, and no longer axed him to yer house, or backed him in his fights. He used to swear at yer for it, and say that he would be revenged, and all sich as that; but still he wouldn't let me leave yer sarvice, 'cause he said I could be useful to him where I was, some day. I liked him well enough to do just as he said; so I continued to live in yer home until yer little Marie was two years of age.

"Well, when the little gal was two years old, the Pet had a big fight with another feller, and killed him. He was nabbed for manslaughter, and tried for it, and got a ticket in the shape of transportation for life. Then he sent for yer, Sir William; and when yer didn't come, he writ to yer, and axed for money and help to have his sentence changed to a fine and imprisonment at home. Yer didn't mind him, and then the Pet grew raving mad. He sent for me, and told me, in the presence of his wife, what he wanted me to do. Don't curse me, Sir William, or trample me under foot; but the big bully did want me to steal the child, yer little Marie, and to go to Australia in a transport, while he went out with the convicts. His wife she tells me to do the same; and when I refuses, they both say that they'll ruin me unless I does. But I still holds out, and then the wife she leaves us alone; and, O, law! I couldn't refuse when he took me in his arms and called me his darling Mollie, and said that he would splice me as soon as his old woman hopped the twig."

Sir William uttered a groan, and was inclined to start up, in his wrath, and do the old woman some damage; but I whispered, "Remember your word."

"I will," he said, "but it is hard to do so."

"Sykes said that I must leave yer comfortable home, Sir William, so that when the child was missed I wouldn't be suspected. He gave me money, and told me just what to do, and where the ship sailed from that started for Australia. After I had secured the child, I was to cut off her curls, dress her in poor clothes, and stain her skin with some kind of juice that his wife got from gypsies. She was to join me, and help me do the work."

"O God, can all this be true?" groaned the unhappy father.

"Sartin; it's all gospel what I'm tellin' of yer. Yer don't

s'pose I'd lie, do yer? No, Sir William, it's truth what you gets out of me. I'm determined to tell it if I chokes — there now.

"Where was I? O, I see. Well, I did just as the Pet wanted me to do. I left yer house, Sir William, and took board with a friend about a mile from the hall. I said I was goin' to try my luck in Australia, where women was dear and men in plenty, and where most any one could have a husband what wished, and didn't look too high. I waited there till I hears from Sykes's wife. One day she met me in the forest, and tells me I must grab the child as soon as possible, and start for Liverpool one week from the day that little Marie is took. The Pet didn't want me to run as soon as I took the gal, 'cos he was afeard that I would be 'spected, and followed. I was to steal the child, 'cos I knew she would go with me; and arter I had done so, Sykes's wife was to help me doctor her, and then run with her out of the county, and find a place to stow away till I jined her, and the ship sailed."

"Do you mean to tell me that you carried out your hellish design?" asked the baronet, in a low, weak tone, as though the confession was too much for him.

"Yes, sir; I did what I told Sykes I'd do. I took the gal one mornin' when she was playin' in the park, and looked so pretty that my heart almost failed me; and if I hadn't told Sykes I'd do it, I shouldn't have had the heart to lay hands on her."

"For Heaven's sake, spare me the details!" murmured Sir William; and then rising to his feet, he staggered to the table, and drank a full goblet of hock.

"I have but little more to add, Sir William," she said. "I took the child, and we doctored it; and then Mrs. Sykes (she was an ugly old thing as ever lived — I hated her) cut for Liverpool, and arter the hue and cry was all over, I started for the same place. From there we took a ship, and sailed over the ocean so blue for Australia."

"And the child," gasped Sir William. "Did it not cry and moan for its friends?"

"O, yes, it almost sobbed its blue eyes out; but arter a while it didn't seem to mind it much, and played with the sailors, and was as jolly as could be."

Sir William's hands worked convulsively, as though they were inclined to fasten upon the old woman's throat, and choke the life out of her in short order.

"What next?" asked the baronet, as soon as he dared trust his voice.

"Well, when we arrived at Melbourne, Bill Sykes was there hard at work on his sentence. His wife she opens a public house with money that he gives her, and I goes and lives with her as a bar-maid, and keep a watch over little Marie at the same time. In about six months, old Mother Sykes applied to the authorities for a servant, and she selects her husband, and says that she will be responsible for him; so he is given a ticket-of-leave, and he marches into the saloon one day, and takes charge of the Red Lion on his own account."

Mother Brown at this stage commenced weeping, but still managed to talk.

"Then began my trials," she said. "I had a hard trial with that Pet and his wife. He wanted me, and she didn't; and betwixt 'em both it was rather rough. But arter my Bobby was born, I had to cut sticks, 'cos old Mother Sykes said that Bill Sykes was Bobby's father; and I guess he was. But the devil claimed her one day, and took her; and then I s'posed the Pet would do the right thing; but he wouldn't marry me, and so I had to sink lower and lower, till at last I was nothing but a poor, miserable, drunken cook for a gang of bushrangers."

While she was sobbing and talking, she tore open the front of her dress, and produced a little bag carefully tied up. She ripped it open, and then placed in the baronet's hands several little golden curls cut from Jenny's head on the day that she was abducted. With a sigh and a groan, Sir William pressed the locks to his lips, and then human endurance could hold out no longer; his head dropped, and had I not caught him, he would have fallen to the floor.

CHAPTER LVI.

PREPARATIONS FOR AN ARREST.—THE PET ON THE WATCH BAD NEWS.

MARDEN hastened to the baronet with a glass of water We wet the man's face, and at last had the satisfaction of seeing him open his eyes and look around, in a doubtful uncertain manner, as though not exactly realizing all that had taken place.

"We must have the fellow arrested for conspiracy and abduction," the commissioner remarked in a brisk tone. "Leave all to me, and I'll see it done. I'll get the warrant out, and see that it is served at the proper time."

"But we must first extort a confession from the brute," Sir William remarked. "I want to be certain that it's my child that I take to my heart and home."

"We'll have it out of him, Sir William; no fear of that," the commissioner replied. "Leave the matter to me, and I'll make him confess, or I'll make him suffer."

"Then we had better start for the Red Lion at once," Sir William remarked.

"I shall have to differ from you on that point," the commissioner replied. "It is too late to obtain a warrant, and if we did we should create such an intense excitement in Mud Lane by arresting the Pet, that the fellow would be likely to expect a rescue, and keep a silent tongue. No, Sir William, there is time enough to-morrow. He suspects nothing, so he'll not leave the city, and the lady knows nothing of what is going on."

"No, of course not."

"Then let us separate, and meet to-morrow forenoon, say at ten o'clock, and then proceed to the Red Lion, where we can have an examination."

"Would it not be better to have one in this room? Can't you bring the lady and the Pet to my quarters?"

"Certainly, Sir William. I can do that in an easy manner."

"Then I'll thank you to do it. I should like to have all of you breakfast with me in the morning, say at nine o'clock, and after the meal we can proceed to business." We all agreed to that.

"Mother Brown had better be kept in the background until we are ready for her," I said. "She must not appear until we have tried other means to compel the Pet to confess."

"I like the suggestion. It shall be acted on. Now, what shall we do with her? She must be kept from liquor, and confined in some room where escape is impossible."

"I don't want to escape," she said, in a determined tone. "I wouldn't leave this work undone for all the gold in the mines of Ballarat. Bill Sykes must suffer for all wrongs he has committed on me and others. Don't fear my escapin'. I'll drink, but not run."

"We must be careful, Mother Brown," the commissioner said. "You can go home with us and spend the night, and then we shall know where to put our hands on you in the morning. You shall have a 'spider' for a night-cap, and bitters before breakfast."

"I'll go with yer;" and the old woman arose.

"A parting glass before we separate," Sir William said.

"I'm agreed," cried Hez and Mother Brown with one accord.

We emptied our wine-glasses, and then shook hands with the baronet, and took our departure. As the night was pleasant and cool, we walked home, and had proceeded but a short distance when we saw the Pet on the sidewalk, looking up at the Nugget House, and in the direction of the room which Sir William occupied. The ex-prize-fighter was so much engaged that he did not notice us as we passed near him. His eyes were too firmly fixed on the room which we had just left to pay the least attention to our movements, although Mother Brown did express a wish to punch his head, and to tear some of his hair out by the roots, and would have closed with him, if we had not held on to her and threatened her if she made the least noise or attracted the slightest attention. When we were some distance from the Pet, I turned and looked back. He was still gazing at the windows of Sir William's room, as though meditating upon some bold and desperate deed. Did Sykes suspect that Sir William was on his track, and determined to pursue him until justice and vengeance were satisfied? It looked so; but how had he learned the fact? Had some one in the baronet's pay revealed the secret, and thus placed the Pet on his guard? I feared so, and wished that we had acted promptly that night, and thus brought the matter to a close. I hinted as much to Murden; but the commissioner laughed at my fears, and contended that there was not the slightest danger of our missing the man. He would be found in the morning at the Red Lion, behind his bar, doing duty, as usual.

Leaving the Pet standing on the sidewalk, we started for home, each one thinking of the morrow, and how Miss Jenny would welcome so great a revolution in her circumstances. To be raised from the position of bar-maid in the Red Lion to that of a baronet's daughter, rich and powerful, would be something of a change; and I was anxious to see if she would assume the position of a lady with a vulgar flourish, or with a quiet dignity that would become her beauty and present education.

We sat and smoked until the mantel clock struck the hour of twelve, and then separated for our respective rooms, with express orders to Tom to call us at seven — instructions which he followed to the letter, confound him! for I was terribly sleepy when he knocked at the door, and told me the time, and also intimated that Murden was up and dressed, and had been stirring round the house for an hour or more. I called to Hez, but that genius swore at me in a frightful manner; so I let him remain in bed, undisturbed. He was getting corrupted by contact with the natives of Australia in the most remarkable manner. Many and wonderful changes had taken place in his disposition since we landed in the province of Victoria, and I feared that it would require all of my Christian-like resignation to get along with him. I left Hopeful snoring, walked down, and found Murden transacting some business with early callers, and sipping coffee at the same time. He looked as fresh and energetic as ever.

"We will move in a few moments," he said. "To tell the truth, I almost repent that I did not take your advice, and arrest the Pet last night. Somehow I don't feel quite right about the matter. Some misfortune is about to happen, unless my nerves are unstrung with last night's drinking. Devilish good wine, though, wasn't it? The Nugget House can do up such things when it has a mind to."

"If some blunder has occurred through your neglect," I said, with a quiver of apprehension, "don't ask me to forgive you, for I never will. You know how strongly I urged you to act last night, and how obstinate you were."

"Yes. I remember all that."

"Well, continue to think of it, for I shall be angry if the Pet has made his escape."

'No fear of that.. If he has left the city I can bring him back. I will find him if he is in Victoria."

Some one knocked at the door.

"Come in," roared the commissioner.

The door opened, and we saw Lieutenant Maurice standing before us, pale and weak-looking, with his arm in a sling, and the limb covered with blood.

"For God's sake, what has happened?" demanded the commissioner.

"I have some bad news for you," the lieutenant replied, in a low tone.

I saw that the man could hardly keep his feet; so I went towards him and gave him an arm, and led him to a seat.

"If you have a drop of wine in the house, I would be thankful for it," the lieutenant said.

"You shall have a gallon, only let me know what disaster has happened," cried the impatient commissioner.

"Well, sir, it is hard news for you to hear, but last night Mad Dick made his escape, and is at large."

The commissioner sprang to his feet. and roared with rage and disappointment. He swore in the most frightful manner, and would not listen to reason, until Maurice turned a shade paler, and then his head fell forward, and the man would have fallen to the ground if I had not caught him.

"Don't be a fool," I said, in an impatient manner. "Don't you see that the man is nearly dead with fatigue and a severe wound, which he has not even stopped to have dressed by a surgeon? Come, be reasonable."

The commissioner swore in a subdued tone, and then assisted me to restore Maurice, who was an old soldier, and could endure much without a murmur. We poured wine and water down his throat, dashed water on his face, and took a hasty look at the limb, which we found injured by a bullet having passed through the flesh of the arm, and escaped the bones, so that they were not broken. We sent Tom for a surgeon; but before the doctor arrived, the lieutenant opened his eyes, and expressed his thanks with a faint smile.

"I did all that I could to recapture the scamp," Maurice said; "but he was too much for me. He had one of our carbines, and when I thought I had him, he let drive, and gave me this ugly wound as a keepsake."

Just at this moment there was a knock at the door, and a servant of the Nugget House entered.

"Sir William Byefield wishes to see you two gentlemen as quick as possible."

Murden and I looked at each other in dismay. What had happened to occasion such a hasty summons?

CHAPTER LVII.

A SUDDEN DISAPPEARANCE. — THE PURSUIT.

Something was wrong, or else Sir William was over anxious, and wished to relieve his mind of some of the care that preyed upon it, in an expeditious manner. But at the present time we could not obey the summons; we had other and important work. We had to attend to Maurice, and then make some arrangement for the pursuit of Mad Dick, one of the most desperate of bushrangers, who, after a long course of depredations, had been captured by Murden and his men, and incarcerated to await his trial. Neither Murden nor myself had the slightest idea that the bushranger could be immediately retaken. But public opinion required that something should be done, and the commissioner was not the man to slight it. He loved praise and feared censure too much for that.

Maurice manifested some symptoms of shame at having fainted.

"I never did such a thing afore," he said, "and hope that I shan't again. But this scratch does jump so like a kicking colt, that I had to knock under. Excuse me."

"Say no more, old fellow," Murden replied. "I dare say that you did all that man could do to bring Mad Dick in. He is a great loss, because he was a bold man; but I think we shall secure him once more."

"I sent four men — all that I could spare — after the fellow as soon as he gave me this keepsake," Maurice replied. "But I have little hope that they will find the rascal. You know him. He is as cunning as Old Nick himself."

We left for the Nugget House, and were soon in the presence of Sir William, whom we found pacing up and down his chamber, in a terrible state of agitation.

"Well would it have been if we had proceeded to the Red Lion last night, when I could have claimed my daughter, and you could have arrested the Pet," Sir William moaned.

"But I can do my part this morning," the commissioner remarked.

"Too late," moaned the baronet.

"Why too late?" I asked.

"Because this morning the Red Lion is closed, and Sykes and my poor child have left the city."

"I am glad to hear that affairs are no worse," Murden said. "I feared that some serious misfortune had occurred. We can easily put that to rights. Never fear but that we shall find them. I'll warrant you that we shall."

"But you do not think of my terrible misfortune — I, who had longed to clasp a daughter to my heart; to tell her how much a fond mother desired to see her. I must now postpone that gratification. It is too hard, when by a little prudence all this might have been avoided."

"Are you sure that they have left the city, Sir William?"

"Quite sure. The Pet must have suspected that some designs were entertained on his liberty, or he would not have left so suddenly."

"I thought so last night, when I saw him standing in front of this hotel. Even then I supposed it was desirable that he should be arrested, but Mr. Murden thought differently; so there was an end of it. Now, we must recover the young lady, and lose no time in doing so."

"You give me hope," said Sir William.

"If my friend will only join me, I shall have no fear of the result," Murden remarked, giving me a strange look.

"You will go with us?" cried the baronet, with an anxious glance.

"I am not a free agent," I said, in a tone that must have convinced both gentlemen that I was anxious to serve them.

"For my sake, for my poor wronged child's sake, do not leave us at this extremity," Sir William cried.

"For her sake I will not," I answered. "For her sake I will again encounter dangers and privations, and even death."

"I will go to the Red Lion, and see if I can trace the flight of the fugitives," Murden said.

"They have been traced by one of my men," the baronet remarked. "They left the city at twelve o'clock last night, in a vehicle. They headed towards Bendigo."

"But I can pick up a few particulars. In the mean time, Mr. Jack, will you go to the house, and make preparations for our departure? We must leave the city within an hour or two," said Murden.

I left the room and hastened home, where I found Hopeful eating breakfast. He uttered a dozen objections against my going, but when I told him he could load the crushers and steam-engine as well as I could, he was somewhat modified, and concluded that I had better go, and let him manage the business alone. My preparations were soon made, and at eleven o'clock we left the city, all three of us on horse back, with provisions sufficient to last a week. But I made one great mistake. I left Rover with Hopeful.

CHAPTER LVIII.

THE HUNT FOR THE BARONET'S DAUGHTER.—A MIDNIGHT ADVENTURE.

We rode on in silence for an hour, raising clouds of dust which almost stifled us, until at last we drew rein at Perry's farm, where we dismounted to obtain a drink of water and to rest our horses, the heat beginning to tell on them in a severe manner. Ten or a dozen teams were in front of the door, the owners having turned their cattle loose until sundown, when they intended to continue their journey with more comfort than they could during midday. I was just about to lift a tin pot of water to my lips when I felt a hand on my shoulder. Turning round I saw my kind friend, Smith, his face none too free of dust and dirt, but looking as well as possible under the circumstances.

"Who'd a thought of seeing you?" he cried, shaking hands with an unction that showed how delighted he was at the meeting. "What's in the wind now?"

I drew him aside, so that none of the loungers could overhear us, and then asked him a few questions before I answered one.

"How long have you been here?" was the first interrogation.

"Ever since eight o'clock this morning."

"You were on the road all night?"

"Yes; I and my teams."

"Did you meet a man and a girl on the road, some time this morning?"

"Yes," was the prompt answer.

"Where?"

"At Fox's station, where we stopped for water at the sink hole at that place."

"Did you notice them in a particular manner?"

"Yes; because they seemed in a hurry, and would not speak with us. The man was a big fellow. I've seen him in Melbourne many a time."

"And the woman; did you notice her face?"

"No; it was covered up, as though she was cold. The air was rather chilly."

"Well, what else?"

"Nothing, only the man watered his horses, and then started as fast as he could urge the animals. But what is up? More adventures and speculations? If I could leave my teams — I have four of 'em with me, for the purpose of carting your machinery to the cave —"

"It won't do, Smith," I said, with a smile; "you are a steady-going man, married to your second wife — a woman who needs more protection and cherishing than Becky, your first spouse. No, no; you have sown your wild oats. You can't go with us."

"But she would never know it," pleaded Smith.

"What! could you deceive your wife? For shame, sir! You don't deserve so excellent a woman."

The honest fellow winked one of his eyes, and said, in a slow and measured tone, —

"Gammon! You know you can't put on such airs to me, and pretend that you would be a pattern. It won't do."

Of course I wilted at once, and no longer attempted to rebuke him; but, nevertheless, I was determined that he should not accompany me on the expedition.

"How did you leave Amelia?" I asked.

"Slowly recovering; but still weak, and agitated at the least thing. She would like to see you. Stop at the house if you have a chance. You know its doors are always open to you and your friends."

I pressed the man's hand, and then along came Murden and Sir William to see if I had obtained any intelligence. In a few words I informed them of the news which Smith had brought. Sir William was terribly impatient.

At two o'clock we started, although it was against our own judgment, and that of the stockmen who were waiting at the house until the heat of the day had passed, before they undertook their journey to the mines, or towards Melbourne. We guarded as well as possible against sunstroke, by placing wet cloths in our hats; but we had not ridden five miles before the cloths were dry, our horses covered with foam, and in such a state of dejection that even the touch of the spur did not cause the least movement of an animated nature. Under the circumstances, there was but one thing to do. That was, to find shade and rest until sundown; and it was well that we determined on such a course, for no sooner had we obtained shelter than Sir William was so overcome that we had to help him from his horse, pour wine down his throat, and bathe his head and neck with water; and, even with such treatment, he was an hour or two in recovering sufficiently to enable him to speak. The first words that Sir William uttered were, —

"My child! what will become of her?"

He made an effort as though to continue his journey, but he was too weak, and his head troubled him; so he sank back with a groan.

"Your child will be as safe a month hence as she is now," I said. "She will be restored to your arms; but it will take some little time to accomplish it. The man who has her in his power will remain concealed for a few weeks, perhaps months, or until he thinks that you have given up the pursuit."

"O, why didn't we arrest the rascal last night?" groaned the baronet.

"Because we were too stupid to do so. We shall know better next time."

This was not as good consolation as I could have wished to bestow, but it was the best I had; and before the baronet had time to find fault with it, I looked up and saw within ten rods of us a native of the Mount Barker tribe, armed with a long spear, a shield made of tough bark, and painted around his body with stripes of red ochre, found in some parts of Australia, and used by the natives for personal adornment. I signalized the native to approach, which he did very willingly, for he scented tobacco and liquor — two things which an Australian takes to. When within ten feet of us, he stopped, leaned on his spear, took a survey of us, commencing with Murden, and ending with Sir William.

"Ugh!" he grunted, the baronet's white hair having attracted his attention; "bissinacy."

He turned to leave us, for he thought he had stumbled upon a venerable missionary and two of his attendants, and if such was the case, he knew that he would have a dry welcome and a long harangue.

"Stop," I cried. "No marimi."

"No?"

"No."

The native drew a long breath, but still appeared unsatisfied. Murden thought that he would convince him; he drew a bottle and held it up. The shrewd native shook his head. It would not do. He had seen missionaries perform that part of their duties with much greater flourish than Murden attempted.

"You d—d fool!" roared the annoyed commissioner.

The oath settled the question instanter. The native stretched out his dark, dirty paw, and muttered in guttural tones, —

"Gib me lub."

Murden poured out a little of the spirit, and handed it to the native. Then we commenced questioning the man, using English and the native language to make ourselves understood, and by that means we were enabled to learn that the fellow had seen the Pet and a lady early that morning, heading for Bendigo. So at six o'clock we thought we could venture to start, and by twelve o'clock we made thirty miles, and were just thinking of stopping for the night, when we were somewhat surprised by hearing a peremptory command of "*Halt.*" As we checked our horses, the same voice that had bid us halt asked, —

"Do you surrender?"

"To whom?" I demanded.

"No matter. Do you surrender?"

"How large is your force?" I continued, in a bantering tone.

"Large enough to take care of a dozen like yours," was the answer.

"I don't believe it."

"Then dismount, and see for yourself."

I was about to dismount, but not with the intention of surrendering, when Murden took up the conversation.

"We surrender," he said, "but we demand good treatment."

"As good as you deserve," was the answer.

"Who in the deuce can they be?" whispered Murden. "I have heard of no gang of bushrangers operating on the Bendigo road. Blast the luck!"

"Put on the handcuffs and disarm the prisoners. Lead the horses to the camp. Close in, men," thundered the captain.

Murden was about to utter an indignant remonstrance; but just at that moment his eyes fell upon the costume of our captors, and he shook with silent laughter, as he whispered, —

"By the Lord Harry, if we ain't in the hands of the mounted police of Bendigo!"

"We swear to you," I cried, as they produced their handcuffs, "that we will make no effort to escape."

"Bah! bosh! don't talk in that way. We are not to be blarneyed by such as you. We know you too well."

Of course we had to submit, although Sir William uttered a deep groan when he found a pair of steel bracelets on his aristocratic wrists, and the commissioner would have uttered roars of rage, if I had not restrained him. The police closed around us, and marched us through the bush for about a quarter of a mile. We then saw a fire, three men sitting around it, and drinking coffee with as much relish as if they had been without for two days. This agreeable occupation was suspended when we were fairly within the light of the flames.

"Well," said the man, who appeared to be in authority, setting his tin cup down on the ground, "you have secured them, have you?"

"Yes, sir; here they are."

"Did they show fight? Did they injure any of our men?" asked the chief.

"No, sir. Lord, they was awful glum when we took 'em. They didn't raise a hand. They didn't seem to have no more spunk than so many sheep. I tell yer we took the fight out of 'em."

"What in the devil's name do they take us for?" whispered Sir William.

"Bushrangers," I answered.

When the chief spoke, I thought that I recollected his voice and form, and I was trying to think of his name; but just as I answered the baronet, some one called the policeman Mr. Commissioner Brown, and then it struck me that I had thus singularly fallen upon my old Ballarat friend, whom I had not seen since I returned to Australia. The idea of our thus meeting was so laughable that I could no longer contain myself, and I roared outright, to the intense surprise of my friends and the policemen who surrounded us.

CHAPTER LIX.

MEETING AN OLD FRIEND.—A DISAGREEABLE SURPRISE.—A COUNCIL OF WAR.

The Bendigo commissioner, after he was once on his feet, surveyed us by the light of the flames with much complacency.

"A worse looking set of ruffians I never saw in my life," he remarked. "Rascal is stamped on every feature."

Considering the darkness we did not think the criticism a fair one, so only laughed at it; not low, in fear and trembling but with a hearty roar, as though we felt all that we uttered. The commissioner started back, astonished and confounded.

"You hardened wretches!" he said, "you'll cry before you laugh much more. Your crimes —"

"O, gammon!" I interrupted. "What do you think of yourself?"

"You insolent scoundrel, what do you mean?"

"Just what I say. I could tell some hard stories of you."

"And so could I," laughed Mr. Murden.

Brown was petrified with rage and astonishment. At last he broke out: —

"You villains! I'll see you hanged before many days. Gallows is written all over your faces. I never saw three men with such ugly mugs."

We renewed our laughter at this. The joke was too good to remain quiet.

"Shall I whack 'em over the head with my carbine?" asked the man who had commanded the party that had captured us.

"Do if you dare!" cried Sir William, who could no longer control his indignation. "If you offer the least violence beyond what you have committed, I'll see that the police department is cleared of such abusive ruffians. These gentlemen," pointing to us, "may think that there is something of a joke in being handcuffed, but I must say that I am unable to see it as yet."

Even Mr. Brown, the Bendigo commissioner, was astonished, for he stopped and pondered over the words of the baronet, as though wondering if it were possible a bushranger could utter them. Finally he managed to ask a question.

"Who in the devil's name are you?" he thundered.

We hesitated a moment, to see if we had carried the joke far enough; but Mr. Brown was impatient.

"Speak. Who are you?" he cried.

"This gentleman," I said, pointing my manacled hands towards the baronet, "is Sir William Byefield, of Lancaster."

The police uttered a shout of laughter. They thought

that we were romancing. Even Mr. Brown allowed his dark features to relax a very little. I waited until the mirth had subsided, and then continued in a calm tone, impressive as possible: —

"This gentleman," pointing to the commissioner of Melbourne, "the man whom you characterize as the ugliest looking ruffian that you ever saw —"

There was a gesture of impatience from Murden. He didn't like such a compliment.

"Is no less a person than Mr. Commissioner Murden, of Melbourne, out on a scout."

There was another laugh on the part of the police, but it was not so loud as before. Mr. Brown did not even smile. He began to meditate.

"And who are you, sir?" he asked, in a slightly sarcastic tone.

"Will you allow me to whisper my name in your ear?"

"Yes; come near me and do so."

I stepped forward, and whispered the cognomen by which I was known at Ballarat during the first year of my residence at that interesting place. Mr. Brown started back, perfectly overpowered with astonishment. For a moment he could not speak. Then he rallied, sprang towards me, tore the hat from my head, turned down the coat collar that shaded my face, gave one long, earnest look, and the next instant, with a yell of joy, he threw his arms around me, and hugged me with as much zeal as though I were a woman, and he in love with me, and had just received permission to take such an important liberty.

"You dear old cuss!" laughed and cried the Bendigo commissioner in the same breath. "How came you here? Who expected to see you just at this time? When did you arrive in Victoria? Speak to me. Tell me something."

"How can I do so, when my hands are ornamented with these bracelets, and when you are squeezing me to death in an embrace like that of an anaconda?"

Mr. Brown suddenly relaxed his hold, and shouted, —

"Take off those irons this instant. Be quick about it.

What in the devil do you mean by putting irons on the best friend I ever had? Off with them."

"And mine too," cried Murden. "I've worn them long enough. Take them off."

"Of course I will. Old fellow, why didn't you utter your name before? If you had but said who you were —"

"But what are we to do now?" asked Sir William, when we had explained matters. "Can't we continue the pursuit? Remember, we are losing time."

"Which we can make up at daylight," answered Mr. Brown. "The fox is heading towards Bendigo. There we can run him to earth in good time. There is no occasion for haste."

"You don't know a parent's anxiety," murmured the baronet in a low tone.

Just at that moment a cry that reminded me of the howling of a pack of hungry wolves started us, and caused us to hold our breath, uncertain whether we were attacked by men or fiends, devils or natives. Once more the yell was uttered; and then we heard the galloping of horses, tearing through the bush as though ten thousand devils were on their backs; but above the tramping of steeds I thought that I could hear a burst of sardonic laughter, as if some fiend were chuckling at our astonishment. The police, who were rolled up in their blankets and mosquito nets, struggled to their feet, and grasped their carbines, as though to resist a desperate attack. For one moment there was silence, and then the hoarse voice of Mr. Brown was heard, as he shouted, —

"Give them a volley, men! Fire high, so as not to kill the horses."

There was an irregular discharge; but as the men could see nothing, and could only judge of the position of the horses by the noise, it was not very effectual. In fact, I don't think that a single animal was touched. For a moment after the guns were fired there was silence, and then came a ringing laugh, a regular ha, ha, ha! of the mocking description, and the sound of horses' feet died away. The police started in pursuit; but Mr. Brown called them back.

"You fools," he remarked, in a complimentary tone,

"don't you know that it's of no use to run after a man who's on horseback? Come back, I tell you!"

The men returned in a sullen, dejected manner, as though they had not been treated just right; while the rest of us looked at the fire. and at each other, and wondered what we were to do, hunting for the Pet and Miss Jenny on foot.

"Tell me the meaning of this confusion, this sudden attack," Sir William said.

"Well, you see, Sir William," returned Mr. Brown, "the confounded bushrangers have rather stolen a march on us. More's the pity, I say."

"Amen to that," muttered Murden.

"What are we to do for horses?" demanded Sir William. "We can't continue the pursuit on foot."

"That's a question that I can't answer, Sir William. All that I can think about is the fact that we have been surprised, and our horses stampeded. Now, who has done this bold, yet neat trick?"

Mr. Brown looked around upon his audience, and waited for an answer. As Murden did not speak, I thought I would utter my sentiments.

"There are none so blind as those who will not see," I said. "You have had repeated warnings of the sudden and stealthy attacks of the bushrangers; yet you will not gain by experience. You knew that Mad Dick was near us, that he must be somewhere in the neighborhood; yet what do I find? There is no guard set over the horses, although you have some twenty men. All lie down to sleep, and trust to fortune to keep Mad Dick at a distance. If you would find your animals, you must seek for them."

"Then you think that that bushranger has done the job?" asked Mr. Brown.

"Yes; he and others whom he picked up on the road."

"Then I'll punch Mad Dick's head the very first time that we meet," said Mr. Brown, in an emphatic manner.

With this resolution he threw out some pickets, while the rest of us rolled our heads in blankets, and went to sleep: for it was useless to pursue at that hour of the night

CHAPTER LX.

IN PURSUIT.—A SURPRISE.—A BLOW ON THE HEAD.—THE CONFERENCE.—A PRISONER.—A FEW REMARKS BY MISS JENNY.—HER VISIT AND ASSISTANCE.

"WHAT shall we do?" asked Mr. Brown, as soon as we had eaten breakfast and packed up our traps.

"Push on for Bendigo as soon as possible," was the general reply.

In a short time we were off, each of us with our blankets strapped on our backs; while the rest of our traps were left behind, under a guard of ten men, who were to be sent for as soon as we reached Bendigo. We were some time in getting clear of the bush and trees; but at last we struck the plain and the road, and although the travel was hard and unusual to most of us, still we trudged on most manfully until near ten o'clock, when we found the sun so overpoweringly hot that we were compelled to call a halt, and seek for rest and shade. Away on the right was a forest of gum trees, and towards that forest we directed our weary steps. Panting, thirsty, and covered with dust, we gained the shade and threw ourselves down, too much exhausted to exchange congratulations on the fact that we had found leaves to screen us from the hot sun. The day passed most slowly. Towards the close of the afternoon I wandered off into the dense forest for the purpose of looking up game; for it seemed to me that activity was better than mopping one's face, and brushing away flies and mosquitos. I found some relief in walking. The insects did not bite as savagely while I was in motion as they did when I sat still; so I continued on until I was warned that I had strayed far enough, and that it was time to join my companions. I turned to retrace my steps; but just at that moment I caught my foot in what seemed a vine. The shock was so great that I staggered, and in attempting to recover my upright position, I grasped at some bushes that grew near me. They were large and thick, and seemed capable of sustaining my weight. As I touched them they yielded, giving way so quick that I was a little surprised; but as I fell I felt that my feet were in something more than the curl of a vine, and looking down I saw, squat behind the bushes, the grinning and repulsive faces of Bill Sykes and Mad Dick.

"Give him a lurch, Bill," said the gruff tones of Mad Dick. "We don't want none of his backers here."

The Manchester Pet, in obedience to the command, did give me a lurch, and a disagreeable one it was; for he suddenly gave a pull, and over I went, head first, into some bushes, so that the free use of my arms was required to prevent my eyes from being destroyed. The cunning rascals had caught me in a trap. The instant I struck the bushes, I heard the Pet say, —

"Let me give him a shot and finish him."

"And bring the whole gang down on us?" growled Mad Dick.

"I should think I might put him out of the way," snarled the Pet. "He's a blasted spy, and don't desarve any mercy from me nor my gal."

"Ain't there time enough for all that?" asked Mad Dick, in a tone that savored of impatience. "Don't we want to learn a few particulars?"

"But, cuss him! he's a slippery customer, and he may get off."

"There ain't no more chance for him than there is for you to go to heaven," returned Mad Dick, in a tone that admitted of no argument.

"Turn him over, and let's see what he's up to now," the bushranger continued.

The Pet seized me with no gentle hand, took my pistol and knife, and then turned me so that they could look at my face. The prize-fighter must have seen something in my eyes that expressed the abhorrence with which I regarded him, for he assumed a savage, prize-ring look, and then, unable to control his temper, raised my pistol and struck me a violent blow upon the head, so hard that it seemed as though he had crushed the skull, for I felt the blood spirt over my face; a dull pain passed over my eyes and shot through my temples, and then all grew dark and silent. When I recovered my senses, I found that I was lying on my back on the ground. My pains were so severe that I had some trouble in moving; but at last I dragged my body about in the dark, felt with my hands, and found that I was in some kind of a room, which was small, and constructed in the rudest manner.

For a short period I cursed myself for visiting Australia for the second time. I thought, what a fool I was to knock my head against every obstruction that I met, and for meddling in matters that did not concern me. Why did I not remain in Melbourne and assist Hez, who was hard at work on his quartz-crushers?

While these subjects were passing through my mind, I thought I heard a movement in another room, and after a while I was certain that my surmises were correct; for some one uttered an emphatic oath, and damned the matches in the most energetic manner because he could not light a candle with them.

I remained quiet, and listened; but after a candle was lighted I crawled to one of the cracks of the partition, and peered through. The sight that met my view was a surprising one. I saw, seated at the table as though they had just entered the hut, the Manchester Pet and Mad Dick; while in a corner, looking as cold and as haughty as ever, was Miss Jenny. The two men were eating boiled mutton, and between them was a black bottle, suggestive of spirit.

For a while the men were too busily engaged in eating to exchange a word; but at last the Pet looked towards Jenny, and, with some show of affection, remarked, —

"Well, lass, has you bin lonesome like, all alone?"

"You know I have," returned the girl, in a cold, calm tone. "How could I help being tired and lonesome, all alone, out here in the brush?"

"Well, well, lass, don't scold. In a few days we will be

off. We has thrown the traps off the scent. They has started for Bendigo as fast as their legs can carry 'em."

"And they has lost the number of their mess," chuckled Mad Dick. "Pass the rum."

"Devilish lucky the young scamp left his dog in the city," remarked the Pet, after he had tasted his liquor. "We should have had to finish 'em both, and that might have been troublesome."

There was silence for a moment; and then Jenny raised her blue eyes, so cold and calm, and asked,—

"Who have you got in that room? I've heard him groan all day, and if you hadn't taken the key I'd gone in and seed him. Who is it?"

"Never you mind," returned the Pet, "who it is."

"But I does mind. Who is it?"

"Why don't you tell the lass," demanded Mad Dick. "She'll be as glad as we is to think that we has him."

The Pet hesitated, and looked at the girl as though he would refuse her request if he dared. At last he said,—

"It's some cove what you hates, Jenny."

"Well, who?" with an impatient gesture.

"Well, it's that police spy, you know. The one what had your daddy nabbed, arter he choked him at the Red Lion."

"O," the girl said, and shut her finely-carved mouth in a resolute manner.

"Yes, lass, it's him; and, now that we has him, we don't mean that he shall get away in a hurry. His friends might just as well settle up his estate, 'cos I don't think that he will claim it."

"O," was all the remark that Jenny made; but she nodded her pretty head several times, as though she comprehended.

"Ye see the cove has gin us trouble enough," continued the Pet. "It's time he was out of the way. He's hurt our business more'n any other man. Blast him! He driv me out of Melbourne. But only for a short time, lass. I shall go back agin."

"To be sure you will," cried Mad Dick, in a hearty tone,

with another pull at the liquor. "Arter we gets a few things settled we all three will jist leave this country, and find a place where we can live like gentlemen. I'm tired of being hunted like a wild dog."

"That's the dodge," remarked the Pet. "I'll jist sell what I has and cut stick. But we has much to do afore that. We must throw the traps off the track, and make 'em think we is lost. Yes, we must keep out of sight, Dick."

"You don't 'spose that I'm goin' to stand out in front of the station, and shout out our intentions, do you?" asked Mad Dick.

"No; but I thought that you seemed a little shaky to-day arter I had cracked the Yankee spy's skull."

Jenny raised her eyes, and looked full at her father's face, as though suddenly interested in the conversation.

"Didn't I tell you that if we had dished the feller that the traps would have hunted for a week but they would have found us, and the place where we is tied up?" Mad Dick asked, in an impatient tone. "Don't I know how much them commissioners sot by him? They would have revenged his death in some way, I tell you."

The Pet grumbled, and acquiesced in the opinion. Then he helped himself to liquor, and appeared to find consolation in the bottle. Jenny, I noticed, was listening to the conversation, although she did not appear to care for it.

"Yes," continued Mad Dick, in a musing tone, "arter all, I'm sorry that you smashed the young kite's head, 'cos I think that if we had been pushed that we could have used him."

"But he's a rat — a spy," hissed the Pet.

"O, gammon! You has been a spy long enough for the traps to know better than that. He ain't no more a spy than I is."

Miss Jenny raised her eyes to Mad Dick's face, and appeared more and more interested.

"Well, what is he then?"

"He's what they call a ventersome Yankee — a feller what likes excitement, and helps his friends. That's what he is; and I'm sorry that you rapped him, 'cos I think that we might have used him."

He took up the bottle as he spoke, but it was empty. Miss Jenny noticed the fact, arose, and took from a box another bottle, apparently full, and placed it before the Pet.

"Well done, lass. I thought that you said we shouldn't swill but one can?"

"I have altered my mind," was all the reply that she made, as she resumed her seat.

"May you keep on altering your mind, if it is as good as this," replied the giant, and filled his glass.

"It's too late to cry about spilt milk," Sykes remarked, as he tasted the liquor. "The feller's head is smashed, and there's an end of it. As far as I'm concerned, I wish that it had finished him; but, as it didn't, why I 'spose we must let him die where he is. He won't forget the blow in a hurry."

The future did indeed look dark and gloomy; and so overcome did I feel, that I was compelled to lay my aching head on my arm, and allow a groan of anguish to escape from me.

"Hullo!" Mad Dick said, "our bird is awake and singing. Wonder how he feels."

"Give me the key, and let me go and see." Jenny remarked.

"No, you stay here," Sykes cried, in a stern tone. "Let the cove die. We has enough to do to take care of ourselves."

Jenny, when she was refused, did not manifest the least disposition to complain. I think that the pain I endured rather stupefied me, for I lost all consciousness, or appeared to fall into an uneasy sleep; and, when I awakened, the light in the next room was burning dim, and the two men were resting their heads on the table, and appeared to be sleeping quite sound, judging from the snoring. Although the efforts which I made were painful, yet I managed to rest my head on my arm, and peer through the crack of the partition. At first I thought that Miss Jenny was sleeping; but, while I looked, she glanced at the slumbering men, then arose in a careful manner, removed the candle from the table, trimmed it, and then put her hand in her father's pocket, and took out a key. It suddenly flashed across my mind that Miss Jenny was about to pay me a visit. I was so much agitated at the thought that I could hardly restrain myself. My heart throbbed wildly, and my wound appeared to bleed afresh, such was my emotion.

I had but just time to lay my head on the ground when Miss Jenny entered the room. For a moment she stood near the entrance, looking towards me, or endeavoring to discover in which part of the room I was. It was so dark that she could not see where I was lying. I remained quiet, watching her motions. I knew her disposition, and was aware that I must permit her to do as she pleased, or she would have a fit of the sulks, and leave me in disgust. So I waited, with a beating heart and aching head, for her to speak to me, and make known her plans.

"Are you awake?" she asked at length.

I did not answer, but managed to breathe as though I was in distress; and, to tell the truth, I was, for my head ached as though it would split open.

"Where are you?" asked Jenny, in a whisper.

I still maintained silence.

She hesitated a moment, and then left me, but quickly returned with the light in her hand. She held it up, so that its rays fell upon my head, and then advanced, and knelt beside me.

I opened my eyes, and looked her full in the face.

"Do you know me?" she asked.

I murmured a feeble "yes."

It was my intention to appear more injured than I really was.

"Then don't talk, but let me help you. Hold still while I look at your wound."

She examined the wound carefully, and I heard her sigh as she did so. Her hands trembled as she pulled aside the matted hair; yet her touch was as light and delicate as a young girl nursing a lover.

"You have a terrible injury," she said. "No wonder your head aches. Sarves you right for not mindin' your own business. What did you want to chase after us for? Didn't you know any better?"

I considered this rather a poor return for the trouble I had taken on her behalf; but I stifled my resentment, and made no reply. I thought that, if she ever learned how much I had done for her, she would feel sorry for her words, and the manner in which she had treated me.

"I jist learned from a friend of my dad's that you ain't a police spy. I can believe him, although the governor says you is in with the traps, and does their spying business. You don't, do you?"

I thought that she spoke in a manner that showed she wanted me to answer in the negative; that she desired the question settled at once and forever.

"I have always told you that I was not a spy," I replied; "but you would not believe me. Give me some water to drink, for I'm parched with fever and thirst."

She left me, and returned with a tin pot full of water. I was so thirsty that it seemed as though water never tasted as well. I emptied the pot, and uttered a sigh of relief.

"Now wait, and I'll wash some of the blood from yer head."

"And if they should wake up, and discover you with me, what would they say?" I asked.

"I don't care what they say. I ain't afeard of 'em. If they talks to me, I'll jist talk back, and give 'em as good as they send."

I could not but admire her independence, although I did not relish the manner in which she expressed herself. It was Red Lion style; but the girl knew no better.

I had half a mind to tell her the secret of her birth; but I thought better of it, and concluded that it would take too long. Besides, I did not know how it would affect her. I thought that my head was of more account, by the manner in which it ached, than a long history of her early misfortunes.

She left me, and returned with water and rags. For the

latter I was inclined to think that she had torn up a handkerchief; for I saw a little needle-work in one of the corners. At any rate, the cloth was soft, and her touch light; but her task was difficult. She had to use a pair of scissors quite freely, cutting off matted hair that clung to the wound, and had dried there stiff and hard. I bore the pain without a murmur; but, in spite of my silence, Miss Jenny would continue to whisper to me, sometimes in a tone of pity, and again in a manner that showed she wanted to scold.

"I don't know what's goin' to become of yer," she said. "Here's one side of yer head all caved in. Yer might have known that the governor could lick a dozen jist like yer. He's a giant. He's strong. Didn't he give yer thunder one day at the Red Lion? Wan't that enough to last yer? No, yer must try yer hand agin. I don't know what's to become of yer!"

"Can't I escape from here before the men awake?"

"Yes, if yer can walk thirty miles afore they moves."

"But I might ride."

"Well, what is yer going to ride in or on?" she asked.

"Horseback."

"Where is yer hoss?"

"I can take one of those which Sykes and Mad Dick stole from the traps last night."

"Can yer?" with a sneer of contempt. "Why, them hosses is on the way to Ballarat, where they will be sold cheap for cash, and the money divided betwix the men what did the trick."

"But can't I use the carriage and horses which brought you here?"

"Them is gone back to Melbourne by the hand of a trusty cove what had his directions how to move."

I uttered a sigh. The Pet had managed shrewdly. He had acted in such a manner that all traces of his whereabouts would be lost.

I had yet another question — one of importance. I was desirous of seeing if she suspected the reason why Sykes left Melbourne so suddenly.

"I don't know as it is any of yer business," she said, in reply to my question; "but I ain't afeard to tell yer, so now. The governor said that the perlice was arter him, and that unless we cut sticks they'd nab us."

"I wish, Miss Jenny," I remarked, in a soft tone, "that you would be a little more choice in your language."

"What do you mean?" she asked; and she suspended her operations on my head to look me full in the face, her large blue eyes extended to their utmost limits.

"Why, don't use words which a young lady ought not to use. Learn to speak properly."

"Why, blast yer impudence! I'm a good mind to leave yer with yer head half dressed. Can't I speak as well as you can?"

I thought that I had made an unfortunate attempt to correct the lady's English, and that I had better postpone the subject until some more favorable opportunity.

"O, yes, you can speak as well, and your voice is sweeter," I hastened to add.

"Then what's the matter with me?" and, as she spoke, she gave my head a sudden jerk which sent such a thrill of pain through my system that I could hardly repress a cry of agony.

She saw me put my hand to my head as the pain darted through my temples; and, suspecting what she had done, an expression of sympathy passed over her face.

"Did I hurt yer?" she asked; and I saw in her beautiful countenance the sweet, womanly feeling so peculiar to a young girl.

"Forgive me," she whispered; "I didn't mean to. But you hadn't oughter have made me savage by slurring me. You know it."

"I won't again," I answered, finding that she grew worse and worse. She was like a young panther, all claws, and, unless you played with her in a careful manner, would get scarred for life.

"You'd better not, unless you don't want to see me no more."

At this point of the conversation she arose and left me; but it was only for the purpose of seeing if Sykes and Mad Dick were still sleeping. Finding that they were, she went to a box, took out a bottle, some rags, and a piece of plaster. With these articles in her hand, she returned to my side, poured out some spirit, and mixed it with water, and then compelled me to drink it. I did not hesitate long about obeying her. Then she poured the spirit upon the wound on my head, saying as she did so, —

"Now grit yer teeth, 'cause it will hurt."

I should think so, and the warning to grit my teeth was not lost. I found it necessary to grind them together in an emphatic manner, to prevent shrieking aloud when the hot spirit touched my wound. It seemed as though it would burn my brains out, shrivel up my flesh, and drive me distracted; and, while I was suffering all this, Miss Jenny remarked, in a cool tone, —

"Don't you make a noise."

I believe that the little witch did it on purpose, to punish me for what I had done in the way of correcting her expressions. If such was the case, she had a fiendish revenge.

"Does it hurt?" Jenny asked, after she had emptied half the contents of the bottle over my head.

"Yes; the liquor is very powerful."

"I should think it was. It even can knock over my governor, and it takes somethin' strong to do that. He's got more strength than two such men as you."

"I have no doubt of it, yet if you will examine his face you will see my mark there."

"Ah, where you hit him with the beer pot. Now, if it wan't for that same lick I could get the governor to let you run."

"But there's nothing to prevent me from leaving at the present time," I remarked, in a quiet tone.

"Ain't there?" with an expression of scorn that was highly amusing, or would have been under other circumstances. "Perhaps you don't think me somethin'," the young girl continued.

"Yes, I think a great deal of you," I remarked.

"Wall, stop that. I don't want no love-making round here. I knows yer and yer intentions."

"You are mistaken," I remarked, in a quiet tone. "I was not thinking of love—I was considering how I should escape from this place and join my friends."

"Them what yer has in the other world?"

"No, those on earth. I have no desire to see those in heaven."

"Humph, there ain't much chance of that. But stop yer noise, and don't talk trash. If yer can cut stick, do it. I should like to see yer walk off, 'cos I tell yer my governor will starve yer to death if he can."

"And will you consent to such a cruel course?"

"I don't know. Yer ain't much to me. 'Tain't so bad as hittin' a cove on the head with a beer pot."

She uttered the last words as though she had found an argument that could be used against me at all times, and with great effect. I quailed a little, but soon rallied, and told her that I would see what I could do in the walking line, for I did not dare to remain and trust my life to the tender mercies of the two men in the next room.

"Wall, let's see what kind of a fist yer'll make on yer feet."

As she spoke she extended her hand, and helped me to stand up. As soon as I was on my feet, I saw that it was impossible for me to walk any great distance; that I was too weak and dizzy to think of it. Jenny noticed that I could hardly stand, and with happy forethought placed one of my arms around her waist.

"I let yer do it," she said, 'cos yer sick. If yer wan't, yer shouldn't, I know."

I was enabled, by holding on firmly to the young lady's waist, to steady myself, and wait until the first paroxysm of pain and weakness had passed away; but still it seemed that I could not walk a mile, even to save my life. The blow on my head had been too severe, and I had lost too much blood to move for a great distance.

"Yer see yer can't walk thirty miles, don't yer?" Miss Jenny said.

"Yes."

"Wall, what yer goin' to do about it?"

"Can't I hide in some of the bushes near at hand, and wait till I gain strength?"

She thought of the question for a moment before she replied to it.

"You might do that. I could bring yer water and somethin' to eat every time I had a chance."

"Besides, I could take a supply with me," I suggested.

"Wall, I think that'll work. Come out in the air, and let's see how you move."

With my arm firmly clasped around the waist of the young girl, so that I could walk steadily, I stepped into the room where Mad Dick and the Pet were sleeping. It would have been an easy matter for me to have killed the two brutes, for their pistols were in their belts, and I had no doubt but that they were loaded. As I moved on very slowly, I noticed that the Pet had my revolver in one of his pockets. As I needed it more than he did, I just took possession, Jenny making no objections. Quiet as I was, however, the Pet moved, and seemed as though inclined to wake up; but he did not, while Mad Dick slumbered on undisturbed.

In a few seconds we were in the open air, cool, clear, and fresh, so different from the interior of the hut, that I felt myself growing stronger. I removed my arm from the girl's waist, and attempted to walk without her support. In a very short time I was convinced that my strength was not equal to such an effort, and I was glad to return to the tapered waist of Miss Jenny, while she saluted me with,—

"There now, you see how groggy yer is! Yer ain't got no wind, and a child could knock yer out of time."

CHAPTER LXI.

A MOMENTOUS QUESTION. — A TERRIBLE STRUGGLE.

"Come," she said, after I had rested, "yer must cut out of this. Time's up. If the governor should suspect yer's out here, there'd be a jolly row. Yer must stow away in the bushes till the coast is clear."

"And starve?" I asked, as I walked by her side, an arm on her shoulder to prevent me from staggering through excess of weakness.

"No, if I can I'll bring yer grub every day, and water too."

"O, Jenny," I cried, "don't say *grub*. It's so vulgar."

"Look a-here," she replied, in a fierce tone; "I'll be dished if I don't drop yer if yer talk in that kind of style. I'm goin' to use just such words as I please; so don't come yer lingo over me."

"But, Jenny," I said, in a soothing tone, "suppose you were rich, and occupied a good station in society; wouldn't you want to speak as correctly as the young girls whom you would meet?"

"No," she answered, in a sullen tone; but I knew, by the manner in which she spoke, that my words were having some effect, for as we moved along she looked up, and in a low voice remarked, "I shan't ever be fit for sich kind of company as yer tells about. I never seed sich girls except the ones what would go by me in their carriages, in Melbourne, and turn up their noses at me, 'cos I was a bar-maid and had to work."

"And yet, Jenny, you would like to be one of those same ladies, would you not?"

"Of course it's better to ride in a carriage than to be handin' out goes of gin, and mixin' spiders, and drawin' 'alf-and-'alf for Mud-Laners, what thinks themselves pretty grand if they gives yer a sixpence of an evenin'. Bah! I'm tired of all sich."

"And would you leave such a life with pleasure, dear Jenny?" I asked, in a low, pleading, affectionate tone.

"Look a-here," cried the fierce little jade, with a sudden stop, and a stamp of her pretty little foot, "if you comes that kind of palavar round me, I'll jist rap that cocoanut of yern till it aches — there now."

"Well, what have I said?" I asked, in a helpless tone, amazed at her sudden temper.

"I'd think yer'd ask," with a curl of her thin red lips and a toss of her head, while I could see a frown on a brow that was handsome enough for a coronet.

"I don't understand."

"Well, I does, and if I ain't a girl of much edication, I can take hints without any kicks — so there now."

"She grows worse and worse," I thought; but I didn't say it. "Dear Jenny," I remarked, in a soothing tone.

"O, bother, don't talk that way to a cove. Say what yer've got to, and done with it."

"I have nothing to say. What did you suppose I wanted to tell you?"

The girl did not look quite so indignant as she did a moment before.

"Well, I thought that it was sass yer was givin' me. Two or three times yer've hinted that I needn't be a bar-maid. Well, if I warn't such, yer mean that yer could take care of me; but yer don't intend that I should be yer wife — there now, yer mean thing."

My heart gave a great leap, and I felt my head grow dizzy. I think that I staggered a little, for I was faint; but when I recovered I found Jenny's arms around me, and my head was resting on her shoulder, as cosily as though we had been life-long lovers.

"Do yer feel better?" she asked, in a low tone, and with all of a woman's tenderness.

"Your cruel suspicions," I managed to say, "made me faint; you must know by this time, that I mean honestly by you."

"Yes, I s'pose yer do," — and I felt a little closer contact from her arms, — "but does yer mean the marrying kind of honesty. That's what I want to know."

Here was a blunt question, and one that I should have to answer, although Heaven knows I was not prepared to; and for the space of about ten seconds, all the time that I knew the young girl, with her suspicious nature, would give me, I reflected.

"I love you Jenny," I said in a low whisper.

Her round, white arms pressed closer and closer to my neck, and her head was turned so that I could feel her breath upon my cheek, as though she was waiting for my decision.

"Yes, but how much does yer love me? That's just what I wants to know."

I stole a look at her face, and saw that it was resolute, determined. She had broken through all maidenly rules for the purpose of obtaining an answer to her question. With her ideas of right and wrong she meant to find out if I loved her, and wanted her as a mistress or wife. And I was so pinned down by the little beauty that I must say yes or no, and lose all of her esteem and respect, if I answered in the negative.

The position was a most unpleasant one. If I said that I was willing to trust her with my name and some of my cares, her proper father, Sir William, would imagine that I had been false to him and the trust which he imposed upon me; that I had extorted consent from Jenny just for the purpose of forming an alliance with his house; and if I made love to the girl and obtained her consent, previous to informing her that she was born to a different position from that which she now occupied, wouldn't she think that I had deceived her a little, and that my affection was increased by the thought that her father was rich and occupied a high position in society? All these ideas passed through my brain while the young girl was waiting for my answer. I had more serious thoughts than ever before in such a short space of time; and in fact I was only prevented from continuing them, by her saying, —

"Yer don't talk much like a cove what cares for a lass."

"But I do care for you, Jenny."

"Well, then, why don't yer say so, and have done with it?"

"Because I don't want to take advantage of your position."

"Humph," she replied, rather sharply, "I'd give yer a whack in the face if yer offered to take any advantage of me out here — so now."

She jerked her arms from around me, and so sudden was her violence, that I staggered and fell to the ground; and it was rather a fortunate tumble after all, for the girl repented of her expression of anger, fell on her knees beside me, raised my head, from which the blood re-commenced flowing, said that she was sorry, and hoped that I would forgive her; and then it suddenly occurred to me that I could postpone her momentous question, for a time at least, on the ground that my injuries were too severe to answer all that she wanted to know.

"Yer mustn't stay here," she said, after a while; "do forgive me; get up and take to the bush, where yer can stow away till yer is strong enough to tramp for it. Come, I'll help yer, and bring yer water and grub. O, I'm so sorry that I pushed yer down! But yer hadn't ought to have made me mad."

"I shall see you to-morrow," I said, as I commenced preparing a place where I could lie down, sheltered from the sun.

"Yes, if I can get away from the hut without the governor's seeing me. I must be shady, yer know."

It was an awful night, the one that I passed. Before morning I had made up my mind to start on the journey to Bendigo, trusting to luck to make my escape. Faint and dizzy as I was, I could not be very sure of my course, or walk long without resting; and as daylight began to appear, I sunk down on some bushes, no longer able to stand. How long I remained in a semi-unconscious state I cannot tell; but I was awakened by hearing the tramp of many feet, and on raising my head and looking up I saw — O, what a thrill went through my heart as I saw the blue-coated policemen of Melbourne, headed by my old friend, Commissioner Murden, whom I had parted with a day or two before in an abrupt manner, through the instrumentality of Mad Dick and the Manchester Pet!

"Hullo, old fellow, is it you?" I asked, almost fearful that he would vanish from my sight.

The commissioner sprang forward, astonished as a man could be.

"My God!" he cried, "who is this?"

"I should think you would ask, for upon my word I hardly know who I am."

"Bring hither a glim!" roared the commissioner, for it was hardly light.

Murden snatched the torch from the man's hand, and held it to my face, looking at me most attentively, from head to foot. At last he seemed satisfied, for he exclaimed, —

"It is he — it's no ghost, as I thought!"

He threw down the torch, flung his arms around my neck, and almost sobbed, so great was his joy at meeting me.

"If I didn't think you dead, may I be d—d," blubbered the commissioner. "I don't know but you are now, but at any rate I'll hold on to you."

"That's just what I want you to do," I answered in a laughing tone, although I met the officer's embrace with one equally warm. "Be sure that you hold on to me. In fact, chain me as a prisoner, if you think it is best. Only don't let me be spirited off again."

"I'd like to see any one attempt it," was the reply, in the regular John Bull style of contempt for an inferior. "I'll blow 'em to pieces if they offer to lay a hand on you."

"I've been on the plains and on the hills, night and day, since we missed you," the commissioner said. "Tell me where you have been, and what has happened to you."

I commenced, and, in as brief a time as possible, related all that had transpired; how Mad Dick and the Pet had damaged my head, and my escape by the help of Jenny, and then informed the commissioner that a dish of coffee would not be amiss at that early hour in the morning. Now that

Murden had rescued me, I wondered if we could do nothing to save the girl, and capture Mad Dick and the Manchester Pet. They might be at the cattle station, even at the present time; and if such was the case, could we not pounce upon them, take them by surprise, and thus restore Jenny to the arms of her father, Sir William Byefield? I suggested the job to the commissioner, while we were drinking our coffee.

"And can it be done?" he asked.

"I think that it can."

"How far is it to the station?" asked Murden.

"Hang me if I know. We may be near it, or miles from it. Perhaps Maurice knows."

The lieutenant was called and interrogated. He knew where the "Haunted Station" was located. He thought that the distance was about five miles, in a south-west direction. I had wandered and crawled so far during the night, in spite of my weakness.

"But our horses," said Murden; "they are about used up; for recollect, I have been wandering all over the country in search of you, and therefore have had no rest."

"I know a place where there is water and grass, out a short distance from here," remarked Maurice.

"Then you had better lead us to it. We will remain there all day and recruit, and start in the evening."

"Agreed."

CHAPTER LXII.

THE HAUNTED STATION. — NO ONE AT HOME. — PERSEVERANCE OF A BLUE MAN. — IN SIGHT.

We found the place where grass and water were to be obtained; so, removing the saddles from our animals, we secured the horses in such a manner that they could not essape, while at the same time they would have plenty of feed during the day. Then we spread our blankets beneath the branches of some trees, and went to sleep just as the sun commenced darting its rays through the eastern horizon. I did not awaken until afternoon, and then, when I arose, more tired and stupid than when I lay down, I found the men hard at work over their horses, bathing their legs, rubbing them down, and otherwise preparing for the journey which we were to undertake as soon as the sun lost some of its heat, and travel would be safe.

"By the way," I asked of the commissioner, "what became of Sir William and Mr. Brown?"

"O, we all went to Bendigo, where we found fresh horses, and started out immediately to hunt you up, while Sir William and Mr. Brown, with the Bendigo fellows, explored a different tract of country, because we hoped that if you were dead we could find your body."

"And yet you did not go near the Haunted Station?"

"No, for I have always given it a wide berth. My men don't like it, and, to tell the truth, I don't."

"I thought that the redoubtable commissioner of Melbourne was afraid of nothing."

"Alive. I said nothing about the dead. I have a horror of being with the dead, or of passing a night all alone in a house where a deed of violence has been committed."

I did not pursue the conversation any further; but I marvelled that a man of the commissioner's nerves should allow such matters to have any influence on his mind. It was the first time that he had made such an acknowledgment.

At sundown the horses were saddled, and we were ready to start. The night was starlight, although so dark that we could not discern an object as large as a man three or four rods from us; so, when we were within a quarter of a mile of the station, Maurice checked his horse, and told us where we were. The signal to dismount was given, and obeyed. The horses were left in charge of two men, carefully concealed in the bushes, while the rest of us stole forward so that we could surround the hut, and if any one was in it effect a capture.

It was a lonely place, miles from any habitation, a long distance from road or trail; and the very ground over which we passed had been the scene of bloodshed and violence. No wonder I noticed more than one of the officers glancing over his shoulder, as though fearful of finding some horrible spectre close to his elbow; and yet all the men in the command were of tried and approved courage, and would not have trembled at facing any odds. At length Maurice suddenly stopped and whispered, —

"There's the hut; but you see no light in it. Every glim is doused, and there's no one there but goblins and demons."

"We will surround the hut," whispered Murden, while we had halted for a moment to consider the best course to pursue. "If the brutes are in it, we will nab them; if they ain't, we will see how long they have been gone, and whether they are likely to return. If they come back, we can take them."

"Good. Dispose of your men to the best advantage; but mind and let me cover the entrance to the hut."

"All right. It's just where I should have placed you."

The commissioner gave a few whispered directions, and the men, in obedience to them, separated, going to the right and left, stealing through the bushes with noiseless tread, until they had assumed the stations which Murden ordered them to take. Then we approached the hut, crawling on our hands and knees, so that we should not offer a mark for an enemy, in case one was concealed behind the walls of the station. We were determined to be cautious in our movements, because we knew how much there was at stake, and how necessary it was that we should effect the capture of two such desperate men, while at the same time I did not want a hair of Jenny's head injured, even by a chance shot.

We reached the door after some effort, and placed our ears to the cracks, to detect the least sound that transpired within. All was quiet. No light was visible: not even a breath was heard. With a long-drawn sigh, I was forced to the conclusion that Dick and Sykes were not there. Murden, after he was satisfied that no one was at home, arose from his knees and tried the door, determined to make an examination of the interior of the hut without a moment's delay. He placed his hand upon the rude latch, and gave the rickety door a push. It yielded, creaked on its hinges in a doleful manner, as though uttering protests at being disturbed, and then we entered the place. I lighted a match, and took a hasty survey of the interior of the building. On the table was a half-consumed candle in the neck of a bottle, some bones, bread, a bit of cheese, and an empty bottle that had at one time contained liquor. I lighted the candle, and then examined the room where I had been confined as a prisoner. In one corner was a pile of straw, clean, and thrown up with some degree of order. I overhauled it, and found sundry articles of dress that had been worn by Miss Jenny. I was folding them up with religious care when that rude Murden snatched them from my hands, and looked them over, or commenced doing so; but I could not permit such sacrilege, and took them from him by force, and replaced the delicate articles of linen where I had found them.

"Hang it, man, no harm in what I was doing," the commissioner muttered, as though he was more than half inclined to laugh.

"Perhaps not; but it seems so to me."

"Pshaw! What a ninny you are! But hang the soiled linen. Let us estimate how long the rogues have been gone. Can you give a guess?"

I looked at the bones, and saw that they were comparatively freshly picked. There was no mould on them, as on the cheese; so I arrived at the conclusion that the game we were in search of had not been gone more than six or eight hours. But would the parties return? That was a question that we could not reply to; so, after a few words of consultation, we concluded to extinguish the light, retire to the bushes, fight the mosquitos, and wait a day or two, and see what would happen.

Carefully replacing everything that had been moved, we retreated from the hut, closed the door, and once more gave instructions to the men. They were to lie in ambush until called out, and on no account were to show themselves, make a noise, or talk louder than a whisper. Murden and I retired to a clump of bushes, where we stretched ourselves, and conversed in a low tone. Then he entered into the most complete details of the manner in which he and Mr Brown had searched for me, after I had disappeared through the agency of Mad Dick and the Manchester Pet.

"Sir William was wild about you," the commissioner continued. "He couldn't have been more concerned if you had been his own son. He almost shed tears when we gave up all search for you."

I was gratified to hear this, for reasons which the reader can readily understand. I loved his fair, but rather coarse-talking daughter, and I hoped she had some affection for me; but I was not certain on that point. I could only surmise that she had some idea of loving me, provided her mind was not warped by prejudice. And then we talked of poor Amelia, the sister of Smith's wife. I repeated the account of her abduction by Moloch, her sufferings, strength of mind, amiability; and then I touched on her beauty and sweetness, and so well did I discourse that the commissioner, to my surprise, did not interrupt me. He seemed to listen, as though he was really pleased to see me so cheerful. How little did I know what was passing in his mind! and how little did he surmise the thoughts that agitated my heart! But at last I fell asleep, even while I was making a comparison between Jenny and Amelia. Both were very lovely; but I had my ideas as to which I thought the more entrancing. Murden had the same; but he did not venture to give utterance to them.

I must have slept two or three hours, when I was awakened by the cold. I was all of a shiver, for I had lain down without a blanket to cover me. I got up without disturbing Murden, and went in search of some of the men, who, I knew, had two or three blankets each. I found them on the alert, and ready to accommodate me. I took my choice of such as I wanted, and returned to my post; but I was hardly settled, when the commissioner was awakened by the same cause that had started me. He looked at the blankets that encompassed me, shivered with envy and cold, and then muttered something about its being a rich thing for one man to be warm while another was freezing, made an attempt to deprive me of one of my treasures, failed most signally, although I pretended I was asleep, and then the baffled policeman went off to his men, and had recourse to the appeal that I had used. He was successful, of course, and, with renewed caution to be vigilant, came back, and went to sleep; but, just as he was dropping off, I heard, or thought I heard, the name of Amelia upon his lips.

The night passed. Morning dawned, and then up came the sun, with all its Australian brilliancy and power. But there was not a sign of Mad Dick and the Pet; and, worse than all, I had not seen Jenny, except in my troubled dream. I was inclined to think the parties had escaped us. I, therefore, was in despair; but the commissioner, with a tenacity that was like John Bull, swore that he would remain in his position a week, but he would catch the rascals.

"Yes," he said, "I'll have those coves if they come back. I want to place Miss Jenny in your arms, and then in her father's, and by that time I shall be satisfied. You know you are dying to see her; so what is the use of denying it?"

"And for the help which you extend to me, of course payment is required."

"Perhaps;" and then the policeman turned away; but I thought I detected a blush on his weather-beaten cheek.

To prevent discovery, we moved back into the woods, where we could secrete our horses, make fires, and be as comfortable as the insects would permit us. We left one of the men in the brush to make observations, and report to us, by a peculiar signal, if Dick or Sykes should appear. With this understanding, we cooked our breakfast and smoked our pipes, lounged under the trees, killed half a dozen snakes, and chased as many more, slept, told stories, and suffered the day to pass as best we could; and yet there was no sign of the parties we wanted. I grew more and more confident that the scoundrels had changed their quarters.

and Murden was equally sure that they would turn up in the course of the day; and faith, to my great joy, he was right, for just about an hour before sunset one of the men signalized that something was in sight.

"Will you go and see what is the matter?" Murden asked; "and, if there is need of an advance, let me know it."

I complied. I worked my way through the brush until I reached the spot where the guard was located. He selected the place so that he could command a good view of the front of the station, no one being able to enter it and escape observation.

"What is it?" I asked, as I crawled to his side.

"See for yourself," he answered, and pointed in the direction of the trail that led towards Bendigo.

I followed his motion, and saw a one-horse vehicle slowly approaching, avoiding the bushes, yet heading for the hut. If Jenny was in the wagon, I was satisfied; and so I sat and watched the horse as he crawled towards the station; and at last I was convinced that Dick, Sykes, and Jenny were near me, and that the animal that drew them had been driven in a most unmerciful manner.

CHAPTER LXIII.

AN IMPORTANT CAPTURE. — THE PET'S REGRETS. — JENNY AND MAD DICK.

I WATCHED the party leave the vehicle with jealous eyes. First Mad Dick jumped out; then Sykes followed him in a lumbering, heavy way, as though he was too ponderous to move rapidly. Mad Dick offered his hand to Miss Jenny, to assist her in leaving the carriage; but the proud girl declined his aid, and I thought that I could see her expression of scorn as she pushed his arm aside, and leaped to the ground. We were not separated by any great distance, so that I could note her handsome face, and almost thought that I could see the color of her calm blue eyes. Miss Jenny gave her dress a shake, spoke a word to her father, and then entered the hut; while Mad Dick, after a coarse laugh, as though he was pleased with her airs and scorn, turned on the poor horse, that was making desperate efforts to nibble a few spears of grass, gave him a kick that sounded as though an empty flour barrel had been thrown from a window, and then swore for five minutes like a pirate of the olden time. Sykes made no attempt to restrain his rough companion. The former entered the hut, but soon returned with a bottle; and it must have contained liquor, for I noticed that the prize-fighter poured out some of the stuff, and handed it to Dick. He took part of it, put it to his mouth, threw back his head, and then returned the cup to Sykes; so that I imagined that it was empty when it reached the burly ruffian's hand. At any rate, the drink appeared to soften the heart of the bushranger; for he ceased swearing, and even was so much mollified that he commenced releasing the poor tired horse from the wagon. Then he removed the harness, and allowed the brute to stray over the prairie, find water and grass where it pleased.

"Go back to the commissioner," I said to the guard, "and tell him that the game has arrived, and that we await his pleasure as to an attack."

In a minute Murden crawled to my side, and was radiant with happiness at the prospect before him.

"I thought they would turn up again," said he. "You know that I told you so."

Of course I congratulated him on his forethought, for I was too well pleased to utter one word of disparagement. Jenny was near me, and I was satisfied.

"Now the question is," remarked the commissioner, "whether we shall pounce on them at once, or wait till they are asleep. If we make a rush, some of us will get hurt. If we wait, we may secure them without a fight."

"True; but can't we play a Yankee trick on them, and thus accomplish our purpose?"

"How?"

"I will tell you. We must induce the fellows to separate. We don't want to kill them if we can help it. Let the hangman do his work on them."

"I'm willing. State your plan."

"It is this. Let Jackson imitate the bleatings of a calf. I think that will call one of the scoundrels to the woods. They would like a change from mutton to veal, and if they hear the bleating, will think that a good opportunity has occurred for substituting one for the other."

"We could then ambush the fellow," muttered the commissioner.

"Yes, and serve him the same way that he served me."

"By the piper, but there would be some fun in that!" returned the commissioner, rubbing his hands with signs of glee.

"Of course there would. Don't you think that I want my revenge?"

"And you shall have it. Here, Jackson, let me hear you cry as naturally as though you were born a calf. If the rascals take the bait, lead them to the thickest of the bushes, and then we'll take care of them. I hope that but one at a time will come."

Jackson chuckled as though he had received a compliment; but after he had become more composed, he commenced bleating in such a manner as to win my unqualified approbation. The cries were similar to those uttered by a young calf, whose mother had deserted and left it without making proper provision for nourishment. After Jackson had uttered three or four mournful bleats, the two desperadoes came to the door, and looked in the direction from whence the sounds proceeded. They appeared to exchange words on the subject, for we saw Dick point to the bushes, where we were going, and then they listened, to be sure that they were not mistaken.

"Keep it up, Jackson," whispered the commissioner. "They are biting in a beautiful manner. You'll draw 'em just like a blister, or I'm much mistaken."

Jackson, still crawling among the bushes, uttered a few more plaintive cries. The listening desperadoes seemed satisfied that a strange calf was in the brush, and that it would pay to capture the same. The question between them seemed to be, who should go in search of the animal. At last it was decided in favor of Sykes, who was probably more tired of mutton than Mad Dick. The giant took a piece of harness from the wagon, and strode in the direction of the bushes; and as he advanced, Jackson receded, while the men glided through the bushes, in obedience to signals, so as to be all ready for the assault, when it should be ordered. Sykes undoubtedly thought that it would take him but a few minutes to return with the prize which he was in search of; but he entered the first line of bushes, and then the second, but still the bleating calf was the same distance from him. I was near enough to the prize-fighter to see his face; and I noted its expression. He hesitated for a moment when he was in the second line of bushes, and looked back, as though he was not satisfied to leave the hut, Mad Dick, and Miss Jenny without his commanding presence. But another and more plaintive bleat of the imaginary calf decided the ruffian. He thought that a few more steps would not take him far from the station, and that he would certainly be rewarded for his trouble by having veal cutlets for his supper. In ten minutes' time, we were a quarter of a mile from the station, and still Jackson kept up the delusion, while the ex-prize-fighter was no nearer the sound that lured him on, than he was when he started. This seemed to enter his thick skull after a while, for he stopped, uttered half a dozen imprecations, and turned to retrace his steps. Then Murden gave the signal to close in upon the man, and secure him at all events, but not to use firearms, except all other resources failed. Sykes had not taken more than a dozen steps, when two stout, active fellows sprang upon him; while at the same moment, two more started up from some bushes that were directly in his path.

The Pet was taken by surprise; but not so much so as to lose his presence of mind. He started back a little, then raised one of his ponderous fists, and planted it full in the face of the police officer on the left, while at the same time, he shook off the man on the right, and rushed forward to encounter the two sturdy fellows who were close upon him. At one of them he aimed a blow; but the man understood something of the art of boxing, and knowing that he could not ward off the huge fist, and that it was dangerous to encounter it, dropped to the ground, with wonderful alacrity, and thus escaped a blow that would have knocked him out of time and shape. The force with which the Pet struck at the officer, caused him to swerve a little from the perpendicular, and before he could recover his former position of defence, the second officer had darted forward, and fastened upon the giant, throwing both arms around his neck, and hugging as close as possible, so as to avoid a blow, or a succession of them, in return. For a moment the two men struggled, and but for a moment. The Pet exerted his huge strength, grasped the body of the officer in his immense hands, strained for a moment, and then raised his plucky adversary from the ground, and threw him at least ten feet, so that he landed in the bushes with a crash, as though every bone in his body was broken. During all this struggle, the Pet had not offered to use his revolver or knife, both of which were in his belt. The prize-fighter was so much more accustomed to natural weapons than artificial ones, that he had not thought of drawing his pistol or using his knife; but now, when he supposed that all his enemies were vanquished, that he could make a rush and escape to the hut where he could secure the assistance of Mad Dick if necessary, he laid his hand on his pistol, and would have drawn it, if Murden had not thought it time to interfere. Suddenly the commissioner, who was concealed in a clump of bushes near the scene of the struggle, arose, revolver in hand, and said, —

"It's no use, Sykes. If you offer to draw a pistol, I'll shoot, and I need not say that my aim is certain. You know me. Surrender, and save trouble."

I saw the brutal prize-fighter glare at the commissioner as

though a combat with fists would be desirable; but the fellow was evidently afraid of firearms, therefore hesitated for a moment, undecided what to do. That moment of hesitation was enough for Murden. Holding his revolver in one hand, he advanced towards the Pet, and I thought that the victory was won, that the giant would yield; but I was rather disappointed in my expectations.

"Come, Sykes, no nonsense. Give up at once, or you will miss it. You know me, and know what I want. I have force enough to take you, and a dozen just like you."

"Yes, I knows, Mr. Murden," the prize-fighter said. "I throws up the sponge. I'm knocked out of time."

He dropped his arms, in token of submission, and Murden putting trust in that sign, returned the revolver to his belt, and then took a step in advance, as though to put handcuffs on the fellow's wrists. Just at that moment, I left my place of concealment for the purpose of joining the commissioner, and as I did so, the Pet, with an angry growl, and an oath that came from his heart, bounded forward, caught the commissioner in his arms, and sought to throw him among the bushes. But the commissioner had no idea of being treated in such a manner. He was small, but with muscle like steel wire; so when he found the Pet was determined to be ferocious and treacherous, he just clung to him with so tenacious a grasp that he could not be thrown off, or even moved, as expected. Sykes strained for a moment or two, shook the slight form that he held in his grasp, but was unable to injure the commissioner, as he anticipated; and before he could proceed to extremities, I had rushed towards the parties, and all the men had done the same, determined to save the officer, even if we had to use our pistols, although orders had been given against firing a shot. As I neared the parties who were struggling, Sykes caught sight of me; and so great was his astonishment, that he dropped the commissioner as suddenly as though he was a ball of hot lead, and had burned his fingers.

"You here?" he roared, and uttered an oath that sounded intensely wicked.

"I'm here," I answered, in a calm tone.

"Curse you; you are my evil genius. I might have known that you was here. D—n you, I'll finish you, as I ought to have done some days ago."

He put his hand upon his revolver, intending to add murder to his other crimes; but one of the men who was in the rear saw the motion, and interfered in time to prevent it; for as the Pet touched the stock of his pistol, the police officer struck the giant a savage blow with his cutlass, and down he fell, with a gash about three inches long in his skull, nearly penetrating to the brain.

"Very well done, Sam!" cried Murden, in a cheery tone, and with a smile of approval. "The blow was well struck, and just in the right time. The least hesitation at such a moment would have cost us dear. Raise the brute's head, and let us see how he fares."

They turned the giant, and looked at the wound, and then at his face. His eyes were closed, and he breathed faintly; but we were not in the least alarmed for his safety. In fact, with a distinct remembrance of the savage blow that he had given me, and which had caused me hours of pain, and nearly a fractured skull, I did not have much pity for the wretch, and was half inclined to feel sorry that my hand had not inflicted the blow; for I owed him no good will after the treatment that I had experienced when we met.

"Put on the bracelets," said the commissioner; "he may be playing 'possum. Bind up his head, some of you. So, that will do."

The Pet opened his eyes when the irons were secured to his wrists.

"Well, old fellow, how goes it?" Murden asked. "Do you feel like making a full confession, and shaming the devil?"

"My head!" the giant murmured.

"O, hang your head. We have got other things to attend to. If you intend to grumble in this manner, I shall begin to think that we have caught the calf which you were in pursuit of."

"You allers was hard on me, Mr. Murden," whined the Pet, whose spirit seemed a little dashed by the treatment which he received.

"Because you never stood up fair and square, and fought like a man. You always struck foul blows when it was just as easy to have given them above the belt. You furnished us with a little information, but you took good care that it didn't amount to much, unless you had a grudge against some poor devil. The fact of it is, Sykes, I've got enough facts to swamp you, and I mean to do it, unless you open your mouth on certain subjects."

The Pet shut his mouth in a resolute manner, and scowled at me as though I was the author of all his misfortunes, and then, finding that it did him no good to make faces at me, turned to the commissioner.

"I s'pose," he said, "that I can make terms, even if I don't throw up the sponge?"

"I know about all that, you know," the commissioner rejoined, in an indifferent tone. "To be sure, there are some things respecting Sir William's daughter which need clearing up; but as Mother Brown has peached, it don't matter much whether you blab or hold your tongue."

"Curse the old hag!" growled the prize-fighter. "If she'd been put out of the way, this wouldn't have happened, and Jenny wouldn't have knowed no father but me."

"It's in consequence of your own brutality, you big rascal," retorted the commissioner. "Had you protected the woman whom you ruined, you would not now be here with a broken head, and a chance on the roads that will require all your days to work out. Mother Brown has only acted like all human beings — she has turned on the one that spurned her, and means to have revenge. I don't blame her."

"Had we not better postpone this discussion until some more convenient time?" I asked. "Already the shades of night are falling, and we are some distance from the hut."

"Right," answered Murden. "We must have Mad Dick before many hours. It won't do to leave him in the company of Miss Jenny for any length of time. He s a dangerous man."

When we reached the clearing in which the station was located, the sun was down, and darkness had already commenced, so that a person moving through the bushes could not be seen unless you were close upon him. I saw a light in the hut, and suggested to Murden that we should crawl towards it, and see what was going on, leaving the men to follow at their leisure. To this the officer assented; and so we dropped upon our hands and knees, and went forward as fast as possible until we reached the hut, when we exercised more caution, and moved deliberately, until we gained a position that enabled us to hear and note all that was going on between Dick and Jenny. They were seated at the table, the former with a glass of grog in his hand, and the latter, looking pale and melancholy, gnawing at a piece of bread as though she was hungry, tired, and out of patience.

CHAPTER LXIV.

MAD DICK MAKES PROPOSALS.—A SCORNFUL REJECTION.—VIOLENCE.—TO THE RESCUE.

For a few minutes, Jenny and Dick, the parties we were watching, did not speak. Dick was too much pleased to open his mouth, except to receive the liquor which he held in his hand, and Jenny seemed too depressed to utter a word. But at last the bushranger emptied his tin cup, and then remarked,—

"Your guv'ner ain't up to time, lass. If he gets lost in the bush, while a lookin' for that calf, it 'll trouble him to find his way out agin."

"He has been gone long enough to eat a calf," Jenny remarked; "I'll go and see if I can't find him."

She started towards the door, which stood open, so that

we could see all that transpired; but Mad Dick sprang up and interposed.

"No," he said, "yer can't go now. I don't care much if yer dad is lost, but I can't afford to lose yer. I loves yer too well, lass, for that. Me and you must know each other better nor we do now."

The impudent scoundrel. I was almost inclined to shoot him down like a dog. In fact I did have my revolver all ready; but Murden restrained me, and kept me quiet.

"Let me pass!" cried Jenny.

"No, girl, yer don't pass out of this hut to-night. I wants yer to listen to me; so yer may as well squat down while I talk."

"I won't sot down!" cried Jenny, in her haughtiest tone.

"Yes, yer will, lass!" and the ruffian advanced towards her, and attempted to throw his arms around her neck; but she retreated, manifesting, however, no signs of alarm. She was too proud to exhibit the least weakness. "Will take a cheer?" asked the bushranger.

"No, I won't — there now," was the answer.

"Yer had better, lass, 'cos I has somethin' to tell yer that will make yer think. Take that cheer, and let's have no more fuss about it."

"The governor must soon return," the girl said, and cast an anxious look at the door.

"Never yer mind him, lass;" and the ruffian commenced filling his pipe. "If he comes I shall cut my yarn short. If he don't I shall jist make them blue eyes of yourn open wide. You see if I don't."

Jenny looked a little scornful and incredulous; but still she had enough of woman's curiosity to listen. The bushranger lighted his pipe, and puffed out volumes of smoke; but at last he said, —

"Does yer know why yer guv'ner brought yer here? why he cut from the city?"

"'Cos the traps was arter him for somethin'."

"Yes, they was arter him, but it warn't for no common thing that they wanted to clap their mawleys on him."

Jenny looked at the bushranger in an attentive manner.

"In fact, lass, it was all on your account that the traps took a notion to trip the Pet."

"Mine! What have I done?"

"You ain't done much; but it is all on your account."

"How?"

"Wall, lass, ye see the Pet ain't yer guv'ner, and never was. That's the long and short on't. You'd know it some time, and I may as well tell yer as another"

"What do yer mean?"

"Just what I say. The Pet ain't yer dad, and never was."

"Not my father?"

The girl arose from the table in her excitement, and looked at the bushranger as though she would read his soul.

"It's a lie!" she said, at last.

Mad Dick smiled, and still continued smoking

"Yer gov'ner told me the whole yarn, this arternoon, while we was waitin' to pick up a team. It ain't likely that he would lie to me."

The girl still continued to gaze at the desperate man, uncertain whether to believe him or not.

"Yer just set down," Mad Dick said, "if yer wants me to continue the yarn. Yer will find it mighty funny"

The girl sat down, and prepared to listen.

"Yes, as I said afore, the Pet did spin the whole yarn this arternoon, while we was waitin' for the wagon what we took from the miner. I hinted to him that it was rather tough for a man like me to be without a nice little wife, and that I shouldn't object to takin' a lass like you."

Miss Jenny started up, disgust and passion on her face at the very thought of uniting her fate with such a ruffian as Mad Dick.

"Keep cool," the man remarked, and continued to smoke in the most placid manner. "I ain't got to the most interesting part as yet. You see, Miss Jenny, I ain't much of a pertic'lar man, so I'd as lives take you, as a gal what could do more work. I told the Pet so, and said that I'd overlook some things, on account of your mug."

"Did yer?" and the girl sneered, as she asked the question.

"O, yes; I yarned it quite free with the Pet. He said he'd like just such a brave cove as me for a son-in-law; but that the fact of it was, he had no darter to give me."

"He said that, did he?" asked Jenny.

"Yes. And more'n that; 'cos when I said that I thought you'd do, he said you wasn't no flesh and blood of his — that he stole you, when you wasn't any bigger than a kitten; and that you was the darter of a rich nobleman in hold Hingland."

"Did he say all that?" asked Jenny, after a long-drawn breath.

"Just as true as anything I ever said," replied the bushranger, in a sincere tone. "He told me the name of the nob what is your dad; but I ain't got much ear for names, and so I disremembers it. At any rate, the Pet said that the old cock was in Melbourne, a lookin' for yer, and a huntin' up things, and that the traps, headed by that blasted old scoundrel of a rat, the commissioner, was all ready to lay hands on him, if he hadn't stepped out as he did."

"O, is that the reason why we left the city so sudden?" asked Miss Jenny.

"Yes, 'cos the Pet wanted time to make terms with the nob, and get a big haul of money. He meant to save his neck and fill his pockets at the same time. He's a smart one, is the Pet, and can even cheat that confounded Murden."

Here the commissioner uttered a grunt of dissent, which attracted the notice of Mad Dick. for he sprang to his feet, and said, —

"The devil, here's the guv'ner come back, arter all. Mum's the word, yer know."

The bushranger came to the door, and looked out; but we had taken the precaution to roll close to the side of the hut, where the darkness was so dense that we could not be seen.

"Is that you, Sykes?" asked Dick, listening for a response. There was no answer.

"It wasn't him, arter all," the fellow said, "But it's most time he come along, if he means to come to-night."

After this cool assurance, the bushranger returned to his chair and pipe.

After a silence of a few moments, Jenny looked up, and said, "If what you has blabbed to me is true, just you take me to my new guv'ner, and let me see what kind of a cove he is."

Mad Dick puffed away at his pipe in a reflective mood.

"It can't be done, just yet, lass. If the Pet shouldn't come back, I'll think of it," returned the bushranger. "In the mean time, don't yer say one word of this 'ere to him, 'cos he has his plans; and them 'ere plans ain't no good to yer."

"I don't believe it," Miss Jenny cried; "you has some motive in tellin' me this."

Mad Dick laughed in a subdued manner. Then he laid his pipe upon the table, went to a pile of straw in one corner, took out a bottle of liquor concealed there, opened it, poured out near a mug full, and said, —

"I gives yer, Miss Jenny, yer 'ealth, and may you soon be the affectionate wife of yer 'umble servant, Mad Dick."

Miss Jenny started to her feet, her face all of a blaze with rage and excitement.

"How dare yer talk to me in that 'ere style?" she asked. "Don't yer do so no more, or I'll leave the hut."

"And where will yer go, my daisy? The natives is around; and if you miss them, there is lots of bushrangers to pick yer up. Come, just be a little reasonable, my chicken; and listen to a man what has his ups and downs, as well as most folks."

"Well, don't yer talk to me about such stuff ag'in," the girl remarked, and down she sat.

The bushranger smiled in a peculiar manner, but did not promise that he would remain silent.

"Yer see, my deary, that I'se a bad man, as the traps says that I is, which don't signify, 'cos they is awful liars. Well, such bein' the case, what can I do? I must do the best I can; that is a sound argament, and no one will dispute it. Wall, what is the best? Let me see; I am a houtlaw, and a price is set on my head. Very good. It's some consolation to know that my head is wallable; but it's worth more to me than it is to any other man. Now, deary, listen to me sharp, 'cos here comes the whole pint of the argament. I've tried bushrangin'. I've seen enough of it to satisfy most any white man. I wants a little rest, and a chance to enjoy the dosh what I has in the ground all over the country. Through you I can do it."

Jenny looked at him with a porter-house glare that reminded me of scenes in the Red Lion, when she and I used to quarrel.

"Yes, lass," the bushranger went on to say, not paying the least attention to the scowl that passed over the girl's face, "you is the one that I has set on to help me out of the bloody fix what I is in. I didn't think of such a thing till the Pet told me who you was, this arternoon. Then I saw a chance for my life, and Mad Dick isn't the one to throw it away."

"What do yer mean?"

"I'll tell yer, lass, in a few vords. I wants a vife to comb my hair and viskers. You is the one for me Yer see, lass, if yer marries me, then I has yer to save my neck. Yer tells yer new guv'ner that yer loves me, and all that, and that he must use his influence to have me pardoned. He does so on your account, and then I becomes a moral and respected member of society. Do yer see?"

"How dare yer make such a proposal to me, when yer know that I hate yer?" demanded Jenny, in a fierce tone. "I will remain here no longer to be insulted. Do yer think that I would marry such a brute as you? I scorn and detest yer. Never speak to me on such a subject again."

"It's most time to interfere," whispered Murden. "The devil is being aroused. We must be prepared, or harm may come to the gal."

"Set down there!" said Dick, in a low but threatening tone, as Jenny moved towards the door.

"Do yer think I'm a nigger, to be talked to in that sort of manner?" the dauntless girl asked. "No, I'm no slave. I'll go where I please, and for all yer!"

Mad Dick left his chair and rushed towards the door, and so sudden was his movement that he reached it before Jenny.

"Go back!" he said, in a low, sullen tone.

"I won't," she replied. "I'm goin' to look for the old man. He'll protect me, even if he ain't my guv'ner, as yer say."

"Yer can't leave this hut to-night; and yer can't speak with the Pet, even if he should come back. Now go and take that cheer, and hear me, 'cos yer must be my wife. There's no gettin' away from it."

He put out his hands and suddenly seized Jenny around her waist, and pressed her to his rough bosom. She struggled fiercely to get free; but the ruffian held her firm, so that she could not move her body, although both of her hands were at liberty.

"Let me go!" she said, in a threatening tone.

"No, I won't," was the answer. "I likes this."

The girl appeared to be aroused to a feeling of desperation at the answer. She turned a little, so that she could use her hands, and then, with a shrill cry, made a dash at his face. Her finger-nails must have been long and sharp, for I saw a few drops of blood follow her savage blows. Two or three times the girl drew blood, and at the same moment she called the bushranger all the vile names that a long attendance in a beer saloon placed at her disposal. At last Mad Dick grew tired of such work, and all the devil of his nature showed itself. He put one hand around her slender, graceful throat, and hissed, between his clinched teeth, —

"Blast yer for a ugly cat, what scratches! You won't be kind to one what wants to be kind to you. Now take this, will yer?"

It was evident at a glance that the man determined to murder her. He was desperate — mad with her scorn, and furious at the number of scratches she had inflicted upon him.

"Help!" shrieked Jenny, who surmised the man's intention, and had no desire to die just then.

"This has gone far enough," I whispered to Murden; "it is time for us to interfere."

"Yes, I think it is," was the answer.

"Come," I said, and arose and stole into the hut.

I was within two feet of the bushranger, and yet he had not noticed me; neither had Jenny. I raised my pistol, intending to knock him down with it; but just at that moment, Murden, who did not believe in half measures, fired his revolver, placing it close to the side of Mad Dick, so that the ball should pass completely through the man's body. The report of the pistol was clear and sharp. The bushranger uttered a yell of surprise, released his hold of the girl, staggered back a pace or two, and then plunged forward and fell to the floor, and the next instant I received in my arms the insensible form of Miss Jenny.

CHAPTER LXV.

AN AGREEABLE SURPRISE. — FATHER AND DAUGHTER. — THE PET'S REGRETS.

The report of the pistol startled the men, who were in ambush around the hut; so they poured into the room in an unceremonious manner, pistols in hand, ready to shoot down all who opposed them. The police looked to Murden for instructions. They did not manifest the least surprise at the scene before them, for they were used to deeds of violence, and had seen too much blood flow to care for the little that oozed from the bushranger's body.

"Take the fellow up, and carry him out of doors," said Murden — "carefully, for he has some life in him yet."

"Not as much as I desire," groaned the bushranger. "I only wish I was on my feet, without this accursed hole in my body, I'd serve you a trick that would repay me for all the sufferings I now endure. But Mad Dick's time is almost up, and what 's the use of his bouncing?"

"Take away his knife and pistol," the commissioner said in a sharp tone, for his eye detected a movement on the part of the bushranger that appeared as though he was still anxious to avenge his injuries.

In fact, Dick had raised one hand in the direction of the butt of his pistol; and, though the movement was a rapid one, the officer detected it. The men obeyed the order, and Dick submitted without a struggle, for it would have been useless in his condition. They bore the man out of the hut, and laid him on the ground, while one of the men, who understood something of surgery, stripped off the bushranger's clothes, and examined the wound by the aid of candle-light.

"Well," said Murden, turning to me, "do you intend to stand there all night, holding the girl in your arms? It is agreeable, I've no doubt, but still rather inconvenient to the lass. I suppose that she would recover in a few minutes if placed upon that straw, and her face wet with water. What do you think?"

I thought so too; so I raised her in my arms, and carried her to the straw and laid her down, then wet her face with water, and at last had the pleasure of seeing her large blue eyes open and rest on my face.

"Do you know me, Jenny?" I asked, in a low tone.

"Yes, I know you."

"And are you glad to see me?"

"Yes, 'cos yer come just in time to save me. But you is still with the traps?"

"Yes, and these same traps saved your life. Remember that, Jenny."

"I will. Now give me some of that water to drink. Yer needn't keep your arms around my neck; I can do without 'em."

She wet her lips with water, and then asked, "What did you go off for the other day? I don't like it."

"To save my life. Your father and Mad Dick would

have killed me, or kept me in custody as long as they could That is the reason why I went."

"You ain't tellin' me lies?" asked this charming maiden, looking into my eyes, as though to discover if I spoke the truth.

"I never tell lies," I answered, in a grave tone, as if to convince her that I was above the common herd.

"O, don't yer? then you is different from other men. I s'posed that all men yarned it a little."

"Then consider me different from other men, now and hereafter. Whenever I speak to you, it will be with a tongue of truth."

"O, hang yer sermons. I want yer to tell me how yer came here; you was just in time, wasn't yer?"

"Yes, thank Heaven. A few moments longer, and it would have been too late. The ruffian had determined to murder you."

"Is yer really glad that he didn't?" asked the young girl; and a look of tenderness shone from her eyes — such a glance as I had never seen in them before.

"Can you doubt it?" I asked in a whisper; for I did not care to have any one hear me when I was in a tender mood.

"O, I don't know; you coves tell the queerest kind of stories sometimes. I've heard a good many of 'em. All the coves — the flash ones, I mean — what come into the Red Lion used to tell me all sorts of nonsense, when I'd listen to 'em. Sometimes I'd hear 'em, and sometimes I wouldn't. It was just as I felt."

"But you will never have occasion to again hear bad language."

"Can yer spell all the hard words yer use?" asked this charming child of nature.

"I hope so," I answered, although I could hardly keep from laughing at the question.

"Then yer must know more'n my guv'ner, 'cos he can't spell at all. But now I think of it, what did Mad Dick mean by saying that Sykes wasn't my guv'ner? Yer can tell me something about it, can't yer?"

"Yes, I know all about it, and could have told you at the time I was a prisoner here."

"Why didn't yer, then?"

"For several reasons. You were cross with me, and suspicious at the same time. If I informed you, I should not have been believed."

"I don't know; perhaps I should have thought your gab was all right."

Just then Murden entered the station. He gave us a sharp glance, saw that we were quite satisfied with each other, whistled a bar of "God save the Queen," and then said,—

"Dick is gone. He stuck out to the last, and died like a bushranger. One devil the less on earth; that's some consolation."

"Is he dead?" asked Jenny.

"Yes; just slipped his cable, and went up. He died with a hardened heart; for although I asked, even begged him to tell me where his money was buried, he said that he'd see me d—d first. And with that he gasped, and went off on a new ranging expedition. Well, a man who won't tell the police where a treasure is buried will never get to heaven; that is one good thing."

"Well," said Jenny, with a shudder, "though the man abused me, still he had some kindness in his heart, and I'm almost sorry that he's dead. He and the guv'ner was just as thick as two thieves."

"Would you like to see Sykes?" I asked.

"Of course I would. Where is he? Dick said he was lost in the bush, while chasing arter a calf."

"He was arrested by the police, while in pursuit of the animal, and is now a prisoner. Let him come in, if you please, Mr. Murden."

"Certainly," said the commissioner. "Bill, bring in the Pet."

The Pet did not present a prepossessing appearance, for the reason that the blood from the cut on his head had flowed on his face, and dried there in spots, resembling a North American savage in the war path

"You're the cove what hit me the rap on the head," the prize-fighter said, as soon as he saw that I stood before him.

"No; I am sorry to state that my hand didn't do that job; but it is some slight recompense for the blow which you gave me a few days ago. You remember, do you not?" and I pointed to my head, which was still bandaged.

The Pet smiled, in a prize-fighting sort of way, as though he thought we were even, so far as punishment was concerned. And then he turned to Jenny.

"The traps has me, at last, girl, and I must do the best I can. They can't do nothin' to you, lass; so you had better go where I told you, and keep quiet till I turn up again. They can't do much with me. They has no proof."

"There is where you are mistaken," I replied. "Here is the proof," and I pointed to Jenny.

"What does you mean?" demanded the bushranger, with a pretended look of surprise, for Jenny had manifested no sign of recognition since he had entered the hut.

"It means," I answered, "that your crime is discovered, and that Miss Jenny is aware of it. Mother Brown has made a full confession, in the presence of the commissioner, Sir William Byfield, and myself. The game is up. You may as well acknowledge it, and make a full confession."

The Pet appeared a little staggered at the thought that his rascality was known to the girl who had so long called him father. He glanced at her, and his face wore an expression which showed he was affected. That look touched Jenny's heart, and I was rejoiced to know it, for it proved that she had one, tender and true, but that circumstances of a peculiar nature were required to bring out the full expression. She went towards the Pet, and threw her arms around his burly form,—his neck she could not reach,—and laid her head against his stout breast; and the prize-fighter raised his manacled hands, and placed them on the girl's head, struggled for a moment to control his feelings, found that he could not, and then allowed large tear-drops to escape from his eyes, and trickle down his rough cheeks.

"It's a pity you couldn't have had a little feeling some years ago," the commissioner remarked, thinking that the display was a hypocritical one.

Sykes made no reply. He was not prepared to resent such sneers or taunts. He was too much humiliated for that. I gave the commissioner a look that he understood, and shook my head. He nodded in reply; and then we had the pleasure of listening to the conversation that ensued between Jenny and the man she had always known as her father.

"Well, lass, I is down now, and the traps is up, and it's all on your account. But I loves you, lass, just as well as though you was—"

The bushranger paused, and seemed reluctant to proceed.

"I knows what yer mean," Jenny whispered. "Yer ain't my guv'ner."

"No, I ain't, lass. I had you took when you was a little wee thing, and I has kept you ever since. But I loves you, lass, just as well as if I was your own guv'ner."

"Yer havn't allers been kind to me," Jenny murmured, tears streaming down her cheeks, "and yer has sometimes made money out of me, 'cos I had a handsome face, and the men liked to look at it. Yer knows yer has made 'em drink when they didn't need any more, simply by tellin' them that I should leave the bar, if there wasn't more calls; but for all of that, I is sorry to see yer down in the mouth, 'cos I kinder cares for yer."

"I hopes yer does, lass," groaned the Pet, the tears still falling.

"Yes, I does care for yer," the girl said. "If you ain't my guv'ner, who is?"

"I can't tell yer just yet," answered the Pet. "Give me a little more time."

"No," she said. "There's no time like the present. I knows most all about it, now. Arter yer was gone for the calf, Mad Dick told me some things that caused my eyes to open; and then he wanted me to marry him, so that my new guv'ner could save his neck"

"The scoundrel," muttered the Pet. "If I'd been here, I'd mashed him. I'd sent him to the devil in no time."

"So you may as well tell me all. Peachin' will do you good."

"You may as well make a clean breast of it," said I, stepping forward. "We know all the means you have employed to steal the child, and transport her to Australia. Every movement has been traced, every act recorded."

"I don't promise mercy," the commissioner remarked. "But still I say, peach, and have done with it."

"I know you has been on my track for some time past," the Pet said, in a reflecting tone; "but I know'd all that was goin' on, and when you got ready to strike, I cut and run, 'cos I thought I could play shy for a time, and that all would blow over."

"You thick-headed fool, what nonsense that was!" returned the blunt commissioner. "You might have known better."

The prize-fighter winced a little, but managed to remark that all were not so full of science as Mr. Murden.

"But that has nothin' to do with my question," Jenny said, in an impatient tone. "Tell me who my guv'ner is."

The Pet gave a mighty gulp, as though something was sticking in his throat, and then sighed as he answered, —

"Your guv'ner is one of the nobs of old Hingland, lass. Me and him was quite intimate at one time. He backed me when I fought the British Butcher, and I won that fight arter thirty rounds, what took just two hours and a half."

"I knows all that," returned the impatient girl. "How many times are yer goin' to tell me of it?"

"Well, you see, lass, it was a game fight, and made a stir in old Hingland at the time. Well, the next fight I had was with —"

"Hang your fights! Will yer tell me the name of my new guv'ner?"

"I hates him, lass."

"And yet you had no cause to hate him," replied a deep, grave voice, that I instantly recognized, although it fell upon my ears so unexpectedly that it startled me as much as if I had heard a response from the grave.

All but Murden were surprised. The commissioner looked as though the interruption was not entirely unexpected. We turned to get a view of the new-comer, and there he stood, apparently as calm as when I last parted from him, his blue eyes looking humid with the emotion that stirred his heart to its foundation. The Pet released Jenny from his embrace, and staggered back as though a bullet had passed through his breast; but as his eyes fell upon the baronet's face, he exclaimed, in a low tone, —

"It is Sir William!"

"Yes, it is Sir William — the man whom you have so terribly wronged, who has been on your track for some months past, and who now has evidence sufficient to bring you to justice."

"Yes, I has wronged you," returned the Pet, with an averted head, and with a voice that was husky with emotion."

"And yet I had never injured you, as you well knew," answered the baronet.

"You wouldn't back me when I was tryin' to make a match with the Northampton Slasher," said the old prize-fighter, as though that was an excuse for his conduct.

"Because I had previously informed you I was to be married, and desired to break with all my old disreputable associates. It was no idle information that I sent. I meant it; and in spite of the efforts that were made to draw me back to the vortex of a wild life, I remained firm. This you were aware of, and yet you thought that you could strike me to the heart by stealing my only child."

Jenny started forward, her hands clasped, and her sweet face expressing all the internal emotions that she felt. She began to comprehend that her real father stood before her.

"Yes, I took her, Sir William," the Pet answered.

"I know you did, and misery enough you caused a happy household by such conduct. Now do what you can in the way of restitution."

"I will, Sir William," was the answer, but in a tone that showed that the heart of the Pet was touched.

"Then restore to my arms the daughter whom you stole from me."

"And if I does, Sir William, will you overlook all the faults what I has committed?"

"I will make no promises. You cannot keep me from my child, even if you lie about the matter. I know her, and all about her."

"She's a good girl, Sir William, and can sell more beer and make change faster than any girl what I ever see'd. She can, indeed."

The aristocratic face of Sir William expressed the deepest disgust at this information.

"I don't want you to have me up afore the beaks, Sir William, on the charge of baggin' the lass, 'cos I has allers treated her well, and she'll say so."

"Tell me, is this the one whom you caused to be abducted?" asked the baronet, and pointed to Jenny.

The Pet hesitated for a moment, as though he would like to tell a lie if he dared to; but a stern glance from the police commissioner decided him, and he answered, —

"Jenny is yer darter, Sir William."

"I knew it all along," was the quiet response; but a deep sigh escaped the father as he opened his arms.

For a moment Jenny hesitated and blushed to her eyes at the thought of having a stranger's arms around her; but at last she rushed forward with a glad cry, and fell upon her father's breast. Sykes uttered a howl and a snivel at the sight; and upon my word I saw tears trickle down his rough face.

"Come," I said to Murden, "let us leave them alone. This scene is too sacred to be witnessed by us."

"Right," was the prompt answer. "We'll go."

He touched the Pet on the arm, and motioned to him to leave the hut; and the fellow obeyed, although he uttered a sob that seemed to come from the bottom of his heart as he did so. Outside of the hut I found camp fires brightly

burning, and a large number of blue-coated police; and ther I learned for the first time that Mr. Brown and his men had arrived in company with Sir William — a fact that was communicated to Murden when he allowed the Pet to have an interview with Miss Jenny. The commissioner had planned the surprise; and an agreeable one it was on some accounts

CHAPTER LXVI.

A LITTLE LOVE. — A FEW EXPLANATIONS, AND A TABLEAU.

In the course of an hour or so, the baronet passed from the hut. Murden, who was all attention, went to meet him, and proffer his services. To my surprise, Sir William put his arm through Murden's, and walked away from the camp fires.

"The baronet is growing considerate," I thought.

I re-filled my pipe, and commenced smoking, wondering how Miss Jenny would now deport herself, since she had found a new father, and a position in society that might turn the brain of many a young and giddy girl.

"Well," I sighed, "it's nothing to me, after all. Her father will take her to England, will give her a good education, and then she will be introduced into society as *la belle Australienne*, marry some one with a title, and forget her Yankee friends." As I thus thought, I looked up and saw the girl standing in the door of the hut, as if she wanted to speak to some one. I imagined that she was waiting for her father, so did not go near her; but Mr. Brown did, and came back saying, —

"Devilish pretty girl, ain't she? Don't want to see me though. You're the one. She asked after you, and said that she wanted to speak to you. Go and see her."

I threw aside my pipe, and went towards Jenny, my heart trembling as though it would deprive me of strength. It was in vain that I attempted to regain composure. I was but a coward in the presence of that girl, ignorant, yet handsome as a picture of the Madonna; proud as a duchess when she was but a bar-maid; wilful in her fancies in her lowly station, what must she be now that she has found herself the heiress of one of the oldest houses in England? These thoughts passed through my mind as I walked towards the young lady, as she stood in the door-way, shading her eyes with her well-formed hand, so that she could look forth and scan the several groups of men who were clustered around the camp fires.

"Mr. Brown informs me that you wish to speak to me," I said, addressing the girl so unexpectedly that she started and retreated several paces into the hut, as though my words had alarmed her.

"Law, how you frightened me!" she said. "I did not know you was so near. Why didn't yer let me know you was comin'?"

"You might have known that I would come if you sent for me," I remarked, in a low tone.

"Would you? Indeed! Well, I'm glad to hear it. But come in. I want you to see me, now I am a great lady. O, I've had such a long palaver with my new guv'ner. He's ever so good, and he kissed me every time I made a mistake in talkin'. What do you think of that?"

"I should like no better privilege," I answered, with a low bow and a smile.

"Jest like yer impertinence. You ought to be ashamed of yerself, that's what yer had."

"I don't think there is much cause to be ashamed of kissing a pretty girl," I remarked, in a jesting tone.

"Did you ever kiss one?" Miss Jenny asked.

"Yes, several."

"Then let me tell you they was mean things, and that if I ever see'd 'em, I'd scratch their eyes out. I don't want any more to say to yer."

She retreated into the house, and would have shut the door, but I followed and prevented her.

"Ah, but let me explain, Miss Jenny. It was before I

had the pleasure of your acquaintance that I kissed the young girls."

"I don't care; it was a mean piece of business, and you had ought to be ashamed of yourself; that's what you had."

"But listen to me for a moment!" I cried. "While I was kissing them, I thought I was kissing you."

This appeared to confound her, and she seemed not to know how to construe my words. At last she said,—

"If you liked me you wouldn't have kissed the mean things."

"It is because I wanted some one to love that I kissed them. Now you should be satisfied."

"Well, won't you make such a mistake again?" the young lady asked, as she turned her diamond rings, which glittered on her fingers, and then stole a look at my face.

"How can I tell? I must have some one to love."

"Well, haven't you got some one?" and the large blue eyes were raised to my face with a look that expressed surprise.

"No, Jenny, no one."

She hesitated for a moment, and then took a step towards me, and held out her hands, while by the poor light which the candle gave, I noticed that her face, so beautiful at all times, in anger and repose, was suffused with blushes.

"Then you don't care for me, do you?"

She laid her hand on mine, and looked up in my face with an expression that an angel might have envied.

"I do care for you, Jenny," I said; and there I stopped.

"Well."

My declaration did not seem to satisfy her. Her face expressed a wish for more forcible language.

"Well," she repeated, and seemed to wait for something.

"I can't speak to you now, Jenny, as I could have spoken to you had your father been other than he is. It is useless for me to tell you the feelings of my heart."

"I don't know about that. If you tell me how much you like me, it seems to me that it would be pleasant sort of gab. Come, go ahead."

She came close to me, so close that her red lips were very near mine, and I felt the sweetness of her breath as it touched my cheek. It was rather a tempting position for a young and enthusiastic admirer of beauty; but I managed to control my feelings, as I asked, —

"What would you have me say, Jenny?"

"Say what is next to your heart," she whispered.

"I dare not. Better that I keep silent."

"Why?" and her large blue eyes were opened to their widest extent.

"On account of your position in life, since you have found a father."

"O, gammon!" she cried, in a petulant manner. "I'd rather have a husband than a father. I'll go ten to one on it. You can't kiss a guv'ner likes what you can a lover."

What could I do or say after such a blunt speech? It was evident that she expected a declaration; and was I ready to make one? I felt her breath fan my cheek, while her red lips were advanced an inch or two nearer my own, and one of her hands found its way around my neck, and the other rested on my shoulder; and then a pair of blue eyes, the handsomest the world ever saw (I thought so at the time, and even at the present moment I have my ideas on the subject), were raised in such a beseeching, seductive manner, that all my self-control vanished in an instant, and I found that I was but a poor, miserable mortal, after all, no more capable of withstanding the blandishments of a handsome girl, than a hungry man can refuse food when it is offered him. In an instant my stout arms were around her, and she was clasped close to my heart, while on her red lips and beautifully formed mouth I rained down kisses, the first that I had ever taken, and the sweetest that I ever knew.

At length, after I had kissed her a dozen times or more, I began to realize what I was doing; therefore was inclined to pause; but the little jade nestled closer, and whispered, —

"Don't throw up the sponge jist yet. I'm game to the ast."

What a horrid way to express her feelings, and to tell me

that she was not tired of the caresses which I bestowed upon her! But I was too much in love to think of her words just at that present time. I only thought of her handsome face, and the remarkable change in her manner. But all things must have a termination; and so at last Jenny raised her head from my shoulder, and asked, —

"Do you love me?"

"Yes, I have loved you for a long time, although I was hardly conscious of it."

"But I mean, do you love me as a wife should be loved?"

"Yes."

"Then you may have me;" and the enthusiastic young lady threw her arms around my neck, and put up her lips to be kissed.

"But you forget that you have a father, who may enter his protest against the arrangement."

"I don't care if he does. I likes you better than I does him. If he ain't satisfied with the match, he needn't bet on it. I stake everything, and run all risks. Don't I?"

"Yes, you encounter some risks, for you have not been acquainted with me more than two months."

"Well, I'm certain that you is a gentleman; that you'll treat me well, and won't love any body else but me."

"And what will you do to insure all this?" I asked, with a smile at her earnestness.

"O, I'll go in trainin'," was the prompt answer.

"Do what?"

"Why, I'll make myself worthy of you."

"How?"

I began to see that she had more character and more feeling than I gave her credit for.

She raised her head from my bosom, placed both her small, delicately shaped hands on my shoulder, and said, —

"You see I ain't had no advantages, don't you?"

"I fear that such has been the case."

"You must see it, 'cos a bar-maid don't know much except how hard most men drinks."

"But I think that most men drink very easy."

"Don't blab just now, but just listen to me," the young girl said. "I never had any larnin', of any account, and now is the time I miss it. If I only knew ever so much, I should be more happy, 'cos you would love me more; so if you want me, you must promise me one thing."

"I will promise you most anything you ask, Jenny."

"That's right. Now hear me. My new guv'ner wants me to return to England with him; but I told him I couldn't, 'cos I liked you better than I did him. He cried when he heard this, and said that he'd only found a child to lose one."

"No wonder he shed tears."

"Well, you know, I was sorry for him, and I said so; and I told him that I would do most anything to make him happy; and on that, he again axed me to go to England with him and see my mother."

"And what answer did you give him?"

Jenny laid her face against my heart, before she replied,—

"I said I'd go, if he'd take you too."

"And what did Sir William reply?"

"He asked me if you had spoken to me about love, and all that; and if you had, at what time."

"And what did you say to that, Jenny?" and as I spoke, I held the sweet girl close to my breast, for I saw the drift of Sir William's questions, and dreaded her answer. The baronet evidently thought that I was a fortune-hunter, and had made love to his daughter after the secret of her birth was discovered.

"O, I told him that you had loved me ever so long (and you have, hain't you?) but that you had never spoken a word about it."

"Such an answer," I thought, "must disarm all his suspicions."

"Did I speak right?" and the sunny face was lifted to mine.

"Quite right, Jenny. But tell me what else he said."

"O, I don't want to;" and she made a feeble effort to twist herself out of my arms; but I held her fast, so that she could not move.

"Tell me," I whispered, and kissed her.

"He asked me if I loved you;" and the fair face was once more buried in my bosom.

"And what was your answer, darling?"

She raised her head, and looked me full in the face, with her large blue eyes, so full of truth and sincerity, that I could not doubt but that it was satisfactory, in every respect.

"What would you give to know?" whispered Jenny.

"A kiss;" and I bestowed a hearty one upon her sweet, red lips.

"You won't laugh at me?"

"Not a smile shall be seen on my face."

"Well, I told him that I had always loved you and hated you at the same time."

She was serious enough now.

"I don't understand you. Explain to me how such feelings could exist."

"Well, when you first came to me, I took a shine to you, and liked you, till the old man said you was a perlice spy; and arter that, I hated you and loved you at the same time. Now, do you understand?"

"Yes."

"And — and you love me a little, don't you?" and the round white arms were thrown over my neck, and that handsome face was pressed close to mine. What man, with blood in his veins, could have remained in a quiescent state, when so much beauty was near him? I could not; so I proved it by catching her in my arms, and holding her in a close embrace, until she begged me to release her, for fear of suffocation.

"Then you do love me?" she whispered, as soon as she could speak.

"Yes, darling, most dearly."

"And you don't want me to go to England?"

"No, not unless I go with you."

"O, that would be so nice! How happy we should be! You could learn me how to talk, and lots of things I know nothing about, couldn't you?"

I smiled and nodded.

"Then"—and the handsome face assumed a determined expression—"I shall tell my new guv'ner that I'll stay here with you; and when you go, I'll go."

"Gently, darling; your father is a very proud man, and must be approached with caution. He is aware that I love you, and have loved you for some time. I will speak to him on the subject, and see what he thinks. We must not let him suppose that his child cares nothing for him; that would mortify him exceedingly."

"Well, but you know I love you," in a petulant tone.

"I hope that you do; and to secure it, I must win your father's respect."

"I don't see what he's got to do with it," pouted Jenny. "If he likes me he must let me have my own way. When I tell him that I want a husband, and that you are the man I have picked out, he musn't make any objection. If he does, I shan't love him."

"Be governed by me in this matter," I whispered, and kissed away the frown that was gathering on her brow; for I may as well own it, Miss Jenny had a will and temper of her own, having been unchecked all through her childhood.

"I will; but remember, I'm not to leave you. If they offer to send me to England without you, there'll be a row, and a jolly one at that, I can tell you."

I soothed her in the best manner possible, and at last obtained her consent to remain passive for the present, or until I could sound Sir William on the subject that was nearest my heart. I had but half accomplished my purpose, when Sir William entered the hut, after his long conversation with the inspector.

"You here?" he asked, in a tone of some little surprise, when his eyes fell upon me.

"Yes, I have been conversing with Miss Jenny," I answered.

"Indeed."

The baronet's face expressed a little annoyance. Jenny telegraphed me with her blue eyes to communicate the subject nearest to my heart; but I signalized her to be silent for a while.

"I suppose the poor child is tired, and desires to retire," hinted Sir William. "Her accommodations are not on a very grand scale, nor such as a baronet's child should have, but I think she can endure them for one night. Here, my poor child, let me overhaul this straw, and see that no insects are concealed in it."

As he spoke, he took the candle from the table, and approached the straw, where the young lady had made her bed for several nights past. According to all rules of good breeding, I should at that moment have retired from the hut, and closed the door, so that the father and daughter could have been together, and exchanged such confidences as they pleased; but somehow, I was forced in a measure to remain where I was, although I could not account for the circumstances. I knew that I was offending, but I silenced all scruples by attributing my feelings to love for the handsome young lady, who was holding the candle while her father stirred up the straw. Suddenly the baronet uttered a startling exclamation, and jumped back; and as he did so, I saw, by the aid of the light, a glittering-coated, hissing little snake dart through the air and strike for one of the fair, round arms of Miss Jenny. Heavens! how the blood rushed to my heart, and then receded, leaving me faint and cold, with the perspiration oozing from every pore of my body, so great was the shock to my system; for, as I looked, I saw the snake, a reptile not more than ten inches long, with spots on its back and sides, of a bright orange color, while its belly was of a creamy white, fasten upon the delicate arm, and then endeavor to enfold it in its embrace. The brave girl uttered a piercing shriek, and turned as pale as death; but still she did not drop the candle, nor faint, as many young ladies would have done. After she uttered the one shriek, she turned her eyes on me, and murmured,—

"Save me, if you love me!"

That appeal restored me to my senses, and once more rendered me firm and determined.

CHAPTER LXVII.

A LIFE FOR A LIFE.

As far as Sir William was concerned, from the time that he saw the snake, until it darted from the straw and seized upon the arm of his child, he had displayed a most shocking want of presence of mind; for he could only clasp his hands and tremble while he looked, not moving one step to kill the reptile and save the child. With no thought for myself, I rushed forward, seized the little reptile near its neck, tore it from the arm upon which it had fastened, and then dashed it upon the floor of the hut, and ground it to pieces with the heel of my boot; and not until the last quiver left the snake's body did I turn to Jenny, and just in time to catch her in my arms, for she had fainted.

"My poor child," moaned the baronet; "she is dead, she is dead! Give her to me."

I did not notice the arms which were outstretched for the purpose of receiving the young girl.

"Man," I said, looking up for a moment, and speaking slow and determined, "if you would save your child, do as I bid you."

"Yes, yes, I'll do anything."

"Quick, then, bring me a bottle of brandy, which you will find on the table in the other room. No words, but go."

Sir William hurried from the apartment, and while he was gone I tore a handkerchief from Jenny's neck, fastened it just above where the snake had inflicted its poisonous bite, tying it so tight that the blood could not circulate in the arm, causing the poor child to moan, even in her death-like faint, and almost unmanning me for the task which I knew was before me. By the time this was completed, Sir William had returned with the bottle of liquor. As he handed it to me, I caught a brief glance at his face. It was pale as death.

"Can you save her?" the unhappy father demanded.

"Heaven has her in its keeping," I answered, in a solemn tone. "We will hope for the best."

I poured a few spoonfuls of the liquor through the clinched teeth of the girl, and it was so strong that it caused her to gasp for breath, and show signs of reviving. Then I examined the wound in the arm; and I looked at it most anxiously, and with a heart full of apprehension. There were the marks of two small teeth, perforations not larger than the point of a darning-needle, red spots that would hardly have been noticed were it not for the swelling just around them — a swelling that seemed to grow larger and larger each moment, and to turn black as they increased in size. Heavens, what agony I experienced, as I looked at the fair round arm, so soon to be drawn out of all shape, and become a bloated mass of corruption! for the girl had been bitten by one of the most poisonous reptiles in Australia. There was but one way to save her, or rather to attempt to save her, for without assistance death was certain in less than an hour's time. But if I saved her life, I run some risk of losing my own; for I encountered much danger in showing my devotion.

"Can she be saved?" gasped the baronet. "Do give me some hope."

"Hold the candle for one moment," I replied. "If she is to be saved, time must not be lost."

He took the light with a trembling hand, but did not remove his eyes from the pale face of his insensible child. Hastily I swallowed a mouthful of brandy, and then with a hope that Heaven would support me, and save us both, I applied my lips to the wound. Sir William uttered an exclamation of astonishment. He now began to comprehend me, and to understand how much I was willing to sacrifice for the sake of his child. I pressed my lips firmly to the spot where the snake had inserted its teeth, and then attempted to suck the poison from the wound. Every moment or two I would cease my labors and eject the saliva from my mouth. I forced more liquor down the girl's throat, and at last had the pleasure of seeing her open her eyes.

"What has happened?" she demanded. "Have I been dreaming?"

"Drink," I said, and placed the liquor to her lips.

"It scalds my mouth," she replied.

"I am sorry, but you must drink."

"For what reason?"

I could not tell her; but I pressed her in my arms, and let a tear drop on her face.

She looked up in a startled manner.

"Ah, now I remember," she cried; and a shudder passed through her frame. "I shall die."

"No, dear, you must live for your father's sake."

"I had rather live for yours," she replied.

Sir William uttered a sob; but the girl did not heed him.

"I don't like to die yet, when I have learned to like you, and to expect your love in return. O, I cannot give you up."

"Courage, darling. I hope there will be no occasion to despair. Swallow the liquor, and attempt to compose your feelings."

She took a deep drink of the strong brandy, and then closed her eyes. In the mean time I stole a look at the wound on her arm, which I had kept wet with the liquor. To my intense joy, I saw that the swelling had not increased; that it was not near so black as when I had first attempted to suck the poison out of the bite. From that moment a feeling of hope arose in my heart, and encouraged me to persevere.

In a few minutes Murden and Mr. Brown, who had been informed of Jenny's accident, entered. Their faces were full of anxiety and trouble, for they feared the worst.

"For God's sake, what does all this mean?" demanded the commissioner, kneeling by the girl's side, and taking one of her little hands, on which sparkled two or three diamond rings, reminding one of the vanities of this world, and the uncertainties of the next.

I informed him in a few words.

"But why was I not told of this as soon as it occurred?" Mr. Brown asked, in an excited manner.

I pointed to the remains of the snake, which had been gathered up, and were lying in a heap in one corner of the room. The commissioner shuddered as he looked, then eagerly felt of the girl's pulse.

"It is the most venomous snake in the country," he whispered; "yet she is alive."

"Yes."

The commissioner appeared more and more astonished.

"I will send an express to Bendigo for a physician. We must save her."

He started up to despatch one of the most trusty men and fleetest horses, but I detained him.

"It would consume twenty-four hours to obtain a physician from the city," I remarked.

"Well, what of it?"

"Only this," I whispered in his ear; "she will be out of danger, or death will ensue long before that time."

"True; I had forgotten the nature of the reptile."

He examined the arm long and earnestly, and then glanced up with an assuring face.

"There ain't the least trace of poison here," he said.

"In the name of Heaven, say that again!" cried the baronet, springing forward, and placing a hand on the officer's shoulder.

"I repeat it; there ain't the least sign of poison here!" Mr. Brown cried in a positive manner.

"What do you judge from? How do you know?" I asked, trembling with hope, for I thought considerable of Mr. Brown's judgment.

"In the first place, I've seen several people after they were bitten by these pests of the bushes — more dangerous than escaped convicts, and more efficient in keeping the ranks of the latter thin, than all the policemen of Melbourne."

"Or Bendigo," echoed Murden, who thought that a reflection was intended.

Mr. Brown did not notice the interruption. He continued: "I've seen men, after they were bitten by those spotted devils, swell up until they nearly burst. I have also taken particular notice of the wounds made by the teeth, and I never saw one that looked like this — never."

He held the candle close to the white arm, and lo, and behold, there was not a particle of swelling to be seen; the inflammation had left, and the black blood had disappeared. Sir William uttered a cry of joy, and then threw himself on his knees by the side of his daughter.

"Darling!" he cried; "do you know me? Do you feel any pain? Speak to me."

Jenny turned her eyes, now wearing a peculiar look, upon the baronet, made an effort to speak, but no sound issued from her lips. So once more she closed her eyes, and only by her slight breathing did we know that she was alive.

"O, my God!" exclaimed the distracted father; "to think that I should find her only to lose her. Speak to me, my child — only a word to say that you love me."

It was with much difficulty that Jenny managed to open her eyes; but they were void of expression, and glassy; not radiant with looks of love and happiness. For one moment she allowed her glance to rest on our faces; then, with a hiccough and a sigh, she said, —

"Don't bother me — let me a-l-o-n-e."

"She's dying!" and the baronet wrung his hands as he uttered the words.

I bowed my head, and attempted to conceal the scalding tears that fell from my eyes. Never had I loved Jenny so well as at that moment, when I was like to lose her forever. Guided by impulse I could not control, I pressed my lips to the young girl's; but as I raised my head, expecting to hear an indignant exclamation from Sir William, I noticed that Jackson had seized the bottle containing the brandy, and was in one corner of the hut, pouring it down his throat with wonderful gusto and rapidity; delighted to think that no one was interfering with his actions. I was about to call

Murden's attention to the matter, when Jenny nestled in my arms, and murmured, interrupted with many a hiccough, —

"Close the Red Lion; it's time to go to bed. You get no more swipes h-e-r-e; now I tell you; so start your stumps."

Mr. Brown had the cruelty to laugh at this incoherent speech. I gave him a glance that I meant should freeze his soul, and compel him to ask a thousand pardons for his indiscretions; but, to my surprise, the man did not seem to be any the less jolly than before I looked at him. He stooped down and put his hand on Jenny's pulse, and for a moment felt its beating. Then he asked, —

"How much brandy did you pour down the lady's throat?"

"About two thirds of a tumbler full," was my quiet answer.

"Humph! not even a giant could carry such a load. The girl is not dead in one sense, but she is dead drunk in another."

"What do you mean?" we all asked, surprised and indignant.

"Just what I say. There is no poison in her system, and consequently the liquor has acted on her brain, and intoxicated her. Or else the brandy counteracted the poison, and then seized upon the blood, and is feeding on it. At any rate, the result is intoxication. I don't understand the thing; but be assured there is no longer any danger. If the poison remained in her system, the brandy would not have affected her in the least. I've seen it tried in the bush at least a dozen times, and never knew it to fail."

"Perhaps we owe her life to this young man, after all," Sir William said, assuming a composure he hardly felt.

"You certainly do, if he gave her the liquor," muttered Mr. Brown.

"No, not on that account; for before the brandy was administered, he applied his lips to the wound, and attempted to extract the poison."

"And he did it!" cried Mr. Brown, with enthusiasm; "although I would not have risked it. However, he loves the girl, I suppose, and was willing to sacrifice his life to save hers. If he escapes, he deserves her."

"Take yer noise out of the Red Lion," muttered Jenny, who seemed to be dreaming of her bar-maid days.

Sir William did not reply to this blunt speech; but I saw that he was in a reflecting mood.

"Come," said Mr. Brown, after a moment's silence, "make up the girl's bed, and let us leave her alone. She will come out all right by morning."

As the advice was sensible, — for it was now evident to all of us that Jenny was under the influence of liquor, and therefore needed rest, — we spread some blankets on the straw and made as comfortable a bed as possible. When we had prepared everything, and were ready to leave the hut, Sir William said that he would remain and watch by the side of his child all night, and let us know if there was any change for better or worse.

CHAPTER LXVIII.

A PRIVATE CONFERENCE. — A PLAIN TALK. — A STERN REFUSAL.

Upon awaking at daylight I saw Sir William standing over me. I thought that Jenny was worse, so sprang to my feet, anxious and trembling.

"She is dead," I said, thinking of the snake bite, and the condition in which I had left her the night before.

"No, my friend, she is safe. She is out of all danger, and now sleeping off the effects of the liquor which she imbibed. Come with me. I wish to talk with you before breakfast, and on matters of importance. Can you spare the time?"

"Certainly, sir."

I shook myself free of the blankets, and arose; following the baronet to the edge of the woods, where we could converse free of interruption.

"Sit down," he said. "We may as well be at our ease."

Down we sat on some dried grass, first stirring the ground, so that we should not sit on an anthill; and then I awaited the communication which the baronet had to make. It was some time before he uttered a word; but at last he turned to me, and said, in a most abrupt manner, —

"You love my daughter, do you not?"

"Yes."

"How long has this passion lasted?"

I thought I detected a sneer in the tone in which the question was asked; so I continued: —

"Ever since she was a bar-maid at the Red Lion."

The baronet, proud of his name, his wealth, and position in life, felt the shot that I had directed, and it made him quiver and flush like a newly-fledged lawyer rebuked by the bench for indulging in flights of fancy not in accordance with the rules of the court.

There was another pause. The baronet appeared to be concentrating for an attack. At last he opened his battery.

"Have you spoken to the young lady on the subject that is so near your heart?"

"Yes."

"May I inquire when such conversation ensued?"

"Certainly. As her father, I have no wish to conceal anything from you."

Sir William bowed, as much as to say, 'That is quite right and proper." I continued: —

"Last evening, when the lady was rescued from a most perilous position, and fell into my arms. After she revived, she spoke her sentiments quite plainly, and I replied to her at some length."

"And will you be kind enough to give me the gist of your reply?"

"Certainly. I said that she had a father who must be consulted on all that related to her welfare."

"Very proper language. What was her answer to that?"

I looked at the man for a moment, and saw that he had assumed a manner that was offensive in the extreme. In an instant all my pride was aroused, and I determined to pay him back scorn for scorn.

"You will excuse me, Sir William," I returned, "if I

decline to answer such direct questions. The lady has reposed some little confidence in me, and I am not the person to violate it."

I saw an angry flush mantle his brow; but he did not burst out in a torrent of passionate reproaches, as I expected he would. He had a purpose to accomplish, and he kept it in view.

"Of course, when you spoke to the honored scion of the house of Byefield, you knew that she was an heiress?"

This made me mad. I could not contain myself.

"The honored fiddlestick," I replied. "The young lady is charming, illiterate, brought up in the most menial of employments, and has no more idea of your position in society than a bushranger. Do you suppose that I would marry her for your money, or that I would take her at any rate unless I thought I could improve her mind. Limited as my sphere is in the world, I should blush to ask your child to enter it unless she would resolve to learn new habits and ideas."

"But you are willing to admit that the lady is capable of great improvement under proper training and discipline?"

"Certainly. She has a strong and active mind, and would apply herself to learning with remarkable enthusiasm, after she once saw the necessity for it."

"I am glad that you admit so much. Now for my conclusions. She is the heiress of an old and honored house; yet, in her present state, she would do neither me nor my wife much credit if we should introduce her to the circle which she is destined to adorn. Two years of careful instruction would give her such advantages that any nobleman in the land would be glad to aspire to her hand."

"I do not doubt it," in a cold, calm manner.

"Well, such being the case, do you not think it would be folly on her part to bestow her hand on you? — a fine, generous fellow I admit, but still not her equal in position or fortune. Come, answer me frankly."

"I will, as frankly as you have spoken; and I hope that you will not be offended if I talk rather plainly."

"Of course not."

"Well, then, let me revert to yourself, and contrast your position with mine, and see which deserves the most praise for character. You were born to inherit a title and a fortune, were you not?"

"Certainly. The Byefields came in with William the—"

"Never mind particulars. Being placed in so favorable a position, you had the advantages of wealth to secure an education."

"Of course. I went to Cambridge."

I did not heed the interruption, but continued: —

"I had no great advantages of wealth, and spent but a year at Harvard College. To pay for the same, I earned money in various ways; yet after I left college, I did not disgrace my name, and that of my family, in the way you did."

The baronet almost sprang to his feet, and his eyes flashed fire, so indignant was he.

"Do you mean to insult me?" he demanded, in a voice that trembled with rage.

"Such was not, and is not, my intention," I returned, in so calm a manner that the baronet resumed his seat, and apparently made up his mind to hear me.

"Listen to me patiently," I said. "You have had your say; now give me mine. I intend to prove to you that an American sovereign is fully equal in position, if not the superior in some respects, to an English baronet."

Sir William drew a long breath, and motioned for me to go on. I should have continued to speak my thoughts without such encouragement, for I had got started, and was bound to free my mind, at all events.

"Yes," I resumed, "I worked hard for a livelihood from the time that I was able to work, until within a few years; and during that period I committed no act that my ancestors would have disapproved of, could they have been allowed to revisit the earth, and take part in the affairs of life. But how was it with you?"

Sir William looked as much as to say, "What the devil is he driving at now?"

"Yes, while I was striving for an honorable position, you were doing all in your power to obtain an infamous reputation. The lowest characters in London were your common associates; and you ate, and feasted, and rioted with prize-fighters, dog-fanciers, horse-jockeys, giving no heed to the position to which you had been born. Come, tell me which has the best record to show, as far as youth is concerned."

"You don't understand that my position —"

"I understand all that you would say on the point. Pray let me continue to the close."

"Your argument is not a good one; but go on; I will not interrupt you. My money —"

"Can your money secure exemption from just censure for crime? or can your title protect you, and make virtues out of vices? Poor as I have been, I never yet stooped to the company of a prize-fighter."

"But you associate with police officers, and think nothing of shooting a bushranger."

The baronet thought that he had hit me hard; but I did not think so, and thus answered him: —

"The police officers of Victoria are a bold, independent corps of men, honorable in most respects, risking their lives for the sake of freeing the country of dangerous characters, never hesitating to relieve when they see distress, and always ready to assist women in their peril. Such are the men with whom I associate; and I leave it to you to say whether they are not superior to such vile brutes as the Pet, whom you made a companion of."

The man winced a little when I mentioned the promptness with which the commissioner and his men avenged injuries inflicted upon women. He knew that the night before, Mad Dick had fallen by Murden's hand, because the bushranger had offered violence to Miss Jenny; but, Englishman-like, he was not disposed to give credit to any one for a noble act, now that he was in an argumentative mood.

"But you don't understand that the customs of Great Britain sanction a little wildness on the part of a rich young man."

"Yes, I understand all that, but must contend that the man who would turn to prize-fighters, instead of intellectual training, must be incapable of sound judgment and moral observation."

Thunder! how mad the man was! He sprang to his feet, his face expressive of the utmost rage; but all such manifestations did not alarm me in the least. I had determined to prove to him that I could return scorn for scorn, insult for insult; conciliation, I found, only placed me in a false light, and gave the baronet a pretence for trampling on me.

"Do you mean to deliberately insult me?" the baronet asked, as soon as he could recover his breath.

"No, I wish to speak plain with you."

"Devilish plain you have spoken, I must say," muttered Sir William. "You mean that I shall understand you, at all events."

"You have spoken your mind, and why should I not do the same? This interview would have amounted to nothing unless we understood each other."

"Do we now comprehend each other's meaning?" asked Sir William, in a tone which showed that he desired to be comprehended.

"I think we do."

"Please to name some of the important points we have touched upon."

"Certainly; it is best we understand each other. In the first place, you do not think it any honor for me to unite my fate with your newly-found daughter."

Sir William bowed.

"Because you desire that she shall contract a marriage with her equal, or a superior."

"Yes, such is my intention at the present time."

"And you do not intend to let her have a voice in the premises?"

"She does not know her own mind."

I think that she does, and that you will find it out before many days."

"But I trust that you will do nothing to incite her to disobey my commands."

"Sir William," I replied, "I am a gentleman, and never associated with members of the prize-ring."

I thought for a moment that he would seek to punish me for the speech; but he choked down his rage, and said,—

"I pardon all your rudeness on account of the treatment which you extended towards my daughter."

"I am glad that you have a memory," I replied. "During our conversation I thought that you had lost all that you ever possessed."

"No, sir; I know how to be grateful, as you shall discover. I have money, and will reward you for all that you have done."

"Keep your money," I returned, with such a gesture of contempt that the baronet actually blushed, and looked uncomfortable. "I have no desire for any part of it. I have more than I know what to do with."

"But I wish to show you gratitude for the care you have taken of my daughter. Remember, last night you risked your life for hers."

"And would again, because such is my nature; but don't talk to me of your gratitude, for you don't know what it means."

There was a moment's silence. I still remained on the grass, plucking it up by the roots, and throwing it into little piles, while Sir William was on his feet, stamping about impatiently, and evidently desirous that the interview should terminate, for he had played his best card, and felt that he had lost the game; that he had not satisfied himself or my honor by the words which he had uttered. At last the baronet turned his back upon me, walked off a dozen steps or so, and then returned to my side, as though one more effort was to be made to appease my wounded pride.

"Let me ask you to pledge your word that you will make no attempts to hold converse with my daughter, unless with my consent. Do this, and I will part with you as one of my best friends."

"I make no promises to a man who has changed so much as you have within the last twenty-four hours. I shall neither seek nor avoid your daughter. If she comes near me, I will talk with her, and tell her why I am so apparently indifferent to her charms. It is but right that I should do this, after what has passed between us."

"Let me beg you to assume all the blame — to tell her that you don't care so much for her as you did a few days since."

"I shan't do any such thing. I won't lie to her to please you or any other person."

"But consider, my dear sir, how hard it is to lose a daughter's love after you have gained it — after you have been years without it."

"Nonsense!" I replied; "it is not near so hard to lose as a lover's. Your sacrifice is nothing compared to mine."

The baronet turned away from me impatiently, and walked towards the camp. I followed at my leisure, but encountered Murden and Brown, who had seen me with the baronet, and suspected what our conversation had been about. As Sir William entered the hut where Jenny was housed, the two officers fastened upon me.

"Is it all settled?" asked Mr. Brown. "When is the wedding to take place? Give me an invite, won't you?"

"If you get her," said the worldly-minded Mr. Murden, "it will be a great lift to you in the social scale."

"Social fiddlestick!" ejaculated the blunt Bendigo policeman. "Isn't he as good as she is, for all of her blood and beauty?"

"But still you know she has rank through her father and mother," urged the commissioner.

"Well, how did she rank before Sir William picked her up?" asked Mr. Brown.

"Rather low," was the honest confession.

"And if our friend had married her, not knowing but that the Pet was her governor, what should you have said?"

"That he had made an ass of himself."

"Plainly; and I should have said the same, and I don't know as I shall alter my opinion even now, if he takes the lady for a wife."

"There's not much danger," I remarked; "Sir William has asked me to relinquish all claim, and even offered me money to do so."

"Did you knock him down?" demanded the impulsive Brown.

"Did you explain who you were, and how much money you were worth?" inquired the cautious Murden.

"Neither."

"Then what in the devil's name did you do?" both men demanded, in an eager tone.

"Why, I did nothing, except to tell him that I was as good as his child, and that I should not dishonor her by marriage."

"Good for you," was the answer. And then I repeated a portion of the conversation which had ensued between Sir William and myself.

Both of my friends were somewhat indignant at the treatment which I had received; and yet Murden was not entirely unprepared for it, as he informed me that Sir William had conversed with him on the subject the night before,—had asked many questions as to my past history, and the reputation which I sustained, and seemed a little disappointed that all that was uttered was so much in my favor.

"I tell you what 'tis," said Mr. Brown, "if you want the girl and she wants you, just take her, in spite of the father. Hang me if I won't help you."

Murden shook his head.

"Better have the consent of the baronet," the cautious commissioner replied. "Keep cool, and I think it can be obtained."

"Hang the baronet!" the impatient Mr. Brown exclaimed. "We can't afford to wait his motions. Run off with the girl, and marry her in spite of him. If that won't do, I'll let some of my men play bushranger for a short time, and take the young lady in spite of the father. Blast it, we'll manage some way, you see if we don't. Your friends won't desert you in this hour of need."

But, to Mr. Brown's astonishment, I declined all such assistance.

"No," I said; "if I marry the young lady, it must be without force and violence. She must come to me and say that my life is as valuable to her as her own, and that without me riches and station were useless."

"Devilish exacting!" muttered Mr. Brown, who did not like such a cool way of reasoning. "The girl won't think you have much love for her unless you are warmer."

"We shall see," I replied. "I only want a chance to speak to her while we are on the march, and I think that I shall be able to set matters all right."

"O, you shall have chance enough this forenoon," both my friends remarked. And then we proceeded to get breakfast, which was awaiting us.

Miss Jenny joined us, looking a little thin and pale after her night's suffering. She was rather inclined to be moody, or sullen, as though something had been said to her that she did not approve of; yet, the instant I bade her good morning, she looked up, ran towards me, and threw her arms around my neck.

"You saved my life!" she sobbed, "and I'll never forget you. No, never! I had rather have you than all the men in the world."

"Pretty little dear!" muttered the sentimental Mr. Brown, almost scalding his mouth with hot coffee; "what a shame to part 'em!"

"Such a fine couple!" Mr. Murden remarked, with a glance at Sir William's face, as though he was fearful of taking too great a liberty with such an eminent man.

Compliments did not soften the baronet's heart. He put an arm on his child's shoulder, drew her away, and said, —

"Your breakfast is waiting, my dear. Better think of that at the present moment. You need it more than such nonsense as you have just exhibited."

CHAPTER LXIX.

ON THE TRAMP. — A WONDERFUL LAKE. — A WARM RECEPTION.

At daylight the police commenced saddling their horses, and packing their effects, and by eight o'clock we were on our way to Bendigo, by the way of Smith's farm, where we meant to stop all night, and part of the afternoon, in case Miss Jenny should exhibit signs of fatigue; and I thought that she would be likely to.

For the first hour we passed over the prairies without exchanging a word, each officer being occupied with the thought that it was decidedly ungrateful on the part of Mad Dick to die in such a hurry, and leave no sign behind him as to the exact section of the country where his treasures were buried.

"Yes," said the commissioner, who was riding by my side, in moody silence, suddenly awakening to life, "I'll never forgive the cuss — never. He might have made us happy, if he had had only a little common sense. I didn't ask much from him, and the least he could have done would have been to make a sign. But he's gone, and with him all knowledge of his money. It's a shame — a swindle — a cheating of honest men out of their rights. But what could you expect from such a low-born villain?"

"Mankind is pretty much alike," I replied. "Peer or peasant, they all look after their own interests before taking care of their neighbors'. You would do the same thing; so don't preach."

"I don't intend to; but you know it was devilish aggravating on the part of Dick; now wasn't it?"

I admitted that it was, although I hardly knew what I was saying, for my eyes were directed towards Jenny, and I saw by her motion that she wished to speak to me. But the baronet kept close to her side, and did not seem inclined to budge an inch, much as I desired him to.

"Are you dying to bill and coo a little?" asked Mr. Brown, with a knowing smile. "Well, you shall, because she's a devilish handsome girl, bright enough to turn the head of any young fellow with a fancy for a pretty face."

"Cease your bantering, and give me the opportunity you said that you would," I replied.

"All right. Just see how I'll do it; keep your eye on me, now."

He fell back a little, and beckoned to Jackson. For a few moments the commissioner and his man whispered to each other, and then Jackson trotted to the front, and Mr. Brown once more joined me. I knew that some plan was on foot, but asked no questions, content to wait developments. Jackson rode far to the front, then suddenly wheeled his horse, and came towards us on a run.

"What's up?" shouted Mr. Brown, as soon as the man came within hail.

"Nothin' perticular, sir; only if you wants to see one of the wonders of Australia, now is the time."

"Hey? What is that?" asked Sir William, suddenly interested, and for the moment forgetting Jenny. He called her by the name by which she was christened; but I ignored it, and stuck to "Jenny," as most familiar. He touched the horse which he rode, and left Jenny's side. Mr. Brown winked in a peculiar manner, and continued to question Jackson.

"What is the wonder you speak of, Jackson?"

"The Devil's Lake, sir. You must have heard of it, sir."

"Of course I have. Who has not? How far is it from here?"

"About four miles, sir."

"And pray what kind of a lake is the Devil's Lake?" asked Sir William.

"Jackson can tell you," was Mr. Brown's answer.

"Sure, sir, it's a lake that is all covered with salt during the dry seasons, and in it you'll see lots of alligators, wedged in as though in pickle, and not a bit can they move till the rains come. It's funny to see 'em."

"Is it possible?" asked Sir William. "I never heard of such a thing. Did you?"

He forgot himself for a moment in turning to speak to me; but not waiting for an answer, continued to address Jackson.

"I've seen the lake many times," the man said, in a sober tone. "Every nob who travels this way takes a squint at it."

Sir William looked a little irresolute; but the next words of Jackson decided him to go.

"No man ever seed such a sight but once in his lifetime," Jackson continued. "Them 'ere alligators is wedged in the salt just as though it was marble, and there 'em lays all the summer, winkin' 'em eyes, and carin' no more for a man than a 'sketer."

"Will you go with me and see this wonderful lake?" asked the baronet, turning to Mr. Brown.

Mr. Brown said that he would; and after whispering the following words, he called to four of his men to accompany him, and left us.

"Now, old fellow, go in and have a good time. Talk to Jenny as much as you please, and if you don't win her to your way of thinking, I shall believe that you don't care for her. I'll keep the old nob at a distance till after you arrive at Smith's."

He galloped off, and was soon lost to view among the bushes. Then I wasted no time. I dismounted from my horse, threw the bridle to one of the men, and took a seat by the side of Miss Jenny, in the miner's cart, disturbing her reverie by the suddenness of my appearance.

"My goodness, where did you come from? I thought you'd forgot me."

"Your father says that I must forget you, Jenny," I replied, meeting the glance of her mild blue eyes with one of such sincere admiration that the girl blushed, and attempted, in a playful manner, to rap me on the knuckles with the handle of the whip which she carried.

"Did my new guv'ner say that you couldn't have me?" asked Jenny, desisting from her rapping project, and looking a little sorry because she had started the skin from my hand

"Yes; we had a long talk this morning, and he informed me that you were above me in station, and I must not think more of you."

"O, gammon!" was the cry. "He knows better than that. He said somethin' like it to me, but I stopped him by jest tellin' him that I was a poor ignorant girl when you fust made love to me, and that I wasn't goin' to throw you aside now that I was somethin' better than a bar-maid."

"He will never listen to my prayers," I said, in rather a despondent tone. "His pride is too great to permit him to look upon me as a son-in-law."

"Hang his pride! you is better than me, anyhow; now ain't you?"

I shook my head.

"You know it's so, for I can't talk like you, and you would never have thought of me if I hadn't had a decent face. Now ain't it so?"

"I tell you what it is," Jenny continued, in a glow of delight at the prospect before her, "if the guv'ner is stiff and won't back down, we can make a livin' in Melbourne by openin' a porter-house. I can tend bar, and force the customers to drink when they has had enough."

"O, Jenny, Jenny!" I cried, "God forbid that we should be reduced to such a strait. I would rather see you in a coffin than behind a bar."

"I shouldn't," was the prompt answer. "I don't think I'd look so handsome in a box as I would behind a bar. Besides, you wouldn't love me half as well dead as alive. You know you wouldn't. Men never do."

"Perhaps not, but still I don't think you will have occasion to hand around beer and pipes to blear-eyed customers. I am able to support a wife if I am fortunate enough to find one."

"And do you still feel that you want me for a wife?" asked Jenny, laying one of her hands on mine, and looking in my face with a glance that told of affection, confidence, and love.

"Certainly I do."

"With all my bad ways, all my ignorance?"

"Yes."

"Well, then, you shall have me, in spite of guv'ner and all his yarnin'. I'll marry no one but you. But—"

"But what?"

"You must let me do as I please till I'm married. Arterwards I s'pose you'll want your say."

I did not contradict her on that point.

"One thing more."

"Yes, let me hear it."

"You knows I ain't fit to be your wife just now, don't you?"

I looked at her in surprise, and wondered what she meant.

"You see, I ain't never had no edication, and that's what I wants most of all. I can be as good as you, and sich company as you would want. You needn't shake your head; you know you'd be ashamed to introduce me to your friends now; wouldn't you?"

"No, Jenny."

"I knows better, 'cos once or twice you has said somethin' to me about my bad grammar — just as though I knew what you meant. But it showed me that I did not talk straight, and I want to learn, and I will learn."

I waited for her to conclude her remarkable statement, for it proved to me that she was much farther advanced than I imagined her to be — that she possessed solid sense as well as great beauty.

"Now don't you think that it would be a good thing for me to learn a little arter I was spliced, or afore I was spliced?"

"I should rather commend such an idea," was my reply.

"Then we think alike on that point. Now for my plan. Arter the guv'ner says I may have you, I'm goin' to school a year or two."

"And leave me?"

"Yes."

"But that is hard and cruel."

"Well, we'll manage so that we can see each other every two weeks. I studies one or two years in some seminary — there's one jest near Melbourne, where any gals is took in and boarded all the time they is there — and then I gets some knowledge of books, and music, and other things, and has a course of study marked out for me, so that I can learn all the time arter I has left school. Now, ain't that good?"

"Yes, as far as it goes. But how can I spare you for such a length of time?"

"Why, you goose, don't you see me once in two weeks by such an arrangement?"

"Yes, but that is small in comparison to seeing you a dozen times a day."

"Ah, but think of the object of my exile. It's to be worthy of your love."

I glanced around, and saw that none of the men were looking in our direction, and then I plucked the freshness from a sweet mouth; and Jenny uttered a sigh of satisfaction as I did so. I was just about to repeat the exploit when Murden rode up. I wished him to the devil, but still had to tolerate him. I believe that he saw me kiss Jenny, and was determined to interrupt me in the business, fearing that I was progressing a little too fast.

"Ahem!" he cried; "it's growing a little warm. Don't you think so?"

I understood him. Sir William might find out that Jackson had humbugged him, and so return and put an end to our pleasant chat.

"Trot!" shouted Murden to his men; and on we went, as fast as I could urge the horse that was attached to the wagon.

For an hour or two we dashed on, raising great clouds of dust in our course, causing the animals to foam and pant under the heat, until at last we began to notice evidences of cultivated soil, civilization, irrigation, and broad pastures. In ten minutes after making this discovery we drew up before Smith's house, with a cheer that brought all the inmates to the door in double quick time, rather astonished at the noise we made. I looked up and saw the grinning face of Hezekiah Hopeful, my partner, the jolly phiz of Smith, and the pale, sweet countenance of Amelia, the young lady who had received such barbarous treatment at the hands of Moloch, before we were able to rescue her, and punish the villain as he deserved. Amelia did not remain more than a second or two at the door. She gave one hurried glance;

her eyes met mine, and then she vanished from sight, and I saw nothing more of her till towards night. Hopeful uttered a shout of joy, and rushed towards me. Smith rubbed his hands and laughed; then, inspired by a bright idea, seized his baby, which was in his wife's arms, kissed it until it cried in terror, and then returned it to the lady, and rushed out to welcome his friends and the company.

Hardly had I set foot to the ground before a solid body dashed against me, nearly overturning me in its struggle to reach my face. It was my brave dog, Rover, that I had not seen for a week or two, and now was testifying the joy he felt at the reunion. Mrs. Smith welcomed Jenny to the hospitalities of her house with a kindness and tenderness that placed the girl at ease at once; while the police, who knew how to procure comfort at a cheap rate, fed their horses, gave them water, rubbed them down, and then began to look after provisions for their own stomachs. Miss Jenny was treated by the hostess to a bath, clean linen, and a fresh muslin dress; and when I saw her, after she had undergone some changes, I thought that I had never seen so handsome a girl; but before I had opportunity to tell her that such was the case, and to prove it to her by word of mouth, I heard a voice in the yard, and looking out, I saw Sir William, Mr. Brown, Jackson, and the four policemen, all of whom had been in search of the wonderful lake, which Jackson was certain "laid off that there, a little ways to the right."

CHAPTER LXX.

A WONDERFUL LAKE. — THE QUARTZ CRUSHERS. — A SEPARATION.

Sir William did not look remarkable for his good nature as he dismounted from his horse and entered the house, followed by Mr. Brown, the inspector.

"I hope you enjoyed your visit to the 'Devil's Lake,' Sir

William," I said, as the frowning man entered the room where Jenny and I were seated.

"No, sir, I did not enjoy it," was the curt answer.

"May I ask the reason why?"

"Yes, sir, you may. The wonders of the lake have been greatly exaggerated. I saw nothing remarkable about it. There was a mass of mud, and a mass of salt; but not an alligator to be seen, nor any appearance of one."

"The fact of it is," said Mr. Brown, "Sir William feels that he has been imposed upon by a traveller's yarn, and that he has wasted time in going out of the way."

Sir William disdained to answer, or to bandy words on the subject. He sat down by the side of Jenny, put his arm around her waist, and kissed her.

"My dear child," he said, "I hope to place you in a different position, in a few days, where you will be surrounded by members of your own sex, and no longer exposed to the wandering life which you have witnessed for the last fortnight."

As this was intended as a hint, I gave Mr. Brown a wink, and left the room, the commissioner following me; but as I closed the door, I heard Jenny say, —

"I don't want to have a lot of ugly old women round me, and I won't — there, now."

"He'll have some work to tame her," muttered Mr. Brown. "She's got a will of her own; now ain't she?"

We met Smith and Hopeful in the front yard. They were relating the trials which they had experienced in moving the crushers and steam-engine; so I had to listen to their account of the journey, the hardships which they had endured; how their teams broke down, their oxen strayed off at night; how some of their men deserted; and a number of other matters that a lover is not supposed to care about.

"And now," inquired Hez, "whar do you suppose the engine is?"

"On the carts," I answered, at random.

"No, sir, it's on the ground, at the foot of Quartz Hill; and in two or three days we can fire up and see what the rocks is made of, and how much gold there is in 'em."

I was rejoiced to hear that such was the case.

"Yes," said Hez, "we has worked rather spry, all things considered. I has hired six men to help us get out the quartz, lug wood, and do other work; and I has stowed 'em all away in the cave. You remember it, don't you?"

Should I ever forget it? Had I not been a prisoner in that cave, surrounded by ferocious bushrangers, and saved from a violent death by the aid of Mother Brown?

"If you have time, we might ride over there this arternoon, and see how things is working," Hez said.

I was about to reply, but Mr. Brown said, —

"Of course, I shall be delighted to go. We have time enough. We don't move from here till to-morrow. Come, I'll find fresh horses."

Off he went, levied on some of Smith's animals, and first making Murden promise that he would keep Sir William and Jenny at the station until we returned, started across the country on horseback, reached the cave at three o'clock, saw that the men were laying a foundation for the engine and crushers, cutting wood, while two experienced miners were wheeling huge blocks of quartz, the sides of which were speckled with flecks of gold.

"It's just the richest vein that I ever worked on," one of the miners said. "There's a mine of goold in this 'ere hill. I only wish I had a claim here, and the tools to work with."

Mr. Brown was delighted and astonished at the evidences of wealth that were around us. On the whole, I was well satisfied with what I saw, and what had been done, and so rode back to the farm house.

"Hopeful," I said, as we neared the house, "how do you stand towards Amelia?"

My friend colored a little, and did not look towards me as he replied, —

"Wal, the fact of it is, I rather thinks I loves Martha Poland better nor 'Mealy."

"Indeed! When did you arrive at such a conclusion?"

"O, this forenoon, I guess."

"How does it happen that such is the case?"

"Confound it! yeou is mighty inquisitive all at once," retorted Hopeful, with a guilty laugh, his plain face suffused with blushes.

"Of course I am when your interest is concerned."

"Ahem — wal, then, if you must know, I don't mind tellin' yeou that me and 'Mealy had a talk to-day, afore you got along, and she said that — O, go long; I ain't goin' to tell yeou."

"Yes, you will; go on."

"How curious you are! Wal, then, she said that she should allers like me as a friend, and all that, but I hadn't better think of her no more as a lover."

"Did she mean it?"

"Wal, I guess yeou'd have thought so if yeou had seen her face. I tell you she was in arnest, if ever a gal was."

"I am glad to hear it."

"Yes, 'cos you want her yourself!" cried the blunt son of New Hampshire.

"There is where you wrong me, Hez. I have no design on the young lady. I have already pledged my heart and hand to another."

"And that other is who? Not Miss Jenny, the barrow-night's darter!"

"The same."

"Whew!" whistled Hez; "she's pretty, but won't she make things fly? I tell yeou, she's got a temper of her own."

"Most women have, Hez. Even your peerless Martha Poland could show a little if she was disposed to."

"Yes, I s'pose so. But what does the daddy say? Is he willin'?"

"No"

"More fool he! You is as good as he is, if not a darned sight better; and I'll tell him so if he talks to me on the subject."

"Thank you; but tell me about Amelia; what else did she say?"

"O, not much, only that her life was blighted, and that she could never be happy again, and that I mustn't speak to her about love any more, 'cos her heart was a ruined heart; and then she shook hands with me and left. I tell you I pitied her. So, that's the way, yer see, that my love all went back to Martha."

I had no further opportunity to speak with Jenny that night. Her father complained that she was tired, and needed rest; so hurried her off to a spare room, and, I think, locked her in; but of that I won't be sure, as I did not venture near her apartment during the evening. But I had an hour's uninterrupted conversation with Amelia, and found the poor child in better spirits and health than I could have supposed. She still remembered the injuries which she had received, and shuddered as she thought of them; but all danger to her mind had passed. Insanity no longer threatened her active brain. But I missed all of her little coquettish airs, which at one time were so charming, and so well calculated to drive a lover or a sensitive person to the verge of distraction; but instead, I found a quiet, womanly grace, a grave, dignified manner, that was full as engaging and delightful as the girlish manifestations which I had so much admired, yet at the same time detested on account of their being so trying to the feelings.

"And now, my dear friend," Amelia said, as she laid her hand on mine, and looked up at my face with an earnest and feeling glance, "they tell me that you are experiencing some trouble. I have told you all that concerns myself; let me have your confidence. Tell me in what manner I can assist you. You know that my gratitude and will are strong enough to do so."

"I know that they are; but still I do not see how you can help me, Amelia. Time may render me some assistance, but at present I am fearful my happiness will be wrecked through the obstinacy of one person."

"That must not be," she said, with a gentle pressure of her hand. "Sir William is not acquainted with your worth, or he would not refuse his consent to your marriage. I am sure that you are as good as she is; in fact, as good as any woman in the world; and most of them would be proud of you as a husband. I will see Sir William and tell him all that I know about you. He must lower his pride. He shall. I will talk to him in such a manner that he will listen to me."

"I fear that it will be in vain, my dear. Better let him pursue his own course. I think that I can count on the strength of Miss Jenny's affection, and that, when the proper time arrives, she will make her choice, and cling to her father or myself. Of course I thank you for the interest you manifest in my affairs, but I think that daylight will be seen before long."

"But I may speak to Sir William?" pleaded Amelia.

"Certainly, my child. You have full permission to say what you please. Only don't praise me too much. He may think that you are overdoing it."

"I will be careful;" and with these words I bade her good night, and retired to rest.

The next morning the baronet stole a march on me; for he arose at an early hour, aroused his daughter, compelled her to dress, and then started for Bendigo an hour or two before we were up. I was astonished when I heard of the movement, and threatened to pursue the parties; but Mr. Brown and Mr. Murden laughed at the idea, and coaxed me to remain and keep cool.

Murden sent the Pet, a most miserable looking specimen of a prize-fighter, all knocked out of time, and no longer able to stand on the defensive, to Melbourne, under the charge of two officers, with orders to make a complaint against the man, and hold him, on the ground of abduction.

"Sykes," I said, as the fellow mounted a horse and was then secured so that escape was impossible, "I may never see you again. I bear you no malice, old fellow, even if you have ill-treated me at different times. Let me hope that you will escape punishment, and live an honest life in the future."

"I don't know what has come over me," answered the Pet; "but I feels like throwin' up the sponge and retirin' from the ring, declarin' all bets off, and no more fights except with the gloves. That's the way I feel."

"I am glad of it. Then there shall be peace between us."

"Yes, I suppose so, 'cos I'm down, and it's hardly fair to hit a cove when he's on his back. Good by, old fellow. If you splices my little Jenny, you gets a clipper, and no mistake. She is as good and pure as old Fay's brandy. I knows it, 'cos I has watched her. At first I thought I'd wait till she growed up, and then I'd sell her; but I has thought better of it, and now I'm glad of it, 'cos much as I hated her guv'ner, I liked the gal. She was just like my own flesh and blood;" and, with a tear in his eye, the prize-fighter rode off, and I did not again see him until he was free, and then he let himself to the missionaries, and travelled round the country distributing tracts, for the charge of abduction was not preferred by Sir William, after he reached Melbourne, for some reason or other. The ministers got hold of the ex-prize-fighter, and made an impression on his mind, and enlisted him in their cause; and a valuable aid he was, going among the miners and natives and compelling them, for fear of his huge fists, to read his religious papers, and to abstain from profanity. It was in this manner he lost his life; for, one day, while insisting that a drunken miner should turn from the wrath to come, should read one of his tracts, and contribute liberally of his wealth for the benefit of the church, they had a quarrel, as the miner differed from the Pet on the expediency of so doing. Sykes was inclined to be fanatical on certain points of divinity; so he called the miner hard names, took him by the collar and shook him in a surly manner,—and then dropped to the ground, with a bullet in his left side, in the region of his heart, the miner thinking that cold lead was the proper manner of ending an argument. It did end it and the Pet's life at the same time, for the wound proved mortal; but before the man died he made a will, and left all his property—some five thousand pounds—to Jenny, free of all control. The ministers begged him to remember the church, but the Pet refused; and so he died, a repentant man, and a better one than his friends expected. Thus terminated the career of a desperate man, and at one time a very bad one. Let us hope that he met with some little favor in the next world, for his life was a hard one in this.

After breakfast we started for Bendigo; but when we arrived, we found that Sir William and his daughter were not there, as we expected. He had met one of the Melbourne stages, secured seats, and sent the horses which they had ridden to the station. Of course this was a great disappointment to me; but I concealed all evidences of it as well as possible from my companions.

"I tell you what it is," said Mr. Brown, while we were seated at the tea-table, and I was admiring the domestic life that he led, "you had ought to be married, and settle, instead of wandering round the country, trying to get your neck broken; that's what you had."

"So he had," remarked Murden; "I quite agree with you."

"You are worse than he is," retorted the amiable lady; "you are older; you should have been married ten years since. It's a shame."

"If you will spare us both, we'll promise to get married at an early day; in fact, as soon as we can find girls to have us," Murden remarked, with a laugh and blush that puzzled me, for he was not accustomed to that sort of thing.

Mrs. Brown graciously promised to comply; so there was no more said on the subject of marriage. We passed the night at Mr. Brown's house; and the next morning, after breakfast, Murden and I prepared to separate, with no expectation of seeing each other for some weeks to come, as I should be engaged at the mines, and he with the police force at Melbourne. At last, we grasped each other's hands, just before we parted, and then Murden said, —

"I shall keep an eye on the doings of Sir William, and will let you know if there is any news of interest. So, good by, old fellow. Take care of yourself."

He mounted his horse, and was off; and after a few words with Mr. Brown, I too turned my back on the town, and slowly cantered towards Smith's station, feeling for the first time that I was homesick.

CHAPTER LXXI.

GENERAL EVENTS. — HASTY WEDDINGS. — CONCLUSION.

I REACHED Smith's house at a late hour in the afternoon I found the ladies at home, but the men were hard at work putting the machines in order, and getting ready to commence operations. I sat and talked with the ladies until Hopeful and Smith returned, which they did just at dark, tired with their day's labor, but in most excellent spirits at the prospect before them; for the quartz looked richer and richer the farther they advanced. In fact, Smith and Hopeful were so convinced that there were millions of dollars in the mountain, that they had staked off additional claims, intending to sell them as soon as the work commenced, for we could not hope to keep our operations secret many days; and we knew that as soon as the news spread, thousands of adventurers would flock to the mine and commence work.

The next day we were up and had breakfast by daylight; and just as the sun showed its face we were on our way to the mine, where we found our men hard at work, and with considerable zeal; for we had engaged a stout young fellow, an American, from Vermont, to act as foreman of the gang and he did not allow idleness when good wages were paid.

In about a week, I received a letter from Murden which contained important information. He stated that Sir William had engaged state-rooms on board the steamer "Bounding Billow," and was to leave for England in a short time. Jenny was reported as being dressed in the most fashionable clothes, and looking quite content at the prospect before her. I don't think that I slept much that night. I thought of the deep love which I entertained for Jenny, and how singular had been our acquaintance; and then I made a resolution not to think of her again, and found that, like most resolutions which men make when a woman is concerned, it was broken as soon as entertained. I think that it was about an hour after daylight that I heard a great commotion in the yard, as though some one had arrived most unexpectedly; but as it was a matter that did not concern me, I turned over and tried to obtain a nap; for since we had got our stamps to work, and a full set of hands, it was not necessary that Hopeful or myself should be on duty at all hours. The labor went on whether we were present or absent. The quartz was crushed and the parts were separated just as rapidly as if we were standing near the machines. In the course of half an hour, after all was quiet outside, I heard some one coming up stairs, and the footsteps sounded like Hopeful's. A knock at the door assured me that it was my friend.

"Hallo!" he cried; "do you intend to sleep all day? Come, rouse up and get breakfast."

"What is your hurry?" I asked; and stepping out of bed, let my friend enter the room.

"O, I don't know; come down stairs."

"Has any one arrived?" I asked. "I thought that I heard a team enter the yard."

Hopeful did not hear me, or, if he did, failed to reply, for he was looking out of the window.

"You'd better put on some of your good clothes; them store clothes, I mean," Hopeful said, when he saw that I was about to mount the suit that I commonly wore at the mines.

"For what reason?" I asked, wondering what possessed the man.

"O, 'cos you've looked rather slouchy of late, and I want to see you spruce up. Come, do it to oblige me."

"Anything to oblige you, Hez;" and on went a neat-fitting suit, with a white linen shirt.

After I was dressed, my partner surveyed me with evident marks of approval, and then led the way down stairs.

"You go into the settin'-room for a minute," he said, and, opening the door, pushed me in, closing the door after me.

I saw a lady sitting in one corner of the apartment, but

as the window-shade was down I did not catch a glimpse of her face until she arose and stood before me; then, to my intense surprise, I saw that the lady was Miss Jenny, with ribbons, silk dress, and all that went towards making a fashionable toilet in that distant part of the world. I was too much astonished to utter a word, for I had not the faintest suspicion that the lady was within fifty miles of me; and while I was wondering if my eyes did not deceive me, the dear girl came towards me, and put her arms around my neck, and pressed her soft velvet cheek to mine.

"Are you not glad to see me?" she whispered.

I could only kiss her and lead her to a seat, striving to still the wild beating of my heart as I did so. I could not speak. I was too much overpowered for words. The surprise was too sudden.

"Can't you give me a word of welcome?" Jenny whispered; and I felt the warm pressure of her hand, as she bent forward to look in my eyes.

I could only throw my arms around her trim waist and kiss her red lips. She appeared to like it, for she made not the slightest objection.

"Tell me how you came here," I said, when I could recover myself.

"In a wagon," was the answer.

"And your father — where is he?"

"In Melbourne, I suppose. I left him there, getting ready to sail for England."

"Then he did not know of your coming here?"

"Of course not; if he had, he would have interfered, and prevented me from visiting you. He said that I was not to see you again. I intimated that I should; and I've kept my word. Here I am. What do you intend to do with me?"

That was a question not easily answered; so I said at a venture, "I'll give you some breakfast."

She pouted a little at the answer, as though she was not pleased with it.

"I don't mean that, although goodness knows I am hungry enough. But I mean —"

She put up her mouth as she spoke; so I took the hint, and kissed it.

"I mean," she whispered, "will you give me up when the guv'ner comes after me? That's what I mean."

"But will he come after you?"

"I suppose so; but I won't go unless you go with me. I have made up my mind to that effect, and nothing shall change me. Without you I should be miserable — with you I shall be happy."

"Tell me how you managed to get here," I asked; for she had not yet related that portion of her adventures.

"O, simple enough. I just fixed up a bundle, hired a man with a horse and wagon to take me, and here I am, a little tired, but glad enough to see you. I have been riding all night."

"You shall have some breakfast, and then retire, and obtain that rest which you so much need," I said. "Come, I think that the morning meal is already on the table."

"Ah," said Hez, as he took his seat at the table, "I reckon some folks is mighty glad that I made 'em change their shirt this mornin'. Some folks look all the better for it."

"Yes, and some folks might have let me into the secret of a certain lady's arrival, and not taken me by surprise."

About twelve o'clock, who should drive up to the house but Mr. Commissioner Murden, his horse covered with foam and perspiration, as though he had ridden many miles at a gallop.

"How fortunate that you are at home!" the officer said, as we shook hands. "I have news for you. Sir William's daughter has disappeared, and we have traced her towards the bush, but cannot find her. She may have fallen into the hands of some prowlers. Will you help me search for her?"

"Yes, come in."

He entered the house, and I presented him to Jenny.

"The devil!" he ejaculated. "Are you married?"

"No. What a question!"

"Then you are the biggest fool in Victoria. A man without enterprise, energy, and pluck, don't deserve a pretty wife."

"What would you have me do?"

"A warm-blooded man, and ask that question! I am ashamed of you."

"Murden," I said, in a grave tone, "all through my life I have been ashamed to do wrong. I cannot think of changing at this hour. I should despise myself for committing a dishonorable act. You would not recommend me to do so."

"No, I don't think I should," answered the commissioner; "but I don't suppose it is dishonorable to marry a girl whom you love and who loves you, as I shall show you."

He crossed the room, put his arm around Amelia's neck, and kissed her; there being no resistance on the lady's part. I was astonished, and my looks expressed as much.

"Forgive me," Amelia said, in a plaintive tone, turning to me as though an apology was due; "but he says that he has long loved me, and I — I rather like him."

"Then be happy, both of you, for happiness you deserve. And to think that I never suspected such a thing!"

"We'll be married this very day!" cried the commissioner; "it's a month sooner than we intended, but Amelia is willing."

The young lady was heard to murmur something about not having a suitable dress; but the remonstrance was drowned in a kiss. Jenny saw this little side-play, and her eyes sparkled, and her cheeks flushed. She put one arm around my neck, and looked into my face with such a roguish glance that I felt my heart melting.

"Come," she whispered, "let's get married at the same time as them does."

"But your father, Jenny!"

"I'd rather have a husband than a father. Can't you act as both?"

"Look here!" cried the stout-hearted Murden; "if you lose time, you'll lose a wife, for Sir William will be here in a day or two, and if he has the legal right, he'll take his daughter to Melbourne in double-quick time, and you'll never see her again. Be guided by your heart, and not by a nice sense of honor."

"Be guided by me," whispered Jenny. "I will not lead you astray. I love you."

At this instant a carriage dashed into the yard. I ran to the window in some alarm, for fear that Sir William had arrived. To my surprise, I saw Mr. Brown, the Bendigo commissioner, dismount, and then help out a venerable old gentleman, who wore a white neck-handkerchief and black coat. I took him to be a clergyman, and I was not mistaken.

"I sent for them," said Murden. "They are on time. I'm to be married within an hour. Will you follow suit?"

"Do," pleaded Amelia.

"Please do," pleaded Jenny.

What man, with ever so nice a sense of honor, could stand up against such entreaties, especially when his heart was interested? I could not; I loved the girl much better than I supposed I was capable of loving. It was my first pure love; so when she held up her red lips for me to kiss, and once more whispered, "Do you want to kill me?" I threw my arms around her slender waist, and pressed her to my bosom, promising to unite my fate with hers as soon as possible.

"Hurrah!" shouted Murden; "the victory is won. I'll send for Hopeful, Smith, and Hackett, immediately. By thunder, we'll have a jolly time of it!"

One of the farm hands was despatched to the mine to call them, while the ladies retired to change their dresses, and get ready for the ceremony. Mr. Brown rushed into the room, as though pursued by a whole gang of bushrangers. First he shook hands with Murden and myself, and kept up the experiment as long as we would consent to such an arrangement. He was in a state of perpetual excitement, and perspired at every pore. Then we went to the dining-room and drank some wine, to keep our courage up under the trying ordeal through which we had to pass; and by the time we had finished a bottle, and Murden and I had changed our clothes for some that were suitable for a wedding, in came our friends, wondering, surprised and withal delighted. They couldn't understand how it had been brought about, but were pleased with the aspect of affairs. Smith hurried to the kitchen, and told the occupants of it to prepare a feast that would reflect credit on the house. There was to be no stint, and expense was not to be regarded; and then the honest fellow tumbled up the stairs to consult his wife on his dress and behavior on the occasion. How she managed I don't know; but when Smith appeared, he had on a white shirt, and a light vest, gloves, and neat boots; and I will give him the credit of saying that a more uncomfortable looking man I never saw while he was thus arrayed. Presently the ladies sailed down the stairs, in all the glory of white dresses, laces, flowers, and other articles of feminine attire, blushing, whimpering, giggling, and whispering at the same time.

"You first," said Murden, in a whisper; "my heart begins to fail me."

He urged me forward, and I found myself leading Jenny to the minister, hearing the reverend gentleman utter a few words, being surrounded, and congratulated, and wished all manner of prosperity; and then I awoke to the fact that I was married, and that a handsome young lady was standing by my side, radiant with happiness, youth, and beauty.

Then came Murden's turn. He led forward a tearful bride; for could Amelia forget the past, even while looking forward to the future with every expectation of happiness? But the police commissioner acted the part of a man, a tender, loving one, and did what he could to cheer her, and whispered words of comfort to her; but tears did not cease to flow until after the ceremony was completed, and Mrs. Smith had folded her in her arms. Then a smile appeared on her handsome face, and the tears were dried up. I stepped forward, and was about to bestow a kiss on the handsome lips of Mrs. Murden; but Mrs. Jenny laid her gloved hand on my arm and restrained me.

"I am sorry to interrupt you in your good intentions," my handsome wife said; "but be kind enough to recollect that you are a married man, and that your wife is rather fond of kisses, especially such as you bestow."

This was the commencement of her tyranny over me, and she has pursued just such a course ever since, strongly objecting to my flirting, smiling, or even kissing any one excepting herself. Well, thank Heaven, I have had no inclination to turn from her sweet face, for I think just as much of her now as the day I was married. Her love is just as valuable as then.

The day passed quickly, for we feasted, and planned for the future, and the ladies consulted as to what they should do, and what they should wear; and Hopeful moped round the house, and thought of Martha Poland, wishing that she was near him, and made queer remarks until it was time to retire; and just as we were debating the question, Rover gave a prolonged howl, as though something disagreeable was near, and into the yard dashed a pair of horses and a carriage.

"It's my guv'ner," murmured Jenny, and drew near to me, and laid one of her hands on my shoulder.

There was a thundering knock at the door. Smith opened it, and in stalked Sir William, my wife's father.

"Child," he said, "what is the meaning of this?"

"It means," answered Jenny, "that I'm his wife, and that there's no use in kickin' up a row; so just give us your hand, and say no more about it. I mean to stick to him, 'cos I loves him, and that's all about it."

"Is this true?" asked the baronet.

"It is true. We were united this morning," I answered

Sir William breathed hard, and his eyes flashed. For a moment I could not tell where the lightning was to strike. Silence reigned in the room. Even a sigh could be heard. I was prepared for violence, but I was not prepared for the manner in which Sir William held out his hand and came towards us.

"You shall both have my blessing, although I am disappointed. But perhaps it is all for the best." He kissed his daughter, shook hands with me, with all those present, and then asked for something to eat, just like the humblest of mortals.

The next morning Sir William and I had a long conference. He made me promise that Jenny should receive a good education, that we would visit England as soon as possible, and stop with him for a long time; and that if I wanted money I would draw on him to any amount. Then he took leave of his daughter in an affectionate manner, and left us to our happiness. I kept my promise, although Jenny was too precious to trust to a boarding-school. I hired a lady teacher, and she came and lived with us, and took charge of Jenny's education; and such was the progress of my handsome wife, that in a year's time she could speak good English, understood a little music, and could read and write as readily as most girls of her age. In the mean time, the stamps continued to work, and the gold to flow into our treasury, until we were rich beyond our most sanguine expectations. At last we had enough, and then we sold out and left Australia for home, by the way of England, leaving Smith and his family, Murden and his family, and Mr. Brown and his family, prosperous and happy; merchants of high standing, for they retired from the police department soon after my marriage, and succeeded in a more engaging business.

I have no more to relate. My wife received a warm, tearful welcome from her mother and father, but our son was more petted than the mother. I was present when Hopeful was married to Martha Poland. He makes her a good husband, and she is all that a wife should be. They are the happiest couple in Hillsboro' County, New Hampshire. Hackett is still in Australia, rich, jolly, and a believer in Illinois and its prosperity. Rover is with me, old, but vigorous.

sides would be equally well guarded, then glanced over the excited crowd, in hopes that Dan would array himself on our side — but that enterprising gentleman had suddenly disappeared, and left us to our fate.

"Stand back," shouted the inspector; "it will be the worse for you. There's many of you present who know me, and know that I have a large force of policemen on hand. If you strike a blow, not one of you shall escape justice.

"Unbar the door as quickly as possible," whispered the inspector, after getting through with his threatening speech.

I lifted the heavy gum wood bar from its place, and then raised the latch, expecting that it would yield, but to my surprise it did not — it was locked, and the key in the pocket of the doorkeeper, who had made his escape from the room in company with Dan.

I almost uttered a groan of agony when I made the discovery, and to add to the perplexity of our situation, the ruffians must have understood our case, and known that the key was never left in the lock, for they uttered a discordant and ironical hoot, and then a shout of sardonic laughter.

"For Heaven's sake, don't be all night in getting that door open," cried Fred, nervously, and I will confess that I also partook of the same complaint.

"Now for a rush — cut them to pieces," exclaimed many voices; but I observed that the cries came from those who were farthest from us, and out of the reach of our pistols, which we were forced to display, in hope of keeping the robbers at a respectful distance.

"Is the door unbarred?" asked Mr. Brown, turning half round, and exposing his side to the knives of the crowd, and quick as thought, a man sprang forward to begin the work of bloodshed; but sudden as were his movements, they were anticipated, for I raised the heavy bar, which I had not relinquished, and let it fall upon his head with crushing force.

The poor devil fell at our feet without uttering a groan, although many spasmodic twitchings of his nerves showed that he was not killed outright. His long knife narrowly missed the side of the inspector, and for the first attempt at our annihilation, it was not to be despised.

The wretches uttered yells of rage when they saw their comrade fall, but none seemed inclined to assume the leadership and begin the attack in earnest.

Not one of their motions escaped us, and as long as they were disposed to brandish their knives at a distance, we did not choose to carry matters to extremities; but change of tactics was suddenly resorted to on the part of our opponents, that placed us in no little peril.

All the tumblers, bottles, and decanters of the bar were taken possession of by the savage scoundrels, and the first intimation that we had of the fact was the crushing of a bottle (empty, of course — they were not the sort of men to throw away liquor of any kind) against the door, just above our heads.

The fragments were showered upon our faces and shoulders, but before we had time to consider on the matter another bottle flew past my head, and hit our prisoner upon one of his shoulders, injuring

as I turned, I managed to keep my eyes on the shelf overhead, so that I could note all the movements that took place. I was repaid for my trouble, for as I fell back and pressed my hand on my side, as though fatally wounded, I had the satisfaction of hearing a triumphant laugh issue from the thicket overhead; and the next instant the repulsive features of Moloch were thrust through the branches of the trees, and he seemed to enjoy the appearance which I presented.

"Bah! you fools!" cried the rascal, in a mocking tone, "do yer think that yer can take me? I vos too quick for yer. Had yer come an hour sooner, yer might have caught me nappin'. But now I jist spits at yer. Ah, fools, I has the voman, and I means to keep her."

I seldom miss with a revolver, especially when the object at which I aim is within reasonable distance; but I must confess that I was nervous and full of revengeful feelings, or perhaps I was too hasty; for I suddenly raised my pistol and fired at the fiend who was grinning at me from amid the branches of the balsam trees. I missed the scoundrel, and yet I would have given a thousand dollars to have sent a bullet crushing through his brain, and killed him on the spot.

"Ho, ho! yer didn't come it," laughed the fiend. "Vait a minute and I'll make yer see somethin' that'll open yer eyes."

He disappeared, and while he was gone I changed position, so that he could not single me out for another shot, in case he desired to test his old horse-pistols.

"You ain't hit, is you?" whispered Hackett and Hopeful in anxious tones.

"No," I answered.

Before they could congratulate me, Moloch, the devil, appeared, bearing in his arms the almost lifeless form of poor, dear Amelia Copey, whose dress was torn and soiled, and whose hair was hanging down in tangled masses, neglected and uncared for.

"Look!" yelled the fiend, in a triumphant tone; "'ere's the gal vot I loves, and she vill love me afore long, or I'll know the reason vy."

As he spoke he held the fair form in such a manner that

THE BUSHRANGERS.

A Yankee's Adventures During His Second Visit to Australia.

BY WM. H. THOMES,

Author of "The Gold Hunters in Australia." "The Bushrangers," "Running the Blockade," etc.. etc.

Moloch appeared, bearing the almost lifeless form. "Look," yelled the fiend, in a triumphant tone.

one else." With these words the merchant took his departure, and I supposed that I should have a moment to myself; but a noise on deck once more aroused me.

I went on deck, and found that Bowmount had returned accompanied by a stout negro, whom I had no difficulty in recognizing as Sam, the coachman, who had helped entrap me the night I was kidnapped by John.

"Do you recognize this imp?" asked the Kentuckian; and as he spoke he cut the negro's legs with a cowhide, which produced a rapid movement on the part of Sam.

"O, golly, massa! don't do dat," yelled the coachman. "Don't you know dat it hurts? O, my legs! Please don't do so no more, massa."

And then followed several blows and several capers.

"Do you see this black cuss?" asked the Kentuckian, suspending work for a moment, to talk to me.

"Yes, I see him. I have met the scamp before."

"And so has I," and here came in another cut on the darkey's legs, that made him jump and howl with renewed energy.

"How did you get hold of him?" I asked, as soon as the noise had subsided.

"Mrs. Gowen sent him to you," was the careless answer. Mrs. Gowen has been on the watch for the black scamp ever since he served you such a trick. This afternoon he was took while I was at the house, and she sent him to you, and says you may do what you like with him. If you takes my advice, you will give him two or three dozen, and then send him to the city jail, whar they'll give him as much more."

"For de Lord's sake, don't do dat," cried Sam. "Dis nig is almost cut to pieces now. Him legs is one mess of rings."

I began to have mercy on the fellow, although he did

RUNNING THE BLOCKADE;

OR, U. S. SECRET SERVICE ADVENTURES.

By WM. H. THOMES, Author of "The Gold Hunters' Adventures in Australia," "The Bushrangers," "Running the Blockade," etc., etc.

ELEGANTLY AND PROFUSELY ILLUSTRATED.

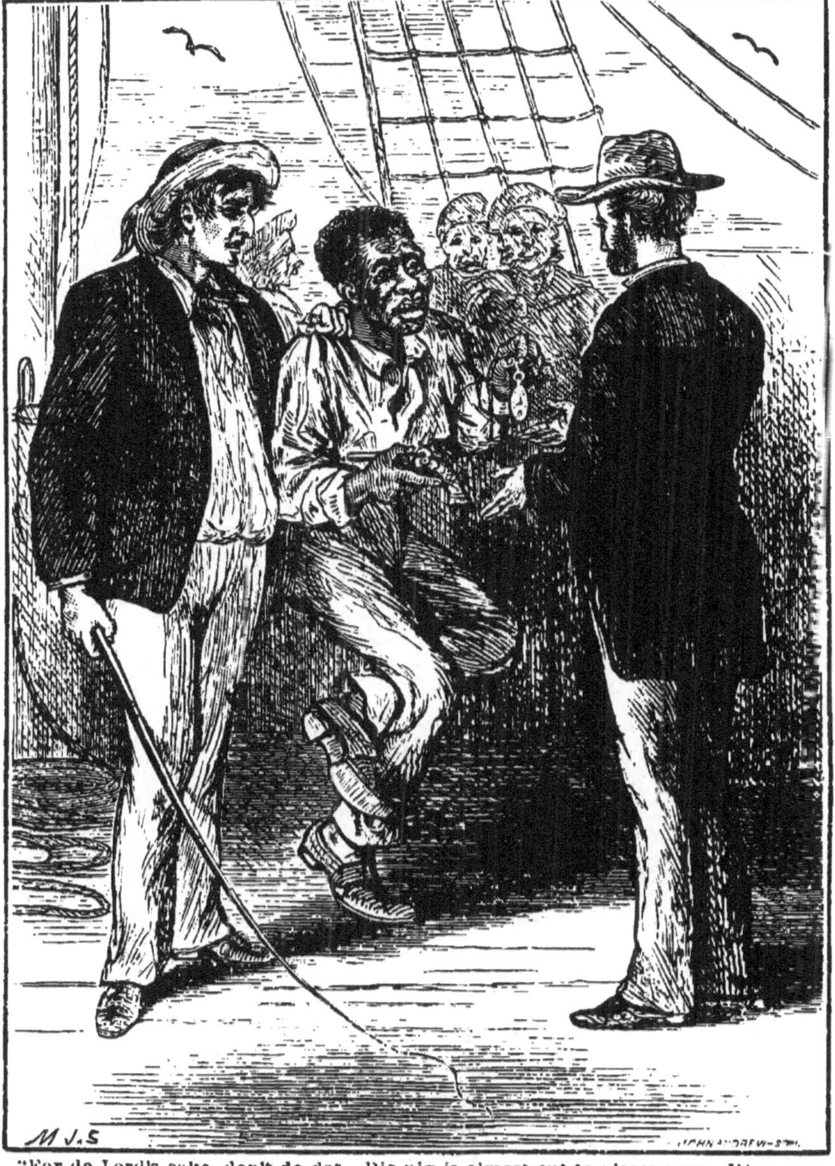

"For de Lord's sake, don't do dat. Dis nig is almost cut to pieces now. Him legs is one mass of rings."

www.ingramcontent.com/pod-product-compliance
Lightning Source LLC
Chambersburg PA
CBHW032011110726
47901CB00004B/1046

9783337180041